STEEL AND PROMISE

Visit us at www.boldstrokesbooks.com

STEEL AND PROMISE

by
Alexa Black

2016

STEEL AND PROMISE

ISBN 13: 978-1-62639-805-4

THIS TRADE PAPERBACK ORIGINAL IS PUBLISHED BY
BOLD STROKES BOOKS, INC.
P.O. BOX 249
VALLEY FALLS, NY 12185

FIRST EDITION: DECEMBER 2016

CREDITS
EDITOR: CINDY CRESAP
PRODUCTION DESIGN: SUSAN RAMUNDO
COVER DESIGN BY SHERI (GRAPHICARTIST2020@HOTMAIL.COM)

Acknowledgments

First and foremost, thanks to Theo. If not for you, this book would still be "that old thing I wrote years ago," and "getting published someday" would still be a dream I'd given up on. Thanks to you and to Toni for believing in this book, and reminding me to believe in myself.

And thanks both to Theo and to Kat for such thorough beta reading, aka putting me through hell to make sure everything worked right.

Thanks to Cindy, my editor, for catching everything they didn't, and for giving me valuable advice on how to turn weaknesses into strengths. And thanks to the rest of the BSB team for being so welcoming and encouraging.

Dedication

To Kat D and Theo T, for their help and for their friendship.

To Lexy P, for her boundless enthusiasm for this book.

CHAPTER ONE

Cailyn didn't know what she expected, but the woman in front of her surely wasn't it.

Everyone knew Lady Nivrai had modifications, and everyone knew she'd spent a small fortune to get them. But Cailyn didn't see any implants in this woman's forehead, face, or short, muscular arms.

That should have been a relief. Less implants meant skin she could touch, caress, comfort. Other courtesans might find modifications sexy, brag to themselves or others about the unique features of the people they had served. But Cailyn liked people she could reach.

Still, this was Teran Nivrai. The sheer normalcy of the woman in front of her unnerved her. High cheekbones, an oval face, thin lips. Sculpted eyebrows, a little angular, but nothing too harsh. Only the color of her eyes looked remarkable—an icy gray almost as pale as her skin.

That fit, at least. She looked like Cailyn should coax her into a walk outside.

None of the rumors agreed on exactly what Lady Nivrai had done to herself. But the whispers all said *elaborate* and *sharp*.

Horns. Teeth replaced with knives. Spines emerging from her back. A barbed metal tail. Daggers that emerged from the skin of her palms to drop into her hands.

She'd even heard that Teran had steel wings, modeled after demon's wings from stories. Whether they were supposed to emerge from under her skin, or whether Teran hid them away under cloaks and capes, Cailyn had never been sure.

As for the real Teran, she wore her short hair too severely to call pretty, cropped bangs slanting at a diagonal across her forehead.

Her eyebrows arched at a sharp angle too, and her lips looked a little bloodless. But they curled up in a smile that seemed welcoming enough.

A little harsh, maybe, but hardly the face of a demon.

Lady Nivrai did wear a cloak, a silver thing that caught the light when she moved. Cailyn stared too long at it, looked for bulges that might pass for wings.

Don't be ridiculous, Cailyn Derys. You're the one standing here naked. Teran Nivrai is just another noble you agreed to serve. Why are you staring like no one has ever hired you before?

Teran laughed, a clear sound. She spread her arms in greeting. "Welcome. Are you looking for my wings or my spines?"

Cailyn blushed. She dropped to her knees with a practiced motion. "Neither, my lady."

Teran stepped closer. "I could punish you for lying, you know," she said. Her hands moved to Cailyn's breasts, and Cailyn tensed. What was she expecting? A blow? A pinch?

But Teran only ran her hands over Cailyn's flesh with slow, deliberate care. Cailyn's nipples hardened under her ministrations. She plans to seduce me, Cailyn thought, and shuddered.

She should have welcomed it. Guild law said nothing about keeping the courtesans you hired happy. And Cailyn was the one whose hands and lips and flesh would offer solace and seduction alike. She never expected from the nobles what she meant to give herself.

But how much should she welcome from a woman who supposedly wasted all her credits transforming herself into a demon, who even the courtesans who served the dark channels avoided?

"But I won't punish you." A hand reached out to pull Cailyn's chin up. "I've never needed excuses to do what I will."

Teran's other hand moved down her body, then paused a moment to lightly caress Cailyn's genitals. Cailyn tried to keep herself still. It might have been better to react as her body, against her own better judgment, wanted to. It was often wise for a courtesan to feign more desire than she felt. To actually feel it was a minor blessing.

Still, she couldn't give away all her secrets. Cailyn tamped down her desire and looked down, letting her hair spill over her face. She hoped it looked inviting.

"I surprise you," Teran said. Her fingers fluttered at Cailyn's throat in a quiet, possessive caress. Then they withdrew.

Cailyn's neck stung, a sharp pinprick of pain. What—?

Her hand flew to the spot. She tapped at it and felt moisture. She pulled her hand away and looked down. Drops of bright red stained her fingertips.

Cailyn's body went cold.

"My lady?" she stammered as the pricking blossomed into hurt.

Half the pain came from the way it unnerved her. If she could calm down it might feel less intense. But how could she, alone and naked in a helldemon's lair with a contract to fulfill?

She looked at Teran, who looked down at her hand, the mild smile still on her lips. Something metallic glittered under the cold lights of the room.

Claws, Cailyn realized. She has claws.

They jutted from the tips of her fingers, polished and bright. A drop of red stained one.

Teran moved her fingers. The claws retracted, leaving what looked like silver-painted fingernails. Cailyn couldn't help but stare.

Teran laughed and extended them again. They locked into place with a soft click.

"Do you like them?" Teran asked. "They cost eighty thousand credits."

Cailyn was too well trained to let her jaw drop. But her eyes widened. Eighty thousand.

Why?

And did she like them? The wound stung. Her neck was bleeding. What kind of question was that? She'd come here to serve Teran, and only Teran's pleasure mattered. At least if Teran wanted to do something like this.

Teran didn't wait for an answer. Perhaps she hadn't expected one. She talked on, but Cailyn couldn't focus.

She heard something about the newsteel the implants were made of, something else about the mechanism that made them work. It reminded Cailyn of a noble she'd once served with a penchant for growing flowers, the way he talked about a strain of rose he'd perfected.

What should she do? Praise them, probably. She'd come here to please her lady, after all. And to offer acceptance. She shouldn't have come here if she couldn't do that.

Her mouth worked, but no sound came.

Teran's other hand rested near Cailyn's vulva. Cailyn lowered her head again, and she glanced down to see similar silver. Teran's hand rested too close to her most sensitive flesh.

I should get out of here. I can make three thousand again easily.

But not from one meeting. It was exorbitant, of course. No one in their right mind would accept an offer from someone like Lady Teran Nivrai if it hadn't been.

No one in their right mind would still be here, she reminded herself.

"You're shivering," Teran said. Sharp metal touched the skin just above Cailyn's vulva, not piercing her skin. Teran's eyes locked on hers.

She's good with those, Cailyn thought before she could stop herself. *She'd have cut me by now if she wasn't.*

Maybe it would flatter Teran to tell her she was powerful. Maybe Cailyn could make a seduction of it. But even now, those strange eyes looked warm enough to get lost in.

"Those things aren't reassuring, my lady," she said. "How do I know you won't harm me?"

Tinkling laughter answered her. "If I wanted to do that, I would have done it already."

Cailyn couldn't answer. Teran's hand, the claws now retracted, moved back to her breasts and moved on them. Cailyn's skin tingled where Teran's hands passed.

She couldn't understand why. This woman could pierce a hole through her nipples. Or cut them off, if she'd heard Teran right and those things were made of newsteel.

"I want to believe that," Cailyn stammered. Two curved pieces of warm, sharp metal encircled her nipple. She tried not to think about it. "My lady."

Teran smiled. "Don't worry. I don't expect you to trust me."

She leaned over to kiss Cailyn. Cailyn opened her mouth in a show of eagerness. She'd trained long years to give pleasure.

She felt fingers and steel in her hair. Would the claws tear it, or not? Lady Nivrai might leave her hair more intact than her skin.

That thought did nothing to ease her mind.

Teran pulled Cailyn's head back, just far enough to be uncomfortable. Cailyn felt fingers on her neck. The claws traced lines down it but did not cut.

"You're very beautiful," Teran said.

Cailyn wanted to laugh. The famous helldemon of Nivrai couldn't think of anything better to say than...that?

She didn't know what might happen if she laughed at Teran. She did allow herself a smile.

"Amused?" Teran asked. She touched the small nick on Cailyn's neck, the trickle of blood dripping from it. She peered at the blood on her finger.

"There's no need to be frightened," Teran said with a chuckle of her own. "I told you before that I have no interest in punishing you."

"You—?"

"I'm quite content to leave that nonsense to guilt-filled flagellants who need excuses. Go ahead and laugh at me, if you like. It won't make me do any more. Or any less."

Cailyn had nothing to say.

"Put your hands behind your back and hold them there."

Cailyn obeyed. She wondered why Teran didn't just bind them. After all, she'd already made her bleed.

Then again, if Teran had such disdain for the way other people did things, maybe she wouldn't rush to tie people up, either.

The tip of a claw rested against Cailyn's chest. She's going to cut me now, Cailyn realized. For real.

It didn't matter if she laughed, Teran had said. So the laugh came: high-pitched, shaky, and utterly meaningless.

The newsteel pierced her flesh, between and above her breasts. It stayed there a long time. Then it moved down. The stinging sensation blossomed in Cailyn's flesh.

She stared at Teran. What did Teran want? What did this do for her? But Cailyn couldn't wonder long. The pain made her vision swim. Tears gathered in her eyes. She held them back.

Another slash down her chest, quick as gasping, and it was over. Cailyn realized, with a shudder she no longer bothered to repress, that the last half of the cut had been fast for a reason.

Mercy.

The kiss that came after relieved her. It felt like what she knew. She opened her mouth to it, and fingers, soft and gentle, grazed her nipples.

And in the middle of it all, impossible to ignore, burned a line of red fire down her chest.

The cloak slid from Teran's shoulders. Cailyn could see little. She wrapped her arms around Teran and felt bare flesh under her hands.

She had nothing on under that cloak, Cailyn realized. She couldn't help but grin.

Cailyn let her fingers wander. She didn't have to feign desire, not now, though that damned cut hurt. She found no other implants on Teran's back. Unless they could hide themselves under skin.

So this was the helldemon of Nivrai's body. Unaltered skin over tight muscles. That wasn't so terrifying. Cailyn brought her mouth to Teran's breasts. Methodical noblewomen weren't the only ones who knew how to tease nipples, after all.

Teran's hands wrapped around her. When the small pinpricks came, in the middle of her back, like the kneading of a contented cat, she expected them. They didn't hurt so much. Not any more. Not in the midst of pleasure.

Cailyn wondered at it. Did Teran even realize she'd pricked her again, or did the instinct come with having claws?

Maybe Cailyn had melted this woman a little. She looked up into Teran's eyes and slid one of her hands downward.

A slender hand gripped her wrist, surprisingly hard. "Not that," Teran said. "Follow me."

Cailyn scowled. Most nobles delighted in being handled by the courtesans they hired. She was here to touch, to caress, to ease. The rejection confused her. The cuts on her chest and back throbbed, as if in sympathy. But Teran only walked away, her steps as unhurried as her touch had been.

Teran led her into a bedroom so small and sparse Cailyn could hardly believe her eyes. Teran was a minor noble, but she did own the planet.

The bed was a decent size, but hardly looked comfortable at all. A nightstand in steely gray sat pressed against it. A low dresser in the same color stood against one wall, under a mirror.

Here, every wall was white, except for one. That entire wall, top to bottom, was transparent, an enormous window. Beyond lay a small garden, a verdant patch of green amid the dull gray. Yellow and red flowers blossomed from the green ground, ringing a small fountain. She hadn't seen anything so bright anywhere in Teran's halls, or anywhere else in Nivrai for that matter.

She wrenched her gaze back into the gray severity of the room. She couldn't even see much furniture, which surprised her almost as much as the garden. Teran might not have wings or spines, but the rumors were right about her tastes. Where were the crosses to be tied to, the benches to be bent over, the floggers or switches that should have hung on the walls? Did Teran have another room for that?

But if she did, she wasn't leading Cailyn there. Or were those claws all she needed?

She watched, puzzled, as Teran walked over to the far wall and pressed her hand to it. The space around her hand glowed. A lock, Cailyn realized. Fancy ones were sometimes keyed to fingerprints.

As the glow faded, a panel slid over the window, the same pale gray of the walls. If Cailyn hadn't seen the window, she would never have known the window existed. A moment later, the wall Teran touched slid back, revealing a hidden alcove.

Which contained most of the things Cailyn had just wondered about.

"It's tiny!" Cailyn said, laughing again.

"Do you think I should be outdoing someone?"

"I—no, my lady."

Teran said nothing. She led Cailyn to a cross and busied herself binding Cailyn's arms.

She stepped behind Cailyn and whispered into her ear. Cailyn expected words of seduction.

Instead Teran only said, "Last I heard, Lord Iridian had six rooms."

"Six rooms, my lady?"

"Each with a different theme. The dungeon, the harem, the examination room. I don't remember them all."

She ran a hand over Cailyn's back. "It makes my eighty thousand seem distinctly insignificant. And it means that to live up to the rumors, I'd need at least ten." She laughed.

Cailyn turned her head. Teran smiled again. Unlike the controlled smile she'd seen before, this one lit Teran's eyes.

Cailyn took some solace in it as she watched Teran take down a flogger from the wall. Cailyn had never served the nobles on the dark channels, and her few forays into mild pain had pleased her clients far more than they had her.

And Teran Nivrai, despite the many ways she'd defied the rumors, still frightened her. A moment of laughter helped.

Extended now, the claws traced patterns over her flesh gently, not breaking the skin. Their dance felt good, a little dangerous. She couldn't stop thinking of what wasn't happening, but so easily could.

The hands withdrew. Something draped over Cailyn's back. She recognized the tails of the flogger. Was that braided? Her muscles tensed as she realized it was.

Just when I started to think the rumors were exaggerated.

She felt Teran's hand on her again, gathering up her hair and setting it out of the way. "If you use that, do you really think I'll stay put enough to keep my hair out of your way, my lady?"

"Maybe not." Cailyn heard the smile. "Then again I could cut it," Teran went on. Her claw sliced through a lock of Cailyn's hair. She held the blond curl in front of Cailyn's face.

For a wild moment, Cailyn wondered if Teran might really do it, steel-tipped fingers shearing curl after curl. She wondered how much money she should ask for in compensation.

Teran moved back. Cailyn expelled a ragged breath. Was she really thinking she'd rather Teran pay for the privilege of cutting off her hair when she could just give her stop word and walk away instead?

She heard the swish of the braided tails moving through the air behind her and tensed again.

"Your back is already bleeding and your front has taken worse. You're more afraid of me using this than you should be," Teran said.

The first blow struck. Fire exploded across Cailyn's back. Any retort she might give became a shapeless, open-throated scream as the thin leather seared her back again and again.

Long years of training had taught her how to listen for the noble's pleasure. But now, she heard no sounds but the ones Teran tore from her. Her own din drowned out the breath she should have listened for, the whispers that would tell her whether the noblewoman was pleased, angry, sated.

She might have known from the rhythm of it, if she could think enough to discern it. But her body burned in every part and carried her mind along with it. Her shoulders. The places on her back where the claws had pricked her. The line cut between her breasts. Even the places Teran had touched gently. Even her lips, where Teran had kissed her. Even her vulva, where Teran had touched her before.

When it ended, she slumped. Teran freed her from her bonds and wrapped one hand around her welted back. Her other hand curled around Cailyn's chin and drew her into a kiss. Cailyn's mouth parted. Warmth spread between her thighs. This she could offer. This she could give.

She hadn't known how to endure the beating. She did know how to give herself up to someone's touch, to relax into her embrace.

She laughed. Teran's tongue darted in her mouth and cut off her laughter. Hands toyed with her breasts, those strange claws familiar now as they ran lightly over her nipples. It felt like sex, like relief. She made a small sound.

The claws retracted with a click. Teran's hand slipped between her thighs again.

Cailyn thanked her patron goddess for small mercies as Teran's fingers moved. Her hips twitched.

"See?" Teran kissed and nibbled at her neck. "Not as frightened as you thought you'd be."

Cailyn didn't answer. She tilted her head back and offered more of her neck to Teran's lips and teeth.

"You did very well," Teran said.

"Why me?" Cailyn's words anchored her. They drew her back to herself. She knew now that these moments of gentleness came with a price.

The dancing fingers slowed. She wasn't sure whether to curse them or thank the gods. The mouth against her neck moved. "What do you mean?"

"I mean…" Cailyn struggled to speak. She could feel Teran's smile. "My lady, there are people who would beg for this, or something like it. There are courtesans who sell themselves on how much pain they take."

The fingers thrilled on her skin again. She gasped and closed her eyes.

"I'm sure you..." She flushed. "I'm sure you know who they are."

Laughter, like glass. "Yes, little one. I know who they are. I know who will come to me and who will not."

"Then why choose me? I never...I don't...well I have, once or twice, but..."

"But."

"Not like this!"

"Do you want all my secrets?"

"My lady, I only—"

"Maybe it's because you haven't. Maybe I don't want one who has. Maybe it's more interesting to me that way."

Cailyn frowned. "Is that all?"

"No." The voice, thick with desire before, went cold. "It isn't."

Damn. Just when she'd thought she might learn something. She bowed her head and, opened her mouth to offer some flowery apology.

Teran had said "I won't punish you." Apologizing might make things worse. She closed her mouth and lifted her head.

"Come here," Teran said. She led Cailyn over to a bench in the same small room.

"You want more of this, my lady?" Cailyn stammered, open-mouthed.

Teran went back to the implements on the wall and took down another. She laughed. "Look at it."

Cailyn looked. Teran was holding another flogger, this one made of soft, wide strips of leather and not braided. "That other was for me. This is for you."

CHAPTER TWO

Cailyn sighed. She knew how to offer herself up to things she would never choose. She enjoyed them, sometimes, seeing the others' enjoyment. But how much of this could she endure? She thought of the stories about Teran. When would a helldemon be finished?

It can't be worse than what just happened, she told herself. And if she hadn't complained at that, how much worse would it be to take issue with this? It seemed Teran meant to be kind—whatever she thought kindness was.

Stifling a sigh, Cailyn bent over the bench and allowed Teran to cuff her hands.

The tails of the flogger danced against her skin. She felt no pain, only her body awakening to its rhythm. She drifted with it, and her fear fell away. She closed her eyes and tried to envision Teran's eyes, her smile, the gleam of light on her claws.

But she could only remember herself, her mouth opening to Teran's lips and tongue, the thrill that tingled through her as the claws ran down her skin, light and delicate, a sharper version of a lover's caress.

She cried out. Her body moved to meet the flogger. She moaned again, a long, low sound.

Why didn't you do this in the beginning?

The welts on her back, the line between her breasts...she could hardly feel any of them now. The sting of her cuts, faint now, left her energized, alive.

Teran must know, know from the way she moved, from the smell of her excitement. That thought unnerved Cailyn, but under her disquiet she felt something like relief. This gentleness came so much closer to her usual, uncomplicated desire. The old familiar need to give herself overflowed through her, soothed and calmed her.

She'd wandered into the lair of someone others called a helldemon. Now she was home.

She drifted. Teran's hands called her back. They moved on the skin they'd warmed and reddened, the tips of the claws tracing patterns over it. Teran reached down to touch her vulva. Cailyn shuddered with a minor climax.

She whispered some formal expression of gratitude as her body pulsed with aftershock and her racing heart slowed. Teran led her to the bed, bidding her to lie beside her. She obeyed, eager to show her gratitude with hands and lips and tongue.

Five pricks of metal at her neck stopped her cold. She looked up.

"You brought something to me tonight," Teran told her, one claw still resting at her throat, keeping her motionless more effectively than any bondage. "I would take it."

Teran's fingers entered her, hard.

She shivered, wanting to respond but too frightened to move. Had Teran retracted the claws on her neck? She still felt pressure there. Was it just Teran's fingertips? She couldn't tell, couldn't think, didn't want to look. Her body ached to move, and she wasn't sure if she could still it.

The face above her curled into a smile, tight and pointed. She could hear, under her own wordless pleas, the low hum of Teran's own sounds, steady growls with short gasps between them.

She didn't even bother to rub Cailyn's clitoris with her thumb. This was use, plain and simple.

Cailyn gave up. Her hips moved and the rest of her body writhed with them. Any moment now, she might feel the pricks at her neck, might freeze in fear. Might feel herself bleed and wonder how deeply she'd been cut.

Long minutes later, she realized that it hadn't happened, and her sigh of relief turned into a cry of pleasure. Teran laughed and kept going.

When Cailyn finally felt the slight prick, she swam through the beat of her own heart and willed her body to stillness. She looked down at Teran's hand to see the fingers still inside her and her thumb, claw extended, digging, just barely, into the skin above her clitoris.

Cailyn opened her mouth to say her stop word. No sound came out.

She stared at the claw and stammered. "Your hand—you don't—it—"

She tried not to shudder but couldn't stop herself.

"Was that fear, or an aftershock?" Teran asked, grinning.

The only answer Cailyn's mouth could form was, "I don't know, my lady."

Teran turned her thumb so the claw pointed away, and withdrew her other fingers. They were clawless.

"Gods!" Cailyn cried, the words bursting out of her now that she knew Teran hadn't hurt her. "You scared the hell out of me…My lady," she added, after an awkward pause.

Laughing, Teran moved her hand away, and Cailyn sat up. Her back stung. So did the space between her breasts. Her body twitched with pleasure and fear.

She heard Teran stir behind her and turned. Teran leaned over the nightstand, looking into a videoscreen. She said something to the image glowing there—a servant of the house, Cailyn reasoned, from the dress and the fact that calling anyone else would make no sense and probably break several laws.

The door slid open, and a servant dressed in the same gray Cailyn saw everywhere brought ointment and cloths to clean Cailyn's wounds.

She turned, expecting the young man to tend to her. He passed the stuff to Teran and walked out without a word.

I should be serving you.

She buried the thought. Teran wasn't the one who needed mending right now. "You do this yourself?"

Teran brought the damp cloth to the cut between Cailyn's breasts. "For others, no. For you, yes."

"Thank you, my lady."

Cailyn tensed, expecting the ointment to sting. Instead, it numbed the burn of the cut. Plain though it looked, it must have been expensive.

And good for healing, Cailyn guessed. Teran had been nothing if not thorough.

She turned so that Teran could tend the welts on her back. "Why do this for me? Why choose me at all?"

"I told you I wouldn't tell you that, little one." Teran brushed her hair away and kissed her neck. She shivered with the pleasure of it.

"No, not that. I mean the claws. You spent eighty thousand on them. But you also told me that you don't care much for flashy things or flashy people. So why spend so much on implants? Couldn't you do all that with a good knife?"

She wondered at herself. How could she talk so breezily about knives, like she knew how they might feel? Like they were nothing. While she sat here on a bed whose sheets had her blood on them.

Teran rested her chin on Cailyn's shoulder. "His name was Mariel."

"His name? You did this for someone?"

"He was one of the gladiators of House Nivrai," Teran said.

Cailyn's eyes widened. Of course some nobles took lovers beneath their station. But if Teran had, why would people bother to spread rumors about modifications when perfectly good gossip would suffice?

Mariel. She tried to place the name but couldn't. She'd never been one for fights, and Nivrai was a backward little planet, hidden at the edge of a system few bothered to visit.

With a demon for a ruler.

"Was, my lady?" she asked at last.

The claws flexed, extending, retracting, and extending again.

"Mariel has been dead five years," Teran said, her voice soft.

"My lady," Cailyn said. "I'm sorry."

"It is not your concern."

Cailyn shook her head. "I understand."

She didn't like saying it. She was supposed to bring comfort.

But that didn't mean foisting it on people who'd asked her not to press the point. She looked down at Teran's hand again, unable to keep herself from staring.

"Go ahead and ask," Teran said. "It's obvious you want to."

"They—you got them for him?"

Teran extended them again. "Yes. They were his idea."

"His idea, my lady? Not yours?"

Teran grinned. "No. Not mine."

Cailyn shivered. What kind of world had she wandered into? "Then he—"

"He liked the idea of weapons that were a part of my body." She smirked. "So did I."

It made sense, Cailyn supposed. If anything here in Nivrai made sense, anyway.

Teran laughed again. "It was also the perfect way to convince the people who had already started to whisper about me that I'd completely lost my reason."

I'm not convinced you haven't, Cailyn thought but didn't say.

"In the end, everyone left me alone, even—" Teran stopped, biting off the words.

"Even who?"

"The rumors got gruesome enough that for anyone to admit desire for me became unseemly. And Mariel was already mine." After a moment, she added, "You have no idea what a relief that was."

For a long moment, Cailyn didn't speak. Then she turned.

"My lady," she said, "I don't know what happened. I don't know what he was to you. But if you're carrying a memory like that, on your own body, it must weigh on you."

The ice-gray gaze fixed on her.

"I'm not him. I'm nothing like him, from what you've said. But please...let me touch you."

Teran lay down and closed her eyes. Cailyn knelt over her. Her hands traced patterns along Teran's skin. She parted her lips with reverence and lowered her mouth to Teran's flesh. Her nostrils filled with the spice of Teran's smell.

A courtesan didn't have to enjoy giving pleasure. Not as long as she gave it well. But the best courtesans did, feeling the stir in their own bodies when the ones they served moaned and bucked.

Cailyn felt it now. A thrill of heat rushed through her as her lips and tongue tasted Teran's wetness. The claws kneaded her back again, piercing her already welted shoulders. In the middle of this, the blossom of pain felt right somehow.

Cailyn traced the folds of Teran's flesh, seeking out the memories buried there. She offered pleasure as a balm, like the salve Teran had spread on her own welts, cool and refreshing. There was so much here. So much life, neglected and left cold.

Under her mouth, Teran tensed. She shook like someone letting loose tears.

Cailyn smiled and touched her breast. A clawed hand reached to cover hers, fierce and possessive like the talon of a hawk.

"I'll go," Cailyn whispered. She pulled her hand out from under Teran's.

The slim hand caught hers. Teran smiled. "This bed has been cold and empty five years. You could stay and warm it."

The hand moved. So did Cailyn, lying down beside Teran.

Teran settled against her. She tapped at a console on the nightstand and the light dimmed to black. Then she wrapped an arm around Cailyn and clutched tight. Her other hand reached to pull up the sheet and blanket.

❖

Light streamed in from the big window. The wall-door of the other room had closed. Cailyn was alone.

"Lady Nivrai?" She blinked, sitting up. "Teran?"

No answer.

Cailyn found her garments, neatly folded, at the foot of the bed. A small tablet with a videoscreen glowed on top of them.

She picked it up. A receipt, she realized, for the transaction. Three thousand credits, transferred into her account.

She turned the tablet around in her hands.

"So no one's going to see me off," she said, her voice a whisper in the quiet room.

She wondered where the bathroom was. Someone as precise as Teran Nivrai would permit her to bathe before leaving. A servant of the house would show her the way if she called.

She decided against it. Better to slip out now. Better to leave this place sooner than later, she thought, turning the tablet over and over in her hands.

CHAPTER THREE

Cailyn gasped. She'd known immediately where the call came from, of course. But she hadn't quite believed it until a familiar face filled her videoscreen and she stared into larger-than-life gray eyes.

"My lady Nivrai." She licked her lips. "I can't say I expected to hear from you again."

Teran smiled. "Your surprise isn't unwarranted. They say that I never see someone twice."

"Yes, my lady. They say."

She'd thought about it, though, more often than she cared to admit. Wondered about that name, Mariel. About the woman who'd made her hands into weapons for him. About the ache she'd tried to soothe, and how much of it her hands and mouth and body had assuaged.

She'd done nothing more about her curiosity, though. Her little tryst with Lady Nivrai hadn't made her any more interested in the dark channels than before.

But she'd wondered. Listened to more rumors than she should have.

Four times a year, Teran Nivrai would hire someone, so the stories went. That was ridiculous even for a minor noble. If the rumors about what she did four times a year hadn't fascinated the gossips, they would've called her close to dead.

Then again, most nobles didn't have retractable steel claws. Much less use them on the courtesans.

Even on the dark channels, the courtesans might turn down her offers. Even if she did pay well.

Cailyn slipped a hand between her breasts, touched the place where Lady Nivrai had cut her. The mark had faded long ago, but she felt a pang anyway.

How long had it been? Six months?

"They are not wrong," Teran said. "If I played favorites, some interesting rumors would start."

"Then they'll start about me if I accept your offer," Cailyn said. She tried to ignore the heat she felt.

"They may. But I will pay well. More than double what you would get otherwise. Besides, I don't think you mind so much."

Cailyn smiled. "There are some things I wouldn't mind so much."

"And the other things?" Teran's voice was rich with amusement.

Yes, that. Pain. Blood. She'd never had any penchant for either.

"I would"—she stopped, looked up at the ceiling, then back at the videoscreen on the wall—"endure the others, for the sake of the rest."

Teran raised an eyebrow. "So you do want to hear my offer?"

"Yes."

❖

A night and a day, as it turned out. That was a long time to be alone with Lady Nivrai.

She remembered the scrape Teran's newsteel had torn between her breasts. It had itched while it was healing. She hadn't minded. But to wake up after a long night of use like that, with scrapes and bruises that still throbbed or burned, only to find Teran rested and eager for more?

That didn't sound so easy.

But Teran had cared about Cailyn's pleasure too. She didn't have to, but she had. And that might be worth a few bruises and some blood.

Cailyn enjoyed giving pleasure. She'd known she would since the first time she'd seen a noble's avid gaze and felt her knees turn to water. But not everyone she served cared much for her, and even her patience had limits.

She thought of her father. How many times had she seen him study himself in a mirror, comb his long blond hair, watching Cailyn's reflection watching him? He'd told her years ago how relieved he had been to retire.

Cailyn hadn't believed it. She'd seen people watch her father, their eyes fixed on his body as he passed. She'd understood even then why they stared, even if she hadn't known exactly what he did with them.

She'd wanted what he had from the beginning. He'd laughed and told her it wasn't all it seemed.

The warning had gone right through her.

She hadn't known just how much effort her father's beauty took. How his hair required hours of styling and care to keep supple. The creams and salves he used to keep his skin looking young. How even the lilt of his soft voice had come from careful enunciation. She had never realized that he never cursed or yelled because he'd learned not to.

She hadn't understood any of it. Not until she'd spent nights under people she hated.

Teran's desires—Cailyn winced at the memories of what Lady Nivrai had done to her.

But Teran had also kissed her like a lover. Whether she was toying with Cailyn or not.

Let her do what she wanted, then. Flog her, make her bleed, whatever else. She'd endured it all already; it was a part of who Teran was, as much as the other.

It wouldn't be easy. But Cailyn had known that the first time.

Cailyn tugged at the fabric of her dress. She'd never fidget in front of a client, but here in the hall, she could let herself be nervous. And she did need to make sure the dress fit right, cupping her breasts and wide hips without bunching up. She'd chosen a deep blue dress made of transparent fabric and rouged her nipples underneath it, wanting to make sure she caught Teran's eye.

She found Teran at a table in a small room. A tubelike seat wrapped around one side of the circular table, arranged so that Cailyn would have to sit beside her.

On the table lay fruit and small portions of a meat Cailyn didn't recognize. Cailyn's fruit had already been peeled, the sections arranged on her plate. Teran's had not.

Teran wore a plain uniform in the standard Nivrai gray. It clung tight enough to reveal the lines of Teran's body but hid her flesh away.

Cailyn looked down at her rouged nipples under the blue cloth. Their hardness embarrassed her. She felt more exposed than she had even then.

She forced herself not to fidget, looked at Teran, studying her reaction to make sure she hadn't noticed too much.

Teran smiled. It looked welcoming. "Hello, little one." She patted the seat for Cailyn to join her.

"My lady." Cailyn slid into the seat beside Teran.

"It's a pleasure to see you again."

"I'm glad to please you, my lady," Cailyn said, letting her smile grow as big as she deemed wise.

"Good." Teran picked up a melon, pierced it with her claws, and drew them down to make slits in the skin. She peeled it slowly, holding it between glistening metal. She pulled out a section of melon and bit into it.

Cailyn took a few bites of her food. The tender meat melted in her mouth. The melon, in contrast, was tangy, a sharp counterpoint to the mild-spiced meat.

Teran watched Cailyn eat, intent as a hawk. Cailyn wondered what she wanted. Did something hinge on her opinion of the food? Confused and exposed, she sipped the wine.

She coughed, the bitter liquid catching in her throat. Whatever the drink was, it wasn't wine. Not wanting to stare, she glanced at Teran, keeping her head down.

Teran smirked. "It's vakren. Traditional, for the worship of one of the older gods. Not much in favor beyond that."

Ancient religious rites to dead gods. How did Teran know about that? Much less enough to buy and drink their traditional beverages? Cailyn wasn't sure she wanted to know. She ate a bite of meat and took a ginger sip of the drink, not wanting to offend.

Teran peeled another piece of melon. Cailyn watched the steel-tipped hands. Her own dress veiled none of her body. She shivered. The claws had moved with that same precision along her skin.

The spot between her breasts ached, a little thrill of phantom pain. She squeezed her legs together and stared at the gray top that hid Teran's breasts.

"How can you wait six months, my lady?" she blurted. "It's unnatural. Especially with desires like yours."

Teran chuckled. "My desire moves slowly through my blood. It's slow to stir and slow to vanish."

Cailyn chewed a piece of melon. Her mouth filled with its juice. Slow to vanish. Did that mean Teran sometimes thought of her?

Teran drummed her fingers on the table with a metallic sound. "And you? What about your desire?"

Cailyn coughed on a piece of meat. "Mine?"

Surely this wasn't just about her. Lady Nivrai wanted something.

Cailyn bit into a slice of melon and hedged her bets. "I'm here to serve you, my lady. My—what I want is to do it well."

"That's not what I asked."

"No, but why should you want to know about me?"

"Your father was a famous courtesan. You follow in his footsteps. Before we met, I thought you did it because of his fame and your beauty." A smile curved her lips. "And that you took my offer only out of curiosity. But you looked at me with desire from the first."

Cailyn fought not to frown. Showing interest was one thing, being obvious another.

Teran picked up another slice of melon. Her claws gleamed. "I don't think my reputation had much to do with that."

Cailyn laughed. "No."

"You asked for my secrets the last time you were here. I gave you one of them. Now I ask for one in return."

She raised the slice of melon to her mouth. Cailyn watched, mesmerized, as she bit it in half.

A secret for a secret.

Very well.

"I remember once when I was a girl. My father—"

"You saw him with a client, then?"

"No. Yes. Yes and no."

Teran said nothing.

"He retired after he had me. But there were still a few people he was...fond of."

Teran's smile widened.

"My mother left for business. My father had made plans. Lord Lerak arrived early, so I hadn't gone to bed when he came in. He spoke to me. I remember he greeted me, smiling."

"You liked him, then?"

"Then I saw him looking at my father. I had never seen such looks. I was fascinated. My father told me to go to bed. I was curious and snuck back out."

"What happened then?"

"I heard them talking but was afraid they'd see if I peeked, so I hid and listened. I heard my father call him 'my lord,' but they laughed like friends. I wanted to know what they were doing. I knew my father's trade, of course, but I didn't know how they would interact.

"They stayed for a long time. They did nothing but talk. Lerak mentioned me."

"Did he?"

"Yes. He said I had my father's beauty." Cailyn blushed. As a grown woman serving the nobles, she worked hard to keep herself beautiful. But all those years ago, the words had flattered her.

Cailyn willed away her embarrassment. "He asked if I would be trained in the same art."

"And what did your father say to that?" Teran purred, then lifted another slice of melon to her mouth.

"He said he hoped not. Lerak laughed. I remember he asked if the nobles were really so bad. My father laughed too and said, 'Not you, my lord!'"

Teran chuckled.

"I hadn't expected to hear them laugh. Not with each other. Not that way. I had to know what was happening between them. As quiet as I could manage to be, I crept to the stairs to look down. By the time I got there, they weren't laughing any more. Lord Lerak looked my father over. His face changed. He walked over with a look in his eyes. Fixed. Hungry. I saw him smile. It frightened me, a little."

Another soft laugh from Teran.

"Then I saw Lerak wrap his arms around my father and pull him close. I remember the way his arms locked around my father's body. Then he kissed my father—sudden, hard. I felt like I'd intruded. Like

I saw something I shouldn't. I rushed back to my room and hoped they hadn't heard me."

The last slices of melon lay untouched on Teran's plate. "And after that, you knew you wanted to be like your father?"

"Yes. I crept back inside. Huddled under the covers of my bed. I wondered what it would be like to be looked at that way. Kissed that way. I imagined eyes like that in the ceiling above me, looking down at me. I felt something stir in my body."

Cailyn fought not to blush. What she had done next, twisted under her covers, for herself and for the pleasure of those imagined eyes, Teran could guess herself.

"From that moment on, I knew what I wanted. I told my father I wanted to be trained. I never told him why. When he asked, I only said I admired him. That I wanted to be like him."

Teran sipped her vakren. Cailyn looked at Teran, her body hidden under the gray uniform. She wanted to draw the fastener down, slowly and with reverence, and expose Teran's skin to her fingers and lips.

Teran's eyes caught and held her. A hand on her chest pushed her down.

Cold light filled her vision as she stared at the ceiling. The dark shape of Teran's face hovered over her. She quivered, pressed against the side of the small sofa.

Bright metal lowered itself to her dress and tore a line. She fought an urge to squirm or flee.

A faint touch of the newsteel rent the fabric, but left her skin untouched. She shook again when Teran moved, unsure if she felt cheated. She blinked at Teran's dark head, wreathed in the light.

The claw came down again. It tore circles in the fabric around her nipples. They came free one by one, bright with the rouge Cailyn had daubed on them. Teran laughed and pinched one. She pulled it up and out. Two points of steel encircled it.

The clawed embrace stung. Cailyn closed her eyes and took deep breaths as Teran pulled.

Cailyn's head turned. She hissed into the fabric under her. Her flesh began to ache, dull and insistent.

"Little one," Teran said. "Open your eyes. Look at me."

Cailyn blinked at the bright light, and she winced again as Teran's other hand caught her other nipple. As before, she pulled.

At least Teran had distracted her first.

"Perhaps I should pierce you," Teran said. Cailyn imagined blood beading up where the metal touched her.

She forced herself to hold Teran's gaze and reached to unzip Teran's bodice. She sought Teran's nipples with blind fingers and ran her fingers over them.

Teran moaned softly, an exhalation Cailyn felt. The claws poked deeper into her skin.

Cailyn slipped her hand down farther and moved her fingers over the skin of Teran's stomach.

Teran twisted the flesh caught between her claws. "Are you sure you want to do that, little one?"

Cailyn swallowed. "You could move your hand, my lady."

Teran's fingers moved to hover just beyond the skin of Cailyn's nipple.

Cailyn slid her fingers down until she found the slick skin of Teran's labia. She moved over them for a moment and sought out Teran's clitoris. How much of the wetness Cailyn felt came from her touch and how much from holding steel so close to her nipples?

Teran's body moved, slight motions Cailyn could barely feel. She took shallow, ragged breaths. Cailyn quickened the dance of her fingers and tried not to think too hard about what might happen if Teran moved too much when she came.

Teran's claws retracted with a metallic clink. She hissed once. Her mouth opened and her body pressed into Cailyn's hand.

Cailyn smiled and brought her fingers to her lips, tasting Teran on them.

Teran's fingertips glittered as they tore open the fabric of Cailyn's dress and pulled it open. Teran kissed her, and Cailyn wrapped her arms around her body.

Claws kneaded her sides, pricking the flesh. Teran's tongue sank into Cailyn's mouth. Pain blossomed in Cailyn's side and faded just as quickly, embers dying on her skin.

Was she bleeding? She wasn't sure.

"Come with me," Teran said.

CHAPTER FOUR

Cailyn stepped out of the remnants of the dress and followed. Out of the corner of her eye, she saw a man and woman dressed in Nivrai gray. They moved to clear away the wine and plates.

But she wasn't here to watch them. She slid her fingers over her sides and felt the roughness of a few pinpricks. Not Lady Nivrai's worst.

She stepped into the bedroom. Teran followed. She heard the footfalls behind her, soft and slow. She caught a glimpse of arms moving—

Without warning, they shoved Cailyn to the ground.

Cailyn scrambled to kneel properly. What was Teran playing at?

A clawed finger traced her chin and slid down her chest. She closed her eyes. Teran retracted her claws and held her clawless hand above Cailyn's heart.

Cailyn closed her eyes and tried to will away her anger and surprise. *I offer myself to you. I came here to do it.*

Cailyn listened to Teran's breath as steel points grew and shrank against her skin. With a last sharp sound, they retracted again.

Cailyn expected to be thrown onto the bed, given the passion in Teran's voice moments before. It must have taken Teran an immense amount of will to do so little. Cailyn wondered why. She'd come here knowing perfectly well what Teran could do.

"You pricked me," she said, opening her eyes and looking down at Teran's hand. "But you haven't cut me."

The claws extended, gleaming on the ends of Teran's fingertips. One rested against Cailyn's chest. She could feel it there when she breathed. If she breathed deeply enough, would it cut into her skin?

Teran's lip curled into a smile. "No, little one, I haven't."

"You want to," Cailyn said.

"Yes." The claw twitched but did not cut.

"Then why haven't you?" From the moment Cailyn had walked in, the memory of Teran's claws and what they'd done to her before had filled her mind. She trembled every time the claws emerged from Teran's fingertips.

She liked the light touches, the steel skating careful over her skin. That didn't hurt, and no one but Teran could do it.

That was reason enough to come back. But it had come with a price before. She would have to pay that price again sooner or later.

Every time Teran touched her, a part of her flinched. With every kiss, she waited for the pinpricks. They weren't so bad in the heat of passion.

She hadn't expected this waiting. Couldn't Teran get on with it?

Right now, Teran stared down at her own claw pressed against Cailyn's skin. Her breath came shallow and ragged.

Of course she wanted to do it.

Her other hand, also clawless, slid lower. It glided down Cailyn's belly to her pubis and paused there. Was Teran really ready to have sex before hurting her, when she so clearly wanted to?

"I will cut you," Teran said, "if you ask me to."

Cailyn hissed. She'd known before coming here that she would have to accept some things she might not want. She would endure them without protest. That was what giving herself over meant. She wouldn't have come if she couldn't acquiesce to them.

She opened her mouth to speak. Teran wanted this, and she was here to give Teran what she wanted.

The words refused to come. Cailyn shook her head. "I can't do it, my lady. Not that."

The claw retracted. Cailyn's skin felt its absence. She wished Teran would touch her with those now-smooth fingers, but they hovered just above her. She sighed.

"You want something," Teran said.

There was no pause. Two fingers sank inside her. She gasped. Teran chuckled and her thumb thrilled against Cailyn's clitoris.

Cailyn shifted to allow better access. *Maybe I could ask now,* she thought. Jolts of pleasure ran through her body as she moved to Teran's insistent rhythm.

Teran leaned over and kissed her. Her mouth opened like her body. That was familiar enough. But with Teran her mouth turned to water.

Teran's fingers drove into her. Even with the claws retracted, they held steel, ready to extend. Cailyn marveled at herself as Teran's rhythm slowed.

"My lady," Cailyn panted. "What—?"

The fingers inside Cailyn slid free. Cailyn gasped at their loss. What had she done wrong? Was this about not asking to be cut?

"Close your eyes." Teran stepped away. "Touch yourself if you wish, but don't come."

All right. Nobles had asked her to put on a show for them before.

Cailyn slid her hand down, making a show of caressing her own flesh. Part of her wanted to turn and look. Part of her felt glad to lose herself, to focus on nothing but the way her fingers moved as they slipped over her slick flesh.

She heard a drawer slide open and froze. When she heard the snapping sound of a glove, she sighed with relief and let her fingers dance again. A jolt of pleasure raced through her as she moved them still faster.

She heard Teran's footfalls behind her. Hands reached down to touch her chest. They slid down her stomach and over her pelvis and paused just above her sex.

Cailyn guessed the touch was a command. She bowed her head and moved her hand away, offering access to Teran's hands.

Fingers filled her again, just like before. They pushed in and out of her in the same powerful welcome as before. One finger thrilled over her clitoris.

Teran's other hand, gloved and slick with oil, sought her smaller orifice.

Glove or no, Cailyn tensed. She thought of Teran probing her there, will alone keeping the steel at bay.

Teran laughed. Her fingers moved on Cailyn's clitoris until her body relented.

It trusts you more than I do, Cailyn thought. Teran slipped a finger in.

Cailyn could ask for pain now. Here in this haze of sex it wouldn't be so bad. And Teran would provide.

But to use her claws, Teran would have to pull her fingers out again. She'd have to stop all of this.

Cailyn could only shake her head as her exasperated sigh became a climax. Twin orifices yawned open as Teran pulled free. She heard the snap as Teran peeled off the glove and tossed it aside.

"What is it you really want?" Cailyn asked.

"You." Teran kissed her.

Cailyn licked her lips. "What will you do now, since you're not going to hurt me?"

Silence. Cailyn listened to her own breath.

Steel wound itself in her hair. A sharp yank pulled her head back so hard she yelped. Metal ran along her neck.

"I never said I wouldn't hurt you." The claw tickled her neck. "I said I wouldn't cut you."

Cailyn swallowed. She shivered as her throat moved, Teran's steel still pressed against it. She blinked up at the ceiling, afraid to move her head with Teran's steel-tipped hand still wound in her curls.

Teran pinched her nipple. She reeled.

Teran rummaged through the drawer in the nightstand. She drew some small clips out. Cailyn frowned. Her nipple still ached. What more did Teran want?

Teran held one of the clips up for Cailyn to look at. Then she fit it over her nipple. Cailyn breathed hard as it tightened over her flesh.

"Have you seen these before? They have a clever little feature." She tapped the side lightly with her finger. The clip emitted an electronic beep and tightened, remorseless. Cailyn bit her lip.

Teran laughed and held up another. Cailyn guessed Teran would put it on her other nipple. But instead Teran's hand moved down between her legs. She shook her head in disbelief as Teran's other hand pulled gently on one of her inner lips.

"You realize I'm not like the others you've seen," Cailyn said.

"Yes, I do," Teran said. She paused to run her fingers along Cailyn's skin. Then Cailyn knew nothing but the agony of the pressure on her pinched skin. She threw her head back and howled.

She'd thought, before any of this started, that giving her stop word would be easy enough. Now she struggled for any words at all.

"Too much," she finally said, the words and a gasp coming out together.

The pressure eased. Relief flooded her before she realized she hadn't heard the electronic sound. She swam back into her body. Pale gray eyes stared at her. It took her a moment to recognize them, or the objects lying, suddenly innocent, in Teran's palm.

She breathed into the paleness of the room. Would Teran be angry? Disappointment seethed in her gut. Then again, if Lady Nivrai wanted to play this game, so be it. She'd risked and lost. It was unfair to demand so much.

To Cailyn's surprise, tender arms wrapped around her body. Teran's mouth sought hers again. Cailyn surrendered to it gratefully, drinking in what Teran gave her. A thrill ran through her opening mouth.

And through her nipple, caught and sore between the metal clamped around it.

The tips of Teran's claws ghosted down her back, not piercing the skin. The nerves under them sang. Cailyn wrapped her arms around Teran and held on.

Go ahead. Cut me now, Cailyn thought. Even the pain of the vise around her nipple, Teran's touch could transform. It burned, a tiny flare of desire, as the steel traced need along her back.

"It will go," Teran said.

"Please, no." Cailyn wanted only this. To melt under Teran's kiss, arch into the lines of the newsteel along her back.

Her voice sounded strange to her own ears, thick with passion. She shuddered, sure it amused and aroused Teran to hear her plead.

Perhaps if she pleaded again and again, it would excite Teran enough to let this go? She felt an unexpected jolt of pleasure, imagining herself prostrate before the infamous Lady Helldemon and begging for mercy.

Teran nibbled at her neck. One of her hands slid along her body, its claws retracted, and down again to her sex.

"Cailyn Derys."

"Yes?"

"Are you not here to serve my pleasure?"

"Yes," Cailyn gasped as two of Teran's fingers slid inside her.

She swallowed, trying to collect herself. "But it's not only my pain that pleases you, my lady."

"True."

"Then why?"

The words sounded as foolish as she felt, fighting not to dissolve into Teran's touch. She held on to them. Here for Teran's pleasure? Yes. Here for whatever kind of use any noble wanted, no matter what? No. Not even for Teran Nivrai.

"Why indeed?" Teran's other hand danced over the clamp on Cailyn's nipple until Cailyn made a small noise.

Teran moved her fingers a few times and then pulled them free. Cailyn turned on her with a frustrated frown.

"I think you're asking the wrong questions," Teran said, moving back with slow, easy steps. "I think the real question is: If you truly hate it, why are you here? It takes more than this to scare you away."

Was she afraid? She winced. She was scared of the pain. Yes. And somewhere hidden under the desire she still felt annoyed.

She didn't know much about the other courtesans, the ones the nobles hired for dominance games. She did know they had their limits, and Guild law said those limits had to be respected. Even Helldemon Nivrai might not break Guild law. After all, she had stopped, moments ago.

"What if it doesn't take more than this to scare me away, my lady?" Cailyn forced herself to ask.

"The door," Teran answered, "is that way."

"You'd send me away? After all this?"

"I wouldn't send you anywhere. The choice is yours and always has been. I would rather waste money than time."

She expected to see Teran pull away. Instead, Teran leaned over her and kissed her, hard.

The hunger in that kiss shocked Cailyn. Did the anticipation excite her so much?

Cailyn kissed her back, unsure if she wanted to lose herself in the kiss or if she hoped to distract Teran.

Fingers probed at her labia before the kiss even ended. She winced to feel them there but didn't want to pull away. She stared at the ceiling, trying not to think of how it would feel.

The pain came again. She heard a strange sound and realized she'd made it. Teran's finger circled her clitoris. Pleasure curled through Cailyn's flesh, and she willed herself to focus on it. Even that couldn't soothe the crushing pain.

She looked into Teran's eyes and willed herself to focus on them. Teran bent down to clip another clamp to her skin. She clenched her fists as the wave of pain came.

Teran's fingers danced along what flesh was left.

She heard Teran's voice telling her to breathe, so she did. When she relaxed, one of Teran's fingers peeked inside her for a moment and then retreated. Cailyn felt herself move after it.

She looked up again. Teran's strange eyes glowed, lit by pleasure. The sight sent a thrill through her, something she finally recognized as desire.

She moved to Teran's touch—her lady's touch, as she was meant to. Reason returned. She imagined Teran laughing, light and amused, as jolts zinged through her body and her fists pounded at air again. Then she realized the laughter was real.

The room slid into focus. Teran smiled down at her and she smiled back, too exhausted to do much else. Faint waves of pleasure moved through her, and on their heels came pain that made her cringe and bite her lip.

Hands moved on her body, gentle, almost sweet.

Was this how helldemons apologized?

Teran reached for the clip on Cailyn's nipple and opened it. Cailyn sighed in a moment of blessed relief.

It didn't last long. A new rush of pain came as the circulation returned.

Teran closed her mouth with another kiss. Her fingers pressed the clip on Cailyn's nipple. Cailyn tensed as it opened. Teran chuckled when she winced.

Again, Teran traced her hands along Cailyn's skin. Cailyn's body, tired of being hurt, ached for the gentle contact.

Just give me this, she thought but didn't say.

Fingers slid into Cailyn's mouth. Cailyn sucked at them. The retracted claws tasted metallic, a sharp promise.

The things Teran did were new to her. But she knew how to give pleasure like this. It relieved her to be on such familiar ground.

The fingers left her mouth and sprouted claws again. Steel ran lightly along Cailyn's lip. Cailyn breathed and opened her mouth. Even with the claws out, it seemed, she missed the contact.

Teran pushed a curl out of Cailyn's face. What did she look like now, sweaty and disheveled from sex and pain alike? She blushed.

"Those should come off," Teran said. Thankfully, there was no gloating in her voice.

"Then do it," Cailyn said with the same seriousness.

"You're not afraid, are you, little one?"

"I am. A little."

Teran's eyes glittered as she reached to pull the clamps off. "Good."

She removed them in rapid succession, allowing Cailyn a brief moment to get used to the pain of the first before overwhelming her with the second. Cailyn winced, cried out, and cursed.

She bit her lip. Perhaps she didn't advertise on the dark channels, but Teran was paying like she did. Learning how to speak with poise and grace came early in a courtesan's lessons.

Teran only laughed. "Nervous, little one? I told you before that punishment holds no interest for me."

She kissed Cailyn's stomach. "In fact, I would say you did quite well for one who is not accustomed to this."

Cailyn flushed with pride. She knew the feeling, a familiar contentment at having done well. With it came a familiar desire, a need to give more, to touch, to offer her all that her art had trained her for.

"What do you want now, little one?" Teran asked. She raised her head, twined a lock of Cailyn's hair around one of her claws.

Cailyn shivered. *I will if you ask me to.* Was that what she wanted? To hear Cailyn ask? After all this, begging to be cut didn't seem so frightening. Those points of steel had promised it already.

"I want to touch you, my lady," Cailyn said. *If I can't give what you want, at least let me offer what I know.*

Teran's lip curled. Cailyn frowned, sure she'd disappointed her, but the twitching mouth settled into a smile.

"Very well." Teran lowered herself onto the bed.

CHAPTER FIVE

Cailyn whispered a short prayer to the courtesans' goddess. She ran her hands down Teran's skin. Was touch like this too mild for a woman with claws?

She closed her eyes and breathed in. She remembered Teran's hand around her wrist the last time they had met, forbidding her to touch.

She parted Teran's slick flesh with care and reverence. She moved her fingers with slow care, seeking out the rhythm in Teran's breath.

Teran's eyes narrowed. Her mouth opened and low sounds came out. Cailyn took it as encouragement and slid her fingers down.

She looked up at Teran, her fingers poised at Teran's entrance. Teran looked back for a moment and nodded once.

Cailyn slid one finger in, slow and careful.

She wasn't sure what she'd been expecting. Eagerness? Resistance? She found flesh, soft and heated, like anyone else's. She moved her fingers without thought, her thumb at Teran's clitoris. Teran's hips moved. Cailyn timed her movements to meet them.

With others it might have been different, all speed and intensity. Cailyn kept her movements slow. From the stream of sound that came from Teran and the glitter of her still-lidded eyes, she seemed lost in pleasure. But that choice was not Cailyn's to make, despite the hum spreading through her own body at Teran's reaction.

So Cailyn waited, taking her cues from the moving body in front of her. Teran moved faster, all at once. Cailyn sped up as Teran cried out and her body locked around Cailyn's fingers.

She remembered that last time, the choked sound. This sound was steady, and the flesh around her fingers pulsed in possession rather than fear.

What had changed in six months? She pulled her fingers free and stared at them like she could read Teran's secrets in the glisten of her wetness. She looked up and Teran quirked an eyebrow at her.

Cailyn lay back on the bed. Teran laughed and told her to get back up.

Teran walked over to the wall and pressed the hidden panel. The wall slid aside to reveal the small flagellary. She walked over to one of the benches and gestured for Cailyn to bend over it.

"My lady?" Cailyn asked again. She would have welcomed even the smallest reprieve, a chance to kneel, listen, know when to let Teran's desire build again. But no.

Teran laughed and gestured again. She moved to the wall to take something down from it. A whip? A paddle? Cailyn didn't look. She climbed, resigned, onto the bench. Locks sealed quicksilver metal over Cailyn's wrists and ankles.

Steel knotted in her hair, harsh and unforgiving. "Little one. Are you so tired after one?"

"No, my lady." Cailyn fought not to sigh.

"Then why should I be?" A claw ran along her chin, sharp and warm.

Cailyn shivered. Why had she ever thought slow lovemaking might calm someone like Teran Nivrai? She laughed at herself.

Claws danced along the skin of her buttocks. Heat rose in her body, mingled with her fear. She let out a slow breath.

Leather draped across her skin. She recognized the braided flogger from last time. Its burn had seared her back. She shivered hard enough that Teran walked over to fist her hand in Cailyn's hair.

"Perhaps I won't cut you tonight," Teran whispered, sharp in her ear. "That much is up to you. But you will bleed."

The hand in her hair withdrew. She felt the weight of her curls like a loss as she heard the whip whistle overhead. Her nipple and labia ached, suddenly demanding her notice.

The tails of the flogger tore fiery lines into her flesh. She clutched at the bench with her hands.

Teran stopped for a moment. Cailyn breathed, gulping in air. The first time, the fire in her flesh had fed her desire, even as she wailed and fought back curses.

She didn't like this, not now. She did not crave it. She endured it. But under it all lingered the wish that Teran would touch her, take her, claim her. Didn't that come to the same thing in the end?

Yes. Yes. She swallowed, seeking out the rhythm in the blows Teran's windmilling arm rained down on her skin. Part of her burned to be touched. Could it kindle to this?

She envisioned the courtesans' goddess, her eyes closed, her head ringed by flowing hair. She focused on the image, slowed her breathing.

Was she bleeding? She might be. If Teran wanted it, she would be soon.

She imagined Teran's smile. She thought of the rich hum in Teran's voice when desire overtook her.

A new image rose to her mind, unbidden: her blood, bright red on steel. Her hips rocked back to meet the whip.

Teran laughed behind her. Pain lanced through her again. Her body moved with the rhythm, the warmth in her body spreading to Teran's will.

The flogger tore screams from her. They no longer mattered. The sensation coursing through her skin was no different from the thrill she felt when Teran touched her. Where one ended, the other began.

A silence fell. Cailyn felt the cool air of the room against her body. The emptiness filled with the sting of her welts, sharp now that the rhythm driving it all was gone.

One of the welts lit with pain as Teran ran a finger across it. Her hips moved of their own volition. Teran murmured approval.

"Am I bleeding, my lady?" Cailyn managed to ask, her voice thin and strange to her own ears.

Teran walked over to the other side of the bench. She showed Cailyn her hand, a bit of blood smeared on one finger. "Some."

Cailyn's mouth opened when Teran's finger touched her lips. There was blood on it, her blood. Still, she'd tasted herself on nobles' fingers countless times. She closed her eyes, tried not to think too hard, and opened her mouth.

Teran purred. It might have made Cailyn laugh if it hadn't unnerved her instead.

Teran pulled her fingers out of Cailyn's mouth and wrapped them around her chin. The claws extended with a sharp sound. Cailyn forced herself not to twitch.

A claw ran along her throat. "So now what, my little one?"

"Go ahead. Cut me."

"Oh?"

"You'll keep coming up with more until I agree to it anyway. That's what you're doing right now."

Teran grinned. "You're perceptive."

Cailyn gave a tired little laugh.

"But if you only want to stop me," Teran said, "you might as well leave."

"No." Cailyn swallowed. "I was thinking of it when you whipped me. I want you to."

Her own words sounded surer than she felt. Still, every caress had made her wonder about the one that would open her flesh. It would be wrong to leave it undone.

Teran nodded and pressed her fingers to the metal binding Cailyn's wrists and ankles. She led Cailyn to the bed.

Cailyn shivered. Teran stroked her leg. "You're afraid?"

"A little, yes."

"You'll like what I have in mind, I think. At least in the end."

Cailyn squirmed. That wasn't reassuring.

The tip of a claw moved to her thigh. A few light scratches impelled her to open her legs. She closed her eyes. What exactly did Teran have in store for her?

The steel pierced her flesh, a thin line torn down the length of Cailyn's inner thigh. She stared in wonder as blood, rich and red, dripped out of it.

Teran lowered her face to the cut and kissed it. Then she opened her mouth and licked its length.

It eased the pain a little. Cailyn heard herself moan. She thought of animals licking their wounds and wondered if it gave them a similar reprieve.

Or did this comfort her because of her desire?

Cailyn tensed as Teran moved to the other leg. As before, Teran rested the claw against her skin. Anticipation made Cailyn's skin tingle.

Pain burst across her body, terrible and welcome. She cried out again.

When Teran pressed her lips to the wound, she was ready. She relaxed as it soothed her, savored the respite it gave her.

A rush of sensation thrilled Cailyn's nerves. She cried out again. Perhaps Teran had been right, after all. Maybe she had enjoyed this.

Teran's lips nuzzled the wound. Cailyn's body rocked with pleasure as Teran pulled away. She smiled with red-stained lips.

"Thank you, my lady," Cailyn said, and blinked. Had she really just thanked Teran for that?

The familiar laughter tinkled through the room. "Little one, did you think I was finished?"

Teran's fingers spread Cailyn's labia. Cailyn froze, but Teran only lowered her head to Cailyn's vulva.

Teran gave a low little gasp of pleasure as she licked. Cailyn wondered for a wild, brazen moment if Teran always did this. The thought made laughter bubble in her throat, frenzied, desperate. She choked it back.

She took a deep breath and willed herself to relax. Her hips bucked harder than she thought they would. Teran's hands wrapped tight around her, possessive but not harsh. She sighed. Teran made her own soft sound in answer.

She tilted her hips again, and strong arms pushed her back down. Pleasure surged through her as Teran held her there, her whole body overfull with it, even the places where she had been cut and opened.

Cailyn's body locked and released, and she found herself staring. She wasn't sure at what, so she tucked her head and waited.

She looked down to find Teran propped on her elbows, looking at her. Teran's smile was still pink with blood. Cailyn's blood, she remembered, as an aftershock reeled through her.

Teran leaned over to kiss her. Cailyn breathed the smell of blood and sex and opened her mouth to admit the vivid taste. Teran's mouth bore down on hers, insistent.

She wrapped her hands around Teran's body.

It was no use, she thought, doing any of this by halves.

CHAPTER SIX

Cool ointment soothed Cailyn's welts. Teran's touch was gentle for now. She savored it.

Her legs still stung. She would have liked the gel to cool their burn, but she didn't feel ready to present the wounds.

"How are you doing, my little one?" said Teran behind her.

"I'm all right," Cailyn said.

"My lady," she added a moment later. Where had her manners gone?

Teran kissed her neck. "Good."

A claw ran along Cailyn's skin. "Turn around and let me see."

Cailyn rolled over and rubbed her eyes. She would just as soon have curled up in these sheets and slept.

Why was she so tired? That had taken a lot out of her, yes, but...

She blinked and stretched. "Did you put something else in that wine?"

"That's against Guild law, little one."

Cailyn sat up and winced. "Then why do I feel dazed?"

"That happens sometimes. Especially with bleeding."

She stared at the lines on Cailyn's thighs. "Maybe you shouldn't have shown me these," she said. Her fingertip ran along the bottom of the wound. Sparks of pain flared through Cailyn's skin.

Teran watched her wince. "They might tempt me too much."

"Gods. Do you ever stop?"

"No."

"What is this about for you, my lady?" she asked. "Why pain, why blood?"

Teran cleaned her wounds. Then the gel-coated fingers numbed the pain as they rubbed the cool ointment over her thigh.

Teran's other hand, still tipped with steel, touched Cailyn's chest near the cut she'd made there six months ago.

"Blood? Blood is a part of you, little one. Like this is a part of you." Her finger traced its way down Cailyn's body to her vulva.

She held up her finger. Cailyn's wetness made it glisten. "Why shouldn't I want both?"

Cailyn let out a slow breath. What could she say to that?

Teran lay down beside Cailyn and wrapped an arm around her. Cailyn turned on her side to allow Teran to better embrace her. Teran had other ideas, her hand resting against Cailyn's back.

"Skin is a barrier," Teran said, the pads of her fingers pressed against Cailyn's flesh. "Isn't it strange how much of our lives we spend with skin between us?"

Five claws extended. They buried their tips in Cailyn's back. Cailyn cried out and wrapped her hands around herself.

She pressed her head against the pillow and flexed her back muscles. The new cuts stung. Teran kissed her just above where she had cut. She wiped the wounds with a damp cloth.

"So that's what you want?" Cailyn asked. "More access?"

"Do you want all my secrets at once, little one? If I told you what I'm up to, you might lose interest."

"I—"

"If you did that, " Clawless fingers traced lightly down her skin, "you might not let me finish."

Finish? Was there more Teran wanted? Cailyn wasn't sure how much more she could endure. But Teran said nothing more.

Relieved, Cailyn settled in beside her.

"Tell me about Mariel," Cailyn said.

She closed her mouth as soon as she said it. But somehow the words fit here, in the dark, when she and Teran both needed rest and neither could sleep.

"You know all you need to know," Teran answered.

"I know you cared for him. I know he died. But you said the claws were his idea. You said he wanted you to have them."

"He wanted everything," Teran said, her voice softening.

"I'm sure he did, my lady, if you spent eighty thousand on implants for him. But how did you know he would? It's not like gladiators can put themselves on the dark channels." She chuckled in spite of herself. "Unless there's something I don't know."

"No." Teran laughed.

"Then what—?"

"I watched him fight."

"Watched him?"

"He was good. Far better, in fact, than most of the others."

Cailyn waited.

"But I noticed things. His fights went longer than most others. He left the ring with a surprising number of bruises."

"He lost to the others on purpose? Just so they would hurt him?"

"I never said he lost," Teran said. Cailyn could hear her smile.

"Then what?"

"I don't believe I ever saw him lose. But it took him longer to win than it took others. At first, I thought he did it to draw things out and keep them exciting for the audience. Until, during a fight with another man he'd always seemed fond of, I watched his face."

Cailyn bit her lip to keep from laughing. So this was what romance looked like to Teran Nivrai.

"You wanted him because you'd seen that."

"Yes." Cailyn felt hands on her back. The touch stung the raw skin, a sudden bite that shocked her to alertness. She twitched away, but the hands didn't move.

Cailyn expelled a long, low breath. She pressed her flesh against Teran's hands and waited for pleasure to follow. She'd learned enough, by now, to expect it.

"I caught up with him between the rounds of the fights. I told him I'd seen the way he looked at Garis. He was nervous to speak with a young noble. Still, he asked me, quivering with indignation, if I thought he wanted a friend to win so badly that he would throw fights. I said, 'You don't want Garis to win. You want him to gore you.'"

Cailyn was glad for the darkness. It would never do for a trained courtesan to let a client see her with her jaw hanging open.

"And what did he say to you?" Cailyn stammered when words returned.

"Yes. I don't think I knew anyone who was as eager for pain as Mariel was." She sighed.

Cailyn blinked. Had Teran ever sighed before? She tried to remember, but could think only of the claws and the whips, the way they stung.

And the haze of pleasure they left in their wake.

Cailyn wanted to smile, to let herself enjoy the story. But a gladiator and a noble? Most of the nobility would like that even less than retractable claws.

"Were you happy together, my lady?" she ventured.

Teran growled. Something sharp pricked Cailyn's back. "Were we? Of course. Was everyone else? Of course not. But you should have guessed that already."

"I did, my lady," Cailyn admitted.

"It is one thing to hire courtesans who specialize in it. It is another to be barely of age and running off after your father's best prizefighter. In the end it didn't matter, though, because I'd caught the eye of Lord Ben Keriel. As long as I agreed to bear him an heir, whatever else I did mattered little enough. So I did it."

"Ben Keriel? On the High Council?" If he'd had a child with Teran Nivrai, everyone would know about it.

Did helldemons lie?

"There is only one," Teran snapped.

"It doesn't sound like you liked him much, my lady."

Cailyn frowned. Nobles used one another for heirs all the time. Most didn't play dominance games with each other. The dark channels thrived because the nobles could do things with the courtesans on them that they could never do with peers.

Not if they wanted to live it down, anyway.

The pricking at her back stopped. Arms encircled her body. Where once she'd felt metal, now she felt warm flesh against her back. Her skin stung, but the warm softness comforted her. She heard herself sigh in the dark.

"No. I didn't like him much."

"The rumors…" Cailyn felt chilled. Had they started because the cold young noble of Nivrai hadn't welcomed her superior's attentions with enough warmth?

"Little one, people never liked me, even as a child."

"You were like this, even then?"

"I talked too little for their tastes. Or too much about things that unsettled them."

Cailyn managed a dry laugh.

"I was cruel anyway."

"And you felt…"

"I felt nothing. They weren't wrong." She laughed again, bitter, sharp. "Then they found out about me. Not about Mariel, but that I… did things. Probably with someone I shouldn't."

"Lord Keriel told them about you?"

"He said things. Some were true. Others were things he thought he knew. People were eager for stories. If I had claws, why not have the tail of a beast or demon? And if I had a tail, why not horns or spines or wings? Even those who weren't so gullible could believe enough to despise me. And Mariel was no fainting boy, eager to be ordered around, only wanting the whip as a sign of it. Between the things my mysterious lover wanted and my age, it was easy to paint me as unnatural."

"I'm sorry to hear it, my lady," Cailyn said.

Teran laughed. "Don't be. I encouraged it, as long as no one knew who Mariel was."

"You encouraged it?"

"It came as no surprise that a demon didn't dote on her son. I had no need to bother with a man I despised. And Mariel and I could do anything we wanted. We were already beyond the pale."

Cailyn said nothing. Was all that really wise?

Teran moved against her. "Do you know, he taught me fighting forms?"

Cailyn remembered the muscles in her back, tight and small. She probably still practiced them.

"I can believe it," she said.

Steel wound in her hair. Lips pressed against her neck, kissing the skin the claws had exposed.

Cailyn wanted to ask more. A big gladiator who almost always won. How did a man like that die so young? But Teran lay silent beside her. Cailyn couldn't break that silence. Not to ask why Teran grieved.

She waited to see if Teran would move, or speak again, or whisper lusty words into her ear. Nothing came. Cailyn closed her eyes and waited for sleep.

Chapter Seven

L ight flooded in from the wall-length window. Cailyn sat up, rubbed her eyes, and looked around. Teran, it seemed, had already gone.

She yawned and stretched. She shouldn't have overslept. She shook her head, thinking of how her teachers at the academy would gasp in horror if they heard she'd done it. But Lady Nivrai had gotten up before her once before. Left her alone then, too.

She walked over to the window and looked out at the garden, the flowers ringing the fountain a vibrant shock of color. Her hands itched to open the door, leave the endless white on gray.

On a whim, she raised her hand to the glass. It was probably a door with a fingerprint lock on it.

The footsteps were quiet, but she heard them. She turned, ready with an apology to Teran, but it was only a young man in Nivrai gray.

"Lady Nivrai is waiting for you in the bathing pool," he said. "If you're ready, I'll take you there now."

Cailyn ran a hand through her hair. This gave her no time to arrange herself properly. Still, if she'd woken up beside Teran she would have looked just the same.

The young man extended a hand. She took it and he led her away. She thought of the two servants she'd seen clear the table before, quiet as ghosts, and wondered if he was one of them.

He pressed his fingertips to the gray door in front of them. It slid open to reveal a bright room with a large pool of water in its center.

Over the pool hung a videoscreen. Cailyn couldn't see what played on it, but low music hummed out of it.

Teran stood in the pool. The water rose halfway up her thighs. She was naked save for a harness. A gray dildo jutted out from it.

Cailyn remembered the rumors. She could easily imagine Teran fitted with wings, water sluicing down them as she rose from the depths. Or picture those same wings enfolding her body like the cloak she'd worn when they'd first met.

She caught sight of the glint of the claws, then looked back at the harness and dildo. She could easily imagine them as more modifications, a strange metal apparatus that snaked out of Teran's skin.

"Hello, little one," Teran said.

"My lady." Cailyn inclined her head.

Cailyn walked to the pool, the tiles slick under her feet. As she walked down the stairs into the pool, Teran put out a hand to stop her. Her claws flashed twice, scoring lines just under Cailyn's breasts.

She moved to let Cailyn pass. Small streams of Cailyn's blood billowed out into the pool as she walked into the water. Teran's eyes narrowed, glittering.

She gestured. "Come here."

Cailyn walked to the edge of the pool. At a gesture from Teran, she bent over the ledge. Teran's arms wrapped around her hips and held on for a moment. Then the tip of the dildo pressed at her opening and plunged in.

Cailyn pushed herself back on the invader and closed her eyes. When she opened them again, she looked up at the screen in front of her. Light played on it, circles of soft color that pulsed in time with the music. The display lulled her into a slow rhythm, the colors changing with the sensation inside her.

Teran's claws dug into her hips, pricked the skin. Low sounds ran wordless into her ears as Teran moved faster.

"You're mine." Teran hissed as she drove deep. "At least for now."

"Yes," Cailyn gasped. Her mind filled with colored lights. Teran raised a hand, clawless now. She snaked her fingers into Cailyn's mouth. Cailyn opened her mouth wide, relieved at Teran's purr of contentment.

Cailyn whimpered. Claws kneaded her skin. Fingers moved in her mouth. She took a deep breath and drove herself back hard over the dildo. The colors on the videoscreen exploded as Teran held her there.

When the fingers left her mouth, Cailyn gulped in air. As her breath slowed, soft lips kissed her neck. They nibbled and then bit.

"Very nice."

Cailyn stood up. Her insides throbbed with aftershock.

"So you're the daughter of Loriel Derys." Teran reached out and wound a lock of Cailyn's hair around a clawed finger. "I didn't think he had curls."

"He doesn't. The curls are my mother's."

"Ah." A claw wandered over Cailyn's lips, pulling the skin taut, as Teran inspected them. "They suit you."

She handed Cailyn a bottle of soap. Cailyn lathered up her hair. What would steel feel like, massaging her scalp?

She dipped her head into the water and watched the soap bubbles float away as she pulled her head back up. Her blood tinted the water around her a faint pink.

Teran's hands circled her nipples and pulled. "Come here."

Half-dragged, Cailyn did, her breasts beginning to ache. Teran pulled her into a hard kiss.

One hand snaked up her back and wound itself in her hair as Teran's tongue explored Cailyn's mouth. With a soft noise as it cut through the water, the other reached out to cup Cailyn's buttocks.

The screen beeped softly. Teran's eyes flicked to the side. Her lip curled. She drew away to fiddle with the panel of controls at the edge of the bath.

"Go over there." She pointed to the other side of the pool. Not sure whether to feel embarrassed or to laugh, Cailyn obeyed.

Teran tapped a finger on the panel and turned around, her hands outstretched along the edge of the tub, claws retracted. The lights faded and disappeared, replaced by a man's face. He had dark brown skin and a close-cut black beard. The two circlets wrapping around his forehead marked him as not only noble, but a member of the High Council.

What would they want with someone like Teran? What kind of man would video her to ask for it?

"Lord Darien," she said. "Your timing is impeccable."

"Teran Nivrai." He chuckled. "You know, if I'm going to interrupt you in the bath, you could always widen the video angle. I can't see much at all."

"My lord, surely you have better reason to call me than that. Unless the council members are interested in seeing me naked."

He laughed again, a deep, resonant sound. Cailyn decided she liked it. "If anyone got near enough to touch you, you'd probably sprout quills and impale them."

"I hadn't heard that one. I think I like it."

Cailyn saw Teran's fingers flex. She didn't hear the telltale sound of the claws extending.

Which means he won't hear it either, Cailyn realized.

"What people claim happens to the poor sods you bed can get pretty interesting. But I'm sure you knew that already. And you're right. I'm here on council business."

"I am the Councils' humble servant."

Teran smirked. Cailyn bit her lip to keep from laughing. "What do they want from me?"

"You heard of the attempt on Councilman Alain's life?"

"Yes, that rebel group who bombed his little..." Cailyn heard a sneer in Teran's voice, "vacation planet."

"We captured one of them. We want to know what they're up to, where they'll strike next. Are they planning to do more, or are they just coordinating random acts of terrorism?"

"I see. But what does all that have to do with me?"

Darien laughed again, a rolling chuckle. How cold this room looked in comparison to his wide grin. Cailyn dipped herself lower in the water, hoping to better immerse herself in it. These walls. They nearly blinded her.

"I thought you might ask that. But they're not planning to tell you. Not until you get there."

"And if I refuse to attend?"

He shook his head. "You think you're alone out here, Nivrai, but you're not."

"Meaning?"

"Meaning you're only alone because you get left alone."

"Is that so?" Teran sneered.

"I don't like it any more than you, Nivrai. But you're coming. Or you're getting escorted there by the High Council's guard."

"What?" Teran's fingers twitched again. Cailyn saw a flash of steel as the claws extended and then retracted again.

Teran blinked. Her face smoothed itself into composure. "I don't suppose it would do much harm to humor the council members in this. Very well, my lord. Thank you for the warning."

"You're welcome." He grinned, the smile wrinkling his eyes. "Oh, and, Nivrai? Be careful."

The face faded out. The colored lights reappeared as the first tinkling notes of the music began again.

The water splashed as Teran walked toward her.

"Turn around," Teran said, her voice cold.

No sooner had Cailyn done so than hands bent her over the side of the pool. She felt the head of the dildo probe at her entrance, then drive in swift and hard.

She could hear Teran's breath behind her, shallow, quick, as the dildo forced her body open. A clawed hand pressed her head into the white tile.

Over and over, Teran drove into Cailyn, her muscles exploding into motion. Cailyn couldn't respond to it, couldn't match Teran's rhythm. She could only hold on. So she did, riding desire Teran forced out of her.

She didn't come until she felt the dildo inside her freeze. Only then did she let herself go. Waves of pleasure submerged her in water and light.

She heard a small click as the claws withdrew. Without the newsteel, the hand on Cailyn's head seemed smaller, though it still gripped tight.

Teran pulled the dildo free. Cailyn's flesh twitched as her body emptied.

She shook her head once and turned to face Teran. She hoped Teran would reach for her now. She hoped Teran would hold her like a lover, as she sometimes did.

But Teran, it seemed, wasn't in the mood. She walked out of the pool with brisker than usual steps and slipped the harness off before Cailyn could even catch up.

One of the ubiquitous servants appeared to take it away. Another offered a bathrobe, which Teran slipped into.

"Come with me," Teran said, finally looking back at Cailyn. A trace of harshness lingered in her voice.

Cailyn let one of the servants slip a bathrobe around her body. At least that felt warm and soft. She closed her eyes for a brief moment, letting herself savor the softness.

But her lady had given her an order. She opened her eyes again and followed.

CHAPTER EIGHT

Thankfully, Teran had let her freshen up. She would have done more, but Teran hadn't given her much time. She'd slipped pins in her hair, spread color on her lips, and practiced a pout to make them look more full. Usually she would paint her face as well, soft coral colors to go with her pale skin. It gave her a way to display what she had to offer. To arrange her curls into something artful. To present herself as worthy of the noble's desire.

But Teran hadn't just been impatient. Cailyn had turned away from her mirror to find Teran leaning against the doorframe. Teran had watched her twist her hair up, her hands nimble with years of memory, and slide the pins into it.

Few nobles saw that part. Most only wanted to see the result, the impossible beauty of a courtesan who'd spent years learning to make herself look like a treasure. The moments she spent in front of mirrors were hers, private in a way her body never would be.

And yet Teran had followed her, stood in the door, and stared like she'd meant to memorize Cailyn's secrets.

Cailyn had wrapped her hands around herself. It hadn't done much to help her hide, and she'd blushed with shame. Her purpose was to serve, and her intent was to give. She'd chided herself and lowered her arms.

But Teran's gaze still seared her. She'd turned back to the mirror to paint her lips and tried to forget Teran was there.

She'd chosen red again. No other color made sense. Not here.

Teran had looked her over and walked out. Cailyn had followed, and they'd sat down and eaten the breakfast brought to them.

Now she lay on the bed, facedown. Teran hovered over her back. "Pretty skin." Teran pressed her lips to Cailyn's back. "Unmarked, too, except for this."

Her lips nuzzled the small dots where her claws had pierced the skin before. "I think I'll keep it that way. For now."

"Whatever you will, my lady," Cailyn said.

She wasn't sure she meant it. But what else was there to say? A courtesan had few better tools than formality and the promise of compliance.

Teran kissed her back again. "Is that so?" Her hands moved to the welts on Cailyn's rear. Her fingers pressed them, reawakening the hurt there.

A claw ran down Cailyn's lower back and slipped between her buttocks. It stopped just shy of the hole. Cailyn's body arched in spite of itself.

The finger drew away, to be replaced with another, clawless, gloved, and lubricated.

"I said it before." She slid her finger in and watched Cailyn rise to meet it. "You're mine. Aren't you?"

What else could Cailyn say? "Yes, my lady."

Another finger joined the other.

"May I touch myself, my lady?" Cailyn asked.

Teran's voice was rich with amusement. "No." She added another finger.

Cailyn rocked to meet the fingers filling her. She probably wouldn't come this way, but that didn't matter. She gave herself over to the sensations, throwing back her head and crying out.

The fingers withdrew.

Cailyn felt empty and open. "What—?"

"That was merely to make a point," Teran said in the same amused voice.

Cailyn let her body fall back down onto the bed. Cloth against her skin wiped away the lubricant still on it. She fought not to frown.

"So what will you do?" She tried to ignore the way her body still yawned open. "Will you answer the Council's summons?"

She couldn't imagine Teran doing it. If a noble needed someone on their arm, the daughter of one of the most famous courtesans living fit the bill nicely. But Teran spent her days hidden in Nivrai and let the rumors show off for her.

She had heard, of course, of the bombing, a clumsy attempt on the life of a member of the Lower Council. By all accounts, the would-be rebels were disorganized and ill-supplied, united by little beyond their hatred of the government. If they planned something more, Cailyn was glad to hear that the council members knew enough about it to pay careful attention.

Still, why consult Teran on this, a minor noble who hid herself on a tiny planet in a corner of the galaxy? What could Teran know that they wanted?

Teran laughed, cold and sharp. "They're not exactly offering me a choice in the matter."

Cailyn tried not to chuckle. She'd have to say this cleverly, if she wanted to say it at all. "Are you planning on taking anyone?"

"Am I?"

"I don't suppose you ever took Mariel?"

"No, I never took Mariel. It would have been too much trouble to hide him." She frowned. "Besides, he had as little interest in politics as I did."

"That must get lonely."

"I don't suppose you're offering."

Cailyn laughed. "Maybe I am."

Things didn't get this interesting every day. And these rooms were big and empty. What must it be like for Teran to live here in them, alone after the death of someone she'd lived with for so many years?

Still, it would mean standing at Lady Nivrai's side in front of anyone and everyone, including members of both the Lower Council and the High.

All those eyes. She remembered Lord Darien's eyes, imagined them, multiplied by tens or even hundreds, staring. Everyone would wonder what Teran Nivrai did with a courtesan who had never even been on the dark channels.

And they would all want Cailyn. Because someone they feared wanted her too.

Metal trilled along her neck. "You would go with me?"

Cailyn shrugged. She felt relaxed now, which made playing dumb easier. "Well, why not?"

"I have half a mind to take you up on that just to know whether you mean it." Teran wrapped her arms around Cailyn and kissed her, claws pressed to the skin of her back. Cailyn opened her mouth. "I don't think you're frightened enough, little one."

Teran clicked the panel on the wall that opened the flagellary. Cailyn watched the wall slide over the window. Maybe she shouldn't have been so nonchalant.

"Now," Teran said, standing in front of an X-shaped cross and looking immensely pleased with herself, "come here."

The lump in Cailyn's throat returned. She stayed silent as she walked over to the cross and held up her arms. Thin metal rings hung from it. Teran fit them over Cailyn's wrists and ankles and pressed her fingerprints in to lock them.

Cailyn felt the metal slide, smooth and cool as it shaped itself to her skin. She sighed, trying to relax into the feeling of immobility.

Teran pulled the pins out of her hair. She turned them over in her hands.

"Pretty," Teran said. She sandwiched them around Cailyn's nipples and wrapped bands around the ends to tighten them and hold them there. Cailyn winced at the pain and blinked as her hair fell down around her face.

"Very nice. I like to see you this way." A claw tapped one of her compressed nipples. It skipped, feather-light, down her breast. "Open, available. Unable to turn away and hide yourself from my eyes." Cailyn shivered as Teran looked her over. She couldn't turn away from that gaze even if she wanted to.

"Or hands." Fingers ran idly along her vulva.

Teran stepped away and sat down. Cailyn gasped. Here she was, stretched out and ready to be used, and Teran decided to ignore her?

It stung even more than the pressure on her nipples ached. "My lady, what are you doing?"

Teran was in front of her in seconds, one claw pressed against her chin. She fell silent. If she moved her mouth again, it would pierce her.

"What was that?" A tight smile spread on Teran's lips. She knew Cailyn couldn't answer.

And apparently liked it that way. Cailyn gulped.

"Do you think I do these things for you?" Teran's eyes narrowed. "Do you think I give you pleasure out of kindness? If I do it, I do it for one reason only: because I want you to feel it."

Cailyn wished she could speak, apologize, say something. But she couldn't, not with a sharp point of newsteel digging into her chin. She looked down and hoped the gesture said enough.

"And if what I want is to bind you and use you as a pretty wall hanging, I'll do that. I promised you something intense before. Do you think I won't deliver it?"

Teran retracted her claw and walked away. Cailyn opened her eyes to watch her sit down and read a small tablet gripped in steel-tipped hands. Cailyn quailed. Then Teran turned her head.

Those eyes had been warm with approval before. Now they burned, too sharp under arched brows.

Cailyn closed her eyes. Why had she even told Teran about Lord Lerak's stare? She should have known how Lady Nivrai would use a story like that.

Helldemons. Cailyn's head drooped. She heard Teran walk over to her and didn't move. Teran's hands wrapped around her head. She let them lift her head up but did not open her eyes.

"Here," Teran said. She slipped something over Cailyn's head. She tapped the side of it, and black panels expanded to cover Cailyn's eyes. "Since me looking at you unnerves you so much."

She kissed Cailyn once on the lips. Steel ran light along the places where her lips had been and withdrew.

Deprived of sight, Cailyn's world narrowed to the dull ache in her nipples and the sting of the scratch in her side. She could hear Teran somewhere on the other side of the room.

Cailyn took a deep breath. She thought of Teran's hands, rising out of the darkness to touch her, somewhere, anywhere. She felt the dull ache in her nipples. Another ache rose between her legs as she imagined Teran returning out of the black to possess her.

Do you think I do these things for you? The remembered voice filled her mind. Had she thought that?

She heard the footsteps first, moving toward her, and the sound of Teran taking something down from the wall.

Fingers tapped at the hair sticks, unwinding the bands fastening them around Cailyn's nipples. A sudden throb of pain rocked her as the blood rushed back into them. She threw back her head and cried out. Teran chuckled.

Something cold and metallic rubbed against her vulva. She winced from the sudden shock of cold, but it was something. She strained to better reach it, but had hardly any room to move at all.

"You like that, don't you?"

The metal drew away. Cailyn felt something else. Smooth, draping, soft, running along her vulva. Leather? The tails of another flogger?

It pulled away and then hit her skin gently. Cailyn tensed as she braced herself.

Stars exploded in Cailyn's head as a sudden thud against her groin let her know that she was right. Her vulva lit up with pain. She would have crumpled if not for the bonds holding her up.

Again and again, the leather crashed into her skin, waves of an angry sea. Cailyn gritted her teeth against the pain. *I don't think you're frightened enough.* The words ran through Cailyn's head as she rode the waves of pain.

The pain vanished, sudden as it had begun. Cailyn sagged. Then the long, thin object moved against her skin again, not so cold now. It ran over her labia and nudged, blunt, at the opening between them. Then it pushed its way inside.

Heat rose in Cailyn's flesh as its motion filled her senses, erasing the ache. She moaned, a wordless plea.

"Yes, I think you do like that," Teran said, and drew it back out again.

Cailyn whimpered, bereft, and the flogger hit her again, right over her vulva, as before. Through the excitement she already felt, the pain set her nerves dancing. Her hands clenched as the impact burst against her flesh again and again.

The flogger withdrew. The metal returned, slid into her waiting and sore flesh. She accepted the reward eagerly. She only wished she had more room to move to meet it.

Whatever price Teran might exact for it, she apparently did like seeing Cailyn climax. Which would happen any minute, unless Teran—

—pulled it out again. Cailyn sighed as Teran swung the flogger again.

"I should make you come like this," Teran said as Cailyn grunted. Cailyn's eyes welled up with tears.

"But you—I can't—" Cailyn gasped. Surely she couldn't, not through pain like this.

Then the metal was back. Cailyn sobbed with relief as the pain became pleasure again. She willed her body to go, finish, now, before Teran changed her mind.

"You can't?" Teran said. She pulled the dildo out and then the hit came, hard. Confused, over stimulated, and stretched to the breaking point, Cailyn responded. Her flesh spasmed hard around nothing and she shuddered with climax.

Cailyn sagged, bewildered. Her heart pounded. Her face was wet. *Tears*, she realized, as the blindfold retracted above her eyes and light flooded them.

She felt a hand on her face. She looked down at Teran's other hand and saw what she'd been holding, a flogger with a metal phallus for a handle.

She laughed, thin laughs that dissolved into hiccups. The hand drew her face up, gentle, inexorable, and pulled her into a kiss. She closed her eyes, thankful for small mercies, and lost herself in it.

CHAPTER NINE

Now it was Cailyn's turn to do something for her lady. That thought suffused her with relief, a warm and comfortable feeling that mingled with the afterglow. She hovered above Teran's back, massaging Teran's shoulders.

She liked the body under her hands, the firm muscles hidden under Teran's skin. She skipped her fingers over them, pressed into them and drank in their strength.

"You did well," Teran said. "Especially for someone who avoids the dark channels." She lifted her head. "Or do you?"

Cailyn's hands froze. "What? No. I've never been on them."

She clapped a hand over her mouth. What was she doing revealing things like that?

And what was this about? Hadn't Teran called her in the first place because she'd wanted something different?

Teran tilted her head. Her lips twisted into a smile. "You've never been on them? Why not? Anyone looking on the dark channels would be delighted with you, little one."

Cailyn blushed. She pressed her fingers harder into Teran's shoulder.

Teran sat up on her elbows. "Last night you asked me for it, as I recall."

"Asked you? You made me."

"Did I? I say you like it more than you think."

The dark channels. What would happen if she offered herself on them? If she could take what Lady Nivrai offered, she could take anything.

Still, if she advertised there, people would assume she craved it.

She leaned down to kiss Teran's back. Her arms ached from pressing and kneading the skin in front of her. And she suspected Teran would enjoy being kissed this way, as if Cailyn were paying homage. She traced a path with her lips down Teran's back, tasted the grooves in Teran's skin.

When she reached Teran's buttocks. Teran tossed her a barrier. "Here. Lick, but use this. I might need your tongue later."

Cailyn spread the thin film over Teran's flesh and held it there. She sought the small hole with her tongue, circled it, entered, retreated, and circled again.

To do this was nothing new to an experienced courtesan. But to tend the most hidden part of someone else's body made Cailyn feel small all the same. She suspected Teran Nivrai knew just how small.

But it felt good to give herself over, to dedicate herself to Teran's pleasure, whatever cruel little joke might lay hidden in it. She had trained for years to serve, and to serve well. Whatever Teran might do, here she was on solid ground.

She reached her other hand around to see if Teran wanted to be touched. She burrowed her fingers under Teran's body, seeking out the sensitive places, and found them, slick with the reward. Teran came with a quiet cry.

After a moment, she turned onto her side. Cailyn lay down, glad to be under her again. Claws tickled her back. She welcomed the feel of them.

"Still blank," Teran mused. "I should change that. Give you something to remember me by."

Cailyn shivered. Blank? What did that mean? Her body tingled with anticipation.

"Frightened again?" Teran asked. A claw ran silver down Cailyn's back. "You're shaking."

"What will you do to me?" Everything centered on that touch, on what it might turn into. "My lady."

Then came the faint click as the claws retracted. "Nothing, for now. For now I have something to show you. Come with me."

Thin fingers pulled her away from the bed. She followed, sad to leave its softness. Still, whatever Teran had in mind now was probably less frightening, or painful, than the memento she'd mentioned. Cool air wafted from the vents on the walls and swirled along the skin of her back.

They stepped into a wide, open room. Mats lined the floor. Soft bags stood on the sides of the room. Mariel's practice room, she supposed.

Against one wall was a small bench, with a large mirror overtop of it. On it sat two smooth stones, set a handsbreadth apart.

Teran walked over to them, took a deep breath, and laid her hands on the globes. They flashed blue for a moment. Teran's face in the mirror winced.

The glow from the stones faded. Teran's thin fingers clutched tight around them. She drew in another long breath, then let it out.

Cailyn walked up beside Teran. Teran's eyes moved to look at Cailyn's reflection in the mirror.

"What is it, my lady?"

"It's an altar. Or at least, it's what one used to be. Very few worship the god it's dedicated to any more." She stepped aside. "The stones helped clear the mind."

Cailyn walked up to the globes and put out her hands. They hovered, reluctant.

Teran pushed her hands down. A shock crackled through her body as her flesh touched the globes. She jumped and tore her hands from them.

The pain, sharp as it had been, vanished in a moment. Strong arms twined around her. She sagged into them. Her head tilted to one side.

Metal tickled her neck and brushed away her hair. Teran's teeth traced the skin of her neck. She tilted her head, offering more to Teran's lips and teeth.

A hand snaked down her stomach. She hadn't liked the pain. She did like Teran's arms around her.

Teran's mouth sucked at her neck, pulling hard at the tender flesh there. She made a sound of her own.

"Don't tempt me." Teran laughed. "This isn't what I was planning."

She kissed Cailyn's neck where she'd bitten it. The mouth was still eager, whatever she'd said. Cailyn wondered if Teran had left a mark. Was she trying to kiss away the pain, or just kissing the sign of it?

Teran moved away. Cailyn missed the feeling of the arms around her. She reached to hold herself.

Teran stood still and stared straight ahead. They did not blink. She breathed in once.

Hands and feet cleaved the air, their movements crisp and sharp. Her small, strong body twirled to face imaginary attackers, blocked invisible blows, spun through counterattacks.

Cailyn had wondered what they looked like, had imagined Teran's small form doing just this, the precision and strength igniting her lust.

And, yes, her flesh tingled at the sight. She ran her hands along the skin of her own arms for the sensation. Her skin tingled where her fingertips had passed.

But this was something between Teran and Mariel, a piece of their history. This was like watching someone else's private video, the laughter and smiles ripped from the context that gave them their meaning.

Teran whirled around. Her fists sliced through air. She stared ahead, unforgiving and unchanging like the metal tucked inside her fingertips.

She moved quickly, all her slow, easy movements forgotten, her small body all force. Cailyn saw little hint of the coaxing touch she'd come to know. How hard would those strikes hit if she were on the receiving end of them? She decided she didn't want to know.

Still, this was beautiful. Beautiful and cold. Cailyn shivered, thinking of the newsteel tipping Teran's hands. The claws were beautiful too, the cruel beauty of any well-kept weapon.

Cailyn watched Teran's hands spin to block imaginary blows. Had she always done this exercise alone, a series of strikes and counterstrikes made into a private dance?

Or was this one half of a routine done with another person?

She looked around the room, doubtless a training room of Mariel's. She pictured a tall, muscular man, lunging at Teran and parrying her blows.

She found it easy to imagine, arms and legs slamming hard against one another as their hearts raced.

The final move came with a yell. If this had once been done in tandem, it apparently ended with Teran winning.

It ended with the claws, finally extended, striking the face or body of an opponent thrown to the ground.

Cailyn closed her lips on a laugh. Yes, this was more than likely half of a duet.

And she felt surer than ever how it ended.

Teran walked over to her, the spell broken.

Cailyn felt a fierce desire to touch Teran, to wrap her arms around her, to soothe her and calm her. To bring the woman out of the weapon and know she'd been the one to do it. Only well-instilled discipline kept her on her knees.

"That was beautiful, my lady."

"Thank you." Teran held out her hand. Cailyn took it and stood.

"But why did you show that to me?"

"I hadn't done them yet today."

A clawed hand caressed Cailyn's cheek. "But that's not what you were really asking, is it?"

"No, my lady."

"Then I'm not going to answer the question you were really asking. You should already know that, little one."

Cailyn sighed. "You did this with Mariel?" she asked, feeling steel move along her chin as she spoke.

"Yes."

"He must have been good at what he did."

"He was. Then again, I was a decent student."

Cailyn would have shaken her head again if there weren't newsteel crawling all over it. "I don't doubt you were." She reached up to touch Teran's face. "You must miss him."

Teran sighed and turned away.

"I watched him waste away," she said, her voice soft. She put a hand on Cailyn's shoulder. "Come on."

❖

• 71 •

Teran bid her lie facedown on the bed and told her to make herself comfortable. She did, remembering Teran's back under her hands. Now it was Teran's turn to run her hands along Cailyn's back.

Strangely enough, the claws stayed in. Teran's touch felt like any other lover's.

That made Cailyn wary, as good as the gentle touches felt.

"Very nice," Teran said, tracing the blades of Cailyn's shoulders.

Cailyn flushed with pride to hear Teran praise her body. But what was Teran studying so intently?

"You've never had an issue with marks before."

Cailyn squirmed. "No, my lady, I never have. Are you planning to leave worse ones?"

She'd looked in her mirror at the marks Teran had left her with before. She'd touched them, studying their contours with her fingertips. The slight pain when she did it had reminded her of Teran, the ice-gray eyes, the silver laugh.

The rhythm of the gentle flogging, the sharp sensation of the braided whip biting into her skin. Teran's smell and taste.

That last flogging had left some new marks, too. She could still feel the welts on her skin, a constant vague sting.

Teran was laughing now. She wound a claw in Cailyn's hair. "Not worse. Different, but not worse."

Cailyn stiffened, not entirely sure she liked that answer. Her eyes strayed to the door. She felt a sudden urge to leave.

Still, she couldn't help but wonder just what Teran was up to. She'd hate herself if she didn't find out.

She let out a slow breath and forced herself to relax. Well, my lady, she thought, hearing the metallic sound of Teran's claws as they extended, let's see just what it is you're up to now.

Her skin sighed open at the first cut, blood and a burning feeling rising together as it did.

The claw traced swirls into her skin. Her hands tightened into fists. Then Teran cut into her skin again, the cut curved like the first. Shorter cuts came after these, sharp, staccato bursts of pain.

It must be a pattern, Cailyn realized. But what sort of design would a helldemon choose to etch into her flesh? She stared ahead in a haze of pain. Her hips shifted.

"Mine," Teran murmured, her voice and breath like water running over Cailyn's skin. The claw seared a new line through her skin.

"Yes, my lady," Cailyn gasped. She fought to hold still. Her shoulder stung, but the heat rose in her body.

An arm pushed her body down, strong, insistent.

"But not for long. So I suppose"—the claw curled into her skin with ruthless efficiency again—"I'll just have to leave you with a reminder."

Wet blood flowed over Cailyn's back. She remembered what Teran had said. *Blood is a part of you.* She pressed her thighs together to keep from shivering.

Teran must not have been doing worse damage than she had before, but this slow tracing hurt far worse. Maybe it came from lying facedown, waiting for something, not knowing what. Maybe it came from knowing that this time the marks were the point.

And even her skin opened to the touch. There was no resisting. It didn't matter how deep Teran cut. Her skin itself was parting at the touch. The skin leaked blood, her very self spreading open. The sting of being cut, the fear that came from bleeding, meant nothing compared to that.

The curling movements reminded Cailyn of the turns in Teran's form. Whatever Teran's claws carved would be elegant. It would beautify her, as much as her lipstick or the hairpins she'd been so glad to wear. She winced as another line seared her, but soon drifted into passivity. Her body hurt, but the skin between her legs prickled with heat.

"Just a few more," Teran said, her voice rich with desire. The claw moved so quickly now that Cailyn felt her skin tear only after Teran finished her lines. Three passes and it was done. Her skin burned in the sudden calm.

Teran's lips pressed against the untouched skin in the middle of her back. "It's finished."

Cailyn drifted. She wanted to rest. She clutched the pillow her head sat on and made a small, irritated sound.

"All that and you don't want to know what it is?"

Teran traced the lines she had drawn with a cloth. The cleanser on it stung so much Cailyn rose off the bed, grimacing.

Her head swam, Teran's eyes silver pinpricks in her vision. As her vision cleared, the calmness in that face infuriated her. Her whole body felt as if it had been through fire, and Teran did nothing but look at her?

She sat up, a move she immediately regretted as her vision doubled again.

"I wouldn't move on your own just yet, little one." Teran laughed, wrapping an arm around her lower back. "But here, if you want to get up."

She guided Cailyn to her feet and led her to a small bathroom.

Cailyn, still wobbling from being cut, twisted around to see the mark on her back in the mirror.

"It's the Nivrai symbol," she whispered.

Or something similar, anyway. To cut all of the twists and turns in a noble's official insignia—her wounds throbbed anew just imagining it. Others who weren't thinking of Nivrai or of Teran might not recognize the simplified design at all. Cailyn might not have recognized it herself if it weren't on all the servants' livery and more than a few of the doors.

Mine, Teran had said. Now she would send Cailyn back into the world with her mark carved into her back. At least until it healed. Cailyn shivered. Wetness seeped between her thighs.

It made no sense to feel this way. She had never wanted to belong to anyone. Not for longer than one meeting.

She thought of Teran's lips on the line she'd carved into her thighs. For a crazy moment, she hoped Teran would kiss or lick this mark as well, liven it with lips and tongue.

If Teran had similar thoughts, she gave no sign. Instead she turned her attention to the cut. To Cailyn's chagrin, she skipped soothing ointment she so often used, instead coating the lines she'd carved with a liquid bandage.

"For when you lie down," she said and led Cailyn to the bed.

The sheets chafed against the cuts on Cailyn's back. She shifted, trying to get comfortable. Teran waited. She settled as best she could.

Teran's fingers entered her, moved inside her, gentle, inexorable. Her will slipped away with the rhythm, and she was grateful for it. Warmth spread through her as her hips moved in time with the fingers filling her. She'd trained for this, to give herself over. She smiled and moved faster.

The sting flared through her skin as her body rose and fell. Clearly, it pleased Teran to see her moan and wince.

Someone else might dive in hard, wrest pleasure and desire from her all at once. But this slow rhythm meant far more. There was no resisting it. It pulled her under, inexorable as tides.

Lightning danced along Cailyn's back. She moaned, half in pleasure, half in the hope Teran would speed up.

Teran's breath came quick, sharp, her eyes narrowed in concentration. She flicked her thumb against Cailyn's clitoris, once, twice, then again.

Cailyn cried out again in despair and relief. To come like this, so quickly, from one touch alone! She hid her face in the pillow.

Yes, she thought as the tension left her body. Yours.

❖

Faces circled their way around Cailyn's videoscreen. They spun to the fore and then faded out as they scrolled by. She tapped her fingers on the table and shifted in her chair.

Her back, still bearing Teran's mark, itched. A flare of sensation flickered through it as it rubbed against her chair.

In the end, she'd begged Teran to let her service her. Teran had wanted her to leave, but she would have none of it.

Her mouth had ached to taste Teran's flesh. "It's what I'm here for," she'd said, dizzy with pain and desire. "Please."

Teran had let her, hovering over her at the head of the bed. She'd drunk in the shining wetness like life-giving water, all thought of skill or technique gone.

Cailyn's lips tingled, remembering Teran's body above her. Then she shivered, running her fingers along her own goose-bumped skin. Marking her had fueled that passion.

And not just marking her. Cailyn wrapped her arms around herself, fingertips touching the cut on her shoulder. Pain flared through it, and she felt an answering pulse between her legs. Teran's design wasn't just any welt from a whip, just any bruise left by a paddle or fist. It was Teran's symbol, carved there by her own hands.

Why should the memory warm her, Cailyn wondered, when she'd bought it with such pain?

But it wasn't the pain she remembered. She remembered blood, her body a river, flowing out and out. It made her think of watching Lord Lerak kiss her father. That had made her knees weak. This had gone through her whole body.

If she could do that, she could surely do this.

She scrolled through the computer's display. So Lady Nivrai wondered why she'd never been on the dark channels. Surely there was no harm in looking at them. Not now that she had bled for Teran, anyway.

She remembered her father's soft, even voice. He'd rested a hand on her head. "Listen to me, Cailyn. A courtesan's life isn't always as fun as you think. And the dark channels are the worst of it. There's a line between service and abasement. If you must follow my footsteps in this, promise me you won't go there."

She'd never promised, of course. She'd never promised him she wouldn't follow in his footsteps, either.

She smiled. As much as he'd argued with her mother over petty things, he'd always been grateful to her for taking him away from that life.

His skill and poise had won too many admirers for his comfort. He'd settled down with his wife in a quiet house with the biggest library his fame could buy him. He still had a few old clients he saw, now and then, like Lord Lerak, but that only happened a few times.

It happened less and less after some unpleasant incidents when Cailyn was young. One noblewoman had decided she had a right to him, Guild law notwithstanding. Videocalls came to their little house in a constant stream. She'd found ways to run into him in public no matter how well the family hid. It was no wonder he'd left that life behind.

Cailyn, for her part, had always felt a sense of loss. She would look at her father, at the long straight hair she hadn't inherited, the bluer-than-blue eyes and full lips she had, and wondered so much.

Her father had tried his best to keep her in the dark, but even he couldn't overcome a young girl's curiosity. She'd caught glimpses of the nobles' faces as they flickered on her father's videoscreen. Retirement didn't mean he never spoke to any of them.

Cailyn had made a game of noticing when he did.

Their cold beauty fascinated her. What would it be like to catch and hold their attention? To be touched by them like something precious, a sculpture in glass? She knew her father was no fool, but she couldn't understand why anyone would give that up once she had it.

She shook her head. She'd understood what she wanted from the beginning. She'd been right about the life she hoped for. But she'd never expected the tedium, the pointless demands, the carelessness of those more interested in use than pleasure.

And although no one who had hired Cailyn had ever defied Guild law, she knew that it didn't always protect everyone. Invoking it after something serious went wrong would be too little too late.

She thought of her father's warnings as the faces swirled though the display on the videoscreen.

The faces looked kind enough. She chuckled, the only sound in the room besides the faint music of the computer. What had she expected? Leering, snarling cruelty? She should know better.

A wide grin caught her eye. She recognized the bearded face: Lord Darien, from the videocall Teran had gotten. She'd liked him. It might be nice to be with someone full of jokes and laughter.

Not to mention the way he talked to Teran. He'd joked to her face about her nakedness, unfazed by her demeanor or her defiance.

Anyone like that was worth seeing, dark channels or no dark channels. She bit her lip and tapped the screen.

CHAPTER TEN

Vaulted ceilings rose high above Cailyn's head. She walked through ornate halls, filigree on the walls accented in gold. After halls as plain as Teran's, the bright gold and twisting patterns looked inviting. She touched the ornate doors, one after the other. They hissed open to admit her.

Lord Darien waited for her in a room at the end of the hall. Its carpet and drapery were a deep red. He sat in a large chair of the same color, one foot crossed over the other. He wore a white ruffled shirt as fancy as the room, and tight black leather breeches that looked like something out of a history book.

How would it feel to unbutton the white ruffles and slide her hand beneath, her fingers moving over his skin?

"So you're Loriel Derys's daughter."

"I am."

"He was the best of the best. I always thought it was a shame that I never saw you on the dark channels."

Cailyn blushed and cast her eyes downward. "You flatter me, my lord."

He stroked his chin. "And now you're on them, apparently. I don't think I've seen you there before."

"I never have been, my lord."

"Then you're new to this."

Cailyn allowed herself a laugh. "Not entirely."

His eyes traced her face, her body. A thrill ran through her as he looked her over and nodded. "But now you're curious."

Cailyn raised her head and met his eyes. "Yes. I am."

He stood up. "Come with me." He took her hand

Velvety drapes and carpet adorned his private rooms. She'd thought the nobles who frequented the dark channels would choose more somber furnishings, not bright gold and white lace.

Maybe she'd grown too used to Nivrai.

She recognized equipment she'd seen in Lady Nivrai's flagellary: crosses, benches, things she couldn't name. Teran hadn't bothered with six rooms. Cailyn wondered how many more rooms Lord Darien might have.

Teran had simple equipment: well made, sleek, comfortable enough for their purpose. These, velvety and padded, would feel pleasant to sink into anyway. She walked over to a bench and reached out to touch the patterned fabric.

He watched her hands move. "You like what you see, don't you?"

She thought of Teran's braided flogger, the thin lines it had seared into her skin. "I expected something more..." she paused, searching for the right words, "...harsh, my lord."

"I'm not the harsh kind."

"That's a relief. My lord."

He walked over and wrapped a hand in her hair, pulling her head upward to face him. Her knees went weak.

He kissed her, hard. His tongue went deep into her mouth, probing. It warmed her palate and she moaned.

She thought of Teran, of a different mouth coaxing her open. Her hips rocked. She felt faithless, already forgetting whom she served. What was she doing thinking of Teran when someone else demanded her attentions?

His hands moved over her thin dress. At first she thought he intended to undress her, but his hands only wandered over her clothes, leaving trails of need behind them.

His fingers brushed her nipples through the thin fabric. Cailyn's body arched toward him in response. He laughed, a rich sound. That, too, warmed her.

His fingers clasped around her nipples, pulled just hard enough to make her gasp. Without warning, he twisted them. Pain flared in her skin. Jolts raced through her.

Cailyn closed her eyes. Teran would pull harder, want to see her wince. But Darien's fingers only whispered along her flesh again, soothing the ache they'd made.

She could learn to like this.

His fingers moved to the fasteners of her dress and slowly drew them down. His hands around her coaxed her out of it. She walked into his arms. The dress fell behind her as she stepped out of it.

He led her to a cross. Leather, rather than metal, encircled her ankles and wrists.

"Have you ever been flogged?" he asked. She felt the tails of a soft flogger trace along her back.

He snapped his fingers once. The lights dimmed. Soft music played.

Cailyn grinned. Sometimes the nobles' lavish tastes could be a good thing.

"Yes." Cailyn gasped out the answer. She thought of the gentle flogging Teran had given her. *That other was for me. This is for you*, she'd said.

And this one, too. The rhythm soothed her. She swayed, presenting her flesh to the blows. With Teran she had to watch herself, but here she could abandon herself without fear.

His next strokes hit her buttocks. The heat between her legs pulsed, spreading outward.

Teran had forced pleasure out of her, coaxing until her body had no choice. This built slowly in her flesh. Cailyn wriggled, hoping he would read her signal and swing faster.

"Please," she heard herself say.

He did. She opened her mouth wide to cry her pleasure, her heart racing, her hair damp with sweat.

He ran a hand along her back as she went still. "You did like that," he said, voice muffled as his lips moved along her skin.

His hands reached around her body to cup her breasts, then tugged at her nipples. Her body arched toward him. Her flesh tingled again with this new touch.

"Yes, my lord," she breathed.

He kissed the restraints as he undid them. He held her hand in his as he led her to the bed.

It was the kind of gesture a lover might make and made Cailyn miss a lover's touch. No one but Teran had touched her like that without someone else in mind.

And even Teran had Mariel to remember.

Teran's claws had left trails of yearning where they passed. But maybe Teran's penchant for seduction wasn't so unique after all.

He undressed, revealing a broad, muscular body. Probably from doing so much of this, Cailyn thought, looking at the flogger in his hand. Teran had muscles too, but limited herself to doing this four times a year, if the stories were true. Were they all like this?

She imagined a room full of them, herself in the center, bound to a bench or table. The bodies all around her, moving through the shadows of the room, each wanting to be the first to reach her.

She was still dreaming of what they would do when he entered her. She moved with him, eager to take him in.

She watched him move above her. His eyes were bright with pleasure. His pace was steady, sure of the lightning each movement sent through her insides. He could use her like this for hours if he chose. She shuddered.

That made her think of Teran again, of the way her fingers had twisted inside her. She moaned again. Darien cried out his own answer, driving into her faster.

She felt like a traitor as the waves of pleasure rolled through her body. A moment ago, she'd been his. Now ice-gray eyes swam in her vision and shone with every thrust. She bit her lip to keep from crying out Teran's name.

He froze inside her, caught and held by her spasming flesh, and then released. She took what he gave eagerly, evidence of his possession. She sighed as it washed her insides.

He pulled out of her gently. He smiled, and his eyes drooped with the lazy haze of his pleasure.

"Thank you, my lord," Cailyn said as her heart slowed and the room came back into focus.

"The pleasure was mine, Cailyn Derys."

He draped the flogger over his shoulder and stood up to put it away. Cailyn stopped him. She wanted him to stay with her, to talk longer. She liked the velvet of his voice.

He let her draw him close. She reached out a hand to toy with the tails of the flogger draped across his back. The light, rich leather felt good to her fingers.

"Curious?" he asked. "You could have fooled me. And half the dark channels."

She laughed, half amused, half worried. Could she really hide her experience?

She wouldn't have to for long. She'd already told Teran she wanted to go with her to that council meeting. Everyone would see her on Lady Nivrai's arm.

There was no hiding that.

Her stomach fluttered. If she wasn't ready for Lord Darien to know that she'd seen Teran, how could she be ready for the council members to see them together? Not to mention the lesser nobles who clung to their coattails, hung breathless on their decisions, craved their favor.

"You flatter me, my lord," she said. She batted her eyelashes and hoped she sounded convincing.

He brought his face to hers. For a moment, she thought he would kiss her. She hoped he would.

Instead, he knotted his hand in her hair. He pulled her head back. "You're not thinking of me, are you?"

She swallowed hard and moved her hands to his nipples, wanting to recapture the feeling of him.

"You were wonderful, my lord," she said.

She hoped it didn't sound glib. It was true. Her body spasmed, remembering him inside her. He had been wonderful, however far away from him her mind had wandered at the end.

"It's all right." He kissed her. "This is a job for you, after all. It's easy for us to forget that. We can have you whenever we want you."

Cailyn sighed and let her fingertips brush the brown buds of his nipples again.

"So who is it?" he asked. "A lover of yours? It must be more fun with them than with us."

Cailyn shook her head. She liked Lord Darien. "No, my lord."

He shook his head. "Whoever you were thinking of, you must like them." He kissed her cheek.

Did she? She'd had clients she liked before. People she looked forward to seeing. People she missed. People she remembered serving, warm desire spreading through her body at the memories.

She wanted Teran; she knew that. She liked the way Teran touched her, like something precious. And, she admitted to herself, she liked wondering what someone like Lady Nivrai would do, the deadly newsteel tipping her fingers.

Lovely as this was, it wasn't the same.

❖

Two servants in Nivrai gray took Cailyn's bags. They said little to her, so she said little to them. Curious eyes watched her pass. Whispering followed her. She could hear the voices asking where she went, wondering aloud if they could trust their eyes.

She watched them carry one bag off. Hidden in it like an iridescent treasure laid a colorful scarf she had bought at a market before coming here. It changed colors under different light. Charmed from the moment she held it in her hands, Cailyn had snatched it up.

Lady Nivrai would hate it.

But now and then, every courtesan had to do something like that. Everyone needed moments away, little things that brought them back to themselves after so long serving others' wills. Somewhere, hidden in her things, was that scarf, shimmering and shifting.

The halls stretched endlessly, a white shining maze, tubes of warm light glowing along the walls. Some bore pictures of council members present or past, circlets glistening.

She stepped into an elevator behind the servants, staring at the plain pale walls, hoping to read something of her fate.

As they led her down the hall, she counted doors, her throat dry. What would Teran do with her?

"Your quarters," one of her companions said. A door slid open.

A small bed filled the middle of the room. A dresser and mirror took up one wall. The other had two doors. One must have led to the bath. The other, Cailyn guessed, would grant quick access to and from Teran's presence.

The servants behind her set down her bags. "You'll find clothes in the closet. You are to dress in them."

With that, they left. The door hissed shut behind them.

Cailyn slid out of her clothes. She ran her fingers along her breasts, stirring her nipples to erection. Teran would like it, she figured. She liked it as well and smiled at the thought of Teran's approving smirk.

She tapped a button on the closet door. It slid open. Inside was a bodysuit, black and shiny. It would cover quite a bit of her skin.

She shivered, remembering the marks that Lady Nivrai had left on her. Perhaps she meant the shining black fabric to hide them.

She could—or Teran could—buy regenerations. The expensive treatments reconstructed damaged flesh, leaving it pristine and scarless. But black fabric solved the problem and wouldn't hide the healing marks. Cailyn shook her head and chuckled.

Still, it raised a question. Did the courtesans who served the dark channels buy them often? Would it gall nobles who frequented them to see someone else's marks on the courtesans they hired?

Or would it fan their desire, seeing bruises, welts, or cuts on the flesh of someone they wanted to hurt? Sometimes jealousy came with its own sharp pleasure.

Cailyn wrapped her arms around her chest, fingertips reaching her back. What did Lady Nivrai have in mind for it now?

She didn't like the black. A stark color like that suited Teran better than Cailyn. Deep, rich colors did accentuate Cailyn's pale skin and hair, but she was no fan of black. Black had no complexity, no richness to draw in the eye.

She shrugged and pulled it on anyway. *It's what my lady wants.*

She turned to the dresser, not bothering to look at herself in the mirror. On it was a simple wand of lipstick, in dark red.

Cailyn sighed again. Red was fine, but that dark? Something else she would never have chosen.

She watched herself trace the deeper red along her lips. Her job dictated making herself over, becoming what others would want of her. Still, the reflection in front of her looked wrong. She closed her eyes and mouthed a prayer to the courtesans' goddess, trying to regain her composure. She'd stayed here too long already.

She stepped toward the door holding her head high. So her stomach was in knots. She'd been trained not to reveal that, trained by the best. Whispering a few more words to her patron goddess, she let the door hiss open and walked through it.

❖

Cailyn's eyes swept over the room. Teran sat in a small chair in the center of it. Sparse, unadorned walls left her with little choice but to look at Teran. For her part, Teran nodded and looked her over.

Teran sat cross-legged in a small chair. She turned something around in her hands. Cailyn could see pale blue metal, shaped into a ring. She laid it down on a small stand near her chair. Cailyn squinted, trying to look without making her staring too obvious.

Teran set the object down. She walked over to Cailyn, close enough to touch her face. Even the warmth that spread through Cailyn couldn't calm her nerves. What exactly had she gotten herself into?

Teran's fingers reached out and touched Cailyn's ear. She fought the impulse to jump. Of all the places Teran could touch her, why that one?

Slender fingers reached out and plucked the gold earrings from Cailyn's ears.

"If you want earrings, let me know and I will provide them," Teran whispered into her ear, voice clear and crystalline.

The gold dangles glinted in Teran's palm. To not have earrings made Cailyn more naked than she had felt in years. She had no trouble slipping out of clothes, but to be denied even earrings? Teran had removed them for her, pulled them out and taken them away like a parent chiding a child for dressing up.

Teran's other hand traced her chin, inspected her, snaked up to wind in her hair. It drew her head back. Teran lowered her head to Cailyn's throat.

"That's better," she murmured against Cailyn's skin. Her other hand snaked under Cailyn's bodice to pinch her nipples.

What did she do with my earrings? Cailyn wondered, until a sharp twist made her hiss.

She sank backward, falling into Teran's embrace. Her nipple throbbed as the pinch faded. Her skin burned, her hips moved. She wished Teran would touch her, ease the burning between her legs, end her humiliation.

"Kneel there," Teran said as she let go.

Cailyn obeyed. Teran walked away. Cailyn bit her lip, determined not to show her anger.

"There's one last thing you need, little one."

Teran took the metal ring off of its cushion. As she walked back over, Cailyn could see that it was made of the same light, thin metal as the restraints Teran had used on her. A collar?

"My lady? I'm not contracted to you exclusively," Cailyn snapped. She glared at the offending ring of metal. It glinted in the harsh light.

Teran laughed. She pressed her fingers to the back of the collar and it opened. "I didn't think you'd planned on looking on the dark channels, little one."

The dark channels? How did Teran know about that?

"My lady?"

"Who else would think of this as anything but a pretty toy?"

Who else? Cailyn's mind raced. She didn't know. She couldn't know.

"You're baiting them," Cailyn realized. "You're making me wear this so they'll be jealous."

"Of course." Cailyn heard the slight click of the claws as they extended. "They expect it."

"I thought you might want to show off, but I never thought you would do that."

"They're going to notice anyway." Metal reached out to stroke Cailyn's chin, sharp, sure. "I might as well give them something to talk about."

Cailyn fidgeted, her hands safely hidden behind her back. Remember your training, she thought.

She raised her head, shook out her hair, and held it up while Teran slid the metal around her neck. It was cold, and Cailyn couldn't hide her wince.

The metal warmed as Teran's fingerprints sealed the lock. It was a part of her now, whatever she'd agreed to. The warm burn against her skin claimed her, like a brand.

"Now go," Teran said, pulling her hand away.

"Go?" Cailyn asked, puzzled.

"Surely you have things to do. People to meet."

"My lady?"

"Surely you didn't expect to spend your every moment here. Besides, I think the others have something to see."

Cailyn glowered. So Teran really did mean to show her off. Still, she had accepted this. She could hardly expect to spend every moment with Teran, tucked under her wing.

"Yes, my lady," she said.

CHAPTER ELEVEN

"Cailyn Derys!"

Cailyn fought not to twitch. She'd walked the halls all morning. No one had so much as spoken to her. Most had stared, their eyes locked on Cailyn's collar, and whispered to one another. All she'd caught from most of them was Teran's name.

And now someone wanted to talk. A shiver of anticipation ran through her. Teran might like people avoiding her. Cailyn hated it.

But Cailyn wore Teran's collar now. Just because someone wanted to talk didn't mean she'd like what they had to say.

Steeling herself, she turned and found herself looking into a familiar face.

"My lady Liana." Cailyn laughed with relief.

"It's always good to see you." Lady Liana's painted lips opened in a wide smile. Cailyn looked her over, pleased to see it.

Dark wavy hair framed Liana's dusky, dimpled face. A diadem, showing her rank on one of the Councils, circled her head. A gem, this one an implant, glistened in the center of her forehead. Jewels winked at her ears. She wore her house's traditional purple, a glittering weave of color that caught the harsh light of the hall and brightened it.

After so long in the gloom of Teran's chambers, Cailyn reveled in it.

"It's been too long, my lady."

"I agree completely." She smirked and looked Cailyn over. "Maybe we ought to do something about that."

Her grin twisted into a frown as she caught sight of the collar at Cailyn's throat. "Unless you're busy for now, with—the woman you're serving."

"My lady Nivrai," Cailyn said, her voice crisp and clear despite the uneasiness she felt.

"Yes. Nivrai. This is all such an unfortunate business. I never thought you'd get caught up in it."

"Caught up in what, my lady? Lady Nivrai hired me to keep her company for this conference. That's all."

Cailyn saw Liana's hand twitch at her side. "Of course, Derys. That's none of my business, really. And I'm sure you're getting something for it."

Her smile returned. "Or at least I hope you are, given what she probably has you doing."

Cailyn bowed her head. "My lady. Like you said, that's none of your business."

"Oh, I agree." She reached out a hand. With a gentle gesture, she tilted Cailyn's head up to look at her again. Warm memories spread through Cailyn's mind at the touch. She let the movement guide her.

"But I meant this whole meeting. This whole thing with Nivrai. It's not something the Councils are meant to demand of someone." She shook her head.

Cailyn opened her mouth to speak, but Liana spoke first. "And seeing you with Teran Nivrai makes it our business. Or at least, some people will see it that way."

Cailyn sighed. "You're probably right."

The fingertips lingered on her chin. "Then you really should make sure to get some pleasure of your own out of all this." She laughed again. "Unless I'm being presumptuous thinking seeing me again would bring you pleasure."

Cailyn felt her cheeks flush. "No, my lady. You're not."

"Then we should talk later, Derys. I'm glad to see you here. I ought to take advantage of the opportunity. Unless you're working only for Teran right now."

"My first duty is to my lady Nivrai right now, yes," Cailyn answered. "But it's not an exclusive contract."

"Thank the gods for small mercies, then. I'll videocall you later, once we're done with some of this damned council business."

Cailyn grinned again. "I'd like that."

"I'm just glad to hear that you can. Nivrai is—" She shuddered.

Cailyn kept her face composed. Was this what she had to look forward to? She'd expected looks and glares, and already gotten a few. She hadn't expected her favorite clients fretting over her on top of it all.

"Even if it were exclusive, my lady, there's no need to worry about me. This is an agreement like any other."

"Like any other," Liana repeated, clearly unconvinced.

"Please, my lady. Don't worry about me. It's a contract, not a prison sentence."

❖

The bedroom was large but unadorned. A cross lay against the wall. Cailyn squinted at it. Had Teran brought hers all the way here from Nivrai, or did the facilities provide for patrons of the dark channels?

Teran slid out of her clothes. Cailyn watched, eyes lingering on Teran's body. Teran turned and took down a harness from a shelf. A large dildo already jutted from it, and Cailyn's pulse quickened as Teran slipped it on. Made of the same shifting metal as Cailyn's collar, it fitted itself to its wearer's body. The metal glimmered as its shape changed.

Then Teran stepped behind her. Cailyn could feel the hard shape of the dildo press against her leg.

"You look lovely," Teran said. She pulled back Cailyn's hair. "A gem in a world of stones."

Cailyn blushed. "My lady?"

Teran's hand slid down the front of Cailyn's bodysuit. Slender fingers teased and pinched her nipples through the garment. Claws grabbed at the fastener and unzipped it with a swift, decisive motion.

Cailyn peeled the bodysuit off. "My lady, you just had me put that on."

"And you expect me to leave you in it when it's been so long?" Teran leaned over to bite her neck.

Cailyn didn't answer. Steel trilled along her breasts. Then Teran pushed her down onto the bed, the delicate curl of the metal replaced by the strength in her hands.

"I thought you wanted everyone to see—"

"I chose you. You ought to take pride in it."

Deft hands moved her hair to one side. Steel tickled her back. "You ought to exult in it."

Teran rummaged in a drawer beside the bed. She drew out a small package and set it beside her. Cailyn twisted to look at it, but a slender hand pushed her head back down.

"Calm down, little one. Here, I'll show you." She held out one of the small cylinders. Metal glinted inside. Cailyn squinted at it. Was that a needle? Whatever it was, it looked small and sharp.

Metal trilled across Cailyn's back. Cailyn was too busy staring to respond.

"A shame I can't just do this with my claws," Teran murmured.

Cailyn gasped, eyes fixed on the metal as Teran drew it out.

Unable to think of anything else to do, she thought back to her training. She'd studied techniques until she was dizzy with desire or sick with boredom. Beyond the lessons in technique, she'd had thousands of lessons in manners. The young hopefuls had learned proper etiquette for every eventuality.

But how, she wondered as she slowed her breathing and visualized the smiling face and flowing hair of her goddess, was she supposed to deal with this?

She could hear Teran breathe behind her, soft and quick. The claws pinched a bit of the skin of her back. Cailyn gasped as Teran pulled it up.

Fire lanced through her skin as the steel pushed through. She cried out at the invasion.

Teran's other hand soothed her. She breathed in slowly, still thinking of the courtesans' goddess, her flowing dark hair, wide eyes, and big-lipped smile.

Another needle pierced her. She breathed out, fought not to tense, and focused on her vision of the goddess's lips as they opened like her skin. Tears welled in her eyes, and she beat the bed underneath her with her fists.

Metal trilled across her back again. The tips of the claws kneaded her back.

Another needle pierced her. The world floated in her mind as the steel invaded her skin. Silver lightning lanced through her again and again. She shook, listening to her own sharp whimpering, and waited for her body to relax again.

"Very nice." Teran laughed. "Was that pleasure or pain?"

Cailyn drew in a breath. "What you're doing is intense, my lady."

Teran's hand slid down Cailyn's body. "I suppose I'll just have to see for myself."

Her fingers reached between Cailyn's legs, probing for wetness. Cailyn slid back to meet them, grateful for the contact.

Then Teran drew her hand away. Cailyn whimpered as Teran's fingers wiped her own moisture on her skin.

"I thought as much. Time to remove these, I think."

Cailyn hissed as Teran drew the first of the needles out, running the point against the channel the steel had made.

She could hear Teran's breath behind her, a faint gasp as the needle came free, quick breaths as she stared at Cailyn's back.

Cailyn howled as a bright spike of pain lanced through her. Teran paused. Cailyn gulped in air. It filled her lungs, pristine and refreshing.

Teran pulled another needle free, ripping at the tranquility Cailyn had made for herself. Tears sprang to her eyes. She muttered a curse.

Teran laughed. Apparently, she'd heard it.

How many more, Cailyn wondered. The room wavered in her vision as tears welled in her eyes and spilled.

I must look awful, Cailyn thought, but the welcome fingers found their way to her vulva again, smoothing away the pain.

Teran's other hand pushed at her back. "Turn around," she said, her voice halting with the desire choking it.

Cailyn did as Teran bid her. Pale eyes, sharp as a hawk's, regarded her.

Then all she felt was the bright shock of being filled. She winced, the pierced skin of her back singing its protest. Teran purred and moved faster inside her.

She twisted, trying vainly to find a more comfortable place for her back, but the pinpricks were everywhere. Each hole in her flesh burned as her body was tossed against the sheets underneath her.

Teran loomed above her, her body a black silhouette. Cailyn stared up at it as the great thing drove deep. She could feel it dividing her. The nerves inside her sang. Shocks of pain thrilled through her back.

She sighed, fixing her eyes on Teran's. They shone, brilliant crystals set in a white face, the mouth slightly open. Pleasure rolled in waves through Cailyn. It crackled through the punctures in her back, spilling out of her like blood.

She opened her eyes as something wide and heavy slid out of her. Her heart raced. She wondered when exactly she'd closed them. Her back itched, the rhythmic hum of pain growing more insistent as her breath and heartbeat slowed.

A clawed finger traced its way along one of her breasts. Her skin opened, bright and alive. Wet blood welled up from the place where it parted.

Teran's lips pressed against the wound. Cailyn closed her eyes again and let go.

The lips pulled away. She moved after them, feeling bereft. When she opened her eyes, metal tickled her chin.

Lips smeared with her blood smiled down at her.

"So, how did they react to you?"

"I—what?" Cailyn stammered. "They stared."

"Don't they always?"

"This—it—" Cailyn's cheeks burned. "It wasn't the same, my lady." At least, not until Lady Liana had appeared to rescue her. But even that conversation had turned to Teran in the end. To this.

Cailyn closed her eyes again. She'd loved eyes on her body, loved the idea of eyes on her from long before. But these eyes she could barely endure.

A gem in a world of stones, Teran had said. *You ought to exult in it.*

"I don't know how you stand it," she said at last.

Teran didn't answer. Silence stretched between them.

Claws tinkled softly against the metal collar. "I wonder how they would react to this."

Cailyn turned her head away, letting her hair hide her face. She swallowed, opened her eyes, and felt warm metal on her neck. She remembered Teran pulling back her hair, urging her to display the collar with pride.

So be it. She would try.

Teran smiled down at her, a few drops of blood on her lips. "That's better." Her hand pushed at Cailyn again. "Turn around, little one."

On her back, she couldn't do much unless Teran wanted to penetrate her again. She hoped that Teran would call on her soon to give pleasure with her hands or lips. She wanted her to feel pleasure as deep as the pleasure she felt now.

Fingers traced their way along her back. It made her fidget, wondering when the fingers would run over the pierced spots in her skin. They didn't. Cailyn sighed and sank into the bed.

A drawer slid open. She listened to Teran sift through it and turned her head to look. Teran drew out a cloth and something else. Probably some version of the ointment Teran had used on her before. Reassured, she turned away again.

A symphony of pain exploded through the nerves in her back. That wasn't ointment. The astringent cleanser burned, its sting a far cry from the cool, soothing ointment.

She twisted away, but strong hands pressed her back down. Then the liquid stung her again. It sent thrills of pain through the punctures in her skin.

She gripped the sheet beneath her, clenching her fists around the fabric. Her eyes fogged again with tears. It wasn't fair, after so much, not to be allowed to rest. Her insides twitched from the penetration. Her mind drifted from the needles.

"You will never be done," she whispered. "Will you, my lady?"

Claws tickled her skin. They withdrew, replaced by the cool touch of the ointment she'd wanted.

She thanked her patron goddess for small, comfortable miracles.

Strong hands guided Cailyn onto her side. Strong arms wrapped around her. She sagged into them, relieved.

Teran reached for her breast and twisted her nipple once, hard. Cailyn hissed as the other arm reached down to stroke her vulva, soothing away the pain. Cailyn's hips bucked. Teran bit her shoulder again. Overwhelmed, Cailyn trembled.

"I wasn't done, no." Teran's fingers, slick with Cailyn's wetness, traced their way back up her belly. "Apparently, neither are you."

Cailyn said nothing. A clawed hand toyed with her hair. One finger reached to her ear.

A claw poked at her pierced earlobe. "You didn't like it when I took these away from you."

"No, my lady," Cailyn answered.

"Why?"

Cailyn winced. *If you want earrings, let me know and I will provide them.* How could she explain how arrogant that had sounded without giving offense?

Still, it would hardly do to ignore a direct question from someone with newsteel-tipped fingers. She cleared her throat. "It seemed... petty, my lady."

"Petty? Little one, you are mine, at least for now. Adorn yourself however you wish in front of others. Not me."

"My lady, adorning myself well is part of my training."

"Of course. But this is the first night you are mine, little one. And for that first night you are mine, I would see you as you are, with nothing between us."

She bit Cailyn's earlobe. A shudder ran though Cailyn's body. Nothing between them, indeed.

Teran's claw ticked against the collar around Cailyn's neck. Her other hand snaked its way over Cailyn's breasts. Metal traced over Cailyn's skin.

Cailyn shivered again. Teran rewarded her with a kiss on the neck that became a hard bite. Pain blossomed through the column of her neck.

She gave herself over to it, let her anger melt as the pain bloomed through her. Naked, just as Teran had demanded.

She sagged against Teran, trusting to her training and her role.

"Much better," Teran said, her voice low with pleasure.

Cailyn heard a faint click as Teran reached over to the nightstand. The lights dimmed. Hands wrapped around Cailyn again, pulling her close.

Cailyn's back burned. Her neck throbbed with the pain of the bite. The heat and softness of Teran's body surrounded her, warm against the wounds in her back. She exhaled and let herself sink against it.

As if in a dream, Cailyn remembered the earrings, their faint tinkle as Teran pulled them from her ears. Was she still angry? She wasn't sure.

Breathing slowly into the now-dark room, she closed her eyes.

CHAPTER TWELVE

Cailyn awoke slowly. The sheets itched her back where spots of her blood had dried on it. She rubbed her eyes and murmured quiet thanks to the courtesans' goddess that, for once, Teran still slept beside her. Waking up alone after that first meeting had rattled Cailyn more than she'd cared to admit.

Teran had chosen to do that. She'd intended to use Cailyn and nothing more, at least that first time. But being dismissed without even a farewell felt wrong, as if Cailyn had left something undone, some service unperformed.

Teran had called her back repeatedly, so she must not see it that way. Still, Cailyn was glad that today, when her lady awoke, she would find her courtesan waiting.

Cailyn touched the metal circling her neck. It felt strange, lying against her skin like it belonged there.

So I'm hers, even now.

Cailyn reached out to touch Teran's face. What did someone like Teran, someone with eighty thousand credits' worth of steel implanted in her hands, dream about?

Teran didn't stir. Cailyn watched the rise and fall of her breath. Somehow Teran seemed so much more human right now, curled up around herself on a bed full of blood.

She stroked Teran's skin, wondering just how she'd gotten into this.

One of Teran's eyes cracked open. Cailyn's hand stilled. Would Teran mind her touch? She hesitated, unsure whether to pull her fingers away or not.

Teran's eyes fixed on Cailyn. A smile crept across Teran's mouth.

Cailyn let out a breath. "Good morning, my lady."

Teran yawned and sat up. Cailyn watched her stretch. Her fingers itched to touch Teran again.

Teran noticed it. "You want something now?" she asked with a laugh.

Cailyn blinked. She hadn't yet washed. Her back had dried blood on it.

"Do as you will, my lady," she said.

Teran laughed again. "Get up. Bend over the bed."

Teran walked to a far wall and took down a paddle. Cailyn could hear her chuckle as she walked back over.

Cailyn swallowed. Her back was already full of small holes from the piercing. If she also had bruises on her buttocks, there wouldn't be much clean skin left, at least not from the front. And she had taken a nonexclusive contract with Teran precisely because she hoped to see some other nobles.

"My lady," Cailyn began, "don't you think that's a bit much?"

"That's no concern of mine."

Cailyn cursed under her breath.

"This is not for you, my little one. This is for me. I will hurt you. Do you understand?"

Cailyn nodded, her throat parched. "Yes, my lady, I understand."

She willed herself to relax. The paddle tapped her backside. It would hit her regardless of what she wanted.

Of course, she could stop it with a word. She would always have that option under Guild law. Teran had even reminded her that she could refuse.

But if she did, Teran might never look at her the same way again.

And Teran might dismiss her. The last time she'd expressed reluctance, Teran had tilted her head toward the door. If she refused, Teran might send her away.

That thought sent a chill through her. The room felt suddenly cool and small. She closed her eyes and then opened them again, resolute.

So be it.

The first hard crack of the paddle reverberated through her. Her bones vibrated with the impact. Her teeth clenched.

Again and again, the paddle slammed into her flesh. She felt like a doll, battered by the force of the blows. There was no part of her they did not reach. No part of her was hidden enough, tucked away far enough, to avoid that insistent vibration. It rocked her, reverberated through skin, muscle, bone.

She did the only thing left to her. She opened her throat and cried out again and again. She drew in shuddering breaths and keened, high wails she could barely believe came from her mouth.

Teran's hand fell to her side. Cailyn heard herself sobbing into the silence. Disoriented, she lifted her head, staring blankly at the room around her. Her buttocks burned with pain.

Clawless fingers traced the bruised skin. Cailyn jumped, unsure if she craved Teran's touch or if she'd had enough. But Teran was gentle now. Cailyn sagged, relieved of the burden of endurance.

Teran's pride warmed her, anchoring itself in the flesh Teran had touched and rising up into her chest. She lifted her head. Her hair spilled across her face. For once, she did not brush it away.

"Thank you, my lady."

Teran nodded and stood. "Follow me, little one. We should clean you up. Prepare you for the conference."

Cailyn twisted to look at the marks on her flesh. Bright bruises purpled her buttocks. She frowned at them. Then she saw Teran staring at them, her gaze unblinking and hungry. She shivered.

She followed Teran into the bathroom, eager to slough off dirt, sweat, and tears. But the purple spread across her buttocks would not rinse away.

She found herself wanting to keep it. After all, it was her lady's mark.

CHAPTER THIRTEEN

The water washed over Cailyn, trailing the soap down her body. Teran did not touch her. Instead, she stood under another jet of water and stared.

Cailyn smiled and preened, glad to be on familiar turf. She stared back, looking over Teran's muscular body, small breasts, and erect nipples.

Cailyn turned to offer a better view of her marked back and rear. She could still feel Teran's eyes on her as the last of the water sloughed away.

With a whir of fans, warm air filtered in to dry their hair and bodies. Cailyn sighed. It meant missing the opportunity to dry Teran herself. Her hands itched to serve. She forced them to her sides, moved to the mirror, and picked up a brush near the sink.

"So, little one." Teran walked up behind her and watched her reflection as she brushed her hair. "How do you like being mine?"

Cailyn reached down to touch one of her bruises. Pain flared out from the tips of her fingers. She sighed. "It's difficult, my lady. But I think it has its rewards."

Teran wrapped her arms around Cailyn and lingered a moment. She let her arms fall and tilted her head toward Cailyn's room. Cailyn nodded and went inside.

Garments lay on the bed, laid out for Cailyn's return. She bit back a sigh. Black pants again. At least Teran had chosen a dark red top to match them.

Like the other garment, it would keep her back covered. The front of the garment hid far less. Wide strips of fabric covered her breasts but left the space between them open. Delicate chains bridged the open space. Rubies cut into faceted droplets dangled from the tiny links.

Cailyn slipped into the clothes. She looked down at the pattern of rubies over her chest and slid on a pair of soft leather boots, red to match.

She liked the red of the garment but crinkled her lip in doubt at the rubies. She might have found it elegant anywhere else. Here, it looked too much like blood. She'd bled for Teran countless times now, but somehow it seemed vulgar to advertise.

Lipstick of the same shade lay open and ready near her mirror. She fought not to frown as she drew it across her lips. Yes, she'd ventured onto the dark channels not long ago. But did Teran have to make her dress the part?

She tugged one last time at the fabric and walked back into Teran's room. Teran stood waiting, dressed in the customary gray. A large Nivrai symbol adorned the left shoulder.

Teran gestured. Cailyn spun around to offer Teran a view of herself from all angles.

"Pretty," Teran said, her eyes fixed on the exposed skin where the shirt parted. "But it's missing something."

Cailyn swallowed. She couldn't have forgotten anything. Everything she'd found laid out, she had put on. "My lady?"

Teran smirked and opened her hand. In her palm rested two ruby earrings. "Didn't I tell you, little one, that if you wanted earrings I would provide them for you?"

Cailyn slipped the earrings into her piercings, half amused, half unnerved. She thought of what Teran had called her before: a gem in a world of stones. Whatever she thought of all this, Teran had sculpted her into someone she would be proud to have on her arm.

She lifted her head and looked with purpose at Teran. She'd trained to do credit to the one who had hired her. She knew how.

She heard Teran walk up behind her. Steel-tipped fingers twined in her hair and pulled her head back. Teran's other hand circled her neck. The claws tinkled faintly as they touched the metal collar and reached up to tickle her chin.

"You look lovely, my little one," Teran said. The claws retracted. Teran slipped on a pair of black leather gloves.

She's hiding the implants, Cailyn realized.

Teran's voice drew her from her thoughts. "Now let's go."

❖

The nobles met in a wide circular hall with tiers of seats. Teran sat on the lowest rung, usually reserved for the members of the Lower Council. Cailyn sat beside her, feeling slightly out of place. A few of the council members had companions at their sides. Some were even courtesans she recognized. But most of the nobles sat alone, their faces smoothed into serious expressions.

She wondered if Teran felt out of place as well. A low-ranking noble from Nivrai would never sit on either of the Councils and could only come to this hall for official business.

Official unpleasant business. She looked for Lady Liana and found her in one of the lower tiers, her dusky face twisted in a frown.

That didn't look right. Cailyn had always seen her smiling. She looked up, searching the higher tiers reserved for the High Council for a glimpse of Lord Darien.

She fidgeted, her fingers turning over and over each other. Like her father, she was far more interested in serving those who hired her than in the intricacies of their affairs. Getting caught up in the nobles' intrigues could be dangerous as well as unpleasant. Cailyn had as little taste for them as her father had.

"Teran Nivrai," said one of the women of the High Council. "The Councils have called you here for a very important reason."

"I am at the service of the Councils," Teran returned, with the same faint mockery Cailyn had heard once before.

Cailyn sighed. Baiting Darien when he called her had been funny, but this was the official council hall.

"That remains to be seen. You've no doubt heard about the recent attempts on Councilman Alain's life?"

"Of course. I trust the councilman is safe now. In fact, I see him in this hall this evening."

"Yes, I'm here," called a sharp voice from the lower circle. Its owner glared daggers at Teran.

"I'm pleased to hear it," Teran said. She flashed Councilman Alain the open smile Cailyn remembered from their first meeting.

Cailyn exhaled, careful not to betray her emotions. Could Teran smile that way at will?

"But tell me," Teran went on, "what does any of this have to do with me? Surely you haven't called me here simply to wish him well."

The woman scowled. "No, Nivrai, we have not. We've called you here because we need your help."

"My help, my lady?"

"Our troops captured one of the men who masterminded the attack," a nobleman beside her put in.

"Excellent. But what does that have to do with me?"

"We have reason to believe that the rebels are planning another," he continued.

"However, the man is not cooperating," said the first.

A frown creased Teran's face. Cailyn could see the black hands under the table, twisting over one another. "How unfortunate. But again, my lords, what does this have to do with me?"

"We have reason to suspect that you might succeed where our interrogators have failed," a third noble said. Cailyn recognized him from his shock of red hair.

Lord Ben Keriel.

The father of Teran's child.

Cailyn looked over at the noblewoman. She thought of Nivrai, the empty mansion on a small planet. Had anyone else visited the lonely rock this year? Even Mariel, the person she'd come closest to loving, had belonged to her.

But Mariel hadn't been noble. As long as she hid their affair, she could use him as she wished. Could a woman like that be a mother?

Cailyn wondered who the child was. Teran had called him her son, hadn't she? How old was he? How much did he know about the infamous Teran Nivrai?

And what did Ben Keriel say when the child asked, "Who is my mother?"

Teran glared back at Ben Keriel. "My lord, what makes you think that I would succeed where trained professionals have failed?"

"Nivrai, we—"

"That makes no sense."

"No sense?" said the other nobleman. "You are a symbol of everything that he and his people fight against."

"You are one of the nobility whose rule he wants to destroy," said the woman who had spoken first. "You have a reputation."

Lord Keriel grinned. "People sit around asking one another just what it is you do, and just what you might do to them if given the chance. You just might intimidate this man when our teams couldn't."

Cailyn blinked. Do what they couldn't? Were they really asking—ordering—Teran to—?

"Teams of interrogators, you mean." Cailyn could hear the faint rustle of leather as Teran's fingers moved in her lap. "Torture? Are the council members really stupid enough to think I would do that for them? That I can do that for them?"

"You don't have a choice, Nivrai," the High Councilwoman said, her voice cold and even.

"Don't I, my lady?"

Cailyn winced.

"Nivrai, you have no right—"

"Those tactics don't work in the first place. You said yourself that you already tried them."

"Some people do talk under torture."

"Anyone can say what he thinks we want to hear. What we want to hear may not be the truth."

"Nivrai," Lord Keriel warned her.

Teran only glared at him "And what do we have to fear from them anyway? It took them this long to try to kill a minor councilman. And they failed at it."

Cailyn bit her lip. Was that true? Cailyn had heard that anyone would break if pressed hard enough. But did Teran know they would lie if they did? Or was she just spinning pretty words to try to get out of this?

"Little to fear? Councilman Alain could have died. Does the loss of life mean so little to you, Teran Nivrai?"

"You caught him. No harm came to Councilman Alain. If any had, that would surely be regrettable." A smile crept across Teran's mouth.

Cailyn stared, startled by Teran's glib words. "That would surely be regrettable." She understood Teran's rage, but this was a council member. Who had been attacked. Did Teran care at all about that?

She winced again. Teran had been cruel to her, yes, but never truly heartless. Hearing her now, Cailyn remembered all the whispered stories about steel hidden beneath Teran's skin in impossible places. If the helldemon's skin could sprout needles and knives, no doubt it would do so now. Cailyn wrapped her arms around herself, chilled by that thought.

She closed her eyes and breathed deep. Her purpose was to serve. In public, that meant being a credit to her client.

She thought of the charge the courtesans' goddess had given those who served her. She focused on that thought and took a deep breath, hoping to clear her mind.

However she might feel about all of this, she could worry about it later. For now, she would focus on her duty.

"Lady Nivrai," the councilwoman said, "why take exception to what we're offering you? You're the perfect one for this job."

"I?"

"Whatever you do to him, the council members promise they will fully pardon."

Teran turned a cold smile on the councilwoman. The quiet hall filled with her laughter. "Fully pardon? So that's what this is about. Did you think offering this would flatter me? That you can toss me anyone at all, like meat to a dog? That you could give me an enemy of the state, someone who despises me on principle, and expect me to think of that as a gift?"

The woman's voice dripped sweetness. "Everything is set up in your favor. Surely you're not going to refuse and aid treason."

Teran sighed. "Is that how it is, then? In that case, I will not defy you."

Cailyn blinked. Had she heard that correctly?

"Maybe so, but the Councils have already made their determination. And assigned you your duty."

"Very well, my lady."

Cailyn looked down at Teran's hands. She saw holes in the tips of the black leather gloves, small dents in the table under her slender fingers.

CHAPTER FOURTEEN

Cailyn didn't trust herself to speak. She walked a step behind Teran, using any technique she could recall to project strength and calmness.

Other nobles loitered in the halls, staring after Teran and Cailyn. Some whispered.

"Cailyn Derys," called one, waving her over. "I never would've expected to see you in such company."

Apparently, Lady Liana wasn't the only one who wanted to talk. Not bothering to stifle a sigh, she turned.

She knew the man, a minor noble ranked almost as low as Teran. He had hired her once, shortly after he'd inherited his estate. Giddy with the power of it, he'd shown off by spending his money on one of the best courtesans he could hire.

For her part, Cailyn hadn't enjoyed their encounter. He had bragged about his skill at seduction, his money, his anatomy. Cailyn hadn't found any of the three impressive.

He'd ground into her for a few minutes, panting comments about himself all the while. Too disgusted to be delicate, Cailyn had shushed him, convinced him to start over. She'd coaxed him into allowing her to touch him. She'd caressed his skin, teasing responses from every part of his body besides the obvious. Chastened, he'd lapsed into silence. Only then had Cailyn straddled him and guided him inside herself.

Once it ended, so had his moment of humility. He'd shooed her out, grumbled about her fee, and waited months before calling her again.

She'd turned him down politely. His face had reddened, but Cailyn had hoped he'd understood in the end.

Apparently, he hadn't.

"The company I keep is mine to choose, Lord Nalar." Cailyn glanced over at Teran, whose jaw was set in a hard line.

"Of course." He stroked his moustache and his lip curled. "But I never would've thought you would be Teran's whore."

Whore. The word went through her like cold water, seeping down into her bones.

She'd heard it before, of course. Every courtesan heard it sooner or later. Sometimes people who disapproved of the nobles' extravagance hurled it at them. Sometimes the nobles themselves sneered it, disgusted with themselves for what they wanted.

And some people just liked the sharpness of the word, when they rolled it around in their mouths.

But this...

"Really," he went on, "are you that greedy, Derys?" His eyes swept over Cailyn's attire. His gaze fixed on the rubies hanging between her breasts.

Cailyn raised her head, willing herself to find her voice. "My lord, it's no one's business but my own what I do. Or how much I'm paid to do it."

"I thought you were better than the dark channels. Those people are barbarians. And even they won't do the things Nivrai does."

"Barbarians?" Teran's voice was quiet and calm. "How do you know that?"

Nalar blanched under Teran's stare. His lips twisted, and his face purpled with rage. "Everyone knows that. And everyone knows about you."

"Do you?"

He opened his mouth to speak and sputtered.

Teran chuckled. "If you don't know, how can you comment on it?"

"Why should I want to know exactly how you ruin a beautiful woman like Cailyn Derys?"

"Ruin? How have I ruined her?"

His jaw worked. His mouth opened and closed, but once again, no words came out. He stared as Teran stepped up to Cailyn's side.

"People like you are the reason the rebel group hates us. It's no wonder they try to kill people when they have monsters like you in mind."

Teran's face was a frozen, bloodless mask, lips drawn in a grim line. A gloved hand clenched at her side.

Cailyn put a hand on Teran's arm, thinking of what the hidden newsteel could do.

"So I should be killed, is that what you're saying? And you say I'm worse than a barbarian."

"Killed? No."

"Then what are you saying?"

"I'm just saying our enemies get their violence from somewhere."

"Somewhere."

Nalar stabbed at the air, at a loss for words again.

Metal glinted through the rips in Teran's glove. Cailyn tensed.

Teran glared at Nalar for a long moment. He blinked, and Teran turned away.

"Come with me," she said. She nodded to Cailyn and swept past Lord Nalar before he could say anything else.

Happy to get away, Cailyn followed.

Teran slammed her against the wall as soon as the doors closed behind them. Cailyn didn't protest. Rough use would drive all those insults out of her mind.

But when the newsteel in Teran's fingers clicked awake, she twisted away. Had Teran really just said she would torture someone?

"Be still," Teran hissed.

Metal clinked against metal as Teran's claws tore through the delicate golden chains on Cailyn's shirt. Numb, Cailyn stared down as the claws broke each chain. When it was done, Teran reached to stroke Cailyn's exposed skin.

Cailyn recoiled.

An unfortunate business, Lady Liana had said. She'd warned Cailyn against getting caught up in it.

She'd thought she could avoid it by accompanying Teran as companion only. But Teran was the one the council members wanted. Now that they'd revealed why—

Could she serve knowing what they wanted?

She remembered her training, the contract, her promises, Teran's touch. Nothing soothed the queasy feeling in her gut.

"My lady," she ground out. "Do you plan to go along with the Councils in this?"

The hand froze, the tips of the claws half-dug into Cailyn's skin. "Plan to?"

"You told them—"

"What they're asking me to do is ridiculous. They have people to do that job. If anyone should."

"But you said you wouldn't defy them."

"Of course I did. What else could I say?"

"Then how can you—?"

"They have to believe that I'm almost convinced." Fingers moved on Cailyn's skin, slow and reassuring.

Cailyn swayed, wanting to believe their promise. The mere suggestion had made Teran angrier than Cailyn had ever seen her.

The hand moved again. It pulled back the fabric, widening the exposed expanse of flesh. Laughter filled Cailyn's ears again. Steel spidered its way along Cailyn's exposed skin.

"Teran's whore."

Cailyn's gorge rose all over again. She flinched. "My lady? You like that someone called me that?"

Teran's voice was smooth as a purr. "I like that he called you mine."

Cailyn twitched. Her flesh slipped open as Teran's hand moved down. She froze, wanting to respond and hating herself for it.

Teran kissed her, hard. The steel tipped hand moved along her breasts. The claws of Teran's other hand clicked as they slid back into Teran's fingertips. Cailyn let out a breath, expectant, as they moved lower.

Cailyn kissed back, her lips chasing the echoes of the words.

Whore. She could hear Teran's voice pronouncing it, slowly, savoring the sound.

And "mine." Teran said she liked that word better. But that wasn't much less frightening.

Teran's fingers slid into her. "Are you frightened of me now, little one?"

"Of this," Cailyn panted as the fingers filled her.

"Of being what they claim?"

Cailyn squeezed her eyes shut, not wanting to nod.

"If they call you dross, take pride in it." Teran kissed her again, her tongue filling Cailyn's mouth.

She drew away and licked her lips. "What better to be than something small-minded people scorn?"

Then the fingers entered Cailyn again, hard and sudden. She gasped.

"Besides, the word means what you do now. Claim it yourself, and it has no power over you."

Cailyn cringed. After all this talk of torture, she wasn't sure she wanted force. Or pain, which would follow soon enough.

She took a deep breath to center herself. Even if she couldn't respond the way she wanted, she could still give pleasure. She'd always enjoyed doing that, at least.

A hand wound in her hair, dragged her head back. "Are you pulling away from me, little one?"

She'd pulled away before. Sometimes the nobles were too boring or unpleasant for even Cailyn to endure with a smile. Awkwardness reflected badly on any courtesan, but it came with the job. Everyone dealt with it. Even her father had, sometimes.

The thought reassured her. The desire she'd felt became a distant glow, waves lapping gently inside her. The gods knew that after so much time with Lady Nivrai, she could use some gentleness.

The fingers battered her, driving in and in. Her body felt limp. The plunging fingers held her up. Their relentless rhythm tore her away from the world she swam in. She heard herself cry, a high, thin noise, and pushed back onto Teran's hand.

She knew by now that Teran would never use the claws, but she found herself imagining them anyway. All memories of decorum or training fled, torn to shreds by the steel-tipped fingers glinting in her mind. She moved with Teran's fingers, no will of her own driving her.

Was she coming? She didn't know. She knew only the ache of her mouth twisted into a scream.

Her body emptied, her sex still yawning open. Arms wrapped around her. She trembled. They gripped her tighter, the response automatic.

"What exactly was that, little one?"

"I don't know, my lady."

It was the only answer she could give without shivering again.

CHAPTER FIFTEEN

The color-changing scarf wrapped Cailyn's shoulders in airy softness. She liked the color, too, after so much gray and black. She wore it with a bright green dress, a lime color she'd never get to wear in Teran's chambers. The fabric swished against her thighs and she walked faster.

She'd looked forward to this meeting for a while now. Seeing a favorite client always offered welcome respite. She needed that now more than ever, no matter what Lady Liana had said that day in the hall.

The door slid open. A lavender gown hung loose over Liana's full-figured frame, sheer enough that Cailyn could see the breasts beneath, the brown of the noblewoman's nipples.

Dark brown eyes crinkled with laughter. "Welcome, Cailyn Derys. It's been too long."

Cailyn grinned. "It's always a pleasure to see you, my lady."

A blush spread over Liana's cheeks. "I don't remember you flattering me this much."

Cailyn laughed, trying to think of an appropriate response. She finally bowed.

"That's a lovely dress," Liana added. "Those things Nivrai puts you in don't suit you."

No, they don't, Cailyn thought.

The room had rich purple walls, a deeper shade that matched Liana's gown. Instead of a bed, a pile of purple cushions filled the center of the room. Golden embroidery winked from the pile.

Light filtered in from large windows overlaid with sheer curtains. Cailyn looked up at Liana, imagining her body laid out on them.

Liana wasted no time in stepping over to Cailyn. She ran her fingers along the soft fabric of Cailyn's bright gown. Her fingers moved to its fasteners and loosened them one by one. "Let's have a look at you."

Cailyn shuddered as the bright green fabric fell to the ground. She still bore Lady Nivrai's marks.

Maybe a regenerative treatment now and then would be a good idea, she thought as she stepped away from the fabric pooled around her feet.

But Liana didn't seem interested in her backside at the moment. Her hands wandered over Cailyn's chest, skipped down her breasts. Cailyn arched her back and pressed them into Liana's hands.

"Come here," Lady Liana said, her voice warm with approval.

Cailyn let herself be led to the pile of cushions, careful to hide the marks on her back and buttocks. It felt strange to shield a part of her body, a body that she made available to people like Lady Liana every day of her life. Did she want to see them, or to pretend they weren't there?

"You're hiding something."

Cailyn froze. Did Liana want her to turn around?

Brown fingers tapped the collar around Cailyn's neck. "So, you just came from seeing Lady Nivrai?"

Cailyn blushed. She'd almost forgotten about the metal circling her neck. "Guild law prevents me from answering that."

Liana ran a hand through her long hair. A frown tugged at her lips. "Either way, working for her must be terrible."

Cailyn said nothing. Guild law meant she didn't have to, after all.

"Your father's very famous."

Not this again.

"My lady, there is no need to—"

"Isn't there some other way?"

Cailyn hesitated. *Teran's whore.* The rumors about her had already begun. If she sounded too eager for Lady Nivrai's company, they would surely only get worse.

"I chose this," she said after a moment. "I told you so before."
Liana's brows knitted. "Well."

Cailyn lay down on the soft cushions and pulled Lady Liana
down with her. "Shh."

She wrapped her hands around Liana's head and drew her into a
kiss, reveling in Liana's mouth as it opened to her.

With deft fingers, Cailyn guided Liana into turning over. There
would be no chance of Liana discovering her bruises if she couldn't
see Cailyn's back.

Liana sank into the cushions and slid out of the loose-fitting
dress. Cailyn reached out to run her fingers along Liana's chest.

She slid her fingers over Liana's nipples. They hardened as
Cailyn caressed them, eager brown buds. Liana's breathing came
sharp and quick as Cailyn's fingers moved.

Cailyn leaned down to kiss Liana's skin, touch it lightly with her
lips. She traced slow patterns with her mouth.

She liked this, her lips tracing kisses along the body of a woman,
seeking the place between her legs.

And there was nothing complicated to do now. Lady Liana
gasped in anticipation and opened her legs. Warmth spread through
Cailyn, and she lowered her head to Liana's vulva.

She waited a long moment and lost herself in the smell and feel.
Lady Liana's hand wound in her hair and pressed her closer. She
opened her mouth and began to lick.

Liana shuddered and tilted her hips, pushed her flesh against
Cailyn's mouth. Cailyn slid two fingers inside Liana and began to
move them. Breathless cries answered her rhythm.

Cailyn drank it in, hungry for Liana's desire. It felt good to serve
and serve well. She drove her fingers in, pushing until Liana bucked
and cried out again.

Cailyn wrapped her free arm around Liana's hips. She held her
there until her spasm passed.

She slid her fingers free and looked up. Liana smiled back at her
and beckoned with one hand.

Cailyn slid up to Liana's side. Liana's arms wrapped tight
around Cailyn's body. One hand reached down to Cailyn's buttocks
and squeezed.

Before she could stop herself, Cailyn let out a small cry.

Lady Liana drew back her hand as if Cailyn's skin had burned it. "What is it?"

"Nothing, my lady."

"Did Teran Nivrai do something to you there?"

Cailyn cursed under her breath. The very question she didn't want to hear.

Right on the heels of Liana's pleasure.

"My lady, Guild law prevents me from answering you."

Lady Liana moved her hand and looked into Cailyn's face. Cailyn willed herself to keep it expressionless.

A courtesan's face must reveal nothing she doesn't want her client to see. She repeated it over and over in her mind, as her instructors had so many years ago.

"She did, didn't she?" A frown furrowed Liana's pretty face. She touched Cailyn's cheek. Then her fingers lowered. They moved down Cailyn's neck and over her chest.

What was Liana doing? Did Cailyn's skin feel different now? Would everyone know who she belonged to now, know it in the tips of their fingers as they traced their way along her skin?

A gem in a world of stones, Teran had called her. She was the gem, but who were the stones? The other courtesans? Most people? Everyone?

Lady Liana's voice cut through her brooding. "I never understood what people saw in those things anyway. What's so wrong with this?" She slid her hands along Cailyn's body, drawing her into a kiss.

"Nothing," Cailyn breathed.

"Then why?" Liana's fingers traced Cailyn's nipple. It hardened at her touch. "You don't seem bored, or jaded, or bitter, like the people on the dark channels."

Bored, jaded, or bitter. Those words certainly didn't fit Lord Darien. What about the other nobles who used the dark channels?

"I'm not, my lady. I like"—she waved her hands, indicating the room—"this."

"Is that so?" Liana chuckled. "You like this, but you still go for a woman who hurt you enough that you feel it when I touch you?"

"I—"

"Don't tell me you actually like Teran Nivrai."

Cailyn tapped the collar at her throat. She thought back to the encounter with Lord Nalar.

"Not many people do, my lady."

"Is that what this is about? Cailyn Derys, friend to the friendless?"

"Maybe." Cailyn thought of Teran's stories about Mariel, of Teran's lean, muscular body as it moved through fighting forms in an empty, silent room.

"Then you pick strange people to help. Nivrai isn't the only noble who could use some cheering up."

Cailyn looked up at Liana's nightstand. The diadem of office gleamed against the rich, deep purple of the table. "Isn't she? The Councils—"

"Gave her an assignment."

"An assignment."

Liana frowned. "It really is unfortunate. But we need the information. And Nivrai likes that kind of thing."

Unfortunate. Was that all Lady Liana would ever have to say?

Cailyn's fists clenched. "It's torture."

"Yes, but—"

"Torturing someone is the same as hiring me?"

"I don't know." Her brow furrowed. "People on the dark channels like hurting people. She's worse than they are. They say she doesn't even go on them because of it."

"Hiring a courtesan isn't interrogation."

"This is Teran Nivrai."

"Which means you think she would want that." It wasn't a question.

"She never leaves Nivrai. She doesn't talk to anyone. She just looks at you with those eyes."

A shudder wracked Liana's body. "Those big, pale eyes. It's like you aren't even there. Even the people on the dark channels don't like her very much, from what I hear." She looked at Cailyn. "How can you stand it?"

What could Cailyn say? She thought of Teran's eyes on her, hard, hungry, unblinking.

She remembered Lord Lerak's visit to her father, all those years ago. The greed and hunger as his eyes drank in her father's body, eager to possess it.

She looked back at Liana, nestled in her sea of purple cushions. How could Cailyn answer those objections when she still had doubts of her own?

Still, Liana was one of the people who had voted to assign that duty not to a professional, but to Teran Nivrai. To a minor noble with a reputation for cruelty. Like that was the same thing.

"My lady," Cailyn finally said, "why would you conscript someone to do that? Based on guesses about her personal life?"

Lady Liana's fingers twisted strands of her black hair. "I didn't do it."

"You voted for it."

"Lord Keriel came up with the idea. I thought he made a good case for it. Yes, I voted for it. I figured that Nivrai would enjoy it. She'd get to do...what she does...and benefit society, for once. I thought she'd be grateful."

Cailyn pulled away. "Grateful? Grateful that you'd force her to torture someone?"

Liana's expression hardened. "Those rebels are terrorists."

"I understand, my lady. But this is—"

"This is the safety of the council members, Derys. The safety of all the nobles. Me, Lord Keriel, Lady Nivrai. Any of the people you serve." Liana reached for her. "And serve so well," she said, her voice low and sultry.

"You could've at least asked her," Cailyn hissed. "Not just volunteered her."

Liana shook her head. "Honestly, I don't think we'd have the guts to ask her anything."

Chapter Sixteen

The door slid open. Teran lounged on her bed, a glass of something—vakren?—in her hand. A piece of black clothing hung on the closet door.

Cailyn peered at it. She'd never seen Teran's walls anything but bare and immaculate.

Even stranger, the garment was black. She had Cailyn wear the color all the time, but Cailyn had never seen Teran wear anything but Nivrai gray.

It might do her some good to wear another color for a change. She'd look lovely in deep purple, Cailyn thought, imagining easing Teran into a long velvet dress.

She peered at the black garment. Official council insignia, conspicuous and ugly, adorned the breast and sleeves. The uniform of an interrogator, Cailyn guessed. Her fantasies of dressing Teran faded as a lump formed in her throat.

Did Teran plan to wear it? She'd said she would defy them. Now the uniform hung in plain sight on the closet door.

"Welcome back, my little one," Teran said, her lips twisting into a smile.

"Thank you, my lady." Cailyn inclined her head and sank to her knees in the fluid motion she'd practiced thousands of times before. She didn't know how Teran would feel about her seeing someone else but wanted to serve as flawlessly as she could right now. Misgivings about the uniform or no.

"You look like you enjoyed yourself." Teran set her glass down and walked over to Cailyn. Steel snuck under the straps of Cailyn's dress. "I'm no fan of that color."

The fabric sighed as Teran's claws slit it. Cailyn's mouth opened in a round O of angry surprise. Before she could protest, the dress fell to the floor in a tangle of bright fabric.

An empty feeling spread through Cailyn's stomach. She liked that little dress. She'd meant to wear it for her other clients. What did Lady Nivrai think she was doing?

"Are you jealous, my lady?"

A hand pushed her head down and brushed away her hair. She jerked as she felt teeth against her shoulder.

"Jealous?" Teran whispered against her neck. "Why would I be jealous when all of this is mine?" She bit again. Cailyn jumped. "Why should I be jealous thinking of someone else touching your body," a clawed hand clenched, digging into Cailyn's skin, "of someone else using you." Strong hands pushed Cailyn back down.

The clawed hands traced their way across Cailyn's body and cupped her breasts. "I'm the one you're coming back to. Not them. This—"

Teran's fingers, clawless now, moved against Cailyn's lips. Reacting by instinct alone, Cailyn opened her mouth to admit them. She felt herself fall away as they pushed into her mouth. Teran slid her fingers back out of her mouth, wiped them off on her chest, then moved them down Cailyn's body.

"And this," she said. Her fingertips glided over Cailyn's labia, slid down to the opening, and peeked in.

Cailyn moaned as they began to move inside her, slamming hard enough to make her gasp. Then they withdrew.

Teran grabbed at Cailyn's bruised buttocks, squeezed and twisted until Cailyn cried out again.

Teran stopped. Her hand traced Cailyn's buttocks. One finger slid over the space between them but stopped just shy of the hole. "This too."

She reached into a drawer on the nightstand and drew out a glove. She slipped it onto a clawless hand and smeared her gloved fingers with lubricant. She brought one finger to the hole, massaged it, and smeared lubricant over it. Then she pushed her way in, quick and sharp.

Cailyn gasped, feeling herself stretched wide by the probing fingers. Teran hissed her pleasure into Cailyn's ear, driving the fingers hard into Cailyn's body. She jumped and hissed as the fingers slammed into her.

She keened, and the cry drove Teran on, Teran's other hand clutching her hard as the fingers inside her clove her.

The claws of Teran's free hand bit into her chest. A current of pain sped through Cailyn's body.

"You like that, don't you, my little one?" Teran whispered, her voice at Cailyn's ear insistent and unavoidable. The fingers tore through her again. She opened her mouth to let loose another scream.

In a quick, sudden motion, Teran's free hand let go. She reached for the glass of vakren and upturned it. The bitter liquid spilled over Cailyn's open skin. It burned where it fell, the wound all fire.

Overloaded, Cailyn cried out. White light danced in front of her eyes.

She slumped and spasmed with aftershock. Little thrills of pleasure lanced through her body. Her chest stung.

She heard the sharp slap of rubber as Teran removed the glove.

"So you do like pain, after all." Teran smirked.

Cailyn coughed and looked down at herself, at her naked flesh smeared with blood and vakren.

She remembered Lady Liana's shock at her bruises. And shook her head. She already had Teran's marks all over her.

"This is getting unsightly," she said. "Are you going to pay for regenerations just so I heal faster?"

Teran stepped out from behind her and leaned over to lick the scrape on Cailyn's chest. "You don't need them. You were famous already. Now you're infamous because you're with me. They'll pay you for that alone."

Her bloody lips twisted into a grin. "I can see them now. Clucking at your marks telling you how concerned they are and paying for the privilege."

Teran had always been so mindful of her pleasure. Was it so hard to also be mindful of her work? "That's easy for you to say."

"Is it?"

"Even people on the dark channels won't want to see your marks all over me."

"So you have been on the dark channels now." A new smile crept over Teran's lips. "I thought you might do that."

"I never said that."

"Didn't you?" Sharp laughter filled the room as Teran moved toward Cailyn.

Cailyn pushed her away. "You ruin my dresses. Question what I do with other people. Mark me until they won't want me anyway. Is this not enough for you, my lady?" She pointed at the blue metal circling her throat. "If you wanted an exclusive contract, you could have asked for one."

"That dress?" Teran looked down at the wrinkled green fabric on the floor. "You can have seven more like it, if you want. All you have to do is ask."

Cailyn threw up her hands, forgetting decorum completely. "That isn't the point."

"Everything I've done to you is within my rights." Teran stared unblinking at Cailyn. "Beyond the rules Guild law obligates me to follow, you set no limit on how I use you. Haven't you figured out that I like their scorn?"

"That's enough," Cailyn growled. She rose to her feet and stepped closer to Teran, her stride wide and determined.

"Do you think I'm here to endure anything you can dream up, no matter how degrading?" She jabbed a finger at Teran. "Are you going to hold me to the letter of Guild law now with no regard for how you actually treat me? Teran's whore, is that it? Does that give you license to destroy my property? Mock my taste? Meddle in things that have nothing to do with you?"

She didn't wait for Teran to answer. She snatched the ruined green dress from the ground with one quick motion and swept off to the safety of her quarters.

The door slid shut behind her. Safe now, she slumped against the wall. Her chest stung. Alone in her room, she had no salve to soothe it. She could call the servants, but she had just shouted at their mistress. Would they bother tending to her when she and Teran had just fought?

Teran called her name again and again, her voice harsh at first and then uncertain. She sank to the floor and didn't answer.

The door slid open, betraying her.

Of course it would. These quarters were Teran's after all.

"My little one," Teran said. "You have so little faith in me."

"Leave me alone."

Cailyn's head snapped up. She stared at Teran. But Teran, for her part, only looked down at the floor.

"I—" Cailyn began, unsure whether the words caught in her throat were words of reproach or comfort.

"Little one," Teran interrupted. She reached out her hand. "At least get up."

Cailyn let Teran take her hand and guide her to her feet.

"You can do what you want with me," she said. "Guild law permits it. But if you do something like that again, I leave."

Teran shook her head. For a long moment, she stood silent. Then she spoke.

"Very well. I will not interfere in your business outside these walls again."

Cailyn nodded. It was a start.

Teran took Cailyn's chin in her hand. Cailyn willed herself not to flinch.

"But understand something, little one. You are mine for as long as you wear that collar. I intend to use you as I will. That has not changed. That will not change."

Teran stared hard at Cailyn. "No matter what else you do on your own time. I will mark you or not mark you as I see fit."

Cailyn looked down at the blood and vakren spattered on her chest. Lady Liana had already seen her bruised. The damage was already done.

And Teran's infamy might be good for business, even if the marks weren't.

"Telling me how concerned they are and paying for the privilege?" She allowed herself a small laugh.

Silver laughter answered her. "If they don't, I'll pay you another five hundred."

Cailyn stepped toward Teran, her movements wobbly from endorphins and the excitement of arguing. Teran put out her hand.

"I am here to serve, my lady," Cailyn said. Strong, lean arms steadied her.

❖

"Go ahead and ask me, little one." Teran twined a clawed hand in Cailyn's curls. "You've been staring at it for the past five minutes."

Teran's glass of vakren was full again. She'd given a sip to Cailyn, passed directly from her own mouth to Cailyn's. She'd laughed, delighted, as Cailyn swallowed the bitter drink without making a face.

"The Councils had it sent to you?"

"Yes. It came this morning, while you were out." She frowned. "Lord Ben Keriel himself delivered it."

Lord Ben Keriel. The father of Teran's child.

Cailyn slid her fingers over Teran's stomach. What had she looked like, her belly big with child? She tried to imagine it, the sharp eyes, close-cut hair, strong shoulders, and small breasts over a heavy stomach.

Cailyn hadn't menstruated in years. Even thinking of her own body that way was strange. What would it be like to grow a child?

Teran knew. Cailyn didn't. Teran, who hadn't wanted to carry a child in the first place. And yet she had. The child of someone she despised had grown in her body. How had those long months felt?

Who was her child? What did he look like? How did he act? How did Lord Keriel feel, father of a child with someone who preferred to hide herself on a distant planet? She'd chosen the attentions of her lover over being a mother to her son.

Teran's voice, sharp and bitter, drew Cailyn out of her reverie.

"Yes, Lord Keriel himself, taking time off from his important duties to the High Council to bring me the uniform he wants me to wear to torture someone."

"Why him, my lady?" Cailyn asked. Teran's claws dug idly into her skin.

"What better way for him to remind me of his authority?" Teran slipped out of Cailyn's arms, walked over to the closet, and ran her fingers along the smooth fabric.

Cailyn's brow furrowed. "He wants you to do this, everyone says. But you said he hated even the things you did with Mariel."

"Of course he did." Teran turned. "My lord Keriel would like nothing better than for me to see the error of my ways. Marry him. Mother our son."

"Marry him? He wanted you to marry him?"

Teran's fingers moved over the fabric of the garment again. Cailyn frowned, feeling queasy. If she meant to defy the Councils, how could she touch their uniform like some kind of prized possession?

"He didn't want an heir. Not really. He wanted me."

"Wanted you?"

"The deal was useful to him, a way to bargain with my parents." Teran shook her head. "It was useful to me for the same reason. Neither of us wanted the child."

Cailyn felt her throat tighten. Was Teran telling the truth?

Teran slid into the bodysuit. The black fabric clung to her muscular frame. The yellow council insignia shone bright and forbidding over her breast and over the muscles of her upper arms.

She crossed her arms over her chest, extended her claws, and stared ahead. "So, my little one, what do you think?"

A chill went through Cailyn. Teran Nivrai, official torturer.

The wisp of heat in her flesh shamed her. A blush spread across her face.

The embarrassment quickly hardened into anger. Teran had said she didn't want to take this job, but here she was trying on the bodysuit like some kind of sexual toy.

Cailyn thought of her own moisture on the steel-tipped fingers and shuddered. "My lady? I thought you said you weren't going to do it."

The smiling mouth hardened. "I don't intend to."

"Then why are you wearing that getup like it's funny? What are you playing at, Teran Nivrai?"

The pale eyes bored into hers. Their gazes caught and held her. She clenched her fists and fought not to blink.

"Is that what's bothering you, my little one? Well then, let me prove it to you."

The steel tipping her hands flashed. Cailyn saw skin peek through black as the patch displaying the councils' symbol tore and fluttered to the ground. The patch over her breast followed, falling facedown to the floor.

A smile spread across Teran's face. "Better now, my little one?"

Cailyn didn't answer.

"Or how about now?" Teran said. The hole in the fabric over her chest widened, her breasts peeking out through the hole.

Cailyn tore her eyes away. The lust rising in her body wasn't right.

Teran knotted her hand in Cailyn's hair and pulled. "I've shown you what you want to see."

Strong hands twisted Cailyn's head around, forcing her to look. Cailyn grunted. Tears pricked her eyes. Her scalp stung.

"You have no reason not to believe me," Teran snarled. Her other hand reached down and tore a hole in the black fabric over her groin.

"Besides, why should I use some fool in a terrorist organization, when I could have a beautiful, trained woman instead?"

Cailyn swallowed hard. Teran pulled her head toward her exposed vulva. "Come on, little one. You know me better than this."

She released Cailyn's hair and traced her hand along Cailyn's cheek. "The only pain I want is yours."

Cailyn's flesh tingled. I want you, too, Teran Nivrai, she thought as those hands drew her toward the warm flesh. I shouldn't, but I do. She reached out her arms, wrapping them around Teran's body.

She opened her mouth, drinking in Teran's wetness with her lips and tongue. Heat surged through her as the hand around her head tightened. Its grip crushed her against the warm flesh.

She abandoned herself to it, her head moving in time to Teran's soft growls of encouragement and pleasure. Teran shifted to allow her better access. She gripped Teran's hips.

Teran moaned as her body locked. Cailyn pushed her down hard, holding her there as she reached release.

"So you do trust me."

Cailyn smiled. "Maybe not, my lady. But I want to."

"That's good enough for now, my little one," Teran said, her hand still wrapped around the back of Cailyn's head.

CHAPTER SEVENTEEN

Cailyn got the videocall the next morning. She had never heard from Lord Keriel before. Now, the day after the meeting, here he was, demanding she see him. She felt sure she knew the reason why.

The thought bothered her. Serving Teran while the intrigue swirled around her was quite enough for Cailyn already. She sighed and moved her fingers down to the smooth metal of the collar at her throat. It was warm from contact with her skin.

Keriel had given Teran the suit.

Or so Teran said.

If it was true, it meant that he wanted to see her torture someone. She didn't want to do it; he wanted to make her. But if even the dark channels made him queasy, why would he do this? The safety of the nobles, as Liana had said, or something else?

Lady Liana hadn't seemed to care much about giving Teran the job either. But Ben Keriel knew more about her than Lady Liana did. He would know that she protected the people she tortured.

Or some of them, anyway. Cailyn slid her fingers lower, down to the mark on her chest. Teran had torn up Cailyn's dress, laughed, and called it ugly.

Could Cailyn really expect better from a woman who scorned everyone?

You look lovely. A gem in a world of stones.

Lady Nivrai had, by her own admission, treated Cailyn uniquely. She had pampered Cailyn, giving her pleasure, coaxing her with sensual touch. Would she bother to do that with someone who had always loved pain?

Had she ever told anyone else about Mariel? Cailyn had drawn the confession out of her just the same as she had drawn pleasure.

Cailyn sighed, remembering their first encounter. When she came, she'd gasped like she was crying. Cailyn wanted that. To be a balm for some of the grief.

But now Teran was making it so hard. Tearing up her dresses. Mocking her tastes. Acting entirely too willing to do awful things.

And she hated Lord Keriel.

Cailyn's chest throbbed. It ached, but still she felt an answering hum between her legs. She wanted to believe Teran.

The only pain I want is yours.

She ran her fingers over the scrape on her chest. Touching it sent flares through her nerves. The small, effervescent burn made her think of sex. The feeling of Teran's fingers inside her, stretching her wide, exploring hidden places.

And hurting her, when she least expected it.

The only pain I want...

She let her hand fall and turned back to the computer in front of her. Why was this so hard?

The videoscreen beeped. She stared at the thin, red-haired face looking at her. What was he up to?

What was Teran up to?

She sighed and tapped the screen.

Cailyn's door slid open. She tapped the screen again and let Lord Keriel's face fade into blackness.

A hand gripped her shoulder. She tensed.

"Little one."

Cailyn turned her head. "My lady?"

In her other hand, Teran held a length of folded fabric. Bright and green.

"My dress," Cailyn whispered.

Teran lifted it up and let it fall. The rip Teran had torn in it was gone. Only a tiny wrinkle at one shoulder gave any evidence that the fabric had been damaged.

Teran ran a hand over the soft fabric of the dress. "Yes," she said. "Mended."

Cailyn swallowed hard. She reached out to touch the strap that Teran's claws had torn. She could feel a slight groove where the fabric had been sewn.

"This comes from a part of your life that doesn't involve me," Teran said. She reached out to touch Cailyn's face. "I shouldn't have meddled in it."

She laid the dress down on the desk in front of Cailyn, her movements slow and careful. Like the dress was precious and fragile. Like she needed to protect it.

"Thank you, my lady," Cailyn stammered. Just what did this portend?

Teran let out a breath. She wrapped her hand around Cailyn's chin. "I want you to trust me, little one."

Cailyn let herself smile. "Is that because my trust is important to you, or because it serves your ends?"

"It does serve my ends." Long fingers wrapped around Cailyn's chin and stroked her cheek. "But that's not all."

"You expect me to believe you after all this?"

Teran's head drooped. "No, little one. I wouldn't if I were you. But I hope you will, all the same."

She nibbled at the skin of Cailyn's neck. "Surely you've noticed that I'm fond of you."

Cailyn bit back a moan. "Yes."

"Do you think that I rub ointment on everyone who comes to me?"

"But that—that's part of what we do together, my lady."

Teran's lips brushed her cheek. "Don't you remember our first meeting? You were surprised I did it back then."

Cailyn's brow knit as she tried to remember. That seemed so long ago.

"I did it on a whim at first." Teran kissed her, her long fingers coaxing Cailyn into turning her head. Cailyn followed the direction but didn't return the kiss.

"Actually, I quite enjoyed it," Teran went on. "Then, when you came back again, I figured I might as well do it again."

One of Teran's hands moved to Cailyn's blouse, tracing patterns along the smooth fabric. The fingers slid over Cailyn's nipple until it hardened beneath the cloth.

Her other hand moved to Cailyn's neck and tapped at the metal circling it. She kissed Cailyn's mouth again. "I want things between us to be like they were before all of this. A matter of mutual desire. You're here for my pleasure. You asked for this. I'm here because the Councils want me here, but I brought you because I want you."

Teran kissed her hard. Cailyn opened her mouth to receive the kiss, wanting Teran to touch her. It would be so much easier to go back to those days.

She peered at the dress out of the corner of her eye. What more would she ever get than this apology? She wrapped her hands around Teran and held on.

"Come with me," Teran breathed. "I have better ways to apologize than feeble words."

To Cailyn's surprise, Teran led her to her own bed and bid her undress and lie down. She tapped at a spot under the mattress with her foot. A compartment sprang out. Inside lay a pair of restraints like the metal ones she'd used many times before. She slid them onto Cailyn's wrists and ankles, then kissed her feet and hands.

Her fingers slid up Cailyn's legs. "How do the others touch you?"

"The others?"

"This is supposed to be an apology." She traced soft kisses over the places where her hands had been.

Then she looked up. Her lips curled into a smile. "You like that, don't you, my little one?"

Cailyn twisted in her bonds. "Yes, but—"

"What?" Clawless fingers skimmed the surface of Cailyn's skin.

"You're not like the others. That's why I see you."

Teran licked the inside of Cailyn's thigh, then pushed her legs apart. Her tongue laved Cailyn's vulva once.

She looked up. "It tastes strange without blood."

Cailyn shivered again. Was that Teran's idea of a joke, or had she really never tasted anyone without making her bleed first?

Cailyn twisted in her bonds, pulling away from Teran's mouth. She wasn't ready for these caresses to soothe away her anger. She didn't want Teran to touch her like this. She didn't want to be calmed.

She could surrender to Teran. That would be easier. She could let herself be torn open by the pain. It could rip forgiveness from her in a scream, vivid and simple.

If Teran soothed her instead, she'd have to feel it first.

"My lady," she breathed, her tone carefully flattering. She tried to ignore the feeling of Teran's tongue against her skin.

Half of a courtesan's work was her facade. She'd never needed it for Lady Nivrai, hated to use it now. But she couldn't bring herself to turn Teran away.

She opened her mouth in an eager pout and spread her legs. "Take me."

"Is that what's bothering you?" Cailyn could hear the change in Teran's voice. "You would rather I was rough with you?" The claws, extended now, dug into her skin. "You'd rather that I—use you—"

"Yes," Cailyn gasped.

One of the hands reached to grip her breast, hard and bruising. "Teran's whore, is that it?"

The resonant voice filled the room, rich with arousal. Cailyn's eyes began to tear as Teran clutched and twisted at her breast.

"Is that what you want? For me to take you, use you, tear you apart with no regard for anything but our mutual pleasure?"

She laughed, piercing and clear. "I could do that." She loomed above Cailyn, her knee pressing hard into Cailyn's groin. Cailyn pushed back against it, her skin igniting to the pressure. Desire flared through her. She ground her vulva against Teran's thigh.

"Yes, I could easily do that," Teran purred, staring down at Cailyn as she writhed, her face swimming in Cailyn's vision.

She let go.

"My lady?" Cailyn blinked to clear away the tears.

"The question is: could you?"

Cailyn's breath came ragged as she gasped. "Could I do what?"

"You're angry with me. You haven't forgiven me."

"My lady, I—"

"It's the truth, isn't it? If I can't fight the Councils, will you still be Teran's whore?"

Cailyn forced her breathing to slow. As much as she wanted to think of nothing but the pulse between her legs, Teran was right.

Cailyn wanted to forgive her. But she hadn't. Not yet.

Feeling tears well in her eyes again, she shook her head. It made a nice dream, a beautiful woman ravishing her until she could no longer remember fear.

But it was a dream. "No. No, I couldn't."

Teran's eyes narrowed. The thigh pressing into Cailyn's vulva moved. Cailyn's skin tingled as Teran slid back down, kissing her body as she went.

"Then let me apologize properly, little one."

With a sigh, Cailyn lay back down. Teran kissed her chest and looked up.

"But you do have a point about not doing quite what the others do with you." She bit lightly at Cailyn's skin.

The small thrill of pain made Cailyn gasp, her back arching to meet Teran's mouth. Teran moaned softly in response.

"That's better," she said. Her lips slid down Cailyn's chest, then her stomach, then farther still. "Now, where was I?"

She didn't wait for an answer. A shudder went through Cailyn as Teran's tongue touched her flesh. She thrashed.

I should be serving you, she thought.

An arm, slender but strong, pushed her back down. Teran's tongue licked her flesh greedily. Powerful hands pushed Cailyn's body closer. She could neither avoid the seeking tongue intent on unmasking her, nor halt the passion rising in response to it.

Teran moaned. Did it please Teran so much to see her overwhelmed by pleasure? She'd done it once before, but made Cailyn bleed first. This time—

With a hungry cry, Teran lapped at Cailyn's clitoris. Cailyn felt herself seize up. Teran's hands clutched so hard she wondered if even the clawless fingernails could draw blood. She cried out as her body released, and she collapsed back into the soft sheets.

After a long moment, she looked down. Teran stared up at her, her gaze fierce and purposeful. She tried to look away, but it held her fast.

"What do you say, little one?" Teran asked. Cailyn blushed as Teran licked her lips. "Do you forgive me now?"

Cailyn floated in the aftermath of pleasure. What could she say? The suit still unnerved her. The memory of the torn dress was still fresh in her mind.

But no other noble she'd ever met would apologize like this.

She laughed as the aftershocks came again. "Maybe I do, my lady."

CHAPTER EIGHTEEN

A young boy answered the door. He had pale skin and a mop of wild red hair no amount of combing could tame, but under it his eyes were dark. He took one look at Cailyn and bounced away into the room.

"Father!" he called. "The woman you wanted to see is here."

Cailyn stepped back. Her father's clients had visited during her own girlhood. Innocent conversation had never done her any harm. Enough nobles saw courtesans that conferences like these almost always had soundproofed bedrooms.

But this boy's greeting made something flutter in her stomach. He'd be only a room away, no matter what passed between her and Lord Keriel.

"Coming, Dion," a familiar voice called.

The child pouted at Cailyn. "You know my mother."

Cailyn's eyes widened. This was Teran Nivrai's son?

She didn't see much of a resemblance. The hair looked like his father's. But the eyes looked nothing like Teran's gray eyes or Lord Keriel's green ones. Teran's mouth was thin and pale, but this boy's thick lips were pink and full.

She looked down at his hands and saw slender, long fingers. He fidgeted, as any child might. But the shape of those fingers—she shuddered.

Yes, those might come from Teran Nivrai.

But should she answer him? Teran had called it all a secret. What would she be courting if she acknowledged it?

And what if she didn't? Didn't this boy deserve to know something about where he came from, even if Teran hid herself from him?

Besides, if he knew who Teran was already, he already knew they'd come to the conference together.

Dion's brow furrowed. He glared up at her, tapping his foot in obvious impatience.

"Yes," Cailyn said at last. "Yes, I know your mother."

"That's hers around your neck."

His stare bored into Cailyn. That, she recognized.

Cailyn swallowed. How much could a boy so young know about what something like that meant?

"Yes, this came from her."

Dion brushed a lock of hair out of his face. "Do you like it?"

"I—what? Yes, I like it."

The boy grinned. He opened his mouth to ask another question. His father's hand on his shoulder stopped him. Lord Keriel's fingers gripped hard at the boy's shoulder. Cailyn could see the creases of the fabric under his hands.

"That's enough, Dion. This woman is my guest."

"But she knows my mother."

Cailyn tensed. But instead of letting loose with the angry outburst she expected, Lord Keriel smoothed his face into a smile.

"You can ask her about that later. Right now, I need to welcome my guest."

The boy didn't retort. He dragged his feet and sulked, headed back toward what Cailyn assumed must be his room.

Lord Keriel extended his hand to Cailyn. "I apologize for him."

Cailyn shook his hand. "He was curious, my lord. I don't blame him."

"I told him I had a visitor coming. I expected him to be gone when you arrived."

"Perhaps we should leave. Or postpone this meeting."

"He can leave instead."

"We can—"

"He is leaving. Now."

She heard a door open behind them. A servant in Keriel green ushered the boy out. He followed without protest, but Cailyn saw him cast a significant glance at her as she went.

"My lord," she tried again. He didn't answer.

Cailyn bit back a sigh. She followed him into a spacious bedroom with deep green walls. Large, pale-curtained windows opened out on a lush view. One wall bore a massive portrait of Dion. His curls fell in an orange blaze around his head. His expression under them was intense, too serious for such a young boy. Did he really glare like that most of the time, or was that artistic license to make him look more like a Keriel should?

Or more like a Nivrai?

Lord Keriel started to sit on the spacious bed in the center of the room. He thought better of it and walked over to Cailyn, his eyes fixed on her.

He stood even taller than Cailyn had thought. Long arms and legs hung from his slender frame. His mouth, thick-lipped like Dion's, smiled broadly, showing whitened teeth. Wrinkles around his mouth showed his age, older than Teran. His eyes glittered under his curls, bright orange as Dion's but less unruly. The double diadem showing his rank on the High Council shone around his forehead. His hands, like Dion's, were restless. His fingers twitched.

He wore the traditional colors of his house, a deep green matching his eyes. Elaborate embroidered leaves twined over his vest. Curls meant to represent their stems snaked between them. Over his heart, the pattern twisted into the Keriel symbol, stylized to look almost like a blooming flower.

He circled Cailyn, studied her from all angles, and came back to stand in front of her. He stared, drinking in the sight of her body. She could see a slight bulge beginning to appear in his pants.

Cailyn flinched under his stare. The bright, avid gaze sent a familiar thrill through her. It should have made her eager. But below the bright eyes, his smile curled into a scowling version of his son's pout.

"So you're the one she wants," he said at last.

His hands fell on her shoulders. He drew handfuls of her hair to his nose to smell its perfume.

"I can see why," he said, letting his hands drop slowly, as if reluctant to let go.

"Thank you for the compliment, my lord," Cailyn forced herself to say. "But I am not here to talk about Lady Nivrai's preferences."

He gripped her exposed shoulders. "Why else would you come here?"

"My lord, you called for me."

"We don't need pretenses."

Cailyn flinched in his grasp. "Pretenses, my lord?"

"You're her creature, after all."

His fingers trailed upward now. They settled around the blue metal of the collar. "You know what she thinks of me."

She flinched. "My lord, I would never presume to—"

His lips brushed her shoulder. "You don't want me. You want to know if she's right."

His kiss was soft and gentle. Cailyn wanted to be soothed, but her skin crawled under the touch. I should leave, she thought.

But if she left, she'd leave behind the chance to hear what happened, all those years ago. She expelled a shaky breath.

"She's wrong, you know. She's a shattered mirror."

"My lord?"

"What she tells you is all broken up. Exactly how she wants it to be."

Cailyn brushed his hand away. She stepped back, unable to bear his touch.

His head snapped up in surprise. "You don't want me. You want to know."

What could she say? True as it was, it felt wrong. Intrigue was for nobles.

"I—"

"I wanted her from the first moment I saw her."

Cailyn tried to move. Her feet refused to obey.

"My family has a spot on the High Council. Everyone treated me well, no matter what I did. They fawned over me, dancing around to catch my eye."

Cailyn laughed in spite of herself. "Nivrai didn't."

She thought back to Teran's welcome that first night. To those first touches, Teran's gentle, skilled fingers moving over her breasts. Even the steel had pierced her with care.

"Teran looked at me. That was all."

Cailyn nodded. Those eyes...

"My knees turned to water. I thought I might fall. She swept past me like I was nothing."

"And you wanted her."

"She was so beautiful. So beautiful and so sure." He reached out a hand, blind and groping. It clutched at Cailyn's arm. "I wanted so badly to touch her."

Cailyn wrapped her hand around his. Pushing him away would be too much, but if she needed to, she would.

"And she didn't want you."

"Nivrai is a rock full of nothing. I thought that she would jump at the chance to leave it."

"To be with you."

The long face twisted in misery. "I thought so, at first. Then, I thought she—"

His head turned. He stared at the door Dion had left through.

"I thought she would want a child destined for the High Council." He shook his head. "I mistook her coldness for ambition."

Cailyn laughed. Only her training kept the chuckles crisp and light. "My lord, that's not surprising."

"But in the end, she did agree."

Did agree. Because he threatened to cause a scandal, according to Teran. Cailyn scowled. Broken mirrors...

"And you got what you wanted," she said, her voice cold.

"Yes." He licked his lips and closed his eyes. "For months, I felt her body, lost myself inside her. I hoped my desire would wake something in her. I hoped I could draw her away from her cruelty."

Cailyn blinked. "You thought you could change Teran Nivrai?"

"I thought if I offered her enough..."

Cailyn said nothing. He slouched, drained, the brightness of unspent tears shimmering in his eyes.

"The child."

"Mothers are kind. Mothers soothe. Mothers nurture."

Cailyn shivered. *I felt nothing. They weren't wrong.* "You thought she would warm to him."

"Yes."

"But she never did."

His twisted face settled into a smooth, calm frown. "She never even nursed him. I decided on his name myself."

"My lord." She shoved down her misgivings and reached out a hand. Offering comfort was a courtesan's duty, one she had always loved.

He looked down. "As far as Nivrai was concerned, the child was a bargaining chip, nothing more."

He raised his head, his gaze fixed on Cailyn. "What are you?"

"What am I?"

"What does she see in you that she would keep you here so long?"

What did Lady Nivrai see in her? Cailyn had never dreamed she would like cruelty before meeting Teran. She'd never thought much of whips or paddles or fingers tipped with knives. Now she stared down at Lord Keriel's wide fingers, at his plain, flesh-colored fingernails. She sighed. How could someone get so deep in her head?

And however pained he seemed, Lord Keriel had no right to know. A courtesan's business was private.

Still, she had to answer his grief somehow. He'd carried it for so long. Now his son did, too.

"I don't know," Cailyn said at last.

"She certainly fancies you."

Cailyn blinked. "My lord, this isn't about me."

"She uses most of the courtesans once. She's called a few back, but only after years."

How did Lord Keriel know that? They couldn't tell him. Unless they ignored Guild law because he favored them.

Cailyn didn't like to think of it. But Lord Ben Keriel was on the High Council, after all.

"What's your secret, Derys? With anyone else, it would be your name. But Teran Nivrai would spit on the High Council's floor if she felt like it. What have you got?"

The twitching hands reached out again. They clutched at her blouse.

Cailyn grabbed at his hands and pushed them down. "My lord."

"Is it your name?" He licked his lips. "Is that what she wants?"

"My lord," Cailyn said again. "You'd have to ask her."

"So I might." His hands twitched under hers, but he made no move to break free of her grip.

"But what would I say?" His eyes darted from their locked hands to Cailyn's face. "Teran Nivrai, why the hell are you falling for Cailyn Derys?"

Cailyn gasped, so startled she let go. Her hand flew to her mouth. "Teran isn't—!"

Lord Keriel smirked. "Maybe you're right."

Cailyn hesitated.

"Go on, then," he said. "If I'm wrong, you have no reason to stay."

Cailyn took a deep breath and lifted her head. Stern and unsmiling, she spoke. "Why do you say that Lady Nivrai is falling for me?"

He snickered. "Because she acts just the same toward you as she did toward that stupid, hulking brute she kept hanging at her side."

Cailyn felt the room tilt. "What?"

"She likes having you," he said. He threw back his head and laughed. "Keeping you. In her room here. In her mansion at Nivrai for the weekends."

Cailyn blinked and put out a hand to steady herself. "Keeping me?"

"She wants to own you. Own you like she owned that brute."

Cailyn put a hand to her collar. She shivered, hearing Teran's voice in her head.

My little one...

Lord Keriel's hands, free now, tore at the fabric of her dress. He reached for her breast.

"Don't worry," he said, patting Cailyn's exposed skin with surprising gentleness. "I don't want to treat you like she does."

"My lord. Take your hands off of me."

He didn't move. "But I do want to know."

"Then you'll just have to be disappointed." Cailyn wrenched his hands off of her. She spat her stop word into the empty air.

He made no further move. He glowered, silent, as she moved away.

She tossed her colored scarf around her shoulders to cover the spot where his hands had torn her blouse and hurried out.

Chapter Nineteen

Teran stared at the colorful scarf. For a wild moment, Cailyn thought that she could see underneath it, see the tear Lord Keriel had made as plainly as if she'd left it uncovered.

"Welcome back. You weren't gone long."

Cailyn shook her head, the movement too violent. For a wild moment, she could think only that her trainers at the academy would be dismayed.

"My lady, you know I can't discuss that with you."

Teran shrugged. Cailyn remembered the computer, her frantic move to hide Lord Keriel's call from her.

"Lord Darien called me while you were out. I thought that might interest you."

"My lady?" Cailyn smiled in spite of herself. The memory of him inside her soothed some of the fear and anger she felt.

"I saw you look at him during the meeting. You certainly looked intrigued."

"I—"

"And if you did go on the dark channels, he's one of the best for beginners."

Cailyn couldn't help but laugh. Teran was entirely too good. "He does sound interesting."

"He called to invite us to a party. He throws them for the people on the dark channels sometimes."

"And you want to go." What was that saying? Too much is never enough?

"No. I don't go to them."

Bright steel pulled back Cailyn's hair. "I prefer to let the rumors feed themselves," Teran said into her ear. "I can't do that if I let them see me."

"Then why tell me this?"

"I have no desire to go. But I thought you might."

Cailyn swallowed, steel at her throat. "You really do want to see me on the dark channels. My lady."

Laughter answered her. "I intended only to invite you. But, yes. The idea does amuse me."

"My lady, I don't see why I would go."

"And I did want to mention Lord Darien to you. I'm meeting with him tomorrow to discuss the Councils' plans for me." She frowned.

Then one corner of her mouth turned up. "I thought I might give you to him when he visits."

"Give me to him?"

"If you consent, of course."

Cailyn thought of his fingers against her skin, of Teran's eyes, watching, staring. She leaned back against the soft lips at her neck.

"I thought you might like that." Teran kissed her again.

Her hands moved down to Cailyn's shawl. Its colors danced as she drew it off Cailyn's shoulders.

Clawed fingertips investigated the skin beneath it.

Teran arched an eyebrow. "Someone must have been excited."

It was Cailyn's turn to frown. "You're not supposed to ask. I thought you said you knew that."

"No, I'm not." The claws trilled along Cailyn's skin. "But since this is ruined anyway, it gives me an excuse."

Cailyn sighed, knowing what Teran was about to do. Still, the fabric was already torn. And this time, its rending would come from desire, not from pettiness or jealousy.

And she could stop it with a word, if she really wanted to.

Teran stared, her hand poised, unmoving.

Cailyn nodded.

A bright flash of newsteel glinted at her chest. The fabric tore. Teran's hands clenched hard around Cailyn's exposed chest. The claws bit into her skin.

"You're in a cruel mood," she said, gasping.

"I've been waiting for this," Teran answered. The claws retracted, but no respite came. Teran's slender fingers grabbed and twisted at her flesh.

Cailyn slid out of her skirt as Teran led her over to the cross against the wall in the bedroom. Teran slipped metal restraints on to Cailyn's wrists. The restraints shimmered as they shrank to seal against her skin.

Teran took down a whip from the wall. Cailyn recognized the braided whip that Teran had used before to. She gulped in air, remembering.

"What is this?" Teran chuckled. "If I'm going to offer you to Lord Darien, I have to make sure that your marks impress him." She laughed again, her voice rich and resonant. "We don't want anyone thinking their helldemon has gone soft."

Cailyn opened her mouth to answer, but the braided leather bit into her back. Her response became a shapeless scream. Her skin burned, as if Teran's strokes laid it open, tearing her flesh, exposing what lay beneath.

She cried out again and again as the thin strips of leather tore at her, the claws of some great animal. She thought for a moment of Teran, claws extended, cutting bloody lines into her back.

Need rose in her. It spread from her back to the space between her legs as she imagined Teran tearing at her flesh, hands smeared with her blood.

She clutched at the chains as Teran's rhythm began again. Her body swayed as the whip buffeted it. Her vision blurred.

Teran growled behind her. Cailyn twisted back to meet the whirling leather. Her mouth opened to let out the energy building in her flesh. A formless sound rose from her throat.

The world swirled in her vision, dancing in time to the rhythm of the whip, until Teran's whirling arm fell.

In the sudden silence, Cailyn gulped in air. The sound of her own ragged breath filled her ears.

She felt a hand against her chin. Teran's fingertips drew her head up.

"I want you," Teran growled.

Cailyn hung, the world still spinning, as Teran slipped on her harness. Teran unclasped her hands and pushed her to her hands and knees on the floor in front of the cross. Cailyn looked around and blushed.

Teran ignored it, entering her swiftly. Cailyn groaned as Teran filled her torn body, slamming into her over and over. The driving movements pushed her open, forcing her body to stretch wider around its invader. Raw heat flared through her nerves. She wailed louder.

Slender fingers gripped her flanks. The steel that tipped them bit into her skin. She could hear Teran behind her, Teran's gasps almost as ragged as her own.

Cailyn's body twitched. The steel dug hard—too hard—into her skin as Teran plunged into her body one final time. Cailyn spasmed hard around the dildo, pushed over the edge by Teran's pleasure.

Then the dildo plunged into her again.

She cried out, her eyes wet.

Nobles had used her like this before, over and over, intent on wringing as much pleasure as they could from her aching flesh. But now she could barely hold her head up. She wailed, desperate for more, desperate for all of this to end, as the endless rhythm consumed her.

Hisses and growls answered her, swirling in the flame that writhed in her flesh. She felt Teran buck harder, and she ground back on the thing inside her. Tears flowed freely from her eyes, blurring her vision again. The lights around the room danced, fey pinpricks of light before her eyes.

She came with a long, desperate sob. Her body clenched around the unyielding thing inside it. She collapsed as the world went white.

The dildo slid slowly out of her body. Without Teran close by to hold her up, Cailyn fell to the floor. She looked up from the ground, her flesh still twitching. Teran stared down at her, the ice-gray eyes bright.

Cailyn blinked under the ceiling lights. Blood moistened her back. Her throat hurt from screaming. Tears stained her cheeks. She couldn't remember crying them.

She reached out feebly to stroke the face above her.

"You liked that, didn't you, my little one?" Her voice was quiet.

"My lady?"

"I think you did. I'd know if you hadn't."

Cailyn nodded once, closed her eyes, and let darkness claim her.

Cool water dripped onto her forehead. The same face stared down above her; the same lights stung her eyes. She felt clean, warm sheets beneath her.

"Hello, my lady," she said.

"You did well."

Cailyn rubbed her eyes and sat up. "I did well?"

Her back stung, her welts rough against the soft sheets. "Was that some kind of test?"

A smile quirked one corner of Teran's mouth. "You could say that."

"And I passed."

It had felt good, too good, that last moment of pleasure cresting through her body.

Slender hands, gentle now, ran over Cailyn's skin. "Yes."

Cailyn's body arched. She willed it back to stillness, not ready to let desire well up in her again.

Teran busied herself with a water pitcher on the nightstand. She poured Cailyn a glass.

Cailyn drank deep. "I've never known anyone quite like you."

Teran leaned down and kissed her. "I've never known anyone quite like you either."

Cailyn blinked.

Teran held up one of her hands. She stared at it, watching the claws extend and retract. "Does that surprise you?"

"I'm surprised it impresses someone like you."

"Are you?"

"I fainted, my lady."

"You did."

"Half the courtesans on the dark channels probably do things like that for fun."

A corner of Teran's mouth quirked. "Probably."

"They probably don't also faint."

Teran laughed, silvery and clear. "You'd be surprised, little one. Two worlds," she said, reaching out to stroke Cailyn's hair. "Yours and mine. How can you span them both so well?"

Cailyn shrugged, trying to laugh it off.

But wasn't this another world? Hadn't Teran led her here? Hadn't she followed, coaxed by the promise of Teran's seductions? Hadn't Teran pushed until she broke?

She'd awoken with Teran's face staring down at her, bright with something like tenderness.

She wants to own you. Own you like she owned that brute.

She stared up at Teran, at the muscular body, at the small, high, proud breasts. She looked at Teran's hands, thought of their hidden, cruel promise. Her back throbbed in sympathy.

She wore Teran's collar around her neck. Teran's mark, obvious to everyone.

Her skin bore still more of them. She couldn't be coy and hide them. Not like she had before.

Which world did she belong to?

CHAPTER TWENTY

Cailyn traced the deep red gloss over her lips, studying her reflection in the mirror. Teran had dressed her in gauzy black garments that left nothing to the imagination, not even the welts and bruises her body bore.

She wondered what Lord Darien would think of the marks. He'd flogged Cailyn with a soft, easy touch. It had felt like any other lover's passion. He'd been sensual, even gentle. Would seeing her like this bother him?

Teran intended for him to see her marks. She would have had Cailyn cover them if she'd wanted him not to. But Cailyn's first concern would always be the one she served.

Besides, the thin mesh stung the marks on her back. The twinges of pain drew her attention, keeping her from focusing on the assignment at hand.

No doubt Teran Nivrai intended that too.

She ran her fingers over her hair, searching for stray curls to tuck in. Teran's servants had threaded pale white gems in her curls. They'd been nothing if not precise. Finding little to fix, she lowered her hands. She looked down at her wrists, adorned with beaded bracelets that matched the jewels in her hair.

The thick bands doubled as restraints. No doubt Teran planned to use them.

She stepped out of the bathroom to find Teran standing near a table. On it lay the stones she'd seen in the gymnasium.

Teran lowered her hands over them. Cailyn jerked as the shock lanced through her. Her eyes squeezed shut.

Cailyn had seen Teran earlier, on her way back from the gym, her body glistening with sweat. Cailyn had ached to touch her. A shower should have been the perfect excuse. But Teran had turned her away.

"I want you hungry when Lord Darien arrives," she'd said.

Now Teran stood silent and serious, her body veiled in the usual Nivrai gray. She opened her eyes and spared Cailyn a brief nod.

Cailyn knelt. When Darien came in, he would find her in the position, already waiting to serve him.

Teran walked over to Cailyn. She ran a gloved hand over her hair, down her chest. Cailyn shuddered with the brief contact.

So Teran really did mean to give her away. Her stomach clenched, even though she'd seen Lord Darien before. Even though she wanted to see him now.

The door slid open. He strode inside. He wore the same fancy clothes as before, his frilled shirt a pale blue. The diadem glistened against the dark brown skin of his forehead and the black of his close-cropped hair.

"Good evening, Nivrai," he said.

"My lord," Teran replied and inclined her head.

Cailyn's eyes widened. She'd never heard Teran say that like she meant it before.

"So why did you call me here?" he asked without even glancing at Cailyn.

Teran smiled. "My lord, I had hoped you would avail yourself of my hospitality before beginning this discussion." She gestured toward Cailyn.

His smile widened. He stepped over to Cailyn and reached down to touch her hair. "I might do that."

Memories flooded Cailyn. What would he do with her? Whatever it was, she hoped he would do it soon. He wasn't even grabbing her hair or pulling her head back! She breathed deeply and forced herself to keep still.

"But I want to know what you're looking for first," he said. He stroked Cailyn's hair but still looked at Teran.

Damn it.

"Looking for? I'm looking for some help with this nonsense the Councils just conscripted me for."

"Nonsense?"

"I have no interest in torturing some dissident foolish enough to get caught."

Lord Darien sighed. "And you think I can fix this for you."

"As usual, they've made assumptions about me. As usual, they're wrong."

"You haven't given them much to counter those rumors, Nivrai."

"Should I?" She moved to stand in front of him. "I think not, my lord."

"Don't play those games with me, Nivrai."

"Games?"

"You can play the little monster with me. I won't bother you. But I can't save you from everyone who will."

"It's not saving I need, my lord. It's advice."

The bearded mouth broke into a grin. "I think I can offer that."

Bloodless as Teran's smile was, Cailyn could see a light in her eyes. "Then by all means, avail yourself of my hospitality."

"What did you have in mind?"

"Use her mouth. The rest of her is mine for now."

"Very well." He unfastened his pants, drew out his length, and moved to stand over Cailyn.

Eager from the long wait, she moved to lick the flesh he offered. She traced her tongue along his flesh and he shuddered. Pleased, she opened her mouth and drew him in.

His hands wrapped around her head, guiding her as her mouth moved over him. Encouraged, she moved more quickly.

His hands tightened around her head and pushed her harder. He wasn't touching her, but little thrills of heat crackled over her flesh as if he had.

Her eyes flicked over to Teran, who lay sprawled on the couch watching them. Her hand dangled between her legs. The thought of Teran drinking in the sight of her as someone else used her, sent a thrill of desire through Cailyn's flesh.

But as much as Cailyn liked the thought of Teran touching herself watching them—what was she doing? She should be concentrating on the noble she served, not staring at Lady Nivrai.

Relief surged through her as Darien's thrusts into her mouth grew more insistent. It forced her attention back on him. She gave herself over to serving him, making her mouth a warm channel for him. Her hips moved as he groaned and pushed deep.

She quickened her pace. He shuddered and threw back his head. His hands tightened around her hair as his seed flooded her mouth. Strong hands held her there a long moment. She opened her throat and swallowed.

Teran chuckled as he drew away. *What are you getting out of all this, my lady?*

"Is that all?" he laughed as Cailyn licked her lips.

"My lord?" Teran asked. She sat up. Cailyn stared, still thinking about Teran touching herself through her clothes. "The flagellary is inside. But I don't know yet how well our negotiations will go."

"Oh, so that's what this is about? If I give you what you want I get to use her again?"

Teran chuckled. "Maybe, my lord."

"That's not very tempting. She already consented to this. What's to stop me from just hiring her after this is over?"

Teran smirked. "Nothing, my lord. But I think it's best to press my advantage where I can."

"You have a point." He tucked himself away and took a seat on the opposing couch.

"So what is it you think I can help you with? The Councils made their decision a long time ago, Nivrai."

"I understand, my lord."

"Warning you about it was the best I could do."

Teran twisted her gloved hands as she looked at him. Did he know what lay under them?

"And I appreciate your warning. Few people would do even that for me."

"Then what more do you think I can do, Nivrai? I defended you when we first met about this. I told the Councils they were both packs of damn fools. But I lost, Nivrai. Do you understand that? I lost."

"My lord—"

"My only advice is to go along with them, Nivrai."

What?

Cailyn wrapped her arms around herself, suddenly cold. The only noble she'd seen listen to Teran was telling her to do the Councils' bidding.

Teran's lips thinned to a narrow line. "Is the person behind this who I think it is? Just answer that for me."

He shook his head. "I shouldn't tell you."

"I need to know, my lord."

"You know already."

Cailyn heard a metallic sound.

"If you want to get out of this, Nivrai, giving him what he wants is the only chance you've got."

"Giving him what he wants." Teran smiled, a bitter, twisted expression that chilled Cailyn.

"I don't like it any more than you do, Nivrai."

"You really mean to tell me, my lord, that if I bed Lord Keriel he can change the minds of both Councils?"

Bed him? Was that what Ben wanted? Cailyn remembered the grasping hands, the long face twisted into a rictus of despair.

He'd said he craved her touch. Would he set all of this in motion just to force her to touch him again?

"Nivrai, listen—"

Teran's voice rose. "That after he takes his pleasure with me, he can simply go to them and say 'Never mind?'"

"Teran—"

"That he can tell them the prisoner had no information after all, and—"

"Nivrai!" Darien barked.

Teran fell silent. She glared back at him with the fierce stare of a hawk.

"I wasn't talking about Lord Ben. I was talking about your son."

"My son?"

"He's asked you to see him. Hasn't he?"

"He has."

"I'm not saying you should give your body to Lord Keriel. Or anything else. I'm saying you should visit the boy."

"I have no interest in the boy."

"Damn it, Nivrai. The boy is your son."

"That was a contract of convenience, nothing more."

Darien's face darkened. "It's no sacrifice to say hello to a ten-year-old boy, Nivrai."

"Sacrifice? No, it isn't. But what will that do for me?"

"Maybc nothing. I don't have the influence to call this off. Keriel may not either. Not anymore."

Teran's hands twitched. "Not anymore?"

"They like the idea. They thought Ben was a crazy man with a vendetta at first, but now they like it. The most feared of the nobility, the one even they worry about, exacting their revenge for them."

Cailyn watched the black-gloved hands clench and heard Teran hiss.

Darien shook his head. "I told you already, I don't like it either, Nivrai."

Teran opened her mouth to respond. She looked over at Cailyn and closed it again.

She turned and nodded to Darien, the movement crisp. "The flagellary is in the bedroom, over there."

"Thank you, Nivrai." He offered a hand to Cailyn. She took it, rose to her feet, and followed.

CHAPTER TWENTY-ONE

Teran didn't follow them. Cailyn cast a surprised glance at the doors as they closed behind her. Did Teran really trust Darien enough to let him do whatever he wanted? She glanced back at the door, remembering Teran's eyes on them earlier. As much as her flesh thrilled to the thought of Darien using her again, she missed Teran's hungry gaze.

Then again, Teran had to be watching.

Darien reached out to remove Cailyn's blouse. He whistled, seeing the welts on her back no longer veiled by the gauzy fabric.

She slid off her pants to reveal the bruises on her buttocks. He patted them, grabbed a handful of bruised skin, and twisted at it. Cailyn gasped, half in protest, half in pleasure.

Lord Darien sighed. "She didn't leave me much to work with."

Cailyn closed her eyes and took what he offered. The part of her that wanted more didn't matter. All that mattered was his will.

He led her over to the cross and bound her there facing him, stroking the pearl bracelet restraints. He grinned in approval as he ran his fingers over her breasts and nipples. She twisted in her bonds, desperate to reach him.

His fingers moved to the long scrape down Cailyn's chest. "That's impressive."

"Is that a compliment, my lord?"

"That depends. Did you enjoy it?"

Had she? She had enjoyed the sex. She had enjoyed Teran's fingers tearing through her. Her skin had opened, suddenly, without warning, in a crescendo of pain. Teran had spilled vakren over the cut, swift and searing.

She had come from it. Come because it overloaded her senses, and because Teran wanted her to. But she'd barely known what was happening.

"That's a difficult question," she said at last. "My lady is not as kind as you are, my lord."

"I'm sure she's not. But you're not—" He bit off the words. Cailyn figured he didn't want to mention their last tryst, just in case Teran might really be watching them.

So he suspected cameras here too, then. Cailyn felt a pulse between her legs.

"—but you're not known on the dark channels. Most people who see Nivrai have experience. I don't need to hear them tell me so to know it. And most of them have a strong yen for pain."

Cailyn nodded. She wished he would stop asking questions, touch her again, hurt her, use her. "I didn't when she first called me."

His eyebrows shot up. "First? You've seen her more than once?"

Cailyn's mouth snapped shut. She'd said too much already.

Still, she did wear Teran's collar. No one would devote herself to a noble for an entire conference without ever seeing her first.

"Don't worry about me, my lord," she said after a long moment. "I can take care of myself."

He laughed. The sound rolled through the room. "I'm not worried about you, daughter of Loriel Derys. If you couldn't take care of yourself, someone would have discovered that long before Nivrai found you."

He kissed her, his lips soft against her own. Her mouth opened greedily. With another broad laugh he kissed her again. His tongue slid deep into her mouth.

She thought of Teran again even as her body sighed open. What would Teran think watching Cailyn surrender to someone else?

Would she feel proud, pleased that Cailyn's service reflected well on her?

Would it make her jealous, fierce, fill her with a yen to take and use what was hers? Cailyn sighed into Darien's mouth, imagined pale eyes sharp with possession.

That change in Teran's voice, the way it went lower and richer when she felt desire. Would she sound that way when Cailyn went back inside?

Darien ran his fingers over Cailyn's nipples again. She strained to better reach him.

"You like that, don't you?" he said into her ear. She gasped out a yes.

He took a soft flogger from the wall and ran the leather tails along Cailyn's skin. They danced over her nipples, teasing them erect.

He let fly with them, the leather crashing against the sides of her breasts. She twisted, wild and desperate, not caring that it hurt. She wanted more, wanted this, wanted him.

He laughed. The sound filled her ears as his motions answered hers.

"Please."

The handle of the whip came up to caress her vulva. She rubbed herself against it, decorum forgotten.

"Easy there." The whip pulled away. Cailyn whimpered. Strong hands reached to undo the restraints around her wrists.

He led her to the bed. His hand pressed against her back as he bent her over it and reached to free himself from his pants again.

Cailyn cried out in relief when he entered her, quick and forceful. She arched back hard against him, gasping at the feeling of his flesh.

He groaned and thrust hard, clutching at her hips as he drove into her body. She moved with him, pleasure rising in her flesh. She could come any moment now.

She gritted her teeth and fought against the heat building inside her. She would hold it for him, release only when he did, take his pleasure as her permission.

He groaned long and loud as he came, his head thrown back as he cried out. Cailyn let out a breath and shuddered around him.

His hands relaxed against her skin as her body pulsed with aftershock. He pulled out of her a moment later.

What would Teran think of Cailyn's body now, full of someone else's emissions? Would it please her? Anger her? What would she think of her courtesan now, slumped over the bed with someone else looming over her?

She shook under his patient hands. He reached out to help her to her feet.

Then he kissed her, hard.

The door slid open. Teran stepped into the room. Startled, Cailyn broke the kiss. She turned to look at Teran, Lord Darien's arms still wrapped around her.

"Lovely."

Cailyn thrilled to Teran's voice—her lady's voice. Her breasts ached, red and sensitive from the whipping. She looked down at them, imagined Teran's hands doing what Lord Darien had done to her buttocks. Gripping the newly marked skin, twisting, prodding.

Running steel over the reddened skin.

Lord Darien couldn't do that.

"I'm glad you approve, Nivrai," Darien laughed.

Teran shook her head. She walked around them, her gaze sweeping over their still-entwined forms.

"Thank you for your advice. I may take Lord Keriel up on that— if I can see the boy without him."

She moved over to Cailyn, who broke from Darien's embrace. A black-gloved hand reached to play with Cailyn's hair.

Darien chuckled. "I'll leave you to your own devices, then."

When he had gone, Teran tossed off the black gloves and extended her claws. Cailyn stared, mesmerized.

Steel against her chin coaxed Cailyn into looking up. "Worried, my little one? You shouldn't be. I gave you to him. You did what he wanted."

Teran's lips were soft against Cailyn's. Cailyn opened her mouth as Teran's teeth worried her lip. She wrapped her arms around Teran.

"Get back down," Teran snarled. Strong arms shoved her back down onto the bed.

Cailyn heard her rummage through a drawer and draw something out. She shifted her eyes, trying to see. A hand on her back let her know that Teran had noticed, and wanted her to be still.

"Someone else left his mark on you just now," she said into Cailyn's ear. "Used you, too."

Something cold and metallic pressed against her entrance. She shivered, her sore breasts aching, as Teran pushed the object in, her body stretching to receive it.

"I'm not so sure I like that," Teran said, her voice still sharp and cold. Cailyn trembled. Teran had given her away, but she felt almost as if she'd snuck out.

She had said once, long ago, that she had no need to punish the courtesans who submitted to her. But she had never, to Cailyn's knowledge, given anyone away before.

"So I'll just have to use you better," Teran finished. "You belong to me. At least for now."

Teran's breath quickened as the cold metal disappeared inside Cailyn. Cailyn bucked, feeling it fill her, driven by the force of Teran's arm. It split her wide, pushed her open, more hard and unyielding than flesh could ever be.

Cailyn gasped as it rent her. A steel-tipped hand pressed her face down.

She steeled herself and moved back on it. Seeing her wince would spur Teran on. She served Teran's pleasure now.

The warming metal picked up speed. She twisted under its onslaught and cried out. Her body gripped it hard and then released.

Teran pulled the metal free. Cailyn whimpered, suddenly empty. Her insides stung from the stretch.

"He thinks I should see my son," Teran said, her voice soft. "What do you think, my little one?"

Cailyn blinked. "You're asking me that now, my lady?"

Teran chuckled. Her fingers moved over the welts along Cailyn's back.

Cailyn willed herself to think about the question. She remembered the boy greeting her, bounding away when Lord Keriel called.

He'd asked about Teran. *That's hers, around your neck. Do you like it?* What would Teran think if Cailyn confessed he'd mentioned it?

According to Lord Keriel, not much. She hadn't even named him.

Cailyn licked her lips. "I think you should see him. I'd like to see him too."

Steel played over Cailyn's skin. "Teran's whore, curious about Teran's son?"

Cailyn winced. Did Teran have to like that word so much? "My lady, if he's half as interesting as his mother is, it'll be a fascinating evening."

Teran's lips slid over Cailyn's neck and chin. She kissed the metal of Cailyn's collar. "Maybe you're right. The son of a helldemon. What has the world made out of him?"

Cailyn sighed, relieved. Teran was intrigued.

That meant she'd see him.

She tilted her head up, wrapped her hands around the back of Teran's head, and kissed her mouth.

CHAPTER TWENTY-TWO

Dion sat across the table, pouting. He poked at the bowl of candy laid out in front of him. He picked one of the candies up, turned it around in his hands, and set it down again.

"They won't poison you, Dion," Teran said. "I don't mean you any harm."

Dion glowered. He made no reply.

Teran sighed. "All right," she said. "If you won't trust me, here."

She slid off her glove and held up her hand. The retracted claws shone silver.

They extended with a familiar click. Dion stared, his dark eyes wide.

Teran gave him a moment to gawk. Then she reached down and snatched up the candy Dion had dropped on the table. With a fluid motion, she sliced it in half.

"See? Nothing."

She dropped the halved candy into her mouth, chewed, and swallowed.

"Now you." She offered him the other half.

Still staring, he grabbed at it. He chewed slowly, his eyes locked on Teran's.

Cailyn looked from Dion to Teran. Teran had always taken such pains to hide her claws. Now she was showing them off at the first opportunity.

That would get around.

At the very least, it would get back to her worst enemy.

Teran drummed her hands on the table. Dion stared down at them.

"Why do you have those?" he asked. He looked over at Cailyn. "Did you get them for her?"

Teran chuckled. "No."

"Then why do you have them?"

"I got them for someone else, a long time ago."

"What were they for?"

Cailyn winced.

"You go straight to the difficult questions," Teran said. "I like that."

"Nobody else does."

"That doesn't surprise me."

Dion tilted his head. "How did you ask the questions you wanted?"

Teran smiled. "I found someone who knew what I wanted to know. Convinced them to give me what I wanted." She clicked the claws on the table for emphasis.

Dion looked up. He scowled again, trying to look menacing. Cailyn bit back a laugh. "Okay. Now tell me what I want to know."

Teran's smile widened. "Tell me exactly what you're asking."

Dion chewed his lip. "I want to know what you do."

"What I do?"

"People say you hurt people. They say you take people away if they misbehave."

Teran Nivrai, helldemon. Did parents say she snatched children up, took flight on implanted wings, and spirited them away to Nivrai?

Teran had the same thought. "Is that what they say? 'Teran Nivrai will get you if you don't clean your room?'"

Dion nodded, his hair bouncing.

"But that's not what I want to know," he added, his tone solemn again. "She's nice. Pretty. And she follows you. Are you cruel to her too?"

Cailyn folded her hands in her lap. She smoothed her face into a mask, glad for the training that had taught her how to do it.

Teran didn't hesitate. "Well," she answered, her voice silken, "I'd think the best person to answer that question would be Cailyn."

Me? Cailyn's eyes widened.

Dion turned his head. His gaze fixed on Cailyn. "Tell me."

Cailyn cleared her throat. "I do what I am bid to do."

A familiar half-smile curled one corner of Dion's mouth.

"Sometimes things—" she glanced at the steel-tipped hands resting on the table "—are difficult."

"Do you have to do it?"

"We choose who we work for. I chose to stay with Lady Nivrai."

"You want to?"

"I wouldn't work for her if I didn't want to."

Cailyn took a deep breath. There. She'd said it.

The words sounded bizarre to her own ears. Had she really done those things? Had she really welcomed them? It felt like talking about someone else, justifying the strange behavior of the wildest courtesan on the dark channels.

Dion stared fixedly at Teran's claws. They gleamed in the light. "And those?"

"The tips can be gentle," Teran said.

"But they're like little knives. You could really hurt people with them."

"Yes, if I chose to."

"It must be fun to have those." He smirked. "You can scare anyone you want."

Teran chuckled. "Most people don't know I have them. But I could frighten people with them if I wanted to."

If she wanted to. Cailyn choked back a laugh.

"Did I frighten you, Dion?"

"A little," Dion mumbled and looked down.

He raised his head and turned to Cailyn. "You could even scare her, if you felt like it." His grin widened.

Cailyn shivered. Had Teran smiled like that as a child?

"If I chose to, I could." Teran's eyes glittered. "But if I really hurt her, I don't think she would come back."

Dion nodded. "That would be bad. She's pretty," he said again. "She likes you."

A steel-tipped hand moved to cover Cailyn's. Teran turned to look at her. The hand on Cailyn's twitched. "She is one of the best. You're right, Dion. I would be a fool to overdo it."

Cailyn fought not to blink. Was Teran trying to be tender, or was she just interested in reassuring her son that she wasn't insane?

And why did she care so much about his opinion, anyway? Ostensibly, she cared because Lord Keriel would value the overture. Offering him candy and making small talk were more than enough for that.

But here she was, telling the boy everything he wanted to know. Including about Cailyn.

Cailyn studied Teran's face, her pale eyes, her bloodless lips. Was she—could she be—fond of him? She'd abandoned him a decade ago.

Dion looked at the claws and at Cailyn. He drummed his fingers on the table, all excited energy. "And you can do whatever you want?"

Teran held up a steel-tipped hand. "That's enough, Dion." She chuckled. "You have plenty of time to learn when you get older, if you want to. I'm not here to teach you."

Dion blushed and covered his face. "I'm sorry."

He grabbed a handful of candies and stared down at them, pretending to be intensely interested in them.

"Mother," he added after a moment.

Teran didn't reply. Silence stretched between them.

Cailyn wanted to say something, save the moment with the wit the academy had trained into her. But the words lodged in her throat.

At last, Teran spoke, her voice soft. "You probably think I owe you an apology."

Dion didn't answer.

"It's true," Teran said. "I do. I neglected and ignored you."

"You did." Dion's face twisted into a snarl. "So why should I forgive you?"

"You shouldn't forgive me, Dion. Not unless you want to."

"I shouldn't?"

"You can think whatever you want about me. You can hate me if you want to, Dion. The gods know you have a better reason for it than most people do."

Dion's scowl uncurled. "Well, then. I don't like you."

A frown flitted across Teran's face. She did not blink and stared straight ahead.

"But most people don't like me either," Dion said.

Teran nodded. She said nothing else.

Dion stood and grabbed another handful of the candies.

"I'm going to go now."

"Very well," Teran said. She slid her gloves back on as she stood. "But I have something to say before you go."

Dion turned.

"Take those silly things out of your eyes. They don't become you."

Cailyn blinked. What did Teran mean by that? She followed Teran out of the room. So did Dion, who rushed over to the cushioned chair where his father sat.

Lord Keriel reached down to give the boy a hug. Dion hugged back and cast a glance over his shoulder. He looked more interested in Cailyn than in his father.

Without a word, he dashed out of the room.

Lord Keriel straightened and faced Teran.

"Nivrai," he said.

"My lord."

"You met with the boy."

"I did." She bowed her head but glared up at him.

He sighed. "Does this mean you're willing to be a part of his life now?"

"My lord?"

"Your fighter is gone. Are you ready to be a mother to your son?"

Teran's teeth clenched. The gloved hands twitched behind her back.

"I did what you asked me to do, my lord."

"What I asked you to do? Nivrai, this is about—"

"You wanted me to meet with the boy," she snapped, cutting him off. "I did. Now will you tell the Councils this whole thing is a farce?"

"I can't do that. You know I can't."

Silver peeked through the tears in the leather. "Do I, my lord?"

"The decision has already been made."

Teran's lips drew back in a snarl. "Has it, now?"

"Nivrai, there's nothing I can do for you."

Teran laughed, a cracked glass sound. "Then do you really want me meeting the boy fresh from a session with the prisoner?"

"Nivrai—"

"If you can't help me, there is nothing I can do for you."

"My lords—" Cailyn reached out a hand and put it between them.

But Teran had already walked away. Cailyn sighed out an apology and turned to follow.

They were halfway down the hall by the time Cailyn asked the question burning in her brain.

"Your son—"

"What about him?"

"You said something about his eyes."

"Yes."

"What did you mean?"

Teran turned. "Dion looks like his father, don't you think? He has his hair, his nose, his features."

"That's true. If I didn't know he was yours, I—"

"It's an advantage."

"An advantage?"

"I don't have to acknowledge it." She chuckled. "And Lord Keriel won't have to mention it for years either."

Cailyn stopped in her tracks. "But Lord Keriel is obsessed with you!"

Teran's brows knitted. Her lip curled in the beginning of a frown.

Cailyn pressed her lips together. Damn it.

"How do you know that?"

"I—from what you tell me, he still misses your attentions."

Teran said nothing for a long moment. Then she spoke. "You wanted to know about my son's eyes."

"I did."

"My eyes are pale. My lord's eyes are green. Both light colors. Isn't it odd that Dion's eyes are almost black?"

Cailyn's eyes widened. "You mean his eyes are light—"

Teran nodded. The claws extended. "His eyes are gray. Like mine."

CHAPTER TWENTY-THREE

Teran's fingers twined in Cailyn's hair. "Tell me about the lovers you've had."

Cailyn blinked up at her. "I can't, my lady. You know that."

"Not your clients. Your lovers."

"My lovers?" Cailyn struggled to focus as Teran's lips and teeth worried her flesh.

"What do you want in someone who isn't us?"

"My lady, that's a very personal question."

"Or do you live only to serve?" She laughed, rich and resonant.

Cailyn looked up. Did Teran want into every part of her life? "No. I've had lovers."

Teran laughed into Cailyn's skin. "Tell me about them."

She shouldn't, Cailyn knew. Teran had no right.

But no noble had ever asked. Not like this. Not without demanding something. Why should they want to know about her life?

And Cailyn had learned quite a bit about Teran's life these last few days. A hidden affair. A secret son. A High Councilman with a disturbing obsession.

Could she hide from someone who'd shown her so much of herself?

"I never had any until I went to the courtesans' academy." She shook her head. "I'd decided my purpose in life early. I thought I should wait."

Teran chuckled.

"That didn't last. I fell for a woman in my classes."

She blushed, remembering. "We ate together, sat together, talked together. At first, I thought we were just good friends, but—"

"But."

"We had lessons: how to touch, why, where. We studied techniques. When we came to the lessons on women, she came to me late one evening. She wanted to see if they worked."

Teran smirked. "I take it they did."

"We spent that evening exploring one another, trying the things we'd read about. I wanted to stay with the things we were learning. I wanted to be sure I had them right. I wanted to be elegant, skilled, refined." She chuckled. "My friend just wanted to try everything."

"Mmm. So she put you up to it, then? She led you, even there?"

"Maybe she did. But I wanted her as much as she wanted me. We saw each other often after that."

"I'm sure you did."

"We would try the things we had learned. Do whatever else we thought of."

Cailyn closed her eyes. Her lover had broad, thick fingers. To an academy that prized delicate features and precise grace, that meant "less beautiful." But Cailyn had never minded. Those fingers and hands had filled her up perfectly well.

Cailyn sighed. She hadn't seen anyone she went to the academy with in years. She hadn't had many lovers either. She'd realized her work wasn't everything, but still had little time for her own life.

"What about you, my lady?"

Teran bit her again. She shuddered.

"Me?" Teran whispered it against her neck.

"I know you've seen courtesans from the dark channels. I know about Mariel. Is that all?"

"Is that all?"

"Were you—were you always—cruel, as you are now?"

"I was always the same, little one." Steel ran across the spot Teran bit and dug into Cailyn's skin.

Blood welled up from the cut. Teran lowered her mouth to the wound. Her tongue traced over it, and Cailyn's worry dissolved into pleasure.

"People stared at me even as a child. They didn't like me, even then." She growled against Cailyn's skin. "I rarely spoke. I had nothing to say to anyone. My parents wondered who they might marry me off to, and despaired of finding anyone."

"And you went on the dark channels."

"I did."

"Because you were tired of people who didn't want the things you did."

Teran sucked at Cailyn's wound. "No. I went on the dark channels immediately."

Why am I not surprised? "You knew what you wanted so young?"

"These people and their gentleness. I never had any taste for it."

"You've touched me gently," Cailyn protested, her voice soft.

"I have. But do you remember the first thing I did when I saw you for the first time?"

"You put your hands on me," Cailyn said, closing her eyes to better remember. She had expected a blow, force, anger. Instead, Teran had caressed her skin, as anyone else might.

"And then what?"

Cailyn reached a hand up to her neck. "You pricked me."

"Yes." Teran sucked hard at Cailyn's wound. Cailyn yelped. Her hand went to her mouth. Courtesans should never make noises like that, she chided herself.

"I like touching you," Teran said. "But do you think I would have stayed interested in you if that had been all I did that night?"

"No, I don't." Cailyn reached out to wrap her arms around Teran. "But I'm glad you did it, all the same."

"So am I." Teran raised her head and licked the blood off her lips. "But that's not why you're here."

Cailyn's mouth twisted into a wry grin. "I know."

"I never understood what other people did. I knew what they wanted, or said they wanted. But why settle for touching someone's skin when I could find my way inside it?"

Her lips brushed Cailyn's wound again. Pain flared through Cailyn's flesh again as Teran's lips dragged slowly across the cut.

Cailyn gasped again. How could she answer? She had never thought of pain at all, not until one of the nobles told her that he'd dabbled on the dark channels, years ago. He'd missed some of the things he'd tried, wanted to flog her. She'd wanted to please him. He hadn't seemed the type to try anything extreme.

It hadn't hurt. Not the way he did it. Like Lord Darien had the first time. The rhythm against her skin had felt like massage. She'd liked the experience but hadn't wanted to repeat it. Why seek out pain for its own sake?

"I don't understand, my lady."

"Why not?"

"People who don't want pain confuse you? You don't want it yourself."

Teran smirked. "Is that so?"

She sat up and gestured for Cailyn to do the same. Wondering what this portended, Cailyn obeyed.

Teran grabbed at Cailyn's hand. She guided it to her other hand and laid it there. Cailyn raised an eyebrow and wrapped her hand around Teran's.

The claws extended, peeking out from under their hands. Teran brought them toward her own chest but stopped just when the claws nearly touched her.

"Go ahead." Teran let go of Cailyn's hand. Her claws hovered just over her own exposed skin.

"I can't," Cailyn said.

It was one thing to let Teran hurt her. By now, Cailyn was used to that. But to hurt Teran? She'd never bargained for that.

Teran snickered. "I've tasted your blood. Don't you want to taste mine?"

Cailyn bit off the words *No, of course not. This is insane.*

Teran Nivrai had said so much about blood and skin. Now she offered them to Cailyn. What would she do if Cailyn didn't take the offering?

"I'll cut you too deep," she mumbled.

"It's my own finger. I only want you to guide it."

Cailyn closed her eyes, mumbled a short prayer, and opened them again. With halting movements, she brought their hands downward.

Teran hissed as the claw dug into her skin. The small sound became a deep, full moan as Cailyn dragged their hands along her skin.

Did it feel the same way to Teran as when Teran did it to her? Cailyn had made vows years ago, devoted herself to her work, to her goddess, to offering service in her goddess's name. If she enjoyed what Teran did to her, she enjoyed it because she liked giving pleasure.

Did Teran like the way this felt?

Cailyn drew their hands away and stared at the bright red line the claw left, vivid crimson against Teran's skin.

Her stomach turned. Had she really just done that?

Teran grinned. "Now taste it."

"My lady, I'm not like you. I don't want the things you want."

A steel-tipped hand circled the back of her neck and pulled her head down. "What makes you think you have a choice?"

Cailyn opened her mouth. Warm, coppery liquid filled it. She choked, coughing at the unfamiliar taste. Teran's hand pressed and held her there, pitiless, unforgiving.

Teran gasped, a ragged murmur of pleasure.

Sometimes Cailyn moaned or pleaded not because she wanted something but to encourage her lady or lord. Did Teran like the pain or just like toying with Cailyn?

Whether Teran meant it or not, heat stirred in Cailyn's flesh at the sounds Teran made.

What the hell was she doing?

Teran's grip relaxed. She snatched her hand away. She stared down at the wound and the smeared blood like it had seared her.

Teran drew Cailyn's mouth to hers. Her tongue lapped at the blood on her lips and in her mouth. Cailyn shuddered, but at least Teran's lips and tongue would wipe away the stain. She opened her mouth to offer better access, wanting all of it gone.

"So," Teran said, "did you enjoy tasting me?"

"I—my lady—you know I've never been one for blood."

"Is that so?"

"I'd never want to do that to you."

"You seem to like when I take it from you." Her head bent to Cailyn's wound.

Her hand slid down to Cailyn's vulva, smearing Cailyn's wetness on her fingers. "See?"

Cailyn twitched. She heard the familiar click of the claws retracting, took a deep breath. She braced herself for the inevitable, and a moment later, the fingers slammed inside her, sudden and pitiless.

Teran's lips sucked hard at her wound. Cailyn shivered as the fingers drove into her again and again. She bucked again, barely aware of what she was doing.

Teran slipped another finger inside. Cailyn writhed, overwhelmed by sensation. Did Teran have to start again so soon?

Cailyn trembled, overloaded. She twitched like a marionette as Teran's fingers moved inside her, panted as they plunged into her again and again. She gulped in air and shuddered. Her flesh clenched tight around Teran's fingers.

The fingers slid out of her as her mind spiraled to earth.

"I ought to arrange something for you," Teran said.

"Arrange something?"

"You're used to me."

Cailyn blinked. "My lady, I don't think I will ever be used to you."

Teran snickered. "You are. Used to me and used to serving. But you were so reluctant just then."

"My lady, I'm not like you. I would never choose to give pain like you do."

"What would happen with someone else?"

Cailyn shivered. "Someone else?"

Teran kissed her. "People on the dark channels would be delighted with you, my little one."

CHAPTER TWENTY-FOUR

S o you're not going to resist, then."
Teran shook her head. "I have nothing to gain from defying the Councils."

"Nothing to gain? How can you say that?"

"Neither Darien nor Ben will do anything for me."

Cailyn kept her hands at her sides, but clenched them into tight fists. "This is about them, my lady? What they're willing to do for you?"

"Without Ben's help, Darien's help, or both, there's nothing I can do."

"My lady, they aren't asking you to make some unpopular political move. They're asking you to torture someone!"

"I know that!" Teran snapped.

"How can you just give them what they want?"

Teran stared down into a glass of vakren. She took a sip of the bitter drink, grimacing as it went down. "It is unfortunate, but…"

Unfortunate. That damned word again.

Cailyn's face must have shown how much she'd grown to hate it.

Teran lifted her head and stared straight at Cailyn. "Defying them won't change anything. We both know that."

"Do we?" Cailyn snarled.

Teran scowled back at her. "They'll just find someone else. The man they've captured will either confess or he won't. Who did what will hardly matter."

"Except to you. And to me."

Teran's thin fingers tightened around her glass. "To you? Does it matter to you more than it does to anyone else? The people who do this professionally have friends, families, consorts."

"My lady, that's not relevant. Not to you. Not to this."

"Are you really so special, Cailyn Derys, that you knowing I'm doing it matters more than one of them knowing the same thing?"

Cailyn winced. Had she ever thought of that? She'd always figured the people who interrogated prisoners must be strange people. People suited to the job of cruelty. Maybe even people who enjoyed it. She'd never thought further than that. Politics was for courtesans who hoped to gain something from intrigue. She'd never wanted or needed any of that.

Then she'd met Teran.

"Listen to me."

A hand gripped at Cailyn's shoulder. She brushed it away, but it came back, insistent. She turned, trapped by Teran's unblinking gaze. The thin lips below them curled into a sneer.

"I have no desire to do this. To beat a man like a piece of meat for a government I don't give a damn about."

A hand reached under Cailyn's chin. Steel sprouted from it. Cailyn froze, afraid to move. The tips of Teran's claws rested against her skin.

Don't touch me. Not now. Not like this.

"And yet he's no less a piece of meat for them if I refuse. And their interrogators are trained for torture anyway."

Cailyn met her gaze. "But you're cruel, too."

"I am cruel." The claws twitched against the skin of Cailyn's chin. "But I'm choosy."

Cailyn steeled herself, ignoring the newsteel crawling over her face. "This isn't funny, Teran Nivrai."

"I didn't say it was."

"Fine. You're choosy. What happens when they choose for you?"

"Is that what you think? That any time I have an opportunity to be cruel, I will?"

Cailyn's jaw tightened. "You toy with everyone. You lied to me."

Steel bit into her chin as Teran's hand clenched around it. She fought not to flinch.

"Why should you trust me? Why should I trust you, Cailyn Derys?"

"What are you saying?"

"You enjoy what you do. Surely that means that you'll jump at the opportunity to get into anyone's bed, no matter how boorish, rude, or stupid. Surely, the mere experience of opening your legs to them is so overwhelming that you simply can't resist it."

Cailyn shook with the effort it took to suppress her anger. "Don't even joke about that."

Newsteel slid back into Teran's fingers with a small click.

"Joke?" Teran snarled. "That wasn't a joke. Do you think everything is sexual to me?" Her hand withdrew. "If it were, why would I need you?"

Her hand slid to Cailyn's blouse and tugged it open. Cailyn grabbed Teran's hand. The thin fingers froze in place.

Cailyn's breast hung exposed, Teran's gaze fixed on it. The newsteel emerged, sudden and shining, but Teran's hand did not move.

"Don't you remember what I said to you? That you are a gem, a rare gift?"

"I remember." With a pang, she thought of Teran's hands in her hair.

Teran Nivrai, the famous recluse, parading her around on her arm. Hungry eyes following as they walked past together. Eyes filled with envy, or longing, or hot rage. Yes, she had enjoyed it.

Cailyn sighed. Teran still wanted to touch her.

"You really don't understand, do you, my lady? You think this is nothing. This is an unpleasant chore, not someone else's body and mind."

Teran jerked her hand away. "They've made their monster, little one. Now they want her to perform."

"And she will. After all she's done—hiding from the nobles, hiding from her suitors, hiding from her own son—she will."

"Cailyn—"

"Is that all this is to you? A performance?"

"Would you do it, Cailyn Derys?" The voice, usually crisp and sharp, sounded heavy and cold.

"Of course I wouldn't!"

"If the High Councils brought you to their meetings, ordered you to bed this man, told you to coax his secrets out of him, would you do it?"

Cailyn cringed. "They couldn't do that."

"Who says they couldn't? Guild law? Surely the Councils could suspend such a thing."

"That's not possible."

"This is a matter of state security. Who says it's impossible? You?"

Cailyn didn't bother to keep her jaw from dropping. Even the Councils couldn't suspend Guild law.

Or so she would have thought a few weeks ago. But hadn't the Councils just done the same thing to Teran?

Their monster, ordered to perform.

What would she do if Lord Keriel came to her and said the state needed her? If he ordered her to seduce someone, told her the security of the galaxy relied on it?

She had never known any life but the one she chose. She'd gone to the academy even as a youth. For as long as she could remember, her friends and peers had been people like her, people destined to serve the nobility.

If she defied them openly, where would she go if they rejected her?

Could she start over? She could try to sell the techniques that had dazzled the nobility. But would it work? Would her new clients exult in her skills and training, or deride her for her disgrace?

They might do both, thrilling to the very idea of using someone the nobility had cast aside. But could she find any joy in a life like that even if they did?

"I—" She stopped herself.

"The others can do whatever they like with me if I refuse them. I don't have much faith in their tender mercies."

The newsteel slid back into Teran's fingertips. Her hand fell to her side. "And we both know they'll have even less mercy for this boy if I refuse. He's already committed treason."

Cailyn looked down at the exposed flesh of her breast. Teran's eyes followed hers.

Teran reached out again to caress Cailyn's cheek. Cailyn let her, wrapping her hand over Teran's.

Teran made a small, pleased sound. The claws re-emerged with it. "Not leaving me yet? I feared you might."

Cailyn shook her head, so firmly it surprised her. "No, I'm not leaving yet. They expect me to be yours, after all."

Teran's fingers tapped the collar around Cailyn's neck. "Good." Her hands traced downward. Cailyn shook.

"I don't like any of this, not any more than you do."

"I know."

Teran smiled, her lips tight. "But you want me to be braver. You'd like me to fight and lose."

Cailyn shook her head. "I'd like you to try to win."

Teran looked down. "I've already lost, little one. There's nothing more to do." Her face hardened. "Unless you want me to give—more—to Lord Keriel."

Would it help? What if it would? Cailyn bit her lip to keep from asking it. How could she even think a thing like that?

"No, my lady," she finally said.

Teran turned toward her room. "Will you come to bed?" She slid down the zipper on her shirt.

"I'll come in," Cailyn said. She slipped out of her clothes and nestled in beside Teran.

Teran made no move to touch her. With a small sigh, she wrapped her arms around Teran.

"I thought you wouldn't want to touch me, knowing what I'm about to do."

"You haven't done it yet," Cailyn answered.

"And when I do, it will poison my touch?"

Cailyn moved closer. "Maybe," she whispered, hoping Teran wouldn't hear.

CHAPTER TWENTY-FIVE

Cailyn's eyes cracked open. The sun filtered in from the windows. Teran still slept, her body pressed up against Cailyn's. Cailyn reached out her hand to smooth away a strand of Teran's hair.

Teran looked harmless now, her hands at her sides, the claws tucked away, the fingernails glinting silver. Flecks of blood still dotted her lips, but they could have been anything: remnants of juice, or wine, or some exotic sauce.

Cailyn slid her fingertips down Teran's face. Was this really the face of a torturer? She traced her way down to Teran's neck and felt for the heartbeat there.

Lord Keriel said she was in love. Was it true? She'd loved Mariel enough to give herself to someone for him.

Mariel.

He'd been strong. Strong and big. How had he died? Teran had said he'd wasted away. Cailyn had heard of sickness like that, especially on remote planets like Nivrai. But she had never seen it, and Teran hadn't told her enough to be sure.

Had he taken a long time to die? What had he looked like, in those final months, the toned body ravaged by disease? Had Teran cared for him herself, like a servant would? She thought of Teran caring for her after their sessions together and guessed Teran had.

Then she'd cared for Cailyn, in ways she said herself she did for no one else. But did that mean Teran was in love with her?

Teran wanted her. She'd felt that desire in the fingertips that clove her skin and the biting leather that tore into her flesh.

But Teran had also lied. She'd promised Cailyn she'd find some way out of this mess, but when it came down to it she'd barely even tried.

Cailyn stilled her hands, and Teran's eyes fluttered open. They looked at Cailyn a moment, then flicked to Cailyn's hand against her skin.

"Go on," she murmured.

Cailyn froze.

"You want to touch me. Do it."

"My lady?"

"You put your hands on me. It's not my desire that sparked this."

She brought a clawless hand to Cailyn's chin and drew it up to look her in the eye. "Is it?"

Cailyn's fingers twitched. This skin under her fingers—could she bear to touch it once it had harmed someone for real?

She wanted to touch it now. For as long as she could before it revolted her.

"No, my lady," she said.

"Then go on. You should know I crave your touch."

"I know. But you want my pain. I can't give that any more. Not when I know what you're about to do."

Teran lifted her hands. The claws extended with a soft metallic sound. She turned her hands over and over and watched the light play on the steel.

"And yet," she said, "these are the same hands they always were. Are they really so infected?" She laughed, a cold chuckle. Cailyn's ears stung, hearing it.

An image flashed through Cailyn's mind: Teran snarling in anger, forcing her down. The bright steel clawing at her flesh, Teran's other hand slamming into her over and over as she bled and keened. Unable to fight, unable to do anything but feel it all, pain, blood, the sting of being torn too far too fast, her own tears running wet down her face.

"My lady, I—" she stammered.

"You want to touch me. I want to let you. Nothing more than that." Her hands moved over Cailyn's again, soothing and soft.

"Do I want to hurt you?" The steel paused, poised to pierce Cailyn's flesh, and held there. She could hear Teran's breathing. "Of course. That hasn't changed. It won't."

The claws vanished back into Teran's fingertips. "But I won't do it. I've lied to you before. I'm not lying now."

Cailyn's skin itched. It ached to feel the newsteel's bite. Maybe she could do it, just one last time.

She swallowed hard. "I understand." She caught Teran's wrists in her hands. "I'm here to serve you, after all."

She guided Teran's hands down at her sides. Teran made no move of protest.

For a moment, they stared at one another. Then Cailyn leaned down to kiss Teran's open mouth.

Teran's breath mingled with her own. Strong arms wrapped around her. The steel at her back touched but did not pierce her.

Moving downward, she kissed a trail along Teran's neck. Her lips slid over the corded muscle. The body under them twitched.

She paused at the cut on Teran's chest. For a long moment, she hesitated. Teran had forced her to lick a wound once, but she had no desire to do it again.

Still, this was about offering what she could, for as long as she could do it. She lowered her lips to the scab and pressed a kiss to it.

Teran's mouth widened. Cailyn felt the tips of the claws against her back. She moved her mouth to Teran's breast, not wanting to linger in the realm of pain.

She bought her mouth to Teran's nipple and sucked. Need sparked effervescent through her vitals as Teran's body rose and fell.

She slipped her hand between Teran's legs. The wetness her fingers found there slicked her fingertips. She ran her fingers along Teran's labia, parted them, touched the nub between.

Teran gasped as Cailyn's fingers slid over her clitoris. Cailyn moved faster, bent to her task. She licked and sucked at the nipple under her mouth.

Teran's mouth opened in a small cry of pleasure. Cailyn seized the opportunity and slid two fingers inside Teran.

Teran gasped. Cailyn moved her thumb against Teran's clitoris to soothe her.

Teran's gaze, at first accusing, grew mild, and she nodded. Cailyn began to move her fingers, slow and deliberate.

There were no tears this time. Teran had allowed Cailyn this privilege once. Now, it seemed, it was hers to use if she wanted. Cailyn pulled her fingers nearly free, then drew back to push deep.

Nothing else mattered now. Not pain, not roles, not politics, not torture. Only the task set before her, the service her body offered. Only the feeling of a woman's flesh around her fingers. Only the rhythm of moving inside it, of hips moving suddenly with her.

The slight sting of metal against Cailyn's back brought her to herself again. Now that Teran was close to coming, would Teran hurt her simply out of instinct?

Whatever happened, freezing up would do no good.

The metal retracted. Cailyn let out a long breath and redoubled her efforts, her mouth sucking at the nipple under it and pushed her fingers hard into Teran.

Teran cried out once, shuddering hard around her fingers.

Thin fingers wrapped around Cailyn's head as she slid free.

"So you do still desire me," Teran said, her voice soft, her hands twining in Cailyn's hair.

The claws extended again. Teran laughed once and retracted them.

"It's a shame you want it this way. I had such plans for you."

Cailyn felt coldness spread through her chest. "Plans for me?"

Teran laughed again. "Relax, little one. I was only thinking about the party coming up for the patrons of the dark channels. If you're going, I thought we might choose someone for you together."

"Someone for me?"

"Yes." Teran nibbled softly at Cailyn's neck. Cailyn hissed. Was this pain? Did it count? She didn't know. "Since I can't do this any more, I thought we might find someone. Do it together."

Cailyn blinked. "Me?"

"Yes." Teran's lips nuzzled her neck. "You belong on the dark channels, little one. You know it. I know it."

"My lady—"

"And for now, you can't take pain. Why not try giving it?"

"My lady, that thing on your chest—" Cailyn stammered. "I could barely—"

"It felt good. To both of us."

Cailyn felt a faint pulse between her legs in answer to Teran's words. Then the ice descended on her again. "No. I couldn't. Not after what you decided."

"No? Not even to someone who yearns for it?" The ice-gray eyes grew hard.

Cailyn reached up to touch her collar. No more pain. Was that really what she wanted, really what she'd followed Teran Nivrai into this world for?

"All right. I'll go. I'll listen to what you have to say. But I can't promise anything else."

Teeth bit into Cailyn's neck again. "That's all I ask."

CHAPTER TWENTY-SIX

S o today's the fateful day," Lord Darien said and stroked his beard.

"Yes, my lord, it is."

"How do you feel about that?" His eyes swept over her dress. Cut low, it scooped far down on her back. Lord Darien had wanted her to display her body despite Teran's marks.

Or perhaps because of them. Whether the bare flesh or the marks intrigued him more, Cailyn couldn't tell.

A few days ago, she would have liked the appraisal. Now she squirmed under his scrutiny. "My lord, it—my lady is just someone who hired me. She's just like anyone else."

Darien shook his head. "Is she?"

"Of course, my lord."

"I've seen the way you look at her." He moved over to her, his hands reaching to pull down her dress. "And the way she looks back at you, for that matter."

"Me? How I look at her?"

"Yes."

"How do I look at her?"

His nearness distracted her. She wanted to concentrate on what he was saying now. Not to feel her skin tingle as her dress slid to the floor.

"Like you want her."

The hands moved again, making her skin ache for closer touch.

"Like you like being hers."

She stepped over the discarded dress. She kept her eyes downcast to hide her knotting brows.

He grinned. "I've been on the dark channels all my life. You think I don't know how people look when they find it for the first time?"

"What?"

"You have it all over you."

Cailyn frowned. "Then maybe I should leave her. Go on the dark channels more often."

Darien shook his head. "You'd have fun doing that. You have fun with me."

Cailyn let herself crack a smile. Why was he shaking his head?

"But I've also seen people in collars."

"My lord?"

"You like wearing that thing. You like that it's hers."

"Teran is going to torture someone."

"So you're here."

"So I'm here." Cailyn sighed. "I want to forget all of this. I don't want to think about her. I don't want to think about…what she's doing right now."

Cailyn felt the chill creep over her again. The room felt small. Her breath came hard. In her mind she could only see one image: slender hands, numb from the cold in a dark room. Those hands, pressed against someone's body as he twitched, cried, flinched away.

A strong hand gripped her shoulder. Warm lips brushed her ear, drawing her back. She opened her eyes and watched the gilded walls glisten.

"I can help you with that, Cailyn Derys," he said. "But I need to know what you'll do after. What happens when she comes back through that door?"

Cailyn leaned into him, wanting his warmth to drive away the chill. "I don't know, my lord."

"I think you do."

Cailyn hung her head. "I—"

"That thing is still around your neck, Derys."

"Fine," Cailyn snapped.

She licked dry lips. "I will serve. As best I can."

She thought of the newsteel tipping Teran's fingers. Would she use them? She'd gotten them for Mariel. Would she defile them, using them on this captured boy?

"You don't know if you can stand it. But you want her." He breathed hot against her ear.

"Yes."

"Then what is it you want from me?"

His hands reached out to wander over her chest. His fingers paused at her nipples, curled around them, and twisted them. "Pain?"

"Yes." The word came out a sharp gasp. She remembered the first time he had taken her. Her mind wandered to memories of Teran. She'd felt faithless to him then.

She felt faithless to Teran now. How could she want pain from him when she couldn't take it from Teran?

He kissed her neck. "Relax," he said, his lips soft against her neck as he twisted harder.

Cailyn moaned. His hand slid down her belly.

Cailyn canted her hips. The fear she carried melted under his broad hands. She arched her back and pressed her chest out in a silent plea for more.

"You want this. Don't you, Derys?" His hand slid lower.

"Yes."

His fingers slid down to her vulva and smeared the moisture they found there. He grabbed one of her labia between two fingers and pulled just enough to burn.

Instinct made her twist away at first. She breathed deep, relaxing into it.

His fingers danced over her vulva. They ran over her clitoris, slipped back to her labia, and pulled again. Her nerves sparked awake and he pulled harder.

Was this pain? She couldn't tell. She knew only that it warmed her flesh, setting it alight despite her fear. She pulled back against the fingers pinching her to heighten the tension.

"I wonder if you could come from that alone," he said into her ear. His other hand, still circling her nipple, twisted hard.

Two fingers slid inside her. Her breath came heavy as they moved, their insistent rhythm driving out her shame.

"Please," she gasped.

But he did not respond. To her dismay, he pulled away. She whimpered, sure he must be toying with her. Perhaps even the gentle ones had their cruel moments.

Instead of taunting her, however, he pushed her down gently. Her body bent over the bed. A sudden burst of desire crackled through her flesh as she waited.

She heard the sound behind her of a drawer opening, a tube of gel being squeezed. The snap of a barrier as it stretched over flesh. Then she felt his hardness, slick with lubricant, at her smaller hole.

Her teeth clenched. She didn't want him to take her that way. He'd spent so long running his hands over her vulva, tugging at her labia until she craved the teasing pain. She wanted him there, inside the nearer hole that already dripped with the expectation of him inside it.

"My lord, not that way."

"No," he said, his voice stern. "I want you to go back to Teran hungry. She's going to need you."

Cailyn groaned as he sank inside her. "Touch me, at least," she heard herself gasp. He grunted and pushed into her harder.

She closed her eyes. What was she thinking? That they were there for her pleasure? She was there for their use. She had no right to decide what they wanted of her.

She pushed back on him. At least she could feel him fill her, even if he'd picked the wrong place.

He wanted her to think of Teran? Fine. She called up her favorite memories, remembered her skin parting to the touch of steel—a touch Lord Darien could never offer.

She imagined Teran watching as Lord Darien used her, as he took what Cailyn had promised was hers. She imagined jealousy and pride in the pale eyes as she met the thrusts inside her.

Waves of heat surged through her. She shuddered, but couldn't release. Sometimes she didn't need anyone touching her clitoris to come this way. But he wanted her to go back to Teran needy.

She closed her mouth on a curse and moved with him. It heightened the sensation, but only frustrated her more.

She focused on his every movement, each little thrill it sent through her flesh, each tiny sensation. It maddened her, each spike of sensation fueling the need he refused to fulfill.

But it was pleasure, all the same. She needed that.

The edge of panic in her cries drove him on. His fingers clutched hard at her flanks as he came inside her. She grunted, envying him as he withdrew.

After a moment, she felt his hands run over her buttocks. The bruises had faded over many days, but yellow traces of the worst still remained. His fingertips ran over them. She ached where they passed, little twinges of pain that made her want more.

He drew back his hand and smacked her buttock.

She gasped at the sharp feeling so soon after being used. His hands ran over her skin, soothing her again. They drew back and he struck again.

Anger flared through her with the impact. How dare he use her like this and not give her release?

She forced herself to be still. What was she thinking, telling herself she should decide what he did with her? She'd come here to serve him.

She breathed with his rhythm. The sensation grew regular. The warmth of it built in her flesh, lulling her into that dreamlike place Teran had brought her to so many times. Her body arched to meet his windmilling hand. She cried out, wanting more.

He laughed and struck again. The impact reverberated through her sensitized flesh. She cried out again. It no longer mattered whether she would come or not. Her body flowed to his rhythm, immersed in the sensations he chose to give her.

Then she felt his hands on her flesh again, soft and soothing against her burning skin.

She turned over to face him. He wrapped his arms around her, patted her hair, then kissed the top of her head.

"Go back to her," he said. "Don't be afraid. Blame us, if you need to blame anyone." He kissed her again. "Blame me," he whispered into her hair.

"My lord." Her voice broke. "I could never blame you."

"You should. I blame myself."

"What? You didn't make the council members vote for this."

"She hoped I would stop them. I didn't try."

Cailyn closed her eyes. "There is only so much you can do, my lord."

"That's what I'm trying to tell you, Cailyn Derys. She had no options. I was in the meetings that made sure of it."

"My lord—"

"She's not a monster. Cold, uncaring, selfish, damn near impossible to like." He smirked. "But not a monster."

"No," Cailyn whispered.

"Derys—"

"My lord," she said, at last finding her voice. "Why hire me just to remind me to go back?"

Darien ran his fingers along her buttock. "That's not the only reason."

She smiled, her reddened skin feeling warm. "I'm glad to hear that, my lord."

He opened his mouth. Cailyn thought he might say more, but he only kissed her, hard. Cailyn opened her own mouth wide, grateful for the respite.

CHAPTER TWENTY-SEVEN

Nivrai servants glided through Teran's rooms. Had Teran said anything to them before she left? Had she seemed nervous, angry, interested, gloomy? How had she looked, wearing that uniform for real?

Cailyn felt her flesh twinge as she recalled how Teran had looked in it before. These things had been half game then. How did she look now?

And how would Teran look to her victim? Cailyn tried to imagine Lady Nivrai as an enemy. Teran had welcomed her from the beginning. But what would those strange eyes, drained of color, look like to a stranger who expected only agony? Teran had smiled at Cailyn that first night, and that welcome had set her at ease. But what would that smile, sharp and mocking, look like to a prisoner, cringing before her and waiting for torment?

She held her hands to her head and sat down heavily on her bed. She moved her hands away and stared at the walls, numb and unseeing.

She'd whiled away the hours since leaving Lord Darien styling her hair. Putting it up, letting it down, putting it up again. It gave her something to do with her hands. She patted the ringlets, then smoothed her clothes.

Teran hadn't chosen her clothes for her. She'd picked a bright red dress, loose and light, easily slipped off. A compromise between the blood-red Teran liked and the vivid colors that would soothe her.

She slid to her knees and waited at attention, hoping the formality would help. Her hands twitched at her sides. She stilled them, chiding herself for the mistake.

Her throat constricted as the door slid open.

Teran walked in, her body swathed in the black of the bodysuit, the Councils' emblem adorning her breast. Her eyes, drained of what little color they possessed, stared past Cailyn, not even seeing her kneeling in waiting.

With a fixed, dull stare, Teran walked into her own rooms, not bothering to shut the door behind her.

Cailyn turned her head to peer as best she could into Teran's rooms. She could hear Teran removing her boots. From the corner of her eye, she saw Teran peel off the bodysuit, her movements frenzied, the fasteners protesting as she tore at them.

Cailyn forgot decorum as she heard the door of the bathroom slide open, the sound of shower water hitting the tiled floor. She stood up before she realized she had done it.

No other sounds came from Teran's rooms. Cailyn slid out of the dress and followed.

No servants stopped her. Perhaps they had been ordered not to interfere. Or perhaps they understood.

Teran stood nude in the center of the wide shower. The water poured down over her body. Powerful as she'd always seemed to Cailyn, she looked small now. Her hands slid soap over her flesh, wiped it away, soaped it again, wiped it away. Her eyes stared, empty and blank, heedless of anything happening around her.

Cailyn watched for a long moment and stepped inside.

Teran did not turn. She ran her hands over her own body again, her movements jerky and unnatural. Her face showed no expression. Her eyes moved only to blink.

"My lady? Don't do that," Cailyn said, reaching back through her years of training for the most soothing voice she could muster. "Please. Stop it," she repeated, over and over. "I'll bathe you."

Teran turned around. She stared ahead, unblinking, but didn't respond to Cailyn.

"Teran?" Cailyn tried.

Teran blinked at the sound.

"Let me do this for you," Cailyn said again. Maybe she couldn't cope with Teran's touch tonight, but Teran clearly needed something.

And the purpose she'd chosen, all those years ago, was about more than giving pleasure. She'd learned to serve so that she could use her body to soothe and comfort. She'd trained her hands, her lips, her flesh itself to serve it. She couldn't fail to use them now.

No matter what Teran had done.

"Please," she said. "Don't make this harder than it is, my lady."

Teran twitched.

"For you or for me."

Teran shuddered. Her body jerked as if to shake off some attacker. It stilled again. She nodded.

Cailyn turned the shower off but left the bathtub faucet on.

She held her hands just above Teran's skin for a long moment. Then she bit her lip and reached for Teran's hand. Teran didn't take it. She wrapped her fingertips around it and squeezed. Teran's fingers curled halfheartedly over hers.

"Come here." She guided Teran into the water with her hands, touching and coaxing. Teran let Cailyn lead her and followed with automatic footsteps.

Cailyn stepped into the tub. Teran walked in after her. She stared ahead without blinking. Cailyn flinched but wrapped her arms around Teran.

Teran shuddered at her touch. Cailyn held her as her body twitched.

"It's all right," Cailyn soothed her, not sure she believed it. "It's all right."

Teran wrapped her arms around Cailyn. Cailyn cooed and reached up to stroke her hair. Teran shook. Cailyn held on while the tremors subsided and repeated soothing words as Teran stilled.

Teran's eyes focused on her. Her mouth twitched once, twice, and then composed itself into a smile.

"I still like your touch," Teran said, her voice soft. She clutched at Cailyn. "You still like mine."

Cailyn froze.

"My lady, I already told you I can't let you. Not now."

Teran pulled away. "I know. It doesn't matter."

Cailyn opened her mouth to speak. Teran shook her head.

"Here," Teran said. "Can you touch me?"

Cailyn nodded. Teran leaned out of the pool and opened her legs to give Cailyn access.

Cailyn bent down and began to lick. She closed her eyes, taking in the scent and feel. Even after all this, it was just like any other skin, soft against her lips and tongue. She lapped at the moisture she found there.

The sounds of Teran's pleasure came as always. Cailyn twitched as she listened to them. Still, her flesh responded to that voice. Her flesh tingled as the body above her ground against her.

Teran's gasps came quick, desperate. Like she expected Cailyn to turn away, at any moment. She pressed her flesh hard against Cailyn's face.

Cailyn hesitated. Even now, Teran sought to take control, to trap and claim her, to turn her offer of comfort into possession.

Cailyn wrapped her hands around Teran's body, wanting as much to still it as to draw it closer.

Her mind went back to that first time. Her lips and tongue had sought Teran's pain. She had licked old wounds, soothed them. She'd pressed her flesh against old scars. Now, the wound was fresh, like those Teran had left.

She breathed deep, taking in Teran's scent. If she couldn't give Teran control, she could at least dive into those memories. She slipped her tongue inside Teran's slick flesh, seeking new poisons by delving for old ones.

Teran shuddered hard as her body opened. She thrashed again. Cailyn's grip tightened to steady Teran as she came.

"Come with me," Teran said. She stepped out of the water and wrapped a towel around herself.

The silver eyes became cold, shimmering ice. They stared past Cailyn, through to the wall behind her. She dried herself with another towel and hurried to follow.

Don't slip away again, my lady.

"Kneel there with your legs spread," Teran ordered her, her lips pressed together in a severe line.

"My lady—" Cailyn stammered. "I—"

Teran tilted her head, cold and imperious.

Cailyn dropped to her knees, graceful and smooth as ever. "I will obey, my lady. But you know I can't let you touch me."

"Relax." Teran lay down on the bed and stared at Cailyn through half-lidded eyes. "I only intend to look, for now." Her hand moved between her legs.

All right, then. If Teran wanted a show, Cailyn would give her one. Nervous as Cailyn was about Teran's touch, she'd done this a thousand times for a hundred different nobles. There was nothing wrong with letting Teran look at her.

She tossed her head, puffed out her breasts, pulled a pin from her hair, and shook out her curls. Her hair fell down her chest and back, ringing her naked flesh.

Teran's gaze swept over every part of Cailyn's body without blinking, the cold stare of a bird of prey. Cailyn shivered.

She thought of her old fantasy from so many years ago: the eyes of a noble, sweeping over her, seeking and capturing her anew whenever she tried to cover herself or hide.

What would she say to that girl-child now if she could?

She remembered her father's warnings. "The life of a courtesan isn't all elegance and romance. It's easy to give your body to some of them. But sometimes they want it when you're not sure you can give it."

She'd frowned up at him. "Guild law says you don't have to do that."

"Sometimes it's not them, Cailyn. Sometimes you want to leave, but don't. Sometimes you know you can invoke Guild law and go away, but you don't."

She'd made a vow to herself that night: whatever she did, whatever offers she accepted, she'd leave if she needed to. She wouldn't let them coax her into things like her father had. No one like that crazy councilwoman would ever come after her. Not if she was careful.

Returning to herself, Cailyn sighed. She wished she could rush back into the study of that old house, throw her arms around her father, and tell him he'd been right after all.

"I bought you these," Teran said, her free hand drawing out a set of clamps from the nightstand. Jewels dripped from the chain that linked them. It glittered in the light.

Teran shook her head. "It doesn't matter now. But I would have liked to see you in them."

"Still, my lady? After all that has happened today, you still want my pain?"

"Always."

Cailyn looked down.

"The things I do stir your desire," Teran said. She turned the clips around in her hands. The jewels flashed as they caught the light.

Teran looked back at Cailyn. "Or, at least, they did before."

Cailyn tilted her head down to peer at her breasts. Her nipples were already erect. They throbbed as the chains tinkled. She wished she could forget all of this, Councils and meetings and jobs and today, and give herself over to them. She wanted the pressure to compress her skin, wanted Teran to press her lips to her neck, bury her fingers deep inside her—

"Yes, my lady," she admitted. "They did."

"Then let me." Teran stepped closer. On another day, she might have bitten her earlobe or kissed her neck. So strange now, to be sure she wouldn't. "I won't touch you after that unless you ask me to. I promise."

Cailyn drew in a deep breath, closed her eyes, and thought of her goddess. She'd chosen the goddess's path. Her training had taught her, from the very beginning, to serve. To give solace with her hands, her lips, her sex. Could she deny it to Teran now?

She nodded once, the goddess's image swimming in her head.

She did not open her eyes. She gasped as the first pinch came. Pressure flared through her nerves. She felt the second, hissed, and opened her eyes.

She looked down at herself. The golden chains shone, a bright adornment that shifted as she twitched. If not for their bite, they could have been jewelry, worn to draw the gazes Cailyn had craved from the beginning.

"You're very beautiful," Teran said, her hand thrilling between her legs. Cailyn watched her hips rise and fall.

Teran had said that once before, so long ago in the beginning. It had sounded wrong then and it sounded wrong now.

"Such a shame I can't use you properly now."

Cailyn twitched in response to Teran's words. Damn Lord Darien. He'd said he wanted to send her back to Teran greedy to be used. He had.

"As long as you don't hurt me," she gasped, as startled as Teran to hear herself say it.

"You want me that badly?"

"Use that," Cailyn said, nodding her head toward the harness and dildo, her voice curt.

Teran's fingers stilled. A smile spread across her face. "Very well."

Cailyn sighed with relief and watched the harness shape itself to Teran's body. At least she'd decided something. At least Teran would settle for using her this way.

Cailyn stared at the transforming metal fitted tight around Teran's flesh, the phallus jutting out from it, ready to claim her. She drank in the muscled body that had used her, explored her, probed every part of her. Her flesh spasmed in anticipation.

Teran stepped up behind her and pressed the tip of the dildo against her entrance. She sighed, expectant.

Teran entered her with one swift, fluid thrust. She moaned as the phallus plunged into the flesh that had burned for it for so long.

This was no slow seduction. Teran slammed into her hard, driving deep and fast. The friction burned, a lightning heat that set Cailyn's nerves aflame.

Cailyn was glad for the speed. She didn't want time to regret it. She pushed herself back on the dildo, desperate to forget.

The chain between her nipples swayed. Jolts of sensation raced through her body as Teran's movements clove her again and again. She threw back her head and cried out, long and loud.

Encouraged, Teran battered into her harder. Cailyn gasped, startled for a moment. Then she opened her legs wider, letting it slide in deep.

Somewhere dim in her mind, she remembered that she ought to be frightened. But it felt so good to be filled, to make herself a vessel for Teran's use, that the ache in her nipples as the chain moved only added to her pleasure.

Cailyn had felt this once before: in the pool, months ago, just after Lord Darien had videoed her to tell her about this conference. Something had driven Teran on, the methodical seduction seared away by the bright pulse of some need Cailyn couldn't name. The same thing fueled her now. She slammed into Cailyn again and again, driving in and in, moving faster and faster as Cailyn's body opened around her.

Cailyn drove back on the dildo impaling her so hard that it hurt too. Her flesh clenched. She cried out as Teran drove deeper.

She was only her body, only the opening, stretching out and out and out.

CHAPTER TWENTY-EIGHT

These will need to come off." Teran touched the small chain. Before, such a delicate touch might have surprised Cailyn, or made her suspicious. Now, Teran was keeping a promise.

"I suppose I should ask permission." Teran's lips twisted as if she'd just taken a sip of vakren. "After all, I can use you, but not touch you."

Cailyn swallowed a retort.

"Go ahead, my lady," she said, her voice as even as she could make it. "I let you put them on in the first place."

Teran bent her head and paused a moment. She reached out to unclasp the clips, her fingers small and fragile with no steel tipping them.

Cailyn cried out as her nipples sprang free. Sensation returned, pure pain now, as the blood rushed back into the compressed flesh. Tears pricked her eyes and she keened.

Why now? Why from so little? It made her angry. She wished the sensation would just go away.

But experience had taught her she'd be sore for quite a while. The thought sent a wave of nausea through her. She thought of asking to be excused to her rooms.

No. She'd done this much. She pressed her lips together. She wasn't about to run off and hide, not now.

Teran exhaled. A smile curled the corners of her mouth. "Thank you."

Cailyn looked down. Her nipples throbbed.

Teran sighed. "He's only a boy. He's so young."

Cailyn froze.

"He could be anyone. Any idealistic fool."

Cailyn hung her head. She thought of her training, all the words a courtesan knew to make a noble feel heard, valued, special.

She could say them now. They might even help. But somehow, she couldn't bring herself to form the words.

"It's not like we haven't done anything. It's not like Councils' taxes aren't ridiculous. It's not like they—not like we—don't live like kings and queens while they starve."

"My lady—"

"It's not like we don't know why they're angry. It's not like we don't know why they try to kill us. What else can they do?"

Cailyn's insides chilled, right down to the flesh that had, just before, clenched with aftershock.

So much remorse in Teran's voice. But this was only the beginning of the long assignment she'd been given.

"And yet..." Cailyn whispered, her voice cracking.

"And yet I do it," Teran spat. "They meant to kill one of us, after all." Her hand toyed with the golden chain of the clamps. "As if that's enough to deserve what the Councils are having me do."

Cailyn had whispered comfort earlier, her arms wrapped tight around Teran as she shook. She'd seen the hurt and reached to soothe it. But what could she do now? Embrace Teran again? Swear that would be all right?

Teran set down the clips in her hand with a soft sound. Cailyn's flesh throbbed as she looked at them, their chains all snaking gold.

The pain sent another wave of nausea through her. She blinked, suddenly woozy. What was she doing here?

"You should go," Teran said, her voice soft.

Cailyn nodded. At least Teran wasn't pressing the issue. She crept back to her rooms, careful to be quiet.

She thought for a moment about searching through her things for a nightdress. She wasn't there for Teran now anyway. The warmth might soothe her. But she gave up after a moment, sighed, and slipped under the covers.

She drew them tight around herself and stared up at the ceiling.

From the beginning, she'd slept beside Teran. Tonight, Teran slept by herself, and so did she.

❖

"Teran Nivrai. I must say I never expected to see you here." The brightly painted mouth turned up in a smile. "And this must be Cailyn Derys."

The woman's red lips and curly dark hair matched the room's red walls, its black, lacy curtains. Jewels dripped from the woman's ears and circled her neck. Her long nails glittered red.

They might have impressed Cailyn a year ago. Now the bright paint on them seemed garish, a bright apology for not being newsteel.

She felt a twinge of jealousy. She'd served nobles alongside other courtesans before, but she hadn't done it often.

Nothing she and Teran could do alone would cut the tension that breathed like a misshapen shadow between them. She agreed with Teran about that. Having someone else around, especially someone Teran could turn to for the things Cailyn couldn't give, could only help.

But Cailyn still didn't like being here. She clasped her hands together behind her back and stared ahead, unblinking.

She wondered what the courtesans' quarters here looked like. Her father's fame had made it easy for her to choose to work for herself. After a few months working for a house near the academy where she'd studied, she'd bought herself a small home and worked from there.

She'd liked her fellow students and had been sad to leave. She'd grown close to the few she'd practiced with and the fewer she'd taken as lovers. But even in those early days, she'd hoped to work alone. Her father's name had given her the chance.

Most of these people didn't have that option. But what about the ones who did? Why might they choose this? Did they get along well with one another? Did they compete for the nobles' attention? What happened when they won or lost? Did that make it hard to come back later, to face their rival?

"Most people don't expect me anywhere." Teran's voice cut into her thoughts.

The madam laughed. Her grin shifted into a smirk. "No, I suppose not, my lady."

"Who do you have that I might be interested in? You should, I think, have some idea of my standards."

"Of course. Your reputation precedes you, Lady Nivrai."

Cailyn stifled a laugh. The woman had barely blinked. Training, indeed.

Teran didn't answer.

"I'll send for Valik," the madam went on. "The man has an endless appetite for pain. I can't promise that you, of all people, won't discover different."

Cailyn doubted anyone else would notice the slight creasing of Teran's brows. "Fine."

Red-painted fingertips tapped at a console. The madam spoke a few soft words and eased back into her chair.

A young man emerged, broad-chested, with warm brown skin. Long black hair fell to his shoulders, its silken smoothness a contrast to his bulky frame. Tattoos twined around his arms and legs. Silvery metal peeked from his pierced nipples. A small metal implant winked from the center of his forehead.

When he saw Teran, he sank to his knees in the fluid manner of any skilled courtesan. "My lady," he said. His hair fell over his face as he bowed his head.

Teran wasted no time. She stalked over to him and wrapped her hand in his hair. He moaned as she pulled his head up.

"You look young," she said, staring hard into his large eyes. "Why should I choose you to serve me?"

"You're right, my lady. I have only been out of the academy two years."

"Is that supposed to interest me?"

"I don't—" he stammered as he struggled to keep staring up at her.

She laughed. Her other hand traced his neck and chest. She drew her arm back and struck him hard. He grunted with the impact.

Cailyn winced, but his hiss became a moan. Cailyn could see a bulge in the small black cloth covering his genitals.

Teran noticed it too. She pressed her boot into his groin. He hissed, his eyes closed.

"Nivrai," the madam snapped. "We're not here to let you get your thrills for free and leave. I don't care who you are."

Teran's gloved hand tugged at a pierced nipple. "I want to know what I'm getting. But since you want me to hurry"—she let go, making the young man whimper—"tell me, Valik, what do you think of her?"

The question startled Cailyn as much as it did Valik, who blinked and looked at her.

"I—I don't know her, my lady," he fumbled.

Teran's eyes narrowed.

"But she's beautiful," he added quickly. He squinted at Cailyn. "She—that's Cailyn Derys. Her father was famous—"

"That's not what I asked." Teran turned away.

"Wait," he called. "Let me look at her." His eyes swept over Cailyn. They lingered over her face, her ringlets, her breasts, the shape of her hips.

"What would you say if I said I wanted to see you together?" Teran said. A thin smile spread across her lips.

"I—"

"Or are you too busy staring at me to answer?"

His brows knitted. "My lady, I would be glad to do anything—"

Teran shook her head, the corners of her mouth upturned. "Of course you would."

"I—I mean that I would be honored to serve alongside someone so prestigious and skilled."

"That's better."

She turned to Cailyn. Without turning back to Valik, she pinched his nipple.

Cailyn frowned. He wanted this. Wanted this in a way she never had. And she wouldn't even look at him.

"What about you?" Teran asked Cailyn. "What do you think of…Valik, is it?"

Cailyn shuddered as she watched the young man's teeth clench. She knew what Teran was asking. Could she handle watching Teran use him?

"He looks skilled as well, my lady."

Teran raised an eyebrow. "Come here."

Cailyn did. Teran reached out, took her hand, and guided it to Valik's chest.

Cailyn closed her eyes. She felt the rise and fall of the young man's chest as he breathed. A tingle spread through her flesh. If Teran wanted to see them together, so be it.

Better that than Teran using her.

"I would be honored to serve with someone as respected as Derys," Valik said again.

"And?" Teran prompted him.

He closed his eyes, suddenly shy. "I like her hand on me."

"Very well," Teran answered. "The end of this week, an hour after the Councils' meeting."

"Thank you, my lady, I will be there."

But Teran had already turned away, talking in a crisp voice to the madam about nothing but the transaction.

She does that, Cailyn thought, watching Valik watching her.

Chapter Twenty-nine

"Valik arrives tonight."
Cailyn pushed food around her plate. It bore the same meat as that first fateful dinner so long ago, spiced in almost the same way, and a cluster of bright berries. She'd picked at them for the whole meal. Her instructors would be ashamed.

Teran smiled and sipped her drink, oblivious to the minor disaster.

She must really want him, Cailyn thought. Since that first night, Teran hadn't hurt Cailyn at all. Just used her like anyone else would, with fingers, tongue, smooth fingertips. She hadn't bound her. Hadn't said a word about pain.

Or about her eighty thousand.

Cailyn, thankful for the reprieve, hadn't pressed the point.

But sometimes Teran reached to touch Cailyn and the steel would suddenly emerge. Teran would blink and sigh. The claws would retract with their usual click.

Valik's visit would do Teran good.

"You should prepare yourself, little one. I'm sure you're wise enough to know I want more from you than just to watch me."

Cailyn looked up. She fought not to frown. "What are you planning for him, my lady?"

"Nothing you can't handle. But I've never made things easy for you, have I?"

"No, my lady."

"I don't intend to start now. Councils or no Councils."

"Tell me what you want." Cailyn speared a mouthful of the meat. The spices, pleasantly mild before, did nothing for her now.

"Other than to use him? To see you with him."

"If you use me alongside him I'll surely disappoint you."

Cailyn chewed her food with exaggerated slowness. Words caught in her throat that she never would have expected to say. *Maybe you should just use him. Maybe it would be better that way.*

They went against everything trained into her, every reason she'd wanted that training in the first place. She'd made a choice to serve. She'd agreed to a contract knowing the rules. Now...

She chewed another bite of meat, searching for resolve.

"I'm doing this for you," Teran said. The hand holding her drink shook, then went still. "You know I'd rather use you instead."

"I know."

Cailyn peered at Teran from under her hair: Her eyes were cold her hair severe. Her mouth showed no hint of the smile that sometimes softened her features. Tight gray fabric hid away her flesh, another barrier between them. In the blue light of the room, she looked more frightening than appealing.

She remembered the wings and tail she'd once imagined, the spines Teran had mentioned, the quills Lord Darien had added to the wild menagerie of rumors.

Once, she'd liked the idea. Now, she knew they didn't lurk in Teran's skin, but the knowledge didn't soothe her.

"That's true, my lady," she said. "You have been kind."

The old smile ghosted over Teran's lips. "I will require a lot of you, yes, but I will not break any promise I have made to you."

Cailyn nodded.

"Unless, of course, you let me."

You did once, Cailyn thought, biting her lip to keep from saying it aloud.

"Yes, my lady," she answered, bowing her head.

Later, Cailyn never remembered watching Valik kneel. She remembered him standing at the door as it opened, his chest bare, his tattoos and the silver metal in his nipples and forehead on full display.

He wore the collar of his house, a darker metal, studded with a large red gem. Cailyn touched her own neck as she looked down at him, knowing he wasn't looking up at her. If he raised his head now, would seeing it make him jealous?

What must it be like, she wondered, to want this like he does?

For a moment, Teran moved like Cailyn wasn't even there, her hands ghosting along the young man's chest with such care Cailyn wondered whether she was intruding.

Cailyn heard a familiar sound, sharp and metallic. Valik gasped. He looked down to see steel poised just above his skin.

"How did you do that?" he breathed.

Steel darted in and out of Teran's fingertips. His mouth opened in surprise.

She ran the steel-tipped fingers down his skin, leaving faint white scratches in the skin where they passed.

He stared for a long moment, disbelieving. Then he threw back his head and cried out his joy.

The claws dug into his skin. He closed his eyes and arched into their bite. Blood beaded up, then dripped down over the patterned skin. Valik drew a ragged breath. As before, Cailyn could see a bulge in the black fabric that barely covered Valik's groin.

She remembered Teran first pricking her. Teran had pierced her neck, hid it with a touch, left Cailyn to puzzle out what had happened from the sting and the bright red moisture.

Had Teran meant to make her into this?

"Cailyn." Teran's voice cut through her reverie. "On the dresser you will find a small box. Bring it here."

Cailyn did as Teran bid her. What exactly was Teran planning?

Delicate patterns twined over the surface of small, thin box. Cailyn thought of shaking it, like a small child with a gift, to guess at what lay inside.

Teran smiled as Cailyn laid it down. Her eyes lingered on Valik, on the lines of blood running down his chest.

Cailyn bit her lip and tamped down a pang of jealousy.

Teran balled her other hand into a fist and punched his chest lightly. He groaned and arched his hips.

"Are you trying to impress me?" Teran hit him again.

He grunted and didn't answer.

Teran grabbed his hair, pulled his head up to look at her, and took his nipple between two shining claws.

His breath came jagged and heavy. Whether from the pain of the punch or simply from arousal, Cailyn couldn't tell.

"Are you?" Teran's teeth clenched as she hissed the words at him.

"Yes—no—I don't know, my lady," Valik stammered as Teran tugged at the nipple caged between her steel-tipped fingers.

She let go. Valik whimpered at the loss. Teran punched him again, her fist catching him as he reeled.

"Why did I do that?" she asked him.

He gulped and looked down. "Because I—because my answer was arrogant, my lady?"

Cailyn couldn't hide a smirk.

"No." Teran snickered. "Why would I give you what you want for that?"

He peered up at her through his hair.

"But that is neither here nor there. You haven't earned my attention." With a metallic snick, the claws slid back inside Teran's fingers. She let go of his head. It lolled, forlorn, as she stepped away from him.

She turned to Cailyn. "But you have earned hers."

Mine? Cailyn looked back at Teran, confused. But Teran only gestured to the box. Cailyn shrugged and slid off the lid.

Inside lay two thin blades. Their handles were a pure white. Filigreed flowers curled over them in delicate designs.

How pretty, Cailyn thought. Was Teran one for flowers? Maybe so, from the garden outside her bedroom in Nivrai.

Were these crafted specifically for nobles on the dark channels? Cailyn guessed so and shivered. Beautiful weapons for beautiful people.

Teran took one of the knives out of the box. She held it up and let the light hit it. "I used these years ago. I don't need them now."

She extended her claws again. Valik's head snapped up at the sound.

"But they can be useful nonetheless."

Teran set the blade back down in the box. She passed it to Cailyn.

Cailyn blinked. "My lady?"

A smile crept over Teran's face. "You'll need them."

"Me?"

"Yes. You."

"No! My lady, it—I can't do that!"

Teran walked back over to Valik. She lowered one hand and ran the tips of her claws over his skin. He closed his eyes and purred.

"You know what this feels like," Teran said.

Cailyn nodded, her throat parched. "Yes, my lady."

She didn't want to think about it. She didn't want to remember. She wanted to ignore it. To forget the hot curl of envy that raced through her as she watched Valik relax into Teran's biting touch.

"You don't think you can do the same thing to him? You can cut with them, yes. But you don't have to. I don't always cut you."

Cailyn stared. "I don't know how to use them. I might make a mistake."

"Is that it? I can guide you." Her voice was a whisper, thick with hidden promise. Cailyn saw Valik close his eyes.

She closed hers too, remembering the feeling of the claws skirring along her skin. Fear came with it all, the remembered thrill of a weapon against the softness of her flesh. The knowledge that she could be cut, that Teran wanted to do it, whether she intended gentleness or savagery.

But light, spidery movement like that left no damage, no mark. She thought of Valik's head thrown back, his hair whipping through the air as he cried out. She pressed her legs together and cursed herself for the heat there, for wanting to fan it.

Teran turned back to Valik. She held up the knife again. "Would you like her to use this on you?"

He looked from the knife to Cailyn. His gaze lingered on her body. He breathed out the word "Yes."

Teran handed her the knife. Cailyn turned it around in her hands. "I'm not like you, my lady."

She looked over at Valik and studied the tattoos that twined over his skin, the metal that glinted in his nipples. She raised her head, looked into wide eyes, a bright silver implant just above them in the center of his forehead.

She couldn't imagine bringing the blades to his skin.

But she did know what it was like to want their teasing touch. She'd missed the sharpness in Teran's fingertips too many times not to know it.

She'd even wanted Teran's steel to bring blood sometimes.

Neither Valik nor Teran was asking her to go that far.

She picked up the knife. Teran laughed, silver and delighted.

Cailyn brought the blade to Valik's chest. She had barely touched the tip to his skin when he took a deep breath, closed his eyes, and stilled under the blade.

"I think he likes you," Teran said.

Cailyn traced the knife along Valik's flesh. His breath slowed. His fingers twitched at his sides. One corner of his mouth turned up in the first hint of a smile. The rest of him was still, minding the blade.

She wondered what her own face looked like. She'd seen Teran before, concentrating, intense. What did it take to do this with such composure?

She swallowed, daring herself to push just a little harder. Valik's answering moan was a great relief.

"Difficult, little one?" Teran asked. Cailyn froze as Teran walked up behind her.

Was this what Teran wanted? To hear her admit how awkward she felt in front of another courtesan? She looked again at Valik. Even now, he puffed out his chest, trying to reach her again.

Whatever terrible things Teran had done, this wasn't anything like them. She moved the blade down, watching a faint white line appear where it passed.

Valik's mouth opened in a wide O of surprise that soon became a gasp of pleasure.

Cailyn cracked a smile. That was…good, apparently. Heat thrilled through her at Valik's response, in spite of the strangeness of it all.

Steadier now, she mirrored the movement on the other side. Valik let out a low moan.

Cailyn blinked. The sounds he made—they made sense as responses to sex, to touch, to kisses. But the twin lines her blade had drawn across his chest were something else entirely.

It made her reel. She pulled the knife away.

"Why, my lady? Why have me do this?"

"Only to see what you would do."

Teran wrapped her hand around Cailyn's and held it steady. Cailyn relaxed as Teran's hand caught and held hers.

With Teran guiding their hands, together they traced patterns on Valik's skin. Cailyn's hand moved smoothly now. It glided over the patterns of his tattoos and veered off into designs of their own.

Cailyn knew how Valik must feel, how the blade traced lines of fire over his flesh. That, she could understand. That, Teran had taught her.

That, she could be part of, in accordance with Teran's will. Her skin tingled as Teran moved their joined hands.

Cailyn's own hand traced that flame over his skin. Teran guided it, yes, but Cailyn's movements were setting his nerves alight. She tightened her grip around the knife handle, hard and determined. A fierce, foreign joy leapt in her breast.

And over it all lay Teran's hand over hers.

Then Teran's hand fell away. Cailyn hesitated.

She pulled her hand away. Once clear of Valik's skin, it began to shake. She tamped her other hand over it to keep it still.

Teran saved her with a kiss. "You can stop now, if you really want."

Cailyn laid the knife down as carefully as she could. Then she melted into Teran's kiss, thankful for the reprieve as Teran's other hand wrapped around her.

CHAPTER THIRTY

"You liked that, didn't you?" Teran stepped closer to Valik and ran a hand over his body.

"Yes, my lady," he breathed.

The newsteel sprang forth from its banks in her hands. She drew the claws down his skin, hard. Cailyn saw red lines where the tips of the claws had been.

She looked down at the box holding Teran's knife. Her hands itched. Were they missing the handle of the knives, or were they just trying to rid themselves of the recent memory?

She clasped her hands behind her back so she could rub them together without Teran or Valik seeing. Her skin felt cold without Teran's touch.

"Look at him, little one." Teran's lips fluttered against Cailyn's ear.

Cailyn opened her eyes and forced herself to study the pattern of Valik's tattoos. Her gaze moved to the cuts, the bright shock of red that dripped from them.

She looked down at her own pale skin. Was that how she looked when Teran cut her?

Her gaze moved down Valik's body. She could see the tiny scrap of fabric covering his straining member. The cloth struck her as ridiculous. It made his desire all the more obvious by so poorly hiding it.

This really is what he wants, she thought.

A hot spike of jealousy flared through her. Valik wanted this. Valik was here as much for this as he was to serve Teran's pleasure. What more would Teran do with someone who craved what she had to offer?

But for the moment, Teran seemed content to pay attention to her. Clawed hands slid over the thin, transparent fabric she wore. A few flicks of the claws and it fell from her body. Deep blue waves billowed around her bare feet.

Then Teran's hands moved on her breasts, as they had on that first day, so long ago. Cailyn's nipples hardened under Teran's fingers. She pushed out her chest to feel more.

Teran took the buds of flesh between her fingers and pinched. Cailyn cried out, more for Valik's benefit than her own. She pulled away just enough to heighten the sensation. Teran growled low.

Cailyn could feel Valik's eyes on her as Teran's claws slid back. Teran ground a fist against Cailyn's vulva and Cailyn rocked against it.

No one had ever watched her do these things but Teran. How did she look, eager for pain?

"Easy now, little one," Teran laughed. "I have another use for you now."

She opened a drawer, drew out her harness, and handed it to Valik. He turned it over in his hands, feeling its shape.

"Undress me," Teran ordered him.

Valik set the harness down next to Cailyn and slid to the floor in front of Teran. Cailyn smiled, thinking of the training it took to make motions like that look easy.

Cailyn stared as he began to kiss and lick Teran's boots. She hadn't thought of that.

Valik breathed deep, clearly savoring the scent of the leather. He licked its length with slow deliberation, pressing his lips and tongue against it with reverence and art, as though he were licking Teran's vulva instead.

Cailyn envied him. She'd been taught to savor whatever she was given. The taste of sweat on skin, the smoothness of a breast, the length of a long neck.

The boots must smell wonderful, she thought. And feel soft against his lips.

Teran reached down to stroke his back. She grabbed his hair as he licked back up the length of a boot. The ends of her mouth twitched. She loosened her grip as he moved back down again.

She dragged his head up. He looked up at her, his mouth still open. He blinked once, bereft, and slid the boots off Teran's feet with practiced ease.

He kissed the fabric of her clothes. She let him linger a moment and pulled him away again.

He whispered an apology and kissed the fasteners of her clothes. With slow, practiced movements, he drew them down and slid them off of Teran's body.

He held out the harness while she stepped into it, then eased it into place with his hands. He watched the metal shift to the shape of her body with shining eyes.

He looked from her to Cailyn, half-stretched on the bed. "Is it me you want to use, or her, my lady?"

"She's there for you. I told you I'd find a use for that."

Valik smiled. He ran a hand along Cailyn's back as he positioned himself. Cailyn twisted to see Teran but could see only the shadow of her body over Valik's.

She sighed and shifted her legs to allow Valik better entry. He froze, not moving until Teran entered him.

She thrust into him and everything changed. Teran's movement drove Valik deep into Cailyn. His flesh opened and warmed her. How unlike Teran's tools, unyielding and cold until her body heated them.

But all this happened because Teran willed it. Valik drove deep into her, pushed her flesh apart, but it was Teran who forced her open. The warm flesh inside her served only as her tool.

Valik thrashed as Teran drove him into Cailyn again and again, as much an object for Teran's use as the apparatus he'd helped her into.

He cried out behind her, his throat opened wide to let out the sound. His fingertips dug into Cailyn's flanks as if he needed her flesh under his hands to anchor him. His frenzied pace told Cailyn just how deep Teran plunged into him.

He wanted Teran, wanted pain at her hands. He'd found only the teasing glide of Cailyn's knives, a few stinging cuts from the newsteel, and this.

Was it enough?

Teran gasped. Cailyn drove back over Valik's member, desperate to reach her. Valik shook, their movements tossing him between them. He foundered and gave in, letting Teran use him fully. As mindless a piston as any other tool, he plunged into Cailyn over and over.

Cailyn felt her flesh cleave, battered like fragile tissue as it opened further and further. She forgot Valik, forgot everything. She felt only Teran, tearing all else away, her flesh flimsy gauze before the force of it. She drove back on Valik's flesh harder. The body between her and Teran only got in the way.

Teran responded, thrusting into Valik with all her strength. He bucked hard and came, flooding her aching insides. That was too much for Cailyn, who felt her own body clench, seizing him as her own spasms overtook her.

Aftershocks ran through her, little pulses of white lightning. She twisted to look back at him as he pulled free. His long hair clung to his head and neck. His head drooped. His mouth twitched, the corners upturned in a dreamy smile.

Teran slid the harness from her body. Sweat glistened on her skin as well. A servant, silent as a cloud, appeared from nowhere to take it away.

❖

"Surely you didn't think I was done with you."

Valik's eyes, half-lidded, fluttered open. "No, my lady," he whispered, still lost in his pleasure.

"You don't want me to be finished with you, do you?"

"No, my lady."

"Then kneel there."

To Valik's credit, he sprang up from the bed and slid to his knees with the grace the academy trained into every courtesan. He lowered his head and peered up at Teran through the dark fall of his hair.

Teran drew out a set of needles from the stand by the bed. Valik stared at them. It looked like nervousness to Cailyn, but from what she'd seen before, it must have been eagerness. Teran reached down between his legs. To touch him, Cailyn assumed, but she only slid a claw over the flesh of his member.

It stirred at her touch. Had they been resting for that long? Or was Valik so greedy for pain that his flesh answered its call?

Teran chuckled in approval and drew out the first of the needles. Cailyn winced as she realized where Teran intended them to go.

Valik hissed as Teran's claws pinched part of the sensitive flesh of his shaft. She pulled the skin up so that the needle could pierce it.

His hissing breath became a cry as the needle drove through his skin. His lips and hands clenched, but he did not flinch or pull away.

Teran ran her claw over the skin near where the needle had pierced it. His pinched mouth relaxed.

"Please," he said. "My lady."

He wanted more of this? He was so young, only just out of his training! Surely it should take years to learn to do this, to come to crave it.

She blinked at Valik as he gasped his way through another needle. So this was what Teran really wanted.

So this was what Mariel had given her.

Cailyn watched, forcing herself to keep her eyes open as the needles went through, one after the other. Valik's hisses melted away with his rising need. Transformed by his need, his grunts and groans became deep, low moans.

Teran's claw trilled over his soft flesh. A helldemon petting her beast. Cailyn peered at a shadow on the wall and thought of wings.

Her skin tingled. She couldn't imagine being pierced through her vulva, but she remembered Teran's needles, sharp and clean.

Her gaze moved to Valik's face. His head lolled, his eyes half-open, his teeth clenched as the needles drove through his skin, his lips open in a wide O as he cried out his pleasure or pain.

Do I do that?

She shifted, letting her thighs rub against one another, sure neither Teran nor Valik would notice. She wanted to feel something, however faint.

Teran admired her handiwork for a long moment. Then she slid the first of the needles free, twisting it as she pulled it back out. Cailyn cringed at the thought of it scraping its way back through the sensitive skin.

Cailyn watched it bleed, mesmerized, as Teran pulled the other needles out, one by one. She watched the metal emerge from his skin, blood running from the punctures.

The dark channels, she thought. She stared at the blood, coursing over Valik's most sensitive parts. Did the academies teach this to students destined to serve on them? Were there classes?

She remembered her own lessons, reviewing them in her mind, trying the techniques on herself in the stillness of her room at night. Had Valik done the same?

Had he pierced himself, whipped himself, dragged the points of knives along his skin? Had he wondered what it would be like to kneel before one of the real nobles, awaiting the same thing at their hands?

Teran took his member in her hand, blood and all. Her fist closed over his shaft with slow, deliberate care. Then her fist moved over his punctured skin.

Cailyn stared at Teran's hand. Blood stained it as it moved. She had seen her own blood on Teran's hands before. But watching Teran's curled hand move over the bleeding flesh, she felt her gorge rise.

She looked up from Teran's bloodied fist to her face. Her wide eyes shone, and she gave a trill of laughter.

This is what she really wants.

She looked up at Valik's face. He'd closed his eyes, and his lips were pulled tight in a grimace. Small sounds escaped him, the rough, sharp sounds of someone forced to endure.

His hips bucked and his breath came quick as Teran moved on him. Then he yipped with disappointment as she pulled away.

"You're done," Teran said.

He opened his mouth to protest, looked down at Teran's loosening grip, and nodded without a word.

As if in answer to a summons, two servants appeared, expressionless and silent. They carried salves, cloths, and water.

Cailyn let out a slow breath. She'd been so engrossed in watching Teran and Valik that she hadn't even thought of the cleaning up he'd need.

Or of the servants doing it for him. Teran had done it for Cailyn so many times herself.

"Lovely," Teran laughed. She nodded to Valik, then tilted her head toward the servants. "Go with them. They will attend to you."

More servants appeared. Valik sagged between them. Cailyn stared at the blood-smeared spot between his legs. Had he really just done all this?

Teran's hand on her shoulder drew her away.

"Not you," the rich voice purred. "I have other plans for you, little one."

CHAPTER THIRTY-ONE

He's out there by himself." Cailyn scowled, her sleepy after-glow gone. "Bleeding. From—from—there." She'd never had any problems calling body parts what they were. Courtesans had no need for false modesty. But now, thinking of what Teran had done to his most sensitive flesh, she could only gesture. "How could you?"

Teran cocked her head. "The servants are attending to him."

Cailyn couldn't believe what she was hearing. Not even from Teran. "You're leaving that up to the servants? The last time you made me bleed like that I went so lightheaded I could barely stand."

Teran chuckled. The sound scraped Cailyn's ears. "Did you think I'd leave him with just anyone? I trained them myself."

"And that's supposed to make me feel better? You poked him full of holes!"

Teran turned. "Lie down."

"You should be out there."

"Like I told you, he'll be well cared for."

"No. You. Not them. *You.*"

"Why? Because I did it for you?"

"Because—"

"I've spoiled you, my little one."

"That doesn't matter. He deserves it."

"Lie. Down."

Cailyn did. She glared up at Teran, her lip curled.

Teran leaned over her. The shape of her body blotted out the light from the ceiling. "I wanted him, yes. To scratch an itch. To do what I had been holding back from doing." Her hands reached down to caress Cailyn's chest.

"But surely you realize the one I really want is you."

The hand tightened around her breast, beginning to squeeze.

"I thought you weren't going to do that."

"Did you think I could hold out forever?" Teran's other hand reached out for her wrist, pushing it toward a waiting restraint. "Remember, I hired you."

Cailyn twisted away. "But you said you wouldn't."

Teran gripped her wrist, tight and bruising. "I've waited long enough. If you wanted to leave me for this, you would have by now."

Cailyn's mouth felt dry. "And if I refuse? You said before—"

"I said before I would not break any promises to you without your consent."

She leaned down, her face inches from Cailyn's. Her grip relaxed. "Go ahead. Refuse me. Leave. I won't stop you."

Cailyn wondered, from someplace outside herself, whether she wanted to stand or to lie back down. She stared at her own body in confusion, wondering what it would do.

Teran kissed Cailyn's cheek. "Go on, if that's what you want. You'll be paid in full. I broke my word to you once. I won't do it again."

Cailyn turned her head, not wanting to look into Teran's eyes. This wasn't her body's decision. This was her decision to make. She would have to make it.

She opened her eyes again, forced herself to look into Teran's eyes. They glinted, fierce, a raptor's stare.

"Did you decide this before?" Cailyn whispered. "That you would hurt me again?"

"No. I meant only to give you the knives. To use him and you at the same time. Then to send him away. I will tell you this, though: If I use you now, I will use you completely. And I will not go back."

Cailyn swallowed. The hand on her breast froze, still pinching.

Cailyn drew in a shaky breath and nodded.

Teran exhaled. The hand around Cailyn's breast tightened again.

Cailyn thrashed. Teran smiled and slammed Cailyn's wrists down into the metal circle. The restraints clenched around them, gripping tight.

Teran drew a thin metal rod from the nightstand. She ran it up Cailyn's thighs and back down again. It was cold and Cailyn winced. She willed herself to be still as it rolled along her flesh.

She sighed. Teran rewarded her by running it over her vulva. Her hips moved to meet it and Teran grinned.

Without warning, Teran drew back her arm. The cane hit her inner thigh. Cailyn tensed at the impact, a bright burning sting. She relaxed and let its burn crackle through her.

Teran drew back her arm again. Cailyn breathed deep to ease herself into the rhythm, but Teran didn't give her time to relax. The sting came again, sharp and sudden.

More strikes came on its heels. Teran rained blows onto her skin, refusing to allow her to ride the sensation. She twisted and turned as the unyielding metal connected with her tender, hidden flesh.

Cailyn panted, a harsh sexual sound. She cried out, half from the pain, half to cover the sound of her breath.

Teran hissed. Cailyn twisted away from the blows, pressing her legs together to shield herself from them.

"Easy," Teran chuckled. She traced the tip of the cane along Cailyn's legs, easing them apart again.

Cailyn cursed under her breath but opened her thighs. It was this or run away. She wasn't running yet.

Teran ran the cane over her inner thighs. It slid over the marks it had made and set them alight with fresh pain.

Cailyn caught herself before protesting. She could answer with a stop word, but not with, "I can't."

"Yes, my lady," she said, her voice breaking.

Teran leaned down to stare at Cailyn's welted flesh. Cailyn winced, expecting another blow. Instead, Teran bit, hard.

The pain washed over her, sharp and pure. She could feel nothing else. She mewled, her nerves overtaken by the sting of Teran's teeth worrying her already sensitive skin.

"Please." She couldn't recognize the sharp wailing sound as her own voice.

Teran drew her head away. Caught up in the fantasy, Cailyn half expected to see blood running down Teran's chin.

"What is it you want?" Teran asked. She grabbed at Cailyn's breast again, twisted it like meat. "More pain?"

"Yes," Cailyn panted. It had been so long.

With a cry, Cailyn abandoned herself to the sensation. She twisted against Teran's grip, desperate to feel more.

Teran's hand slid down Cailyn's body. Her claws traced welts as they went. Then their pointed tips reached Cailyn's labia. Cailyn froze, trying not to twitch or arch into Teran's touch.

"Please," she begged her. She wanted Teran inside her. She wanted the freedom to move against the fingers that speared her.

She heard a snick as the claws retracted. She felt the fingers, smooth now, explore her wetness. She pushed against them, wanting to feel them enter her.

Two of Teran's fingers sank into Cailyn. Her body yawned a welcome, her nerves already electrified. They flickered to new life as Teran moved inside her. She ground against Teran's hand and whined, a greedy, shapeless sound.

Teran drew back to drive in again, deep, pushing a third finger in alongside the other two. The sudden stretch stung Cailyn's opening, the ache complementing the burn in her thighs.

Teran's thumb danced over Cailyn's clitoris. She rocked back against Teran's fingers, all resistance gone.

When Teran squeezed lubricant onto her hand and added a fourth finger, Cailyn writhed in time with every motion.

Her training had taught her, above all else, to focus on the nobles' pleasure, rather than her own. Teran had turned all that upside down.

Did those eyes above her, pale as gems, reflect pleasure? She could see only concentration, fierce and unyielding.

Yet she rode Teran's fingers, drawn away from any thought of Teran's enjoyment by the silver threads of sensation running through her body. The thumb moved off her clitoris and she whimpered, only to wriggle as it slid down to her entrance.

She whined again, a shapeless, needy sound, as Teran's thumb slid in, stretching her impossibly. She recovered herself enough to breathe as the last of Teran's hand slipped inside. The stretch burned for a moment. Then Teran's hand settled inside and rested there.

Cailyn paused to catch her breath. She panted, unable to silence herself.

All this was bad form, she knew. She also knew that Teran didn't care.

Teran moved inside her, gentle and sure. Cailyn mewled, her reason slipping away as the sensation flooded her mind. She knew nothing but Teran's movements.

"You are mine," Teran whispered, her voice sharp.

Cailyn heard the words from a great distance. She heard the pleasure in them but wondered at their meaning. She whispered a response. Whatever Teran wanted, she wanted to be.

The hand moved inside her. Her head rolled back. Sounds came from her mouth. She was beyond thinking, beyond orgasm, beyond everything but the movement inside her. She strained against the bonds, sensation overloading her, until Teran's hand grew still, then slid free.

She sobbed into the silence.

"Yes," she gasped out. "Yours."

Teran ran her fingertips over the bonds around Cailyn's wrists. "My little one." Teran smiled down at Cailyn.

"You may see to Valik now," Teran said, pushing a small bottle of salve toward her. "If you still want to."

Cailyn swallowed, her mouth dry. She wished Teran had given her time to prepare. But if she meant to do this, she would have to do it now. Regardless of her gaping flesh, the sweat plastering her hair to her head, the ache in her thighs from Teran's cane.

This was an indulgence.

"Valik?" she asked as the doors hissed closed.

"Derys," he said. Cailyn could see bruises on his chest from Teran's fists. For a moment, she thought of pressing the tender skin. She shook her head and the moment passed.

She did not look down at his groin. She didn't want to.

"How are you doing?" Cailyn asked, setting the salve and cloths down. She hadn't had the training Teran's servants had, but she would make the best of it.

He stretched and yawned. "You're very lucky, you know. Teran Nivrai favors you. Most of the dark channels can't say that."

How do you know? It's not like we go around telling one another our business.

"I am lucky. But it's difficult for me."

Valik smiled. "She's fond of you. She wouldn't have spent half her time talking to me about you if she weren't." A grin flitted across his face. "Or bothered letting you use her knives on me."

Cailyn swallowed, a hard lump in her throat.

"You weren't as bad at it as you think, you know."

"Do you need anything?" Cailyn sat on the edge of his bed. "I don't like that she left you after all of that."

"She's Teran Nivrai. I expected it."

He stretched, then winced and sighed in lazy satiation. "They took good care of me. I'm a little woozy, but I'll be all right."

"Let me at least treat those bruises."

He grinned and lay down. Cailyn spread salve on his skin. When her fingers ran over the marks, he trembled.

"You really do like it."

He raised an eyebrow. "Are you saying you don't?"

Cailyn looked down at herself. Sweat coated her body. Bruises and a new scrape speckled her chest.

She shook her head. "I want to please my lady. I enjoy serving. With Teran that means pain. But what she did to you—" She flinched.

"You were eager for it."

He laughed. "No wonder I'd never seen you on the dark channels before!"

"I never expected to be here."

She thought of Teran, of the changes in her voice when it became rich with desire, of the sensations she felt when the pain no longer frightened her. "But yes. I like it."

"You took an assignment from Teran Nivrai without ever having been on the dark channels before?"

She nodded, then wiped the salve off her hands. "I couldn't pass it up."

Valik gave her a knowing smile. "I should ask you why you stayed around."

Cailyn busied herself picking up the cloths and the bottle of salve. "And I should be getting back."

"All right." Valik nodded and waved. "Good luck."

"Thank you," Cailyn said and walked back out.

CHAPTER THIRTY-TWO

Teran drew back the bedcovers as Cailyn entered. It was the sort of thing a courtesan would do. But there was no mistaking the look in Teran's eyes. This was no invitation. She slid into the bed next to Teran, trying to be graceful.

Strong arms wrapped around her, holding her fast. Teran bit her shoulder. Her neck arched, the response automatic.

"You're greedy now," Teran purred. Her breath moved on Cailyn's ear.

Cailyn's flesh, raw and open, twinged at Teran's touch. "I'm tired of fighting you, my lady."

"It's you I want."

Teran traced kisses down Cailyn's back. Cailyn didn't want to shiver, but the response came anyway. She trembled under the sudden gentleness.

"And I think you feel the same," Teran went on. Her fingers moved to Cailyn's nipples. Cailyn closed her eyes, imagining the gleam in Teran's eyes.

Teran rolled Cailyn's nipples between her fingers and twisted them. Cailyn's hips bucked, a marionette's hips, responding only to Teran's touch.

"How much would it cost to keep you?" Teran nibbled at Cailyn's back.

"What?" Cailyn snapped.

Teran nuzzled Cailyn's back, her lips feather-gentle. "It seems a shame to let you go when this is over."

Cailyn rubbed her eyes. "Stay with you?"

"Teran's whore, they call you. How would you feel if it were true?"

Cailyn winced.

"My lady, I am the daughter of Loriel Derys. I didn't choose this so that I could withdraw from it. I have no interest in serving anyone exclusively. Not you or someone else."

"Exclusively? I wouldn't dream of it. I have no interest in taking you away from your work." She wrapped her fingers in Cailyn's hair. "It suits you."

She pulled Cailyn's hair just enough to sting. "Serve whoever you want. Go wherever you want. Make whatever money you want. None of that matters to me. You have your father's gift. It would be a shame not to use it."

"Then why suggest that I stay with you?"

"Because you would come back to me. No matter where you went, no matter who you served, you'd be mine in the end. That's all I want. For you to do as you like and return to me. Just like here. Just like now."

To return to this, over and over. It would be too easy. Too easy to wrap her hand around Teran's head, draw it down to her lips. Too easy to forget anger and fear and open instead.

She sighed. This thing with the Councils, whatever Teran thought of it, Cailyn would never feel comfortable in the bed of a torturer. Not fully. Not enough to leave it and return to it over and over. Lazy and warm as she felt now, her misgivings would catch up with her.

But if none of that had ever happened? If Teran had asked her the same question after a long, leisurely stay?

Could she have said yes?

She could spend her nights at Teran's side, never leave lonely and tired. Never sleep alone after serving someone who unnerved her or who took liberties she didn't want. Never wonder if new clients would be fools born into money who considered a courtesan's body their personal playgrounds. Never wander onto the dark channels, the yen for pain nipping at her heels, without knowing if the noble she found knew how to give it well. Never fear that serving meant going without her own pleasure.

"My lady." She kept her eyes trained on the ceiling. "You know I can't agree to that."

"I know."

A flick of long fingers, and the lights dimmed. Cailyn settled against Teran's body. Was Valik spending the night in the other room, attended by silent servants in gray? Or had they sent him off already?

He thinks I'm the lucky one, she thought as her eyes closed.

❖

Lord Keriel lounged on the same bed as before. "Hello again," he said.

He held something in his hands, flat, thin, and gray. A tablet of some kind, though its screen lay black and dormant. Rather than read it, he toyed with it, passing it back and forth between his hands.

Cailyn stared ahead. She held her chin high, imagined the metal around her neck shining like armor, a talisman clasped there to protect her. "My lord." She bowed, curt and cold, with all the precision she'd learned over the years.

"Still attached to Nivrai, I see." He cast a pointed glance at the collar.

"My lord?"

"I didn't expect you to stay."

"I agreed to a contract," Cailyn said, her voice cold. "I intend to honor it. In full."

"Fair enough. But there is something I think you should know about her."

"My lord?"

He shuffled the tablet from hand to hand. "I gather you were surprised when Teran told you she'd take this assignment."

"That is a personal matter."

"Is it, Derys?"

"What my lady does for the Councils is between her and the Councils."

"And not you?"

"If she tells me anything, my lord, that is no business but mine."

The tablet froze in the cage of his hands. "Of course. But there is something I wanted to tell you."

Cailyn looked at the muted brown and green of his shirt. She didn't answer.

"Teran is no one's friend, but she has her own idea of honor. It doesn't include torturing rebels."

His long fingers curled over the surface of the tablet. *What is that thing?*

"You heard her tell us off. She came as close to refusing us as anybody ever could."

"My lord, I don't understand why you should bring that up now, after you told her you couldn't stop this."

"You know her well enough to know that she would never obey us without an incentive."

Cailyn blanched. "An incentive?"

"They promised her something they knew she would accept, no matter what."

Cailyn's hands shook.

"Tell me," she said, regretting the words as soon as they left her lips.

"You."

The room spun in her vision. "Me?"

"You."

She put a hand to the wall for support. "But that's impossible. Guild law says—"

"Guild law doesn't matter." He sat up and stared straight at her. "The Councils have already promised her a full pardon for anything she does."

"With the prisoner."

"With anyone. Surely you don't think the Councils give a damn what she does with you."

Cailyn's mouth opened, closed, opened again. Teran had always been scrupulous about Guild law. She'd never needed reminding of it, unlike some clients who'd been far less violent.

"My lord, I'm already promised to her until this conference is over. Unless you're trying to tell me you think she would go against my wishes."

He ran his fingertips over the dead screen of the tablet. "She wouldn't want to. But she might if she thought she had to."

"Had to?"

"Tell me: have you ever refused her?"

"My lord, I can't—"

"Of course you can't tell me. I don't need to know."

"She would never have done such a thing to Mariel," Cailyn whispered.

His eyes shone bright, greedy green. "Mariel was her slave, Derys."

"Mariel was—" She bit her lip. That was Teran's private life, and Cailyn would never spill those secrets. Especially not to Ben Keriel.

"Mariel was a gladiator. Entertainment. He'd live and die in service to Nivrai no matter what. The only thing Teran taking him home changed was how. Then he caught the wasting sickness and faded away." He chuckled. "She should be glad no one knew about him. She tore apart a man for fun. A few years later, he became weak and sick."

"My lord!" Cailyn cried. "You're not saying you think she—"

He chuckled, low and harsh. "I'm not saying a damn thing. But there are plenty of people on the Councils who would think that's a little too convenient."

"She would never harm him."

The hand holding the tablet clenched tight. "She never had to."

"My lord!"

"Derys, surely you don't think she obeys Guild law because she believes in it."

Cailyn raised her head. "My lord, if Mariel was just entertainment, then so am I."

He looked down, muttering. "I see you're going to be harder to reach than I thought."

His restless hands moved again, curling over the thin edge of the tablet. "It's hard to get her out of your blood, isn't it, Derys?"

Before she could answer, he turned his head away. Cailyn's gaze followed his to the portrait of Dion.

"It doesn't matter right now," he said. "But what will you do when the conference is over? When she calls for you again and you can't refuse?"

"What?" Cailyn cried. "They can't—!"

"They already did."

"Already did? What are you saying?"

"You belong to Teran Nivrai now. She just hasn't told you yet."

Cailyn's mouth worked. Numbness spread through her body.

"You're lying," she choked out.

"No, Derys. I'm not. What do you think it took days of meeting to decide?"

"What—if you're right—what will she do with me?" Cailyn whispered.

"You'd know that better than I would. All I know is that she doesn't want to let you go."

How much would it cost to keep you?

"My lord," she said, choosing her words carefully, "Lady Nivrai has always paid close attention to my limits and needs."

He looked down at his hands. "I'm sure she has."

"My lord?"

"You're a challenge for her."

"A challenge, my lord?"

"You're not on the dark channels. You're not the sort to swoon over her from the beginning. So she took her time seducing you. Surely you didn't think she did it out of kindness?"

He looked back at her, his gaze sharp. "She has you wrapped around her fingers."

"What?"

"Teran's whore. That was her plan. It's got nothing to do with respecting you and everything to do with winning you over."

Teran's whore. Everyone knew it. Everyone said it.

"But my lord," Cailyn stammered, trying to find words. "Lady Nivrai understands that my life is my own. She's told me so herself."

"The proof will come when you want to leave and she lets you," he answered. He gripped the tablet hard.

"No!"

"I was in the room where the Councils decided it."

"My lord, just saying that isn't proof."

He shook his head. "I thought she wanted your love, at first."

Cailyn quieted. She wanted to leave, to protest, to insist on Teran's innocence.

But Teran had already lied once before.

And long conversations with courtesans sometimes loosened nobles' lips. Especially if they wanted to keep talking.

Which, apparently, he did. "I thought she wanted that gladiator's love, too."

Cailyn bit her lip.

"I asked her about you. I told her I thought she wanted your love. But if she did, how could she agree to what the Councils offered?"

"And what did she say?" Cailyn asked, putting on her best expression of breathless interest.

"She said 'Love? I don't want her love. I wouldn't know what to do with it if I had it. I want her loyalty.'"

Cailyn shuddered.

"She doesn't care what you think or how you feel, Derys. Not as long as you're hers."

She raised her head to look at the painting. She'd noticed the eyes before, lovingly rendered.

His eyes are gray, Teran had said.

She'd also said that Lord Keriel lied.

"That remains to be seen, my lord."

"So it does." He swept a long arm in front of his chest in a conciliatory gesture. "But I thought you'd want to know."

"Thank you, my lord," Cailyn spat, the words bitter ash in her mouth.

"You say she's been kind to you. She's never kind without a reason. She wants to claim you for herself. But trust me. If she can't, she has no problem coming to the Councils for backup. She was willing to torture to keep you, Derys."

Cailyn said nothing more. Her voice would break if she tried. She summoned up all of her training to give him one last imperious look.

Then she fled down the hallway as quickly as she could.

CHAPTER THIRTY-THREE

Teran hadn't laid out any clothes for the night. At first, Cailyn had hoped that it meant Teran would give her time to choose her own outfit, to dress and primp before Teran returned. The little rituals of grooming calmed her, and she needed them now.

But the videocall had been absolutely clear. She was to be naked and positioned over the bed when Teran came in after her shower.

She'd chosen her earrings, bracelets, and anklets with absurd care. Teran wouldn't notice them, but it gave her something to do.

And small details could matter. Noticing someone's favorite color, for example, could be the difference between giving someone a pleasant evening he'd soon forget and giving him a delightful evening he was sure to remember.

Cailyn fidgeted as the door slid open. Teran hadn't frozen up—not like before. But what would she do now, fresh from the interrogation room?

Nothing, apparently. Teran didn't touch her or prick her or even greet her. Instead, Cailyn immediately felt the tip of Teran's dildo pressing against her opening.

"My lady Nivrai?"

She twisted to look at Teran and caught a glimpse of glittering eyes and a hard-set mouth. A clawed hand slammed her head into the bed sheets.

The device rammed relentlessly into her, the force of it stinging as it pushed her open.

Again and again, it ripped into her, its strokes measured and cold. She writhed in a desperate attempt to make herself comfortable, a twisted parody of pleasure. Teran snarled and drove into her harder. The force froze her in place.

Behind her, Cailyn could hear the clipped, harsh panting of Teran's breath. Teran made no other sound, neither moan nor snarl nor hiss. Cailyn willed herself to be still as Teran's motions grew more insistent.

They tore at her, cleaving her. Wetness oozed onto her thighs. But she took no comfort in it. When her body clamped hard over the dildo, she thought she might retch.

Teran snarled and drove in deep. Cailyn wasn't sure if it was worse or a relief, not even when Teran finally collapsed over her body.

She slid free of Cailyn's stinging flesh. The hand around Cailyn's head withdrew.

Cailyn turned to look and saw the same expression as before. Teran's eyes stared ahead, fixed. Her jaws clamped shut. Cailyn shivered and turned away.

She heard the hiss of the doors sliding shut as Teran left her alone. For a long moment, she did nothing, lying there in the empty room. Her flesh yawned open, wide and obscene. It burned with the sting of Teran's roughness.

No servants came. Why should they? This was sex. If it stung, that hardly mattered.

With a sigh, Cailyn stood up, drew back the covers of the bed, and climbed in. She wished she had someone to talk to. Lord Darien. Valik.

Even talking to Teran, whatever black mood she was in, would be better than being alone now.

CHAPTER THIRTY-FOUR

"Did you sleep well?" Teran sipped at a glass of vakren. "You look tired."

Cailyn took her own sip and coughed. How dare Teran ask a question like that?

"No, my lady," she answered in as calm a voice as she could muster.

She looked down at her goblet. She knew many ways to smooth truths over, but she wasn't sure which to use now. When things went badly, a courtesan smiled. She found something to compliment, unless something truly bad had happened and she wanted to take it up with the Guild.

"Last night," she said. "You didn't say a word. And you had just come back from—from your work for the Councils."

"I had, yes."

"It unnerved me, my lady."

"Of all the things you could take exception to, you choose that."

Cailyn glared. Teran laughed.

"My experiment must be going well, little one, if you object to hard use more than pain."

Cailyn dropped the fork she'd been holding, the food on it untouched. "Experiment?"

"I've been seeing you for months now. You don't think I would've kept calling you back if I didn't have something in mind."

"Experiment?" Cailyn said again. "I was an experiment to you, my lady?"

"Of course."

"I thought I was your gem in a world of stones."

"You were. You are. But do you really think I would have taken the care I did to seduce you just because I liked you?"

Cailyn felt the world tilt under her chair. "I don't understand."

"You are one of the most famous of the courtesans. One of the best there is—beautiful, intelligent, and skilled. But I've rarely called anyone back. And never hired anyone I didn't find on the dark channels. Until you."

Cailyn felt the blood drain from her face.

Teran speared a bite of meat. "It should have been obvious I had a plan."

Damn it.

Teran had asked so many questions. About her lovers. About her preferences. About her desires. She'd volunteered more information about herself than she ever gave to anyone.

"A plan, my lady? What plan?"

"You know already, little one."

Cailyn's teeth clenched. "What plan?"

"The dark channels are nothing to me. You know that. I have never known anyone as eager for pain as Mariel was. And Mariel served me personally."

"What does that have to do with me, my lady?"

"Even those who do kindle to pain only go so far. People like our friend Valik"—she licked her lips—"are few and far between."

Cailyn chewed a bite of food. It tasted like chalk in her mouth.

"And even people like Valik get boring far too soon."

"I—my lady—again. What does all this have to do with me?"

"People on the dark channels wanted me. At least, the people who weren't too afraid of me to see me. The people off them? I couldn't hire them, as far as I knew. As far as I knew, I was their favorite monster."

Horns. Wings. Spines. A tail. The fangs of a demon. Hell made flesh. Cailyn had known the wildest of the rumors couldn't possibly be true, but wondered about them anyway. What might it be like to bed a woman with wings?

Teran chuckled. Cailyn put a hand to her ear, not liking the harsh sound. "You were intrigued. Weren't you, my little one?"

"Yes," Cailyn breathed, her stomach sinking.

"Which is exactly what I wanted." The claws emerged, gray and gleaming. "Someone from outside the dark channels. Someone intelligent, curious, skilled enough to be worth my time."

"I know," Cailyn said. The vakren stung her throat.

The newsteel slid in and out of Teran's fingertips. "I wanted to train you, my little one. To take someone who'd never wanted pain and teach them—"

"To want it," Cailyn finished for her.

Teran nodded. The newsteel at her fingers sparkled as she raised the glass to her lips.

Cailyn dropped her fork. It clattered against her plate. "You called me back to see if it was working. Not because I impressed you. Because you had more work to do."

Teran raised an eyebrow. "Of course you impressed me. Would I have called you back if you hadn't?"

Cailyn chewed and swallowed, the movements automatic. So all Teran had wanted was someone to seduce.

"That's all I am to you," she said. "An experiment."

She thought of her other assignments. Of the clients she'd visited after seeing Teran. Of the delight she should have felt in serving them. Of all the moments she'd thought only of newsteel-tipped fingers.

I don't want her love. I wouldn't know what to do with it if I had it. I want her loyalty.

"You were manipulating me," Cailyn whispered. "All this time, you were—"

"Manipulating you?" Teran slid out of her chair and walked over to Cailyn. "Of course I've been manipulating you." She reached down to touch Cailyn's hair. "I've been manipulating you from the beginning. Are you telling me you didn't know?"

Cailyn brushed the steel-tipped hand away. She squirmed in her seat to tamp down the heat rising in her flesh.

Not now. Not now. Not now.

"You became a courtesan for the same reason as your father. You enjoy serving. It fulfills you, as it did him."

"Leave my father out of this, Teran Nivrai."

Teran's lip curled. "Very well. But you knew what you were getting into when you chose to serve me, little one."

"I knew this? I knew that you'd hurt me, yes. I agreed to that. But not to this." She glared at Teran. "Not to being your test subject."

"You didn't know what I'd do with you. But you knew that I would challenge you. That I wanted to."

"No!"

"I did. I enjoyed it. Did you expect anything different from a helldemon?"

Cailyn glowered. "Don't call yourself that."

"I called you back. I tested you again and again."

"Tested me?" Cailyn thought of that first night. She remembered the heavy flogger, made of braided leather.

Too much for a beginner. Too much, too fast.

A test.

A gods-damned test.

Teran nodded. "You passed them all." A smile spread over her face. "You should be proud of yourself, not angry with me."

"Proud of myself?" Cailyn swatted away Teran's hand, heedless of the newsteel's danger. "For what? For letting you manipulate me?"

The ice in her chest spread out through her veins. It chilled every part of her. "You wanted to change me. To make me into what you wanted."

Her lips pulled back into an ugly snarl. "Did you ever stop to think about what would happen to me if it worked?"

"What would happen to you? You've already been on the dark channels."

"I don't give a damn about the dark channels! This is about you. You didn't give a damn about what experimenting with me would do to the rest of my life." She set her glass down hard. It rang as it hit the table. "Or you wanted it that way."

"Cailyn, listen to me."

"That's it, isn't it, my lady? That's what you wanted."

"Cailyn, I—"

"That's what you meant yesterday. The end of the experiment. Me becoming yours. Me coming to Nivrai to serve you permanently."

"Cailyn—"

"Say it. Just say it. You've twisted the truth enough, my lady Nivrai."

Teran let out a slow breath. "I would like that, yes. But that was never part of the plan."

"Wasn't it?" Cailyn snarled.

"You were just an amusement to me, like any other. I didn't think I would even call you back."

She laid a hand on Cailyn's shoulder. Cailyn pushed it away. She glared at the food cooling, uneaten, on her plate.

"You don't give yourself enough credit, little one. I was looking for someone to toy with. I admit that. But it never would have become more than that if you hadn't impressed me."

She leaned in, her face inches from Cailyn's. "I could have chosen anyone. I chose you." Her hand moved to Cailyn's neck. Metal clinked as Teran's claws tapped her collar. "Yes, you've been my experiment."

Cailyn flinched. Teran didn't move. "But you never would have been if you hadn't earned my respect first."

Cailyn wanted to believe it. To delight in the gesture. To give herself up to the possession.

But how could she?

"If you respect me so much, my lady, why did you come in last night like I meant nothing to you?"

"Teran's whore, they call you, but you get angry when I use you like one." Her hand clutched Cailyn's shoulder. The newsteel pricked it. "If I didn't know better, I would say you missed the pain."

A growl welled up from somewhere inside Cailyn. "How can you say that?"

"Pain is what we do. It would remind you of my desire for you—and of yours for me." The clawed hand released Cailyn's shoulder. Newsteel skipped over Cailyn's skin.

Teran leaned down to kiss her hair. "We both know the experiment worked."

Cailyn closed her eyes. She bit her lip, used the sting to recover herself. "You didn't even speak to me."

"I wanted to lose myself, little one." Teran looked up, her eyes bright as crystal. "There's the Councils' work: dirty, thankless, and difficult. There's you, and you are mine."

"So you do think you own me, then," Cailyn snapped. She pulled away.

Teran made no move to draw Cailyn back. "I asked you yesterday to come with me to Nivrai. You refused."

The proof will come when you want to leave and she lets you.

"I did."

"Your life is your own." Her eyes glittered, the gleam in a hawk's eye just before it descends. "Unless you're reconsidering."

"No," Cailyn answered. She studied her fork to avoid Teran's gaze, then speared a bit of fruit. "I can't leave my life behind for you, my lady. That hasn't changed."

"Then I have nothing else to say."

Cailyn bit her lip. Teran had lied. That much she knew. Had Lord Keriel lied too?

Would anyone around her tell the truth?

CHAPTER THIRTY-FIVE

"Will you be going to Lord Darien's party?"
Cailyn stopped. She hadn't even thought about that.
A party for the dark channels. If she went, the nobles who patronized them would see her. Use her, if she let them.

Some would surely call her afterward. That would be fine from someone like Darien. But what about the rest? Even if she wanted them, could she serve them now, knowing she craved what they offered only because Teran made her?

Then there was Lord Darien himself. He would want to see her. It would be nice to see him too. She thought of the soft touch of his hands, the odd gentle sting of his whips.

Kneeling to him would be easy after all of this intrigue with Teran, too. No matter where her desires came from.

"We should go," she said.

"We, little one?" Teran's lip curled like she tasted something bitter. "I told you I wasn't going."

Cailyn breathed deep. She thought of the claws opening her skin, of Teran's head bent down to kiss the wounds. She cursed herself for the little thrill of heat between her legs.

"Besides," Teran continued, "I have a reputation to uphold."

"By not showing up."

The claws extended, retracted, extended again. "As impressive as these things are, they're nothing next to wings and a tail. Much less a retractable metal phallus. Their imaginations can come up with far worse than I ever could."

She reached out to stroke Cailyn's hair. Cailyn froze. She didn't want to respond.

"If I send you alone, they'll go on believing whatever they want about me. And you'll get to see some people I suspect you miss." Teran grinned. "My lord Darien, for one."

Cailyn cast her eyes downward.

"Embarrassed, little one?" Teran pulled Cailyn's head up by the hair. Newsteel tangled in Cailyn's hair, and Teran leaned in to kiss her parted lips. "You shouldn't be embarrassed. You never were before this."

Cailyn let Teran kiss her. Her anger hadn't cooled, but she had agreed to serve. She'd have to break her contract to refuse.

And she still couldn't do that. Not when she didn't know the truth.

Teran's tongue slipped into her mouth. She distracted herself by thinking of Lord Darien. She remembered his warmth inside her and moaned around Teran's tongue.

She'd thought so often of Teran when others touched and used her. And now she thought of him while Teran touched her.

How had things gotten so turned around?

"Nervous, my little one?"

"A little," Cailyn answered. "What can I expect, my lady?"

"I don't know. I've never been to one."

Cailyn blinked. "Never?"

"No. Why would I? When I first came of age, I hired someone from the dark channels to teach me technique. I did nothing on them since. I had Mariel for that."

"Mariel." Cailyn tasted the word.

She had meant to ask Teran so much more about him. About how he'd died. She didn't want Ben Keriel's words to be the last ones she heard about that.

But she had so much to think about. The boy. The Councils. Teran's duty here. Her strange, distant behavior after the sessions.

And she'd rejected Teran. She couldn't just ask how Mariel died.

She'd asked about their relationship, his service. She'd never asked about who he was. About what he wanted. About how he'd taken sick. What happened after.

Why Lord Keriel would call him a slave.

"He wanted to serve you?"

Teran chuckled and shook her head. "He wanted pain. In the arena, he let his opponents hit him. He pretended it was for show, but I knew better."

Of course you did, Cailyn thought.

"I don't think he ever expected it to get anyone's attention."

"But it got yours."

"Why go to the dark channels and pay when a man let others bruise him in front of me in the arena every weekend?"

Teran chuckled. "Why bother with politics? I had what I wanted already. I just needed to claim it."

Claim it. She thought of Teran braving the sands of the emptied arena. What had her body looked like before she'd met Mariel, before she'd practiced fighting forms with him and torn into him at the end?

It would still impress him. Cailyn had no doubt of that. Teran had said she was always cruel, after all.

Cailyn envisioned thin fingers pressing into Mariel's bruises. Mariel's answering hisses, filled with sweat and hunger.

Had he felt any of the same misgivings she felt now? "He went to you—"

"I goaded him into it."

"Goaded him, my lady?"

"I taunted him. I told him I could see his desire. I worried his bruises, kissed his cuts."

Her hand moved as if the remembered flesh lay under it. "He wanted me to stop, to leave him alone. He didn't want to want me. He knew what it would mean." She chuckled again. "But he couldn't have refused me anyway."

Cailyn pulled back as if burned.

Teran's head snapped up.

"Nervous, little one?"

"A little, my lady."

"Do you want me to finish the story, or not?"

Cailyn swallowed. "Yes," she said. She felt faithless. Teran didn't know what she was asking, not really.

"No. I snuck into his rooms in the arena after most of the fighters had gone to sleep or left. We hoped that the sounds we made would seem enough like training that no one would care if they did hear us."

Cailyn winced again. "That was a risky thing to do, my lady."

Teran shrugged, claws sparkling. "I didn't give a damn. My parents wanted an heir. I couldn't have cared less. I mocked those who visited. Or ignored them. Or stared until they quailed and ran away."

Her mouth curled as if she tasted something sour. "But there was one person even I couldn't scare off."

"Lord Keriel." Cailyn thought of hands on her dress and his hot greedy breath. *What's your secret, Derys?*

"Yes. My lord Ben." Teran spat the words. "But I didn't care. Not then. I loved those stolen moments." She smirked. "To think, I did it all right under the lords of Nivrai's noses."

Cailyn stared, dumbstruck. "The lords of Nivrai? They were your parents."

"I was never fond of them. I was never fond of anyone until I met Mariel. They owned the house where I lived. That was all. I snuck out more and more often to see him. It delighted me to see my marks on his flesh, to watch him try to muffle his cries of pleasure."

"But Lord Keriel found you."

"Yes."

"How?"

"He'd already come to my parents, offering me the favor of carrying a High Councilman's heir. Finally, someone willing to breed with their silent, sullen daughter."

"But you didn't want him."

"Of course not." Teran's hand flexed as if to strike. Cailyn shuddered.

"One interminable afternoon, my parents insisted I dine with him. He tried to woo me with expensive food, promises of wealth, professions of desire." She snickered and slipped a hand over Cailyn's.

Cailyn flinched but let her do it.

"I thought he was talking with my parents, making plans for their alliance."

"He wasn't?"

The grip around Cailyn's hand tightened. Cailyn forced herself to be still.

"He followed me. Watched me go in to Mariel. I heard him slip away after we finished. I thought little of the sound. I thought only of Mariel." She shook her head. "I should have paid attention."

"He told on you," Cailyn said, her voice flat.

Teran's grip was painful now. "He told my father. He threatened to tell everyone else. Unless I agreed to bear his child."

"So you did it." Cailyn pulled her hand out from under Teran's. Once free, she flexed it, trying to work out the soreness.

"No."

"But you've told me—you had Dion—"

"Not because Ben Keriel threatened to spread rumors. True or not."

"Then why?"

Teran's expression hardened. "You don't know my lord Keriel, do you?"

"I—" Cailyn snapped her mouth shut.

"He made a deal with me. That's what he does."

"My lady?"

"He made my parents promise that if I agreed to bear his child, they would let Mariel move into Nivrai proper. And become my personal servant."

You belong to Teran Nivrai now. She just hasn't told you yet.

Mariel was her slave, Derys.

Cailyn's mouth fell open. "Lord Keriel—"

How could she ask it?

"He did that for you?" she tried.

Teran's mouth puckered. "Lord Keriel did that for access to me. He knew I wouldn't refuse."

"And you agreed to it? Knowing…what he wanted?" Cailyn couldn't bring herself to say it.

"My parents would have banished Mariel. Or killed him. This way, he was mine."

Cailyn cringed, thinking of Teran alone in Nivrai, seeing no one.

My desire is what it is. It moves slowly through my blood, little one.

It's slow to stir and slow to vanish. If she had lost her lover to violence and politics, would it ever have stirred again?

"So you agreed."

"Yes. With a stipulation of my own."

"That you wouldn't raise Dion."

Cailyn winced. What it would be like to have a mother—or father—who had never held her as a child?

"Yes. And that he leave me alone after Dion was born." Teran drummed newsteel-tipped fingertips on the table. "A rule he has trouble obeying."

She turned away. "Mariel didn't understand that I didn't want the child, not really. He had big hands. He would run them over my belly, laughing as he felt the kicks. It made me feel ill to have something of Ben Keriel's growing inside me, but it made Mariel laugh to feel it."

Cailyn remembered her shock at the thought of Teran pregnant. At the thought of pregnancy at all. Female courtesans kept their own cycles suppressed.

Still, she could understand how Mariel felt. A child grew inside the woman he loved, safe and warm within her body. Unlike one of the courtesans, Teran could have the experience of growing a life inside her without retiring—or disappearing.

And yet Teran had never considered herself lucky. She hardly knew Dion even now.

Teran's hand reached out to cup Cailyn's again, gently now. "He wanted me. Delighted in serving me. But if I had never found him, his life would have been very different from the life I demanded of him." She looked down. "I never asked him if he had regrets."

"My lady—"

"I don't think he had any. But I think he hoped that when Dion was born, he would get to play father. I never gave him that chance."

Cailyn didn't answer. She waited, silent.

"I had Dion. I gave him to his father. I had Mariel to myself again, without—" Teran shook her head with a violent motion. The grip around Cailyn's hand tightened again.

"Then I watched Mariel die. He—his body, all muscles and strength—"

Cailyn shook her head. "I'm sorry, my lady."

"He was so small when he finally died. Smaller than me."

Teran's head lowered. Cailyn followed her gaze, looking down at Teran's hand on hers.

"I couldn't believe that," Teran said. "I couldn't believe that he'd become so small."

Her grip relaxed. She held up her hand and watched her claws catch the light. A thin smile turned up the corners of her mouth.

"Now he is gone. And I have this."

Cailyn looked at her, worried. But her smile widened and her eyes brightened.

"You do." Cailyn allowed herself a small laugh. "I'm sure they make quite a memento."

Teran retracted them and extended them again with a laugh of her own. "They are a part of my body. A part of me. So is he."

They'd been his idea. So Teran had said. He'd wanted his lady's hands to be her weapons.

Or better weapons than they already were, Cailyn thought with a wry smile.

Had the claws frightened him at first? Had he wondered where his life was taking him? Or did his desire rise immediately as he first watched metal spring free from his lady's hands, eager for the rending of his flesh?

Had he reacted, from the beginning, as Cailyn did now?

She swallowed hard. Teran had called her an experiment. Had he been one as well, to a young, bored noble who snuck out to ease her boredom?

Or had he been hers from the very beginning, as Teran had said?

The ice-gray eyes watched Cailyn intently.

"I'm sorry, my lady," she said again.

CHAPTER THIRTY-SIX

Cailyn twisted around to get a better look at herself in the full-length mirror. Religious application of Teran's expensive salve for several days, coupled with an even more costly regeneration treatment at Teran's expense, had made her marks fade. Now she bore a few scrapes, the yellow remains of healing bruises.

Teran had reminded her of the rumors. "Nothing I do will be violent enough to satisfy them," she'd said. Her smile had showed teeth. "They expect me to be a demon. They'd be disappointed if you didn't show up half-dead." She'd stretched, the claws glinting. "I want you as flawless as possible. I want to surprise them."

Cailyn looked over her nearly pristine body. She pressed her fingers into her skin. She'd gotten used to pressure making her nerves blossom with pain. Now she felt oddly numb. She shrugged and slipped into the bodysuit Teran had chosen for her.

It was the same black bodysuit Teran had bid her wear when she first arrived. The one that revealed so little.

She hadn't liked it then. Didn't like it better now. She slipped a pair of plain black shoes onto her feet. At least their heels were high, and at least she'd put her hair up. And at least she had her lipstick. As usual, it was a blood-dark shade of red, not the brighter red Cailyn would have preferred.

She patted her hair once to be sure it was all in order. She didn't want to linger. Teran had gone off by herself. Probably off to the gymnasium to practice her forms. Or attack targets until she tired herself out.

Trying not to think too hard about Teran's tight, muscular frame, Cailyn snatched up a bag with her essentials and hurried out the door.

Despite her nervousness, she slowed her pace as she headed to the elevators. Racing wouldn't do anything to calm her nerves. Besides, even if she couldn't calm down, it was a bad idea to let everyone know it. She took deep breaths, envisioning the courtesans' goddess: serene, closed eyes, flowing hair, voluptuous nakedness.

She opened her eyes to find someone staring back at her.

Lord Nalar. The one who'd called her "Teran's whore."

This was all she needed. She pressed her lips together, determined not to react.

"Cailyn Derys." His lip curled.

"My lord," she answered, her voice clear and musical despite her annoyance. "I hope you'll pardon me. I have somewhere to be."

"Not so fast." He stroked his moustache. "I want to ask you something."

"Ask me something, my lord?"

"You think you're too good for half the nobility. How can you crawl to Teran Nivrai?"

"Teran Nivrai asked, the same as anyone else." Cailyn's grip on her bag tightened. "Now if you'll excuse me, I need to get going."

He moved to block her. "You had me fooled then, Derys. I didn't think you worked for anyone."

"My lord, I have the right to accept or deny any proposal. For any reason."

He laughed, a short, mirthless bark. "Teran's whore. Prancing around the dark channels. I should have known."

He stepped closer, his face inches from hers. She clutched her purse, ready to hit him with it.

She hoped she wouldn't have to. The last thing she wanted right now was an altercation she'd have to explain. Guild law protected the courtesans, yes. But that didn't make hitting nobles look good.

"You should know no one will hire you after this," he spat. "You bow and scrape in front of Teran Nivrai and flaunt it. You use your father's name for fame off the dark channels, and then expect us not to notice when you have Nivrai's collar around your throat?" He mimed wrapping around a neck and squeezing.

"Stay on the dark channels. If they even want you there." His spittle sprayed her face. "Keep. Away. From. Us."

His lip twitched. Cailyn dropped into a defensive stance and glared at him.

He snarled, turned on his heel, and fled down the corridor.

Cailyn stared after him. *Do you think I'm turning into Teran, or do you think she's coming to save me?*

It didn't matter, not really. She mouthed a prayer of thanks to the courtesans' goddess. Her grip on the purse relaxed.

Before her stood another set of doors and a tall, well-muscled doorman with a small computer tablet in one hand. He looked at it, looked Cailyn over, then pressed a button. The heavy doors behind him slid open.

Cries and moans filled Cailyn's ears. From all directions came the sounds of hands, leather, and other things striking flesh.

Cailyn looked around. Near her, she could see a large section of sofas, tables, and padded chairs, upholstered with soft, supple material. Beyond that, she saw a small tray of food and drinks.

Equipment filled the rest of the room. She saw at least two of every cross and bench she'd seen in Teran's or Darien's flagellaries. And plenty more she hadn't. Almost all of the equipment was occupied by writhing and twisting bodies.

She gaped at the crowd. She'd always heard that the dark channels served people who'd tired of other forms of pleasure. She'd imagined most people weren't bored enough for them. Teran was different, but Teran was Teran.

Then again, even Lord Darien didn't seem like the sort who'd lost interest in other things.

She closed her eyes, listened to the sounds around her. She'd thought she would hear screams, winces, protests. Instead, the noise that filled the room sounded more like sex than pain.

Impacts rang from everywhere, and yelps or barks of pain followed them. But Cailyn heard just as many gasps and pants and quiet currents of pleading.

She opened her eyes and let out a breath. Maybe this wasn't so different after all.

She scanned the room for people she knew. In a far corner she found Lord Darien. He slid clips onto the plump, round breasts of a woman bound to one of the crosses. He grinned and ground his knee against her vulva.

Cailyn flushed and turned away. She hadn't come here to stare at Darien.

Valik stood nearby, bound to a ladderlike frame. A tall pale man with salt-and-pepper hair flogged him. Cailyn recognized him from the High Council.

Valik's member jutted upward. He groaned as the mop of thick leather crashed into his back. He grimaced as it hit, but his face relaxed a moment later, the lines of pain smoothing. His back arched to meet the whip and he cried out all the louder.

The heat in Cailyn's flesh kindled to a jealous fire. Her hand slid over her own nipple before she recovered herself and dropped her arm to her side.

The nobleman's arm dropped. The tails of the whip hung down over his hand. His other hand wound tight in Valik's hair. He pulled Valik's head back, leaned down, and kissed him full on the mouth. Cailyn heard Valik moan.

"Like what you see?"

Cailyn blinked and turned around. A woman stood in front of her. Bright red hair, as curly as Cailyn's own but less controlled, cascaded past her shoulders and down her back. She wore a deep purple corset that left her breasts bare and cinched her waist. Cailyn whistled softly. She'd never tried it, but she'd seen enough in the academy to know how much dedication such training took.

Was it painful? Her gaze lingered on the pinched waist, moved up to the bare pink breasts. Colored rings glinted in the woman's nipples.

Cailyn realized she must be staring. "My lady," she said and lowered her head.

"Lady Nivrai isn't with you, then?"

"No. She told me I could come alone if I chose." Cailyn breathed deep, relaxing. "So I did."

"We're glad to have you here." She reached out a hand and shook Cailyn's.

"My name is Elana Teth. I always hoped I'd see you on the dark channels. Your reputation precedes you, as your father's preceded him."

"Thank you." Cailyn shook the offered hand and smiled.

"Here, let me show you around. Explain to you what everything is." Her grip on Cailyn's hand tightened, promising.

"I've seen most of it already." Cailyn squeezed the hand encircling hers. "But I would be glad to come with you."

Lady Teth smiled and led Cailyn past couples and groups of every description. Cailyn felt of her depth. What should she ask for? She wished Lord Darien had found her instead.

"My lady," she finally said and pointed, "look at them, there."

She would have asked what they were doing, except that it was obvious. A woman, her skin shining with oil, reclined on a table while the man held a lit candle, dripping wax onto her nude body. The woman moaned and twisted her body to meet the falling wax.

Cailyn had seen candles before. She served the nobility, and plenty of nobles had a taste for antiques. They lent charm to old-style rooms, made them glow with soft, seductive light. If you felt like bothering to find them and buy them.

Now it seemed they had a practical use.

"You've never done that?" Elana asked. Cailyn shook her head.

Elana peered at her, clearly curious. "Most new people try that."

She laughed. Her finger reached out to caress Cailyn's collar. Cailyn froze.

"But maybe that's why you haven't," Elana said. "Maybe it doesn't hurt enough for Teran Nivrai." She screwed her face into a scowl and held out her hands in mock threat.

It was a terrible impression of Teran. Cailyn laughed anyway. "Maybe not."

"Cailyn Derys," Elana said, her voice still mock serious. "You're missing out. But there is another table over there."

Cailyn let Elana lead her. She began to pull off the black bodysuit clinging to her skin, but Elana reached to finish it for her. Cailyn relaxed under her hands.

Elana peeled the cloth off with care, like peeling a rare fruit. Eager to taste it, not wanting to damage it.

Cailyn's face burned as she climbed onto the table and lay down. Lady Teth took down the bottle of oil and opened it. She tilted it slowly and let the oil fall onto Cailyn's skin.

She spread the thick oil over Cailyn's chest, her breasts, her stomach, even her hands and arms and legs. And, of course, along her vulva, with the same light touches. Cailyn whimpered and shifted to better meet her hands.

Elana slid her fingers over the soft flesh again, her laugh full of promise. Then she pulled her hand away.

She reached for a blue candle. Its flame illuminated her face, casting a warm glow around her for a moment. Then she tilted it down.

The bright river of wax fell. The warm burn made Cailyn gasp. It wasn't pain, not exactly. Intense warmth that woke her nerves and set them singing. She writhed and moaned as the wax dripped over her nipples.

Lines of heat crossed her body, over and over. Her chest, her stomach, her thighs, all ignited by Elana, her nipple rings glinting in the warm light of the candles.

Elana set down the first candle and picked up another, this one a bold red, then a bright, vibrant green, then others. Cailyn looked down at herself and saw the bold colors spattered on her flesh: red, green, blue, purple, yellow.

Elana set the candle down and bent to kiss Cailyn. Cailyn opened her mouth, thinking of how Elana's fingers would feel, turning and twisting inside her.

Then Elana drew forth a knife. It glittered in the candlelight. Cailyn shivered with a familiar fear.

She froze when the sharp, cold metal touched her skin. She didn't think she could deal with blades. Not now. Not after everything that had happened with Teran.

She opened her mouth to protest, but it had already moved over her skin.

It did not cut. It only scraped away the wax dripped on her body as it glided over her oiled flesh. She marveled at the grace of it.

Such skill with such dangerous things. Lady Teth, Lord Darien, the roomful of people around her. Their knives, floggers, paddles, clips. Had they spent years practicing to do these things, like Cailyn had spent learning to serve?

Elana's fingers ran soft along her cheeks, pulling her out of her reverie. The blunt nails felt different from Teran's metal. Elana smiled and ran them down her neck and chest, teasing her nipples to erection.

A languid warmth spread through Cailyn. Her eyelids drooped. She murmured as Elana's fingertips traced the places where the wax had been.

She opened her eyes and gasped. A crowd had gathered around them, just far away enough not to intrude. They smiled, joked, pointed. Elana leaned over Cailyn. "It's all right," she cooed.

Cailyn pushed her head away, the room a blur of candlelight and bright red hair. "I'm all right." She propped herself up on an elbow, little pieces of wax all around her. "I'm used to people seeing me."

"Be careful when you get up." Elana guided Cailyn to the edge of the table. Cailyn shook her head to clear the dizziness as she righted herself.

Elana wrapped her arm around Cailyn. People moved aside as they made their way to the cushioned sofas. With a light touch, Elana guided Cailyn onto the soft cushions.

Cailyn sank into them. "Thank you, my lady."

Elana reached for her again, but Cailyn pushed her away. She was here to enjoy herself. Not to attach herself to one person.

Elana nodded. She flitted away to join the other revelers, sparing Cailyn a last wink. Cailyn closed her eyes and luxuriated in the soft cushions.

Someone sat down beside her. She opened her eyes and looked into the bearded face of Lord Darien.

"I saw you over there. Very nice."

Cailyn reached out to touch his muscled arms. She remembered their strength—and the subtle things his fingers could do.

"Did you enjoy yourself?" he asked. She nodded. He grinned. "You looked like it. Will you do more tonight?"

She blushed. "I'd like to, my lord."

"You'd like to?" He eased an arm around her, which she welcomed. "Plenty of people here would love a turn with you. You could go talk to them."

"It's not them I'm frightened of."

With one of his booming laughs, he said, "They can't do worse than Teran Nivrai."

"No, my lord. It's not that. It's—I feel wrong without her here. Taking pain from strangers."

"You've taken it from me."

"That's different."

"Maybe it is. But this isn't all about pain, you know. You learned that from me." He grinned. "Or should have."

"Yes. I did learn that from you, my lord." Cailyn's mouth twisted into a smile.

"You could save pain for her, if you want."

"Here?"

He chuckled again. "Maybe not completely."

He pointed to an empty leather sling hanging in a corner. "But we could put some cuffs on you and bring everyone over for sex rather than for pain."

Her smile widened. She watched the nobles pass by, staring, waiting. What would they do with her?

He'd said she could forbid them pain. Would that frustrate them? Would they take it out on her in other ways, cleave her with hands and members and devices, worry her skin with fingernails and teeth?

"That might not be so bad, my lord."

CHAPTER THIRTY-SEVEN

Cailyn hurried to the sling while Darien spread the word. Supplies lay near it already: gloves, lubricant, a few small implements of pain. How many would the nobles use by the time they finished with her?

Darien returned, alone for the moment. Others hovered a respectful distance away. Their eyes swept over her, and she shivered, heat building in her flesh.

For a moment, Darien did nothing but look at her. The position tilted her vulva toward him, pink and obvious. She watched him watching her, wished she could feel his fingers against the silky flesh. Instead, he reached to close and lock cuffs around her wrists.

He ran his hands along her body, reached down to unfasten his breeches, and drew himself out. He teased her vulva with his member as he had with his hands and rubbed his erection over the slick skin. Cailyn tilted her hips, but he laughed at her frustration and moved away again.

Hands reached down to caress her. From the delicate shape, they couldn't be Darien's. She tilted her head to look, saw light skin and purple fingernails. Elana.

Good. Two people she knew would take her first.

The slim fingers slid up her torso and neck. They tapped against her cheeks, her lips. She opened her mouth to take them in and felt Lord Darien pressed against her entrance again. She moaned around Elana's fingers as Lord Darien plunged in.

The others gathered close. She saw faces, hungry, avid. But the fingers and flesh invaded her, waves of pleasure drove all else away. She knew only that they watched, stared, waited.

More hands descended on her all at once. Some ran along her flesh, their movements slow and tender. Others grabbed at her. They twisted at her breasts, squeezed and slapped at her exposed skin.

She tried to focus on them, but the rhythm of Lord Darien moving inside her and the fingers probing her mouth made it impossible.

Gentle touches soothed away the roughness. She swam through the sensations and closed her eyes again.

Slaps and pulls shocked her back to the room and the people in it. They fought over her, almost, clutching at every bit of flesh they could.

When Lord Darien came inside her, she thrashed with both pleasure and panic, knowing he would soon be gone.

Gloved and oil-coated fingers pushed into her smaller orifice. She had no idea whose. Frenzied, they drove into her, trying to outdo the man who'd used her just before. Someone else drove without warning into her open mouth.

They pushed and pulled, forced her ever more open, prodded her with too many hands. Someone suggested putting clamps on her nipples. Lord Darien paused to see that she didn't object. Twin stars of pain flickered in the middle of the forces tearing her.

Flashes of pleasure flared through her as whoever used her found his stride—or hers, as women's fingers, dildos, and men's flesh became a blur, one diving in when the other left her open.

They moved in her, a great machine. Her body locked and spasmed, over and over.

How many times had they used her? Others stood back, staring with hungry and unblinking eyes. Were they waiting their turn? Had they taken it already? She'd forgotten. Moments flared gossamer in her mind, each driven out by the next.

She didn't know how many times she came. Sometimes she welcomed it. Sometimes her body responded, automatic, a reflex driven by the will of the assembly. Flushed, sweaty, exhausted, no longer hers. Pleasure built in her, burst through her, awakened her, left her drained. Again and again and again.

A hand swept down to remove the clamps. She grimaced, shook, and came again.

The last of them withdrew. She panted. Little trills of sensation sparked through her sweating flesh. Her body ached in a hundred places. She wondered if there would be bruises. Lord Darien had promised they'd restrain themselves, but Cailyn couldn't remember enough to know they had.

She opened her eyes. He hovered over her. His fingers ran over her hands and wrists. She blinked away the fuzziness in her vision and smiled up at him.

He stepped aside. Everyone else fell silent and followed.

What—?

With effort, she bent her head up to see what had happened.

In front of her stood Teran Nivrai.

She neither smiled nor frowned. Her mouth was set in a harsh line, her expression unreadable.

Gloves hid her hands, as usual. But while one hand wore her usual leather, the other had already slipped on a black rubber glove. Cailyn winced as Teran squeezed lubricant onto her gloved fingers.

Damn her. Couldn't she see that the others had done too much already?

Cailyn stared at Teran. She wouldn't refuse. Not now. But why had Teran come here? She'd told Cailyn not once but twice that she had no interest.

Teran smirked, not returning Cailyn's gaze. She slammed her fingers into Cailyn's smaller orifice.

Cailyn shrieked as they entered. Teran's harshness had always come with seduction. Even when Teran was cruel right away, gentleness would follow.

Now Teran was staring past her. Now she could have been anyone. Now she felt only a relentless burn in an orifice the others had already used. She cried a shapeless word of protest. The fingers drove into her harder.

She screamed a desperate welcome and hated herself for it. She stared up at the blank face. Her body tightened hard around Teran's fingers. She bit back a curse, closed her eyes, and tried to slow her breathing, force herself to relax.

Teran paused as Cailyn tensed. Then her movements sped up again, plunging in as the flesh around them loosened.

If she'd really meant to be cruel, would she have bothered?

Cailyn looked up. Through the haze of sensation, she could hear the others gasp around them.

Cailyn blinked at them, curious. Her breath grew hard and fast. She bit back a plea for more.

Teran's mouth twitched as she drove her fingers in again. Amusement? Desire? Cailyn had only a moment to wonder.

The orgasm washed over her at last, so strong she thrashed in her bonds. She yelled again, a strange foreign sound she never thought she'd hear herself make.

Teran slid free. Cailyn watched, heart pounding, as Teran peeled off and discarded the glove. She slipped on her usual leather one in a quick, fluid motion.

She reached down to release Cailyn from her bonds, but made no move to help Cailyn stand. Cailyn held on to the frame of the sling to steady herself. She looked out at the audience, hoping they might help. None did.

They did whisper, hissing recriminations at Teran. Gloved hands clenched and Teran scowled. Cailyn thought she might say something, but she stayed silent.

Steady now, Cailyn looked down. Someone had laid her clothes next to the sling. Teran ignored her. Cailyn shrugged and slipped them on.

Teran turned and walked out, her stride long and swift. She stared straight ahead, not glancing at Darien or Valik or anyone else. Cailyn hurried to keep up.

❖

It wasn't until the elevator doors hissed shut after them that Teran said anything to Cailyn.

"You put on a good show back there, my little one," she said, reaching out a gloved hand to caress Cailyn's cheek.

Cailyn flinched. "You were so cold in there. Now you want to touch me?"

"I had to give them what they wanted. How do you think they would have reacted if they'd seen me treat you well?"

Cailyn opened her mouth to speak. Teran's hands moved down to her breasts, circling her nipples. Pain flared through them at the light touch. They were still tender from the bite of the clamps and the fingers pulling and twisting at them.

Cailyn laughed, too tired to argue. The doors slid open. Cailyn followed Teran into their rooms.

"Get yourself cleaned up," Teran ordered. Cailyn hastened to the shower, eager to rinse herself off.

As she shook out her hair, she remembered the wax dripping onto her flesh, the warmth of it falling onto her skin. If she'd known people on the dark channels did things like that, would she ever have taken an offer from the queen of helldemons?

She turned off the water, dried herself, and wound towels around her hair and body.

"I didn't tell you to leave," a familiar voice said. She looked up to see Teran with a braided whip in one hand.

"My lady?" Cailyn stammered. She dropped the towel in surprise and stepped back as Teran advanced. "Don't you want to go into the other room?"

"No. I want you right here. Put your hands up on the wall."

Cailyn shivered but obeyed. "You want this now?"

Teran walked over to her and draped the falls of the braided whip along her back. It might have felt good. If Cailyn didn't know what it promised.

"Our time here is almost over," Teran whispered, her breath close in Cailyn's ear. "The boy is on the verge of breaking."

"My lady—don't—"

"Before we part, I want to have you everywhere. Not just in my bed. Or the flagellary. Or our rooms." A hand slid into her hair, gripped tight.

Cailyn blinked through the swoon threatening to overtake her. "The boy—"

"There's something he doesn't want to tell me. I left him crying. Shaking. Huddled in the corner of the room."

"Teran, I don't—"

"Maybe he'll break down. Tell me the rebellion's plans. Maybe he'll scream something he thinks I want to hear."

"Don't."

"I will present whatever he says to the Councils, just as I have been. They'll decide what to do with that information."

Cailyn gulped in air. "And it's over after that?"

"Yes. I won't see him again." Teran sighed. "Or you."

"You don't think he knows, do you?"

"I think he does know. I just don't think pain will wrench it out of him."

She shook her head. "Then this foolishness will be a memory for everyone involved. I won't be sad to see it end." She kissed Cailyn's neck. "But I will miss you."

Cailyn pressed into the wall, suddenly cold. "Why turn your back on me? You still want me."

She swallowed hard. "I still want you."

"So I was right." Teran ran a still-gloved hand down Cailyn's naked back. Cailyn trembled under her touch.

Cailyn swallowed hard, thinking of the boy. Teran would break him, even if it didn't yield results, just because the Councils made her. Lust alone was no good reason to stay.

And yet, the Councils had forced her into it all. Even Lord Darien thought so.

Then there was the ache she felt. The long, stretching hollowness that filled her, hearing that Teran had finished with her. That the experiment was over. That she would never see Teran again.

The gloved hand pressed against her back. She whimpered, wanting to feel the newsteel digging into her skin. Her flesh stung where the others had used her. She should have wanted to lie down, to sleep. She should have told Teran to just let her rest.

Given what she'd just gone through, even a helldemon would understand that.

"And if I called you months from now? If I asked you to come to me?" Teran's lips, cool on skin the bath had warmed, pressed against her ear. Her teeth worried Cailyn's earlobe. Cailyn gasped, grateful for the small bloom of pain.

"If you called me, I would come."

Steel pierced her. She could feel Teran's smile.

"Please," she gasped.

The claws tore into her skin, electric and sharp. She threw back her head and screamed.

Teran kissed her, light as the touch of an angel's feather.

She stepped back, then swung the whip at the air in front of Cailyn's back. Cailyn gulped in air. She would have no time to prepare herself. Not now. Not like this.

The braided leather tore into her back. Her breaths became screams.

There was no sensuality in it. The strikes laid her flesh open. Every part of her back stung as they tore into it. Cailyn's nerves flared to unbearable life as the tails of the whip tore through her illusions.

She screamed again and again, her mouth wide as she cried out in welcome and relief. Her body burned with long hours of use already, but she'd had so little pain.

Her nerves drank it in. She shrieked until she lost her voice. Still her throat opened, again and again.

Behind her, Teran panted, her breath heavy with exertion and desire.

She thought of Teran's thin fingers, of how quickly they would cool in a chilly interrogation room. Or would it be cold? She didn't know, but as soon as she thought of it, she could feel it, the chilled fingers a counterpoint to the ragged fire rending her back.

At that thought, Cailyn shuddered, as violently as she had from the blows. But this too was a part of her now, whether Teran had wanted it or not. Those hands had done things Cailyn couldn't imagine.

She could feel that too, sharp slivered ice behind the flame. It would always be there. She twisted away from the flogger, then arched back to meet it a moment later.

Whatever Teran had done, whatever Teran would do, Cailyn needed her now.

Teran would use her again. As many times as she could before the end. But this desperate slicing into her skin would not happen again. If Cailyn wanted it, she would have to seize it now.

She pushed her back out to meet the whip again. A snarl of aggression and delight answered her, and fire burst over her skin.

She shuddered. Everything went white as she slumped against the wall.

From the corner of her eye, she saw Teran's arm fall. Hands ran over her skin, warm from the shower's humidity. Teran's arms held her up as she sagged against the wall. She leaned on them, feeling faint.

Generous now, Teran steadied her, led her back into the bedroom. The journey felt infinite.

Cailyn collapsed onto the bed. Teran helped to ease her down. Her head lolled as she sank into the soft sheets.

Steel tickled her cheek and chin. "Quiet now."

The ceiling glowed. The dark silhouette of Teran's head bent down over her. Hands cradled her head. Her sex throbbed. Her back stung, sudden pinpricks of sensation curling through it.

Her lips cracked into a smile. Teran's head leaned down to meet her lips. She opened her mouth, closed her eyes, and sank into the black.

CHAPTER THIRTY-EIGHT

M y lord."
Cailyn fidgeted. Everyone got nervous, but a courtesan was trained to hide the worst of it. Yet here she was, her hand skittering like she hadn't been in the academy a day. She quickly clapped a calmer hand over her rebellious one. "I have something to ask you."

His shirt lay half-undone, showing her a hint of the dark flesh beneath. Her mouth watered to see it. She wanted to lick, kiss, bite. To end this with him spearing her.

She looked around the room. Light filtered through lace curtains, burnishing the soft velvet of the couch she sat on. Sex and laughter would be so much better than this confrontation.

Lord Darien had mastered both. But she wasn't here for that.

"What is it?" His smile wrinkled into a frown.

"It's Teran." Her hands stirred in her lap again. "It's this whole thing. This assignment. This—" She waved her hands, helpless. "Torture."

"She's angry as hell at the Councils. She has good reason to be." He smiled as he shook his head. "We're lucky she isn't a helldemon after all. We'd all be picking pins out of our ribs by now."

Cailyn stood up. It would be easy to lose herself in the soft sofa. She couldn't let herself do that. "How can you joke about it?"

"I'm not joking about it. What they did was terrible."

He chewed his lip. "What we did. I shouldn't pretend I'm not one of them."

"What you did."

"The others thought it was a great idea. The nobility takes its revenge. Without middlemen."

His hand went to his forehead. "Gods. They thought it was poetic."

"They thought she'd like it." Cailyn shifted in her seat. The fabric of her clothing scratched against last night's welts.

To be naked, her torn flesh pressed against soft upholstery, would be so much nicer than this. To feel him above her—

Her lips opened in a half-sigh. She snapped them closed.

"I tried to talk them out of it," he said. "We've got people trained for that sort of thing."

"I know."

"Hell, I'd try to talk them out of that, too, if I thought I could manage it. I even told them I'm on the dark channels myself."

Cailyn's hand flew to her mouth. "You told them that, my lord?"

He nodded. "I told them. Right in the middle of a Council meeting."

"And?"

"They think she's different. They think the rules of the dark channels don't apply to her." He turned to look at her. "They think she's their monster, Cailyn."

Cailyn lifted her head. "Tell me what they told her."

He sighed. "You were there, Cailyn. There's nothing to tell."

"Nothing to tell?"

"They gave her a duty. She accepted it."

"No."

"That's all."

"It isn't. It can't be."

Damn it. She'd blurted enough out already. Now she'd have to say it.

"She planned to defy you. She told me. She promised me."

He sank into the sofa and winced. "She lied to you, Cailyn."

"No." She stared at his indolent, open shirt. Her palm itched to slap his face. "She was telling the truth. Something happened. Something else."

"Cailyn, I—"

"Tell me what it was."

He sighed again. "Nothing else happened."

She opened her mouth to protest. Before she could speak, he corrected himself. "At least nothing I saw."

"Nothing you saw?"

"If something else happened, I can't tell you what it was."

"I have to know, my lord."

He looked down for a long moment, then up at her again. "But I can tell you that we…talked, in the Council meetings. About how to convince her."

Cailyn swallowed hard. "What kind of talk?"

"They said she'd do it anyway. Said she'd appreciate it. Said she'd see it as a gift after all the shunning and ridicule."

"She wouldn't. She didn't."

"I know. So did some others."

"Who?"

"Lord Keriel, for one."

"Lord Keriel?"

"He thought she'd need convincing. He had an idea. He thought that they—that we—should find something she wanted. Something she valued. Tempt her with that."

Cailyn's heart sank into her feet.

"What was it?" she asked, her voice cracking.

He shrugged. "Nobody knew."

"Nobody—"

"Teran Nivrai lives on a rock in the middle of nowhere. If you believe the rumors, she turned herself into a demon. What would she want enough to bother with us?"

"What indeed?" Cailyn echoed.

"No one could think of anything." He wiped a sweating brow. "I was relieved."

Cailyn's hands clenched. Could she believe him? "They left it at that, then?"

"They left it at that." He squinted at her. "You think the Councils bribed her. Teran Nivrai. The last person in the galaxy to give a damn about bribes. Or about us."

"I know they did." Cailyn face hardened. "I know what they promised her."

"Then you know more than I do, Cailyn Derys."

Could she believe him?

It would be easy. Convenient. She could let this go. She ran a finger over the fabric of the sofa, savored its texture.

Why believe Lord Darien was lying when she could believe Ben Keriel was lying instead?

"Maybe I do, my lord."

She hurried to the door. "Thank you. That's all I wanted to know."

Lord Darien rushed after her. He grabbed at her shoulder as the door slid open.

"Wait."

Cailyn turned.

"What the hell do you mean, Derys? What could they possibly promise her? She never sets foot outside that little hellhole if she can help it."

"Me."

Cailyn twisted out of his grip and stepped through the door.

Teran sat cross-legged on the floor. She held something in her hands. Cailyn stepped closer, saw the stone globes from Teran's gym.

It seemed a lifetime ago, now.

She'd hesitated. Teran's hands had pressed down, hard, forcing her palms against the stone. A jolt of pain had shivered through her. She'd fallen back into Teran's arms. Teran's lips and teeth had soothed it all away.

Cailyn tapped the place where Teran had bitten her. Her neck had been bare then. She'd arched her head back to meet Teran's mouth.

Now metal circled it, warm against her skin.

She looked over at Teran. The globes crackled with energy. Teran shuddered. Her lips twitched as the shock went through her. Her expression twisted into a rictus of pain. She gasped, hissed, bared her teeth.

Cailyn winced. She tapped Teran on the shoulder.

Teran turned and glared at her. "What do you want?"

Cailyn gestured toward the globes. "What are you doing, my lady?

"I'm leaving to torture someone. Until he breaks." Her body twitched with another jolt. "It's only fitting I do this first."

"More pain won't help."

"Maybe not." Teran laid the spheres on a small table. "But it will clear my head."

Cailyn touched the tight shoulders, still tense from the shocks. "I could help you with that."

"I'm tempted. But not now." Teran pushed her hands away. "I'll need your services more afterward." A steel-tipped finger skirted along Cailyn's cheek and chin.

Afterward. Cailyn's stomach sank, a hard, despairing rock beneath her flesh. She didn't want to think about what would happen when Teran came back. Didn't want to think of steel-tipped hands touching her after defiling someone else.

She remembered that first time. Teran's numb, dead shock and wide, sightless eyes. She'd drawn a bath, then led Teran in. Her hands gave pleasure and solace, soothed as they caressed.

That was what she'd always wanted.

She was Teran's creature now. She would be until their contract ended.

No refusals remained but one, the one she'd never used. The stop word she'd almost forgotten she had.

She wouldn't use it now. She promised herself that, tried not to remember how many vows she'd broken.

She forced herself to look at Teran. "Of course, my lady."

CHAPTER THIRTY-NINE

Cailyn stared into the computer's display. Faces spun, grew larger, then retreated again. The long dance soothed Cailyn. She recognized many of the faces. She'd served more than a few. They smiled the glittery smiles of those who ran the world.

Could she call one of them now? Serve as she had so often before? Let her fingers dance along their skin? Open her flesh to their members and fingers?

She had hours to do it, if she wanted. Spur of the moment meetings had their charm. It took skill to craft an experience with almost no preparation.

Teran prepared things so carefully. Was it so surprising that she'd planned it all from the beginning? Teran had eased her so carefully into pain. Changed her.

Marked her, no matter how many regenerations she had. She wrapped her hands around her shoulders and felt her back. Her probing fingers found the ragged parts torn by whip and steel. They found old marks too, submerged and made invisible by rejuvenated skin.

However healed her flesh, they would be with her forever. She tapped the screen and watched it darken.

How did Teran feel now? She'd talked to her son after years of never seeing him. After not wanting him.

But once she'd carried him and bore him and given him up, had she missed him at all?

Mariel had liked her pregnancy. Had she really remained indifferent? Had she ignored new life, kicking and stretching inside her? Had she wanted the child in spite of herself?

She wanted her son's trust, at least. When he shied away from taking the candies, Teran had extended her claws, cut one in half, and eaten it in front of him.

She could have just broken it. Instead, she'd let the boy see her. Just like she'd let Cailyn see her. Perhaps ties of blood mattered to Teran after all.

She'd neglected Dion. Admitted it, even. To his face. But she hadn't seen him since.

Maybe the helldemon had done nothing but discharge a debt.

Cailyn wrapped her hands tighter around herself and massaged away a chill.

What about this assignment? It was a debt too. To the Councils. A task to be completed. Then Teran would go on with her life.

Without Cailyn. Before meeting Cailyn, she'd spent months alone. Waited until the urge seized her. Chosen someone. Used and discarded him. Done the whole thing again.

Would she go back to that once Cailyn was gone?

She'd been looking for a break in the monotony. Cailyn had given her that. Was that it? Was that all?

Teran had told her about Mariel. The words bled out of her just like the cuts in Cailyn's skin. She'd carried those words for a long time. And Cailyn had drawn them out with lips and tongue and hands.

And yet Teran had left today to break someone.

Would he scream from the beginning, or only when he broke?

Or would he break quietly, the din of his body dimming to silent, choked sobs?

Would Teran's claws dig into him? Or were they reserved for lovers? For Mariel, for courtesans she hired, for Cailyn?

If she did use them, what words would she draw out with his blood? True ones? Or only lies?

Teran would bring them back like trophies. It would be enough. It would have to be.

Cailyn tried to picture the boy. She imagined a young man, handsome, all hard jaw and bright wet eyes. And the raggedness of captivity: wild-growing hair, scraggly beard, sweat and dirt.

She pictured his mouth, open obscenely wide, the bright pink flesh of his cheeks and palate and the hoarseness in his throat as he screamed.

Would she trick him, crisp silk in her movements and voice, and coax him between agonies? Or did she save that gentleness for lovers?

Cailyn's back twinged. She rubbed it against the back of her chair for the sting.

She wanted it. Wanted more.

Even now.

She wanted Teran with her. She wanted steel tracing slow along her skin. She wanted the rich voice to soothe her, to tell her that it was all over.

She wanted desire clouding reason.

Pain forcing it out of her head completely.

She pressed her fingers to the smooth desk in front of her. Faces danced in it again. Lord Keriel's swirled by.

She tapped the screen.

The image of him looked away at first.

"Dion!" he called, his brows knotted.

He turned to the screen, and his expression changed. He smiled, relaxed and open. "Derys. Always nice to hear from you."

Cailyn didn't want to hear it. "The deal. The one the Councils made with Teran. I want proof."

"I thought you might." He held up a thin tablet. "Come see me and I'll give it to you."

Cailyn swallowed hard. He'd toyed with a tablet the last time she saw him. He hadn't shown it to her; she hadn't pried. Had he been holding Teran's confession in his hands the whole time they'd talked?

If he had, why hadn't he shown her then? She never would have doubted him if—

She pressed her lips together to keep her thoughts from slipping out. "Yes, my lord. Thank you. I will come for it after my lady returns."

"Not now? She'll want you when she gets back."

"She will." Cailyn closed her eyes. "I've made my peace with that."

"Have you?"

"I have."

"Then I'll see you tonight."

She smiled, her face composed as she'd been taught. For the first time in weeks, she felt proud. "Very well, my lord."

She tapped the console. His image winked out of sight and she let herself sigh.

❖

The door slid open.

If this really would be her last day, she would behave as perfectly as possible. She would take refuge in her training, just as she had in the beginning.

There would be time later for her misgivings. For now, her only purpose was to serve.

She walked through the doorway and knelt, quiet as falling snow.

Teran swept past Cailyn without seeing. She stared ahead, unblinking, and stopped in the middle of the room. Her lip twitched. With a loud metallic sound, the claws extended.

Cailyn bit her lip. Teran stared past her and crossed her hands.

Cailyn waited for the sting, but the claws never cut her. Instead, they tore through Teran's bodysuit with such speed and violence Cailyn hoped Teran hadn't cut herself as well.

Teran threw aside the tattered scraps of fabric. She didn't watch it fall. The claws ripped at her clothes again and again. Jagged black scraps of cloth littered the floor.

Cailyn saw scrapes on Teran's skin. Some bled, red trails flowing from the cuts.

Cailyn rushed to Teran's side.

"My lady—you'll hurt—you'll do yourself harm." She grabbed at Teran's arms, trying to pull them down.

But the best gladiator in Nivrai had taught Teran to fight. Practicing forms and wielding whips kept her body strong. Her arms didn't budge.

Damn. How could Cailyn stop her if Teran didn't even know she was there?

She could move the steel-tipped hands to her own flesh. Maybe the offering would ease Teran into gentler pain.

But what if it didn't work?

The newsteel would tear Cailyn's skin like paper. Without Teran's will to hold it back, Cailyn shuddered to think what it could do to the meat beneath. It was a wonder Teran had only bloodied herself.

But maybe this would become sex if Cailyn offered herself. Maybe this strange mood of Teran's only meant descending to another level of pain. Maybe all Cailyn had to do was steel herself for it.

She looked at Teran's eyes. They stared ahead, cold gray stones. Cailyn blinked.

No.

"Please," she said.

Teran snarled. She cast aside the last of the fabric and pushed Cailyn away. Cailyn fell to the floor in a graceless, twisted heap.

"There is only one thing I want you for," Teran said. She walked over to a shelf behind her, took down her harness and dildo, and slipped them on.

Cailyn swallowed hard. This hissing, bleeding thing was not the woman she knew.

"Here," the thing with Teran's face said.

She didn't move.

A clawed hand pointed to the bed.

"Now."

Steel tore at Cailyn's dress. It fell in tatters of cloud around her feet.

The claws didn't cut her. She wasn't reassured.

She bent over the bed, not looking back at the strange thing in Teran's skin. She'd said she would serve until the end.

A hand pressed her head into the bed sheets. Long fingers trapped it in a sharp steel cage. Behind her, the dildo pressed against her flesh. Too cold. Too thick.

Was this it? After everything Teran had done to her? Every seduction that had changed her? Was this the end of the experiment? This cold coupling with a woman so distant she might never remember it happened at all?

Cailyn writhed under the alien grip, trying to twist away. This was no awakening, no play on long-primed nerves.

This was violence, cold and ugly.

"At least give me pain," Cailyn rasped. Maybe if she begged, Teran would remember.

Maybe it would reawaken the seduction, the slow planning, the clever mind that eased her partner into craving what she gave.

Cailyn needed that slow descent now. Without it, she couldn't endure this cold-eyed thing in Teran's skin.

"As you wish."

The claws tore through Cailyn's flesh in a biting flash. Pain flared through the wounds. The wetness of blood dripped down her legs.

"Please," Cailyn tried again.

Teran drew back.

"Wait!"

With one mighty thrust, Teran battered her way in. Cailyn screamed, a raw, wet sound.

The dildo ripped through her. Her nerves sang a cacophony of lust and hurt. Her own panting response made her shiver. All artifice gone, she breathed, ragged and harsh. The air stung her throat as she inhaled.

Behind her, the woman working in her snarled, driven on by something Cailyn couldn't name.

She forced herself back on the thing inside her. Maybe pretending to want this would hasten Teran's pleasure. Maybe this would be over sooner that way.

The claws pierced her flanks. Teran drew back, drove deep. Cailyn shrieked as something tore inside her.

Was this what she'd expected, all those months ago? A helldemon, rending and tearing, half metal and half flesh? Was this the cruelty she'd invited, once the seduction was finally finished?

"No!" she cried.

Teran snarled louder and plunged in again.

The pain was nothing to her now, not after such a litany of it. But this wordless desire, this impossible hardness on the heels of torture, gave her vertigo. She choked.

This would destroy everything. Every memory, every seduction, torn to pieces by the thing rending her.

She spat out her stop word, trembled as she cried out. Would the monster behind her listen?

The dildo froze inside her.

She drew in a long breath, the sound of it ragged in the sudden silence. Would Teran understand?

Would she honor it? Lord Keriel had called Cailyn her slave.

After a long moment, Teran withdrew.

A hand tangled itself in her hair. Tears filled her eyes. She blinked them back and stared into ice that barely saw her.

She opened her mouth. Teran was supposed to stop, not—

Before she could speak, Teran shoved her forward. Rough hands parted her hair.

The claws retracted with a sharp click. Fingers pressed the metal at the back of her collar. It unlocked with a soft sound and fell to the ground in front of Cailyn.

Cailyn looked up, but the door had already hissed open. Numb, she watched Teran leave.

"Wait!" she called, a moment too late.

She got to her feet. Her flesh throbbed; pain demanded her attention. Something had torn inside her. It would need to be treated.

Servants swarmed in, supplies and salves in hand. She sat back on the bed and waited for them.

She reached down. Her hand closed around the band of metal. She stared down at it, turned it around in her hands over and over.

The servants closed in around her, gray birds fluttering in concern.

CHAPTER FORTY

Cailyn's insides stung. The servants had treated her with their usual care, but they couldn't help the itch as her injury knitted together. Good doctors could minimize that, or simply dull the pain with drugs, but servants weren't doctors. Even servants extremely well versed in first aid, with plenty of supplies, had limits to their skills.

If they'd had their way, they'd still be tending Cailyn now. But she had an appointment to keep. She rushed down the hall and pounded on Lord Keriel's door.

It slid open. He stood in the doorway and spread his arms wide in a gesture of welcome.

She sat down, fighting not to wince.

"The recording," she said. "Where is it?"

He turned away and rummaged around on a shelf on the other side of the room, found something, and turned back to Cailyn.

He kept one hand behind his back. The other held up a thin tablet, just like the one she remembered.

Had he had it all that time?

"It's right here, Derys. Right here."

"She confesses?" The words spilled out of Cailyn. "On that recording?"

He nodded and moved toward her. "Of course."

Cailyn held out her hand. He didn't move and stared at Cailyn with unblinking eyes. His mouth twitched, and so did the hand that held the tablet.

"My lord?" Cailyn reached for the tablet.

His other hand came down. A heavy weight hit Cailyn full in the head.

She blinked at him, confused, and everything went black.

❖

Her eyes cracked open. Her head throbbed. Pain made her want to close her eyes again. She tried to move a hand to the wound, but metal cuffs held her hands fast behind her.

Lord Keriel sat in front of a videoscreen. Cailyn tried to look at it, but looking at it hurt her head. It went black again, and she sighed with relief.

The tablet sat on a table, just out of her reach. Was there anything on it at all? Or was it just a prop from the beginning? He'd never let her look at it.

Lord Keriel crossed over to her, a strange light in his eyes. One hand held a gun.

"My lord," she croaked through the pain in her head. "Why?"

His hand, a bony spider at the end of a thin arm, fell to her breast. She recoiled but couldn't twist away.

His hand slid over her flesh. His eyes strayed to the door.

But whoever he was looking for, the distraction proved short-lived. His hand moved down her stomach, toward the space between her legs. His fingers grabbed at her clothing.

She tilted her head and tried to bite.

"Relax," he hissed. "It's not you I'm after."

True to his word, he moved his hand away.

His gaze moved to the table. Cailyn's followed. On it, she saw another pair of cuffs.

Cailyn bit back a gasp. All his talk of unnatural desire, and here he was using cuffs to set his trap?

And touching her while she was helpless.

"What about your son?" she snapped. "You talked so much about being good to him. You wanted Teran to be a better mother—"

"He left hours ago. I promise I won't need you for long."

Cailyn recoiled.

The door slid open. Cailyn felt no relief seeing the familiar silhouette. No thrill seeing the shape of a gun in her deliverer's hand.

"What is this?" Teran's voice was rich and musical. Cailyn had heard those tones before, in the midst of passion. She shivered again.

"You haven't taken enough?" Teran said.

He pressed the gun to Cailyn's temple. "You know what I want from you, Nivrai. I'll shoot her if you don't."

Teran's lips curled into a misshapen, twisted little smile. "Will you?"

"Yes."

"Then do it."

Cailyn blinked, too stunned to feel betrayed.

Lord Keriel did the same. "What?"

Teran laughed, ugly and cold. "I have no interest in submitting to you. Go ahead. Do it."

Lord Keriel's mouth worked. It opened and closed, showing the wide pink inside. "You'd let me kill her? You were willing to torture to claim her!"

"I've been looking for a reason to kill you, Ben Keriel. What better reason can I have than revenge?"

Lord Keriel's hand shook. "You really are a monster."

The claws emerged with a flourish. The ice-gray eyes stared, cold as a creature from legend.

Lord Keriel's lips moved. Cailyn could barely hear him, but what she caught sounded like a prayer to his patron god.

Teran snickered. "You're even giving me a reason to do it slowly."

The hand holding Ben's gun twitched. Cailyn hoped he'd drop it. "You don't care about her, then."

"Of course I care. But look at you."

His grip tightened. "At me?"

"If you make good on your threat, I kill you. Or you kill me before I manage to do it."

She frowned. "Either way, you don't get what you want. You don't have any leverage if you kill her." She stared down at her claws and grinned. "You have no power over me."

"You'd leave her here with me?" He blinked again. "To my tender mercies?"

"Tender mercies? Do you think you're scaring me?"

"I'm telling you I'll—"

"You'd never get your hands dirty." She snarled. "That would be barbaric."

Without another word, Teran turned away.

Lord Keriel's teeth gnashed as he watched Teran go. He shot Cailyn a wild look and slumped to the floor.

He walked back over to Cailyn with the same flat look she'd so recently seen in Teran's eyes.

He reached out a hand. For a moment, Cailyn thought he might press his fingers to the lock on her bonds and let her go.

His hand fell onto her skin. It gripped the meat of her breast hard enough to bruise. His lips pulled back in a slow snarl. Cailyn thrashed, alarmed at the transformation.

"Then you won't mind if I use her like you have," he said.

Cailyn saw Teran's turn, her silhouette dark against the light coming in from the open door. Silver glinted on her fingertips. Her eyes were bleached pools in a cold face. They looked from Cailyn to Lord Keriel and back again. The beginnings of tears glinted in them.

"No," Teran whispered.

She walked back into the room with slow, measured strides. She slid to her knees in front of Lord Keriel with a grace that made Cailyn gasp in protest.

"It's me you want." Her eyes sparkled with contempt as she opened her hand. Her gun fell to the floor. "Let Cailyn go."

Lord Keriel picked up the cuffs on the table. He eyed Teran's claws as he crossed to Cailyn and pressed his fingertips to the lock.

Cailyn stood, too stunned to do anything but stare. Teran knelt before her enemy, the hawk-eyes sharp, the face twisted with hatred.

"Go," Teran snarled. "It's nothing he hasn't done before."

Cailyn crossed the room with strides fueled by despair.

Her foot caught on Teran's gun. She looked down at it, then back up at Teran. The cuffs locked Teran's wrists behind her. Her claws, extended and gleaming, twitched as she watched Lord Keriel free his member from his clothing.

Still snarling, Teran lowered her head.

Cailyn didn't think. She dove for the gun and yelled. Lord Keriel turned to face her. She fired again and again. She didn't stop until he fell. Bright red spurted from his head. She watched him twitch, then let herself blink when he went still.

Her eyes met Teran's. Swallowing her revulsion, she reached out for Ben's hand and pressed his lifeless finger to the lock.

The cuffs opened and fell. Teran rushed to Ben's body and pried the gun out of his hand.

"Come on," she said. "We have no time to lose."

Cailyn cast a longing look at the tablet on the table.

She shook her head and hurried on. Teran had submitted to Lord Keriel to save her. That would have to be enough. Her own hands had trusted that. Her mind would have to follow.

Gathering the servants proved easier than Cailyn expected. Teran had made plans, long ago, for a getaway from Nivrai, should even her own planet prove unsafe for her someday. She'd half-assumed some rumor would catch up with her for years.

The rumor that she'd killed Mariel for pleasure long ago. The rumor that she wanted to kill Lord Keriel.

The servants had joined them without question. One sat silent as ever behind the helm of their shuttle.

Teran had kept the cuffs. Lord Keriel had keyed them to his fingerprints. Teran could at least claim that she and Cailyn had needed to defend themselves.

It gave them time. Cailyn slipped away to her quarters to watch the stars in a window and think. It made her head throb, but she needed to do it.

Needed to think about many things. Escape. Alibis. Defenses. Lies.

But all she could think of was Dion. He'd been so curious. He'd wanted to know what they did, what they knew of one another, what they enjoyed.

Now Teran's whore, loyal to the last, had killed his father.

But when she thought of Lord Keriel, she could only remember the light in his eyes as he advanced on Teran, the cold hatred in Teran's voice. Cailyn's hands twitched like they still held Teran's gun.

Was it really so easy to kill? Or would what she'd done catch up with her as she snuck through tunnels under Nivrai? Would she remember the blood, the hole in his head? Would she slump against the wall, her every cell steeped in sudden understanding?

She was numb to it now. All she could think of now was a curly-haired boy, shuffling his feet as he stood in the doorway. She remembered dark eyes. Teran said he hid gray ones under lenses.

She heard footsteps behind her. She welcomed them. She belonged to Teran now, in a way she never had with that collar clasped around her neck.

Teran's whore. She'd hated those words. And now she'd killed for her.

Teran's whore. So be it.

"I wanted to kill Lord Keriel." Teran purred into Cailyn's ear. It sounded like romance.

Cailyn choked but didn't pull away. Claws slit her clothes; steel-tipped fingers skated sharp along her flesh.

She'd become the monster the Councils had made Teran. What reason could she have to pull away?

"I always thought I would do it," Teran said. "Someday when I didn't care enough to protect myself."

Cailyn arched her head. Steel thorns pressed against her neck.

"Just one thing," she said.

The hands froze.

"Is this what you want, my lady? This, and not—what you did before?"

"What I did before?"

Cailyn swallowed hard. Steel pricked her moving throat. "You were so harsh."

The points pierced her skin. Blood welled up around them. "I can't promise you I won't be harsh."

Her other hand moved down, found Cailyn's wetness, and smeared it over the silken flesh.

"I don't want you to promise that," Cailyn stammered between heavy breaths. "Just don't do that again. Don't go away when you use me. I need you here."

Teran smiled. "I promise."

Cailyn's lips and flesh opened in the same moment, to Teran's tongue above and fingers below.

She'd remade herself. Teran had begun it, rearranged her passion. But Cailyn had finished it herself. She'd shot a bloody hole in a High Council member's head. She hadn't even blinked.

She had no shame left. She howled as her nerves sang, awakened by the touch she'd so long craved, by the steel that pricked her neck.

She threw herself onto the driving fingers, snarled and laughed as she opened to them. They thrilled against every nerve. Waves of light rushed through her flesh. Teran's mouth swallowed her cries.

The other hand, tipped with steel, reached behind her back. It tore its mark on her skin.

Cailyn came, overwhelmed, crying into the mouth sealing hers. The blood felt good, right, proper: a monster sealing a monstrous pact.

Cailyn huddled closer to Teran, grateful for the claws' bite.

CHAPTER FORTY-ONE

The videocall came too soon. There hadn't been time to rush into the tunnels, fake the documents, alter Cailyn's fingertips so they wouldn't match her prints. Dread filled her as a High Council member's face filled the videoscreen.

What had she expected? This would mean her life. Had she really thought she could slink away, eke out a new life somewhere? Where would she go? Her father was famous even in the outer reaches of the galaxy. Who would she serve, hiding out on backwards planets? Without extensive surgeries to change her appearance, she wouldn't last days on the run.

She settled into her seat and looked at Teran's hands. She'd killed someone. Death was coming for her.

Maybe she should let it.

Dazed, she heard the caller ask Teran if she knew anything about Lord Keriel.

"Should I, my lord?" Teran asked, her tone as crisp as ever.

"We found him dead in his rooms," he answered, his lips thin and grim. "Shot in the head. The last two people cameras captured headed there were Derys and you."

"That's disturbing news indeed, Lord Xanas. What about the camera in his rooms? What did it show you?"

"It wasn't on."

"How unfortunate."

That phrase again. Cailyn bit back a wild laugh that threatened to undo her.

"I was hoping you could tell us about that, Nivrai."

"My lord, are you telling me I turned off a camera that wasn't even on when I got there?"

She snickered as he stammered.

"I know there are rumors I have powers, but I wouldn't expect the Councils to believe them."

"Nivrai, this is no time for mockery."

"He disabled that camera himself, my lord. Or destroyed it."

"Why would he do that?"

"You found metal cuffs in his room, didn't you?"

Xanas nodded.

"Keyed to his fingerprints. When I arrived, he had Cailyn bound in them."

Cailyn bit back a gasp. How much would Teran tell?

Her eyes darted to the door. Could she find the tunnels herself? Maybe the servants could guide her.

"Easy, Nivrai. I don't want to hear about lovers' spats now."

"He took her hostage. Meant to rape her, or worse. I went there to stop him and found her bound in those."

"I don't suppose you have proof of this, Nivrai."

"No, my Lord Xanas."

"Then I'm afraid I—"

"But you might."

The knotted eyebrow rose. "I might?"

"He called Derys to lure her there. If most of the cameras on the planet were working, in my rooms or his, you might discover how he did it."

Cailyn felt her cheeks flush. The tablet.

She'd wanted it. He'd used it to lure her into this mess. Would they have recordings of that, too, her bald-faced need to know? If she was taken away—put to death—would Teran ever see it? It shamed her now to think she might.

But not because she'd forgiven Teran. Teran had meant to claim her without her consent, and had been willing to torture someone else for the right to do it.

Cailyn's rage cooled to a numb scar somewhere beneath her chest. If she had time left in her life, she would have to unearth it.

But right now, she could think of only one thing: Teran dropping to her knees in front of Lord Keriel. Buying Cailyn's freedom.

"And what will we find, Nivrai?"

"I don't know, my lord. Derys and I argued. I left to attend to other business—" Cailyn winced, remembering the collar falling from her neck and the door closing, leaving her alone—"and she went to see Lord Keriel. Sometime later, I got a videocall from him, showing Cailyn bound and telling me to come to his rooms."

"And?"

"I told you already. He had her bound. He threatened to rape her, kill her, or both." She took a deep breath. "I shot him before he was finished explaining it all. He died surprised."

Cailyn froze. Had she heard that right?

The face on the screen blinked. "You're admitting that you did it?"

His answer was a brittle smile. "Of course I did it."

"But—"

"My lord, I've wanted revenge on Lord Keriel for years. I have no reason to be bashful about taking it."

"You know what this means."

"Of course. I'll come peacefully."

"No!" Cailyn cried, her voice cracking.

She fought not to tremble and rose to her feet. "No. That isn't how it hap—"

"Enough!" Teran thundered.

Cailyn kept her eyes fixed on the screen. If she looked over at Teran, she might lose her nerve.

"That's not how it happened," she said again.

Lord Xanas's eyes, enlarged by the screen, widened, speckled rings of brown surrounded by bloodshot white.

Cailyn swallowed hard and continued. "What my lady says is true. Lord Keriel lured me there. He said he had..." she hesitated, "... said he had something I wanted. I went. He knocked me out and bound me, as Lady Nivrai says. She came to rescue me, and he threatened to violate me, as she said."

"And what happened then?" Xanas's brows knotted in puzzlement.

Cailyn could guess why. The helldemon of Nivrai had just confessed to murder. Could she convince him that a monster was innocent? She licked her lips and spoke again.

"She took my place. She traded her freedom for mine. I walked away. Then I turned back, and I saw them—"

Her voice broke. She closed her eyes to block out the memory, but it remained, burned into the backs of her eyelids. "I saw her kneel in front of him. I couldn't stand it. I picked up the gun—"

"Enough!" Teran cried again.

The words spilled free from Cailyn now, heedless of Teran's command. "I picked up the gun and screamed. When he turned around, I fired. I shot until I knew he was dead."

She stared straight at the screen. "It's me you want, Lord Xanas. Not Teran Nivrai."

"No—!"

"It was me," Cailyn said again. "My fingerprints are on the gun."

"You mean to tell us—"

"If my lady had come in, shot Lord Keriel, and set me free, why would my fingerprints be there too?"

Xanas's brow furrowed and he frowned. "You do understand what you're confessing to, Derys?"

Cailyn bit her lip. They already believed Teran. Why shouldn't they? She was the helldemon who snatched disobedient children away.

And she'd already tortured one person and enslaved another.

"You think I don't understand murder and treason, my lord?"

"I just want to be sure you know that you don't have to obey her. We will protect you if you need it."

Damn it. Did everyone think she was nothing more than Teran's toy?

"I'm telling the truth, my lord."

His eyes flicked to Teran. "Is she, Nivrai?"

The silence stretched. Cailyn wrapped her bare arms around herself, suddenly chilled.

Xanas spoke again. Pink lips parted to expose a pinker tongue. The size made it obscene.

"She is, isn't she?"

STEEL AND PROMISE

"My lord," Teran said finally, "it's not right to punish her. This
was between me and Ben—and Lord Keriel."
"You meant to kill him."
"I went there to kill him. I went there to rip him apart."
"But you didn't do it. Did you, Nivrai?"
"I say I did."
"That's not—"
"Take us both and decide. Or better yet—"
Teran looked up, a light in her eyes.
"What is it, Nivrai?"
"Serving me led to this. Don't kill her for that. Let her stay here
with me."
"Nivrai, you've already spoken your piece, and that was a lie."
Teran smiled, a bloodless smile Cailyn knew well. "We'll both
remain here, far away from any intrigue."
"I'm supposed to take your word for this, Nivrai? One or the
other of you just committed murder and high treason."
"Let me finish." She laughed, a cold chuckle that chilled Cailyn
even though she'd heard it before. Xanas cleared his throat, apparently
just as unnerved.
"You believe Derys, I think, and not me," Teran continued.
"Well, then, if she ever leaves Nivrai—if anyone even so much as
sees her in a shuttle leaving the planet—her life is forfeit."
She purred at his answering blink. "As is mine."
"You're saying she'd become your slave." His mouth pursed in
disgust. "You're asking us to deny her rights."
The claws emerged for a moment and then retreated. "You've
done that already."
Cailyn froze. A chill spread through her.
Had she heard that right?
Teran was still talking. "All that would change is that you can
kill me if she leaves."
"Nivrai, we could never allow that. That's barbaric."
"Barbaric, my lord?" Teran snickered, a sound of pure contempt.
"You already know you won't get the information you need from me
if you destroy something you promised to me."

Ash and acid clogged Cailyn's throat. So it was true. They had traded her body and freedom for atrocity.

A gem in a world of stones.

She'd basked in being prized. But now they'd bartered and offered her. Traded her like a shining thing with no will or needs of its own.

She thought of her father, of his styled hair, rouged cheeks, lipsticked mouth. Even after years of retirement, he'd painted himself like a courtesan. Had he wanted it that way? Or had he done it for her mother? She'd whisked him away from a life he'd no longer wanted. Had he kept himself polished for her?

What about the crazed client who'd come after him no matter where he hid? Cailyn had never paid much attention to it. Now, seeing what Lord Keriel had done to Teran, some part of her understood.

Xanas nodded. "The Councils will have to meet. But mark my words: Nivrai is surrounded. If you try to escape, you will be shot down."

Teran nodded, all business. "Understood."

CHAPTER FORTY-TWO

"You can't do that!"
          "I can't do what?"
Cailyn's fist slammed against the table. Her voice shook as she fought tears. "You can't just trade away my freedom! It doesn't belong to you!"

The dam burst. Cailyn's vision blurred. She blinked to clear it. "But it does."

"What?"

"Your freedom. It already does belong to me."

Teran looked at Cailyn. "Guild law doesn't matter, little one. Not if the Councils say it doesn't."

Cailyn dug her nails into her palm to keep the tears from coming again. "I already know what you're about to say, my lady. Lord Keriel already told me."

"They gave me immunity. Not just for what I did to the boy."

Cailyn said nothing.

"I could use you when I liked, even if you refused. I could keep you with me, even if you wanted to leave."

Teran's lips pulled back in a grimace or a grin. Cailyn couldn't tell which.

"I know," Cailyn said, her voice flat.

"Then you know I had that right and didn't use it."

"You—"

"I didn't want to force you. I still don't. I'd much rather you choose to stay with me."

"Then how can you do this?"

"But that doesn't change the facts. You're already mine, little one."

She chuckled, sharp and harsh. The sound turned Cailyn's insides to water. Fortunately, she was already sitting down. She thanked her goddess for the small mercy of her knees not buckling.

"I couldn't keep Mariel alive. Claws and rumors don't fight a sickness that wastes someone away from the inside. But I can keep you alive."

A claw tucked under Cailyn's chin. "If I have to keep you here to save your life, I will."

"You can't do this!"

"I don't give a damn about your consent."

"I turned myself in. It's over."

The claw sank back into Teran's fingertip. Teran stood up, the gray suit she wore hugging a body Cailyn still itched to touch.

Long fingers twined in her hair. "Is serving me really so terrible?"

The richness of the voice made tears come to Cailyn's eyes again.

"Would it really be so awful to belong to me forever?"

Cailyn pushed Teran's face away. She couldn't stand to feel her breath on her skin.

"No," Cailyn said. "No. It wouldn't."

"Then come with me." Newsteel glinted as it slid down her cheek.

"I'm offering you everything," she said. "Everything I have and more. I will make this place a paradise for you. Forever."

But what kind of paradise could there be without freedom?

"You like this," Cailyn spat. She turned her head away. "You like the thought of keeping me. It excites you."

Teran's lips touched Cailyn's cheek. "Of course." The other hand slid over Cailyn's chest. "So do you."

"No." Her hands found their strength. She seized Teran's fingers, trapped them fast. "I won't trade my freedom for your pleasure."

"If it weren't your life on the line, I would understand," Teran returned, her voice sharp as a cracked mirror. "I would let you go. If that's really what you want."

"It is."

"But now I am your life. My pleasure is your survival. This is your only hope."

"I had a life out there. I had lovers. Clients. Friends. You were part of it. Not all of it. You can't be all of it now."

Teeth slid along her neck. They bit, sudden and sharp. The hand at her breast tightened. Her blouse tore.

"No!"

"No?" The richness at her throat became a growl. "If I went ahead, what would happen?"

Thin fingers reached through the torn fabric. Metal curled against Cailyn's skin. Fingers ran over her nipple. It hardened at their touch.

"You would surrender, wouldn't you?" Warm lips kissed their way down her neck. "You'd be mine. All of this would be over."

Cailyn closed her eyes. Maybe Teran was right. Would she really buy her freedom at the cost of her own life?

A part of her wanted Teran to end it, her fingers plunging in, driving out her confusion and fear. She yearned for it, even as she knew it would tear her asunder.

Now she had a choice. Between death with honor and life as a broken toy.

A toy cloven by pleasure and pain, drowning in one or the other or both at once.

"No," she whispered. She said it again, her voice loud and strong. "No." Tears came. She didn't check them. "You'd save me from rape so you can do it yourself?"

Metal pricked her. The hand on her breast tightened, hard.

With a cry, the claws pulled away.

Cailyn blinked away the tears blurring her vision. "I'm going. Now. I'm taking a shuttle and turning myself in."

She took the first step forward. The next would be easier, and the next, and the next, until she sat in the cockpit of a shuttle. Ran her hands over the controls.

Left Nivrai behind her.

Like all the courtesans, Cailyn had been trained in self-defense. Guild law didn't always deter the obsessed or the violent.

But Lady Nivrai had been trained by the best. The blow came, a solid hit to Cailyn's solar plexus, before she even thought to expect it. She hit the floor gasping for breath.

The pain of it overwhelmed her. Its purity shocked her senses. She choked and sputtered and struggled to sit up.

After that, she would have to stand. And then—

Servants surrounded her, a silent swarm. Teran loomed over her, every part of her a weapon: claws, elbows, thighs, teeth.

A voice rang above her, a tempest in her ears. She struggled to make sense of its words.

"—to the cells down below. Care for her well, but don't let her out."

Hands wrapped around her arms. They pulled her up and dragged her out.

Cailyn supposed she should be grateful for the warm, padded bed. Grateful for the meal, simple but nourishing. Grateful for the servants who peeked in. They never said anything aloud. They waited until she told them she was well and left.

Teran could have thrown her in a box, cold and alone, on a cot that hurt her back. She could have made the light sear her eyes.

She could have done countless things to make sure Cailyn would break.

Cailyn stared into the lights on the ceiling. She'd break eventually, whether Teran was kind to her or not.

Her mouth watered. Memories of Teran's smell and taste washed over her when the walls and bed grew too boring to stare at.

More memories followed. The five stinging cuts on her breast where Teran had grabbed her. Teran's voice, telling Lord Keriel to go ahead and kill her.

And the worst image of all, replayed over light she gazed into: Lord Keriel's head, blood pouring from it and pooling around him on the ground. His sightless eyes, wide in what should have been triumph.

She'd killed a man. He'd hit the floor leaking life from punctures she'd made.

She slipped, fell to the floor, and retched.

She couldn't imagine the thing she'd done. She remembered it but couldn't hold it in her mind. It slipped away, a bright-colored image without meaning.

Dizzy, she hauled herself up.

She blinked. Teran stood above her. The doors had already closed behind her.

Cailyn stared up at the clean lines of the gray uniform. Her stomach turned again. She'd gone from serving the helldemon of Nivrai to lying on the floor in a cell and fighting not to vomit.

She lifted her head, scrounging for dignity.

"The Councils accepted my proposal," Teran said. "You will live."

"If I leave—" Cailyn began.

"If you leave today, they'll take you. Execute you. Otherwise you're going to live."

She reached down and offered her hand. She'd retracted her claws, but still the silvery promise glistened in her fingernails.

"I did it," Cailyn said. "I deserve justice."

Teran's hand wound itself in her hair and dragged her up. "You mean death. I could do that too, you know." She stroked Cailyn's tear-stained cheek with a hand festooned with knives. "If death is what you want, I could just kill you myself."

"I don't want to die."

"Then come."

"We can use the tunnels, escape through them—"

"No."

Cailyn winced. The hand in her hair stung her scalp. "Then I have no other choice."

Steel ran over Cailyn's lip, down her cheek, over her chin. It stilled at her neck, sharp and deadly. "If you're so set on dying, why let them kill you? They don't give a damn about you. They'll try you and they'll dispose of you, toss you aside, broken, like—"

She fell silent. Cailyn saw tears glisten in her eyes.

"If you're so sure they're right, at least let yourself die well." Steel-tipped fingers tickled the flesh over her jugular. "At least take pleasure in it."

The room spun in Cailyn's vision. "Is that what you want, my lady? Is that how this ends? You train me to love pain so I'll come when you kill me?"

"I watched Mariel die by inches," Teran spat. "Do you really think I want to watch you die too?"

"I—"

"But if you insist on dying, I can give you something those fools can't. I can make it beautiful."

Cailyn closed her eyes. She imagined herself hanging naked and bound, the claws running soft as leaves over her flesh and then digging in, drawing out sighs and screams alike.

Would she die that way if Teran did it? Would she drown in her own red? She imagined the dizzy sparkle as she gave herself up to the pain.

It would be unnatural, horrible as anything else in this litany of atrocity. But it would be hers. Chosen. Private.

An execution wouldn't be. A roomful of people who'd been taught to despise her would gawk as she took her last breath. Teran and old friends and lovers would weep in some far corner as she drifted to her last sleep.

Was that really what she wanted?

She let Teran haul her up. Steel danced against her neck.

"Now?" she whispered.

The hand froze. "No. Not now. Let me take you back up first."

Cailyn slipped her hand into Teran's and followed, not sure whether she meant to consent or to slip away once they left the cells.

She watched for the servants, learned to predict when their gray shapes emerged and disappeared into rooms or shadows.

More than once, she saw opportunities.

She'd only have to make it as far as the shuttles, after all. If the cruisers still lurked in orbit around Nivrai, even opening the hangar doors would have them on alert.

But that wouldn't work. Teran had said she would forfeit her own life if Cailyn ever tried to leave.

And Teran, not Cailyn, was a helldemon with newsteel tipping her fingers and a taste for blood and screams.

Cailyn tried to slip her fingers out of Teran's grip, but they wouldn't move. Her feet wouldn't either. The only way to make them move was to follow and follow, until the familiar door to a familiar bedroom stood before them.

Cailyn looked at the large window, the garden and fountain beyond it. She walked over to it and put her hands to the glass.

"I'd like to go out there, my lady," she said.

"Very well." The glass glowed as Teran's fingers touched it. The window slid open. She watched Teran walk outside, unhurried as always, and followed.

Scents flooded Cailyn's nostrils: the flowers, the leaves, the grass. She slipped off her shoes, let the grass touch the bare skin of her feet. She bent down to touch a flower, straightened up again, and waited.

Teran peeled off the gray uniform. The water shone behind her as gleaming fingers slit Cailyn's clothes.

They faced one another, naked and silent, their eyes meeting. The waterfall bubbled behind them.

Newsteel flashed out, scored deep lines just above her breasts. Cailyn sobbed in relief. Her flesh throbbed with desire she hadn't known she felt.

The steel sang in her skin, again and again. Blood flowed down her breasts, her belly, her thighs.

It was no worse than anything Teran had done before. But at the end of it, a bright light that would take her away from this, from violation, from torment, from lifeless bodies with gaping holes in their skulls.

The claw twitched, a ragged tear inside her skin. She raised her head to look.

Teran held out her hand like a penitent making an offering to her patron god. Blood ran over her palms and down her fingers.

"My lady—Teran—what ?"

She looked up into Teran's face. Her eyes overflowed with tears and her mouth twisted into a grimace.

Cailyn's cuts stung anew as she looked at Teran. Sympathy sang in her flayed nerves.

"I can't see," Teran whispered. Her shoulders heaved. "These tears—I can't stop them. I can't stop them and I can't see. I can't do it if I can't see."

Cailyn reached out. The flooded eyes looked up at her touch.

Teran turned away.

"Go if you have to," she said. "Call them and tell them you mean to die, if that's really what you want."

"I don't want death," Cailyn said. "I want freedom. I can't have it without leaving."

Teran shook again. "Then go."

"I'm sorry," Cailyn said. Fear twisted her stomach.

"I know."

Cailyn walked to the door, her feet heavy, like she was moving through thick oil. Was her body rebelling, some survival instinct resisting the motions her mind told it to make?

The world beyond the garden was too real. Too cold. She didn't want to bleed in it.

She thought again of Teran's face, the pale mask contorted with sobs. She'd seen her grief before, the first time her lips touched Teran's flesh.

She didn't know if Teran had cried when she came. She hadn't looked.

And now...

Teran had wanted Cailyn to die hers if Cailyn died at all. Cailyn had agreed to her wish.

Teran's body had rebelled against what she wanted to do. And she had let Cailyn go.

After all she had done to force Cailyn to stay, she'd let her go.

Did she even know what she'd just done?

Probably not. Mariel had wanted to serve from the beginning.

Teran had found Cailyn and submerged her in desire and pain. The need had stayed with Cailyn even when she surfaced. She'd scrambled for it. From Darien. From Elana Teth. From the pack of nobles at the party.

Did Teran need her too?

The deal with Lord Keriel said yes. The tears said more than need could move her.

Cailyn turned and walked back through the open window. Her steps grew lighter as she did. Slipping to her knees was even easier, as easy as the first time.

"You understand," Cailyn said. "You let me go."

"Leave now. Don't make this harder than it already is."

"You let me choose."

"I—"

"That means I belong here."

Cailyn bowed her head, offering her neck.

"With you."

Newsteel twisted, harsh and welcome, into her hair. Lips met hers. They tasted like tears.

She opened her mouth.

CHAPTER FORTY-THREE

Cailyn had expected sex. They'd denied their desire long enough. And now—she'd thought Teran would tear at her. Rip through her with savagery born of relief. Especially here in the garden, the fountain singing behind them and the grass tickling her knees.

It didn't happen.

That must mean Teran wanted to put the collar on her first. To lock it around her naked throat, never to be removed again.

Teran owned her, after all. Now everyone could finally admit they knew it.

Instead she ordered Cailyn to kneel facing away from her, pulled her long curls aside to expose her back.

The claws dug into it, too deep for pleasure.

Wet blood ran over her back as the newsteel opened her skin. The sting shivered her senses a moment later, delayed like thunder after lightning.

She did not scream. She balled her hands into fists at her sides. Her eyes filled with tears, and she stared ahead through their mist.

She let the tears fall. Teran had cried over her, after all.

She had done this once before. The claws had dug deep, curling and twisting into elaborate shapes as they carved their mark into the skin of her back. Slow and deliberate, they'd scored the Nivrai symbol into Cailyn's shoulder.

Had she known what Teran meant, that first time her claws etched the sigil into her back? Teran had teased her with it, a mark that would heal over, a hint of what she wanted. The experiment's purpose and eventual result, cut into her skin long before she'd understood it.

The mark had faded like any other. She'd remembered the precision and the passion that drove it, but nothing more.

Now the newsteel cut deep enough to scar.

For the rest of Cailyn's life, she would wear the symbol of Nivrai, etched into her skin by the hands that had held her, soothed her, torn her open, sent her reeling.

The newsteel traced flame down the nerves in her back. She cried out at last, unable to keep silent.

Memories flooded her mind, their sting washed away as she bled. Lord Keriel dead on the floor of his room, blood pooled around his head. His hands toying with the tablet without revealing what it held. Teran tearing at herself, ripping the black bodysuit to shreds, slicing her own skin.

Cailyn's dress, torn and mended.

The memories rose before her eyes, then burst like bubbles. The blood carried away their sting. Desire rose where despair had passed. The flesh of her back opened to Teran's touch, as eagerly as her sex would the next time Teran used her.

Teran's breath came quick and shallow. Cailyn heard her murmur, a low purr of contentment and desire. That too would remain with Cailyn always. Everything that passed between them, the scar would seal inside her skin. Whenever she wrapped her hand around her shoulder, she would feel it and remember.

Opening to Teran had become second nature. She cried out. Fire raced from the seared nerves of her back down into her sex and up into her screaming throat.

She did not know it was over until the burning stopped and every part of her throbbed.

Her head drooped. The steel-tipped hand withdrew. Teran stood over her, casting a shadow over the grass and flowers.

A hand, its claws hidden away, reached for Cailyn's cheek. She opened her mouth and kissed Teran's fingers. She tasted her blood, opened her mouth to lick and suck it away. Teran's fingers sank into her mouth.

Heat rose in Cailyn's shoulder and inside her sex. White fire licked at her back. Teran's fingers sealed it in her open mouth. It flooded her, returning and returning.

Teran had transformed her. She could do nothing but take pleasure in it. She thought of the steel tucked inside Teran's fingertips and shivered in fear and exultation.

❖

One videocall remained.

The image flared to life, nobles sitting around a circular table. Circlets ringed the nobles' heads.

That only made sense. Teran had made her deal with the Councils, after all.

Some, Cailyn recognized as former clients. She remembered their hands on her. Knowing what she'd done, would they shudder when they remembered her touch?

Would there be rumors about Cailyn now? In the beginning, Cailyn had half-expected a helldemon to swoop down and carry her away. In the face of so many whispers, the claws that pierced her had both amazed and disappointed her.

What would they say about Cailyn? Would they whisper about a courtesan driven to murder by the passions of a demon?

Even the servitude she'd chosen would become a story. She would be an object lesson. A beautiful woman who had paid for her twisted passion with her freedom, forever condemned to remain in the demon's thrall.

Now she understood why Teran laughed.

"Cailyn Derys," one of the High Council members said. "We have considered Nivrai's proposal and decided to spare you. Provided you agree never to leave Nivrai."

Cailyn nodded. "I understand, my lords."

"If you ever do leave, both your life and Teran Nivrai's will be forfeit."

"I understand."

"No second chance will be given. To either of you."

"I understand."

The woman's diadem shone. "Then you agree to these terms? If you do not, and you're found guilty of murder and treason, you will be executed."

"I agree to the terms," Cailyn answered. "I will—" She stopped and swallowed, unable to hide the catch in her voice.

Memories flooded her mind. That stolen moment between her father and Lord Lerak so long ago. The fierce joy in the nobleman's eyes as they kissed. Laughing with the other courtesans-to-be about the things they studied. The first time a door irised open and a noble walked in. The first time a noble's gaze swept over her, naked and kneeling as she waited to be used.

It would all end here. Her flesh itched, the fresh scar already re-knitting. She looked over at Teran.

It was enough. It would have to be.

She spoke again, the tremor in her voice gone. "I will remain in Nivrai and never leave."

"You're a lucky woman, Derys, to get out of this with your life."

"Thank you, my lady."

The noblewoman blinked. Cailyn didn't blame her. Just hours ago, Cailyn had thought she'd rather die than agree to this. "Then here."

A panel blinked near Cailyn, the agreement written on it. Cailyn swallowed and signed. It vanished when she finished. Her freedom vanished with it.

She watched the faces in the videoscreen. What did they think of her, courtesan turned murderess turned slave?

The video blinked out. Teran walked up behind her. Clawed fingers curled around her unmarked shoulder.

"It's done, then," she said.

Cailyn nodded.

Teran's hand slid to her neck. Steel pricked her where the collar had been.

"I will make this place a paradise for you," Teran whispered. Steel glinted at her fingertips, bright as the metal of the council members' diadems.

The fabric of her clothes began to tear. She looked down. Would she dress in the finery of a courtesan now, or would she wear Nivrai gray?

Teran's hand moved to cup her breast, the metal flitting against skin and nipple. Cailyn arched back as Teran's other hand slid down her chest and stomach. The claws retracted with a click. Cailyn stood and spread her legs.

Teran's fingers speared her in a quick, smooth movement. She moved against them, her flesh opening and opening to Teran's fingers.

Now, whatever else she'd lost, there would be no end to this. She ground hard into Teran's hand, gasping, her flesh alight. Her back stung in time with the building heat inside her.

Her eyes opened. The whirlwind of memories peaked and broke.

Teran slid her fingers free. Cailyn lifted her head in answer. Teran's smiling face filled her vision.

Steel moved to cup her chin, slid over her cheek.

"Welcome home, my little one," Teran said.

THE END

About the Author

Alexa Black lives in the Washington, DC, area where she works as a peer mentor and advocate for people with disabilities. She has a master's degree in philosophy from Georgetown University, but has always returned to her passion for writing. Though a philosopher by training, she would rather inflict complicated questions on her characters and take readers along than lecture about them. When not writing, she can be found gaming, seeking out new restaurants to try, or drinking ridiculous, fancy coffee. *Steel and Promise* is her first novel.

She can be found online at: http://writeralexablack.blogspot .com/ and www.facebook.com/alexablackwriter and emailed at alexablack44@gmail.com.

Books Available from Bold Strokes Books

18 Months by Samantha Boyette. Alissa Reeves has only had two girlfriends and they've both gone missing. Now it's up to her to find out why. (978-1-62639-804-7)

Arrested Hearts by Holly Stratimore. A reckless cop who hates her life and a health nut who is afraid to die might be a perfect combination for love. (978-1-62639-809-2)

Capturing Jessica by Jane Hardee. Hyperrealist sculptor Michael tries desperately to conceal the love she holds for best friend, Jess, unaware Jess's feelings for her are changing. (978-1-62639-836-8)

Counting to Zero by AJ Quinn. NSA agent Emma Thorpe and computer hacker Paxton James must learn to trust each other as they work to stop a threat clock that's rapidly counting down to zero. (978-1-62639-783-5)

Courageous Love by KC Richardson. Two women fight a devastating disease, and their own demons, while trying to fall in love. (978-1-62639-797-2)

One More Reason to Leave Orlando by Missouri Vaun. Nash Wiley thought a threesome sounded exotic and exciting, but as it turns out the reality of sleeping with two women at the same time is just really complicated. (978-1-62639-703-3E)

Pathogen by Jessica L. Webb. Can Dr. Kate Morrison navigate a deadly virus and the threat of bioterrorism, as well as her new relationship with Sergeant Andy Wyles and her own troubled past? (978-1-62639-833-7)

Rainbow Gap by Lee Lynch. Jaudon Vickers and Berry Garland, polar opposites, dream and love in this tale of lesbian lives set in Central Florida against the tapestry of societal change and the Vietnam War. (978-1-62639-799-6)

Steel and Promise by Alexa Black. Lady Nivrai's cruel desires and modified body make most of the galaxy fear her, but courtesan Cailyn Derys soon discovers the real monsters are the ones without the claws. (978-1-62639-805-4)

Swelter by D. Jackson Leigh. Teal Giovanni's mistake shines an unwanted spotlight on a small Texas ranch where August Reese is secluded until she can testify against a powerful drug kingpin. (978-1-62639-795-8)

Without Justice by Carsen Taite. Cade Kelly and Emily Sinclair must battle each other in the pursuit of justice, but can they fight their undeniable attraction outside the walls of the courtroom? (978-1-62639-560-2)

21 Questions by Mason Dixon. To find love, start by asking the right questions. (978-1-62639-724-8)

A Palette for Love by Charlotte Greene. When newly minted Ph.D. Chloé Devereaux returns to New Orleans, she doesn't expect her new job, and her powerful employer—Amelia Winters—to be so appealing. (978-1-62639-758-3)

By the Dark of Her Eyes by Cameron MacElvee. When Brenna Taylor inherits a decrepit property haunted by tormented ghosts, Alejandra Santana must not only restore Brenna's house and property but also save her soul. (978-1-62639-834-4)

Cash Braddock by Ashley Bartlett. Cash Braddock just wants to hang with her cat, fall in love, and deal drugs. What's the problem with that? (978-1-62639-706-4)

Death by Cocktail Straw by Missouri Vaun. She just wanted to meet girls, but an outing at the local lesbian bar goes comically off the rails, landing Nash Wiley and her best pal in the ER. (978-1-62639-702-6)

Gravity by Juliann Rich. How can Ellie Engebretsen, Olympic ski jumping hopeful with her eye on the gold, soar through the air when all she feels like doing is falling hard for Kate Moreau, her greatest competitor and the girl of her dreams? (978-1-62639-483-4)

Lone Ranger by VK Powell. Reporter Emma Ferguson stirs up a thirty-year-old mystery that threatens Park Ranger Carter West's family and jeopardizes any hope for a relationship between the two women. (978-1-62639-767-5)

Love on Call by Radclyffe. Ex-Army medic Glenn Archer and recent LA transplant Mariana Mateo fight their mutual desire in the face of past losses as they work together in the Rivers Community Hospital ER. (978-1-62639-843-6)

Never Enough by Robyn Nyx. Can two women put aside their pasts to find love before it's too late? (978-1-62639-629-6)

Two Souls by Kathleen Knowles. Can love blossom in the wake of tragedy? (978-1-62639-641-8)

Camp Rewind by Meghan O'Brien. A summer camp for grown-ups becomes the site of an unlikely romance between a shy, introverted divorcee and one of the Internet's most infamous cultural critics—who attends undercover. (978-1-62639-793-4)

Cross Purposes by Gina L. Dartt. In pursuit of a lost Acadian treasure, three women must not only work out the clues, but also the complicated tangle of emotion and attraction developing between them. (978-1-62639-713-2)

Imperfect Truth by C.A. Popovich. Can an imperfect truth stand in the way of love? (978-1-62639-787-3)

Life in Death by M. Ullrich. Sometimes the devastating end is your only chance for a new beginning. (978-1-62639-773-6)

Love on Liberty by MJ Williamz. Hearts collide when politics clash. (978-1-62639-639-5)

Serious Potential by Maggie Cummings. Pro golfer Tracy Allen plans to forget her ex during a visit to Bay West, a lesbian condo community in NYC, but when she meets Dr. Jennifer Betsy, she gets more than she bargained for. (978-1-62639-633-3)

Smoldering Desires by C.E. Knipes. Evan McGarrity has found the man of his dreams in Sebastian Tantalos. When an old boyfriend from Sebastian's past enters the picture, Evan must fight for the man he loves. (978-1-62639-714-9)

Taste by Kris Bryant. Accomplished chef Taryn has walked away from her promising career in the city's top restaurant to devote her life to her five-year-old daughter and is content until Ki Blake comes along. (978-1-62639-718-7)

The Second Wave by Jean Copeland. Can star-crossed lovers have a second chance after decades apart, or does the love of a lifetime only happen once? (978-1-62639-830-6)

Valley of Fire by Missouri Vaun. Taken captive in a desert outpost after their small aircraft is hijacked, Ava and her captivating passenger discover things about each other and themselves that will change them both forever. (978-1-62639-496-4)